She was a headstrong
  beauty with a dar...
to best a hot-blood...
  in a duel of hear...

Jake deliberately closed the door and walked over to where she was sitting. "I didn't expect to find you here."

His voice came so softly that she almost didn't hear it. "I'm sure you didn't. I'm sorry if you're disappointed."

"Disappointed? Now why would you think that? You're a very beautiful woman."

There was no concealing her surprise, nor the blush that spread across her face. "Is there something I can do for you?" she asked, then thought about what she'd said and cringed. Of course he came to Miranda's room expecting something.

His smile widened and he narrowed his eyes. "Are you considering changing your profession, darling?"

Dallas started. He was challenging her, and she found herself responding sharply. "Would you pay for my services if I did?"

"Are you expensive?"

"Very. In fact," she added with what she hoped was a warning, "I don't think you could afford my price."

"Try me?"

"I might, if you have something to offer that I want."

The suggestive words had come unbidden, teasing and curling around her tongue.

She stared at him in the mirror and knew that he was as caught up in the moment as she was. She wished she hadn't come here. Jake Silver was no gentleman engaging in a genteel flirtation. And she didn't have a Pinkerton agent hovering in the background, ready to come to her aid. She was on her own, and she was in big trouble. . . .

REBEL IN SILK

Rebel
in Silk

Sandra Chastain

BANTAM BOOKS
NEW YORK • TORONTO • LONDON
• SYDNEY • AUCKLAND

REBEL IN SILK

A Bantam Fanfare Book/April 1994

FANFARE and the portrayal of a boxed "ff"
are trademarks of Bantam Books,
a division of Bantam Doubleday Dell Publishing Group, Inc.

ISBN 0-553-56464-1

Published simultaneously in the United States and Canada

Bantam Books are published by Bantam Books, a division of Bantam Doubleday Dell Publishing Group, Inc. Its trademark, con-
sisting of the words "Bantam Books" and the portrayal of a
rooster, is Registered in U.S. Patent and Trademark Office and in
other countries. Marca Registrada. Bantam Books, 1540 Broad-
way, New York, New York 10036.

PRINTED IN THE UNITED STATES OF AMERICA

OPM   0 9 8 7 6 5 4 3 2 1

Dear Reader:

The tales of ancient Greece are timeless stories and legends that continue to fire the imagination and teach us the lessons of love and life.

The settling of the American West embodies the best and worst of man, proving once again that nothing is new. Range wars were only a new name for an age-old confrontation.

When I began to think about setting a Once Upon a Time Romance *in the West,* I remembered another epic struggle for land and the legendary manner in which it was settled. I was thinking of the story of Lysistrata, the woman said to have changed the course of history in ancient Greece. Had our pioneer women studied Greek literature, they might have brought the brutal territorial disputes to a hasty conclusion.

Rebel in Silk *is the tale of how one woman might have taken Lysistrata's story to heart and settled a range war in Wyoming in 1874.*

Sandra Chastain

Rebel in Silk

Prologue

West Kansas—1868

I need you, Jake.

The anguished voice jolted Jake Silver from a restless sleep in the middle of the night. His eyes flew open. A cold sweat poured from his skin while his heart pounded against his chest like the frantic drumbeat of an Apache war dance.

Jake automatically reached for his gun and waited for his senses to focus on the intruder. But this presence wasn't real. Sarah wasn't here. She couldn't be. Still, he searched the darkness, wishing as he had a thousand times that she was lying beside him, and finding nothing but cold, empty space. He took a deep breath, forcing himself back to reality. This wasn't the dream he'd carried with him for months. This was a cruel joke, a waking nightmare.

Then her voice called again, *Jake!*

He came to his feet, left the rustic cabin, and plunged out into the bitter cold, his deep howl of rage filling the night. The falling snow neither erased the pounding nor stopped the voice tormenting him, the voice of the woman he'd been forced to leave behind.

A dozen times in the first month, he'd almost gone back for her.

Almost.

But he hadn't let himself. She didn't belong to him any longer. She had no right to call out to him now. Still, her sorrowful cry sliced his mind with pain, then slammed into his gut.

The plea for help hadn't totally surprised him. It had been that way from the first with Sarah. Long after she'd made her choice, her voice had reached out for him, tormenting him, following him across the prairie. And then it hushed. And he'd thought he was finally free.

Until a few days ago, when he had known that something was wrong. The feeling started innocently enough with an uneasy sensation that had him looking over his shoulder. It mushroomed into an overwhelming sense of impending disaster. He hadn't know what, but he'd known trouble was coming. He'd rechecked his supplies, snapped at Wu, his Chinese cook, and paced his room at night.

His longhorns had been rounded up. His men were ready and waiting for the trek north to the Wyoming Territory, where he intended to stake out a section of land. The worst of the winter weather was over and spring was at hand, yet he'd delayed their departure, the ever-present feeling of urgency persisting.

And then he'd heard her voice. *I need you, Jake.* And the pain of his loss came hurtling back.

It was Sarah. Sarah was in danger. And no matter what he'd promised, he had to get to her. Nothing else was important, not that Sarah was married to another man, nor the signs of an approaching storm. Sarah needed him.

He felt her pain.

He felt death.

With provisions for three days, he'd left his ranch and ridden straight into the storm. Now three days had turned into four, and the snow showed no sign of abating. He was no longer sure he was heading in the right direction. There was a good possibility that he would never reach her. She'd never know that he loved her. She'd never know how hard it had been to ride away.

"Don't give up on me, Blackjack!" he begged his horse. But his words were caught by the wind and tossed away.

Jake Silver drew his lean frame lower, hugging the laboring animal's body in a hopeless attempt to absorb warmth. He tried not to breathe any more than necessary, for each breath further frosted his already ice-laden mustache. The blowing snow and icy wind had taken their toll. He could no longer move his feet, and his hands felt as if they were frozen to the reins.

He only hoped that his stallion could find the way. God knew, there was a time when he and his horse had made their way back to Sarah in worse weather than this.

Until Sarah had fallen in love with Jake's best friend.

Until Sarah had chosen Elliott.

Blackjack stumbled and stopped, forcing Jake to shake off the pain of his memories. He raised his head and glanced around, squinting his eyes to focus them on the snow-covered shapes around him. The horse hadn't just stumbled, he'd stopped—in front of the barn where he'd always found shelter. They were home.

No, that was wrong. This small Kansas farm wasn't his anymore. It belonged to Elliott—and Sarah.

The wind dropped suddenly and the blowing

snow gave way to a scene that wrenched Jake's heart. There was no smoke coming from the chimney, no lamplight shining through the glass window that had been Sarah's pride and joy, no sign of life.

Jake tugged his boots from the stirrups and dismounted, dropping Blackjack's reins. He considered digging the drifts of snow away from the barn door, then apologized to the big black horse, who was near exhaustion.

"Sorry, boy. I have to check on Sarah, then I'll look after you."

The snow was knee-deep, higher in spots, until he reached the narrow corridor between the barn and the house that had been swept clean by the wind.

The door to the house was standing open. Snow had drifted inside, collecting on Sarah's braid rug and across the bed, which had been pulled close to the fireplace.

"Sarah?"

No answer. The other room, Sarah's room, was empty. He raised his head and glanced at the loft. It was obvious there was no one there.

"Sarah!"

Jake made his way to the bed, swept the snow away and swore. There was no hiding the blood-stained sheets, frozen in wrinkles that clearly revealed its occupant's slide from the bed.

The ashes in the fireplace were long cold. There was no oil in the lamp. The cabin was empty. He was too late.

Sarah was gone.

Jake let out a bellow of anguish and raced out of the cabin, studying the surrounding yard.

The barn. Maybe she's in the barn.

This time he broke through the frozen crust of ice and, with hands that no longer had feeling, dug the snow away from the barn door. Once he opened the door, Blackjack followed him inside.

The cow had broken from her stall and was chewing the last of the hay that had been stored in the corner of the building. A few chickens skittered nervously about. A few chickens and one cow. What had happened to the other stock?

At least the horses were gone. Surely that meant that Elliott had taken Sarah away. But when? And where? And why did Jake still have this sick feeling in his gut?

Blackjack had edged the cow away and was stamping his feet as he vied for the last of the hay. Jake glanced at the hayloft and saw that there was some feed still there, at least enough to keep the cow alive for a time after he left.

Then Jake noticed the saddle, Sarah's saddle, draped across the stall wall. Wherever they'd gone, Sarah hadn't ridden her horse. The wagon? Through the doorway, Jake saw a snow-covered shape that made his breathing quicken. A closer examination confirmed that he'd found the wagon.

He'd known it from the start. Something was wrong with Sarah. Elliott was gone, as was his horse, but Sarah's saddle had been left behind and they hadn't used the wagon. "Where are you, Sarah?" He turned his head, willing himself to hear her speak the words he'd heard in his mind for days.

I need you, Jake.

But this time, the voice was silent. Frantically he stumbled through the yard, searching for shapes that revealed familiar objects: her washtub, a feed bucket, the plow.

And then he saw it, a low, flat mound of snow beside the open gate. With sinking heart, Jake kneeled and brushed the snow away.

"Sarah?"

Lying there, in a bloodstained nightgown, was the body of the woman he loved, the woman he'd walked away from when she'd chosen his best friend and partner to be her husband.

"Ah, Sarah." He broke her free of the crusty snow, turned her over and lifted her in his arms, understanding at last what had happened.

Sarah was pregnant.

Sarah had died, trying to give her husband a child.

And she'd died alone.

Jake was halfway to the house when he heard the sound of horses approaching. He never stopped, nor looked back. Inside the house he laid Sarah on the bed and covered her lifeless body with his duster.

"Sarah?" A scream of animal-like pain. It was Elliott.

The sound of Elliott's voice hardened any last trace of friendship Jake might have felt for the man he'd served with at the Battle of Shiloh, the man who'd saved his life and become his best friend, the man who'd followed him west to become his partner in a new land.

Jake couldn't blame Elliott Parnell for falling in love with the beautiful young widow they'd discovered alone on the trail. Her wagon had been separated from the train and left behind when the wagonmaster discovered that her husband was suffering from a fever. Jake and Elliott buried the man, but they couldn't ride away and leave Sarah alone. She'd joined them in grateful appreciation.

Such an arrangement might have seemed unacceptable back in Charleston, but out here, on the lonely Kansas plains, it had been a necessity. And the three of them, Jake, Sarah, and Elliott, had built a farm. They had called it their Hope and made plans to turn it into a plantation like the ones they'd known before the war. Jake was the leader, Elliott the follower, and Sarah the peacemaker.

There'd been only one problem. They'd both fallen in love with Sarah.

Gradually, Sarah had watched friends become rivals. Jake understood what was happening but he was powerless to stop it. Sharp words that had no rightful origin became commonplace, and the relationship between two men turned into hate. Neither man would allow Sarah to leave; each man had sworn to take care of her. Though she loved them both, Sarah was finally forced to make a choice. She told Jake that she chose Elliott because he needed her the most.

Jake accepted her decision, but he couldn't watch another man marry the woman he wanted. He pulled up stakes and left, turning over the responsibility for Sarah to Elliott.

Now Elliott had left Sarah, and she was dead.

Elliott burst through the doorway, caught sight of Sarah on the bed and swayed. "No! No! Sarah, I brought help. I came as quick as I could, but the storm . . . Oh, Sarah!"

Jake didn't know he was going to do it before it happened, but he hit Elliott. Hit him and sent him sprawling in stunned confusion.

"Jake?" Elliott said, as if he'd just seen his old friend. "Jake, you came back!"

"Not soon enough, you bastard!" Elliott tried to get up. Jake hit him again. Blood trickled from the corner of Elliott's mouth. This time he didn't try to rise.

The men who'd ridden in with him entered the cabin and started toward Jake.

"Now, see here—" one of the strangers began.

"No point in doing more damage," another

added, "Elliott came for the doc. We been trying for two days to get here."

It only took one look from Jake to still Elliott's friends and force them to move away.

"I trusted you to look after Sarah," Jake said. "I left her in your care."

"But the baby wasn't due yet. Oh, Jake, you don't know how it was. After you left, everything went wrong." The man was sobbing now. "Oh, God, I'm so sorry."

"Maybe God will forgive you, Elliott, but I won't."

"I loved her, Jake. I tried to take care of her. I swear!"

"No, you let her die," Jake said and went out the door. He would never allow himself to care for anyone or anything again. From now on, he swore, Jake Silver traveled alone.

Chapter 1

Wyoming Territory, May 1874

FEUD BETWEEN CATTLEMEN
AND FARMERS ESCALATES!

Dallas Banning studied the headlines of the *Green Willow Gazette* as the Union Pacific freight train on which she was riding bounced along.

The ink-smudged headline was followed by a more detailed article explaining the cattlemen's concerns over the loss of open range needed to feed their herds. A second article of equal length outlined the United States government's generous offer of four hundred and fifty acres to homesteaders with the suggestion that this was a better deal than buying from land speculators.

The *Green Willow Gazette* was a good newspaper, in spite of the poor quality of the paper and equipment used to print it. The headline would have appealed to Dallas's adventurous nature even if it hadn't been the last newspaper her brother had printed before his death.

Dear Jamie, so kind, so fair, as always, covering both sides of the issue. Who could have murdered him? Had he angered someone that much? She could see where the cattlemen and the land specula-

9

tors would be upset; the ranchers over losing the grazing land and the land agents over Jamie's suggestion that the government land elsewhere was better for farming. But resorting to murdering a newspaper editor seemed absurd.

James Augustus Banning shouldn't have been the one to go west. He wouldn't have if she'd returned to Philadelphia as she'd promised. But she'd been caught up in her own bid for independence and she'd put Jamie off. If she'd been there, he'd never have chosen such a drastic way to prove that he was as much of a newspaperman as his brothers. Sadly, any of her three older brothers would have been better suited to survive the settlement of a new territory. But not idealistic, gentle Jamie.

Dallas swallowed a lump in her throat. Not only had she failed him once, she'd done it a second time when Jamie had written and begged her to come to Wyoming. One man, he'd said, held the solution to the trouble, a man called Jake Silver.

Then Jamie was dead, brutally killed in a way that still hadn't been explained. Dallas swore then that she'd find Jamie's killer. And she'd start with Jake Silver.

Her family, back in Philadelphia, would have received her telegram by now. They would know and understand why she had to be the one to find his murderer.

For she was the only Banning qualified, both as a detective and a journalist. Dallas Banning, daughter of the famous Wesley Banning, member of the Banning newspaper family of Philadelphia, was also, until last week, an operative of the Pinkerton Detective Agency.

Dallas had first met Allan Pinkerton shortly before he'd suffered a debilitating stroke. At that time he'd been a vibrant, active man who'd inspired her with his acceptance of women in his company. He believed that women should use their minds and their abilities to the fullest. She'd been expected to succeed and she had. But after Allan Pinkerton's stroke, the agency was filled with uncertainty, and Dallas had to work even harder to prove her worth to those now in charge.

Then, eight months ago, Jamie had been killed, and Dallas had waited for the local law officials to make an arrest. It was bad enough that weeks had passed before the family learned about his death, but when months went by and no arrest was forthcoming, she'd known it was up to her. But she hadn't expected the last leg of her journey to be on a freight train. In spite of heavy blankets and a wood-fed stove at the back of the car, blowing snow and fierce winds sent icy fingers through the small passenger car.

One of the freight cars on the train actually carried a small group of German immigrants. She worried for their comfort, for there were children and elderly people among the families. But short of giving up her blanket, there was little Dallas could do except hope they arrived soon

Since the train had last stopped for wood, there had been hours of slow tortuous movement up the snow-covered incline that hugged the Rocky Mountain chain. The track ran through tunnels that split sheer rock, leaving walls of frozen granite on either side, under snow sheds built to keep the track free of drifts, and across bridges that made her dizzy just to see the ragged rocks spanned by the wooden structures. Now, according to her guidebook, just ahead was the six hundred fifty foot free-span bridge over Dale Creek, then Laramie city and the Continental Divide.

Dallas closed the book and peered through the

grimy window, trying to catch a glimpse of the snowy peaks in the swirling light. They'd left Cheyenne and headed toward Laramie, skirting the mountains to the flatlands where Green Willow Creek was located. Only a few more hours and she'd be there.

At that moment there was a shout from the back of the rail car, where a poker game had been taking place for most of the day. Though the car had been half full when they crossed into Wyoming, one passenger after another had departed, leaving only Dallas and several rough-looking cowboys who were gambling with a well-dressed gentleman.

"Well, I'm cleaned out," one cowboy said, and lumbered to his feet. "Good thing I'm nearly home, or I'd be eating my saddle."

"Come on, Pete. You know Jake will stake you," one of his companions said.

Jake. Dallas perked her ears. The name of the man Jamie had mentioned.

"Yeah, and he'll send me to the north range and I'll disappear like that prospector last fall in the Green Mountains. You've been there as long as I have, Slim. It takes a lot to get Jake Silver riled, but you know how hard he can be."

"For my money, it takes him too long to act," Slim argued. "Sometimes he has a mighty funny way of looking at things, like the way he stays away from people."

"Yep," the third cowboy said, "but all you have to do to get along with him is follow orders and keep your mouth shut."

"No alibis, no excuses," Pete added. "He ain't going to like us getting back late. He sure as hell won't be happy about you bringing another group of foreigners to Green Willow Creek, Parnell."

Elliott Parnell listened to the cowboys' conversation with more than casual interest as he studied his cards. Until he'd brought the first group of immigrants to Green Willow Creek last summer, he hadn't known Jake was there. Had he known, he might not have taken the job. It had been five years since he'd seen Jake, and in the short time he'd spent getting the first group of farmers settled, Jake hadn't come into town. He must have known that Elliott was there; the appearance of the farmers was too threatening for Jake to be ignorant of it.

A lot of water had washed over the dam since Jake had accused Elliott of murder, and a lot of pain. Since then, Elliott had done things he was ashamed of, but he'd survived. And he'd never seen Jake again. But that couldn't go on indefinitely. Elliott was in Green Willow Creek to stay. He took a deep breath and asked, "Jake mention me?"

"Nope," Slim answered. "Not by name. But ain't no doubt how he feels about them people you're bringing in. Jake is the biggest cattle rancher in Wyoming, or he soon will be, if he can find a way to keep your farmers from fencing the open range."

Elliott had tried, without success, to convince the land speculator to hold off bringing in more Germans. Once he'd seen the land being sold, Elliott had doubts about the potential for success. Only time would tell. The plains grew range grass, but he had seen little evidence that anything else would grow. The agent had refused. The Germans had money; they were buying a dream, and the speculator was getting rich.

In the end, Elliott had known that he would have to seek Jake out, but not until he'd finished the job he'd been hired to do. This job offered him a chance for a new life. His pay for bringing in the immigrants was expenses, a salary, and his own piece of land. Until he had the land in hand, he'd wait.

"All the range isn't open," Elliott said automatically, repeating the phrase again with no more acceptance from these men than from the others he'd faced in Green Willow Creek, "not any more."

"It ain't fair," Slim argued. "Them railroads got millions of acres of land from the government in payoffs and bribes. Now they're getting rich all over again by selling it to a bunch of crooks who're bringing in them foreigners."

Elliott knew it was useless to argue, but he tried to explain. "It will be settled sooner or later. The government Homestead Act opened up the West to the farmers. Free use of the range is gone forever."

The ranch hand called Pete walked to the stove and warmed his hands. "As far as Jake's concerned, it's still open range. I don't think he's gonna like more dirt farmers coming in. You'd better watch your back, Parnell."

"Yeah, I'll do that," Elliott agreed.

He had good reason to know the truth of Pete's statement. Elliott knew there'd been a time when Jake had wanted to kill him. Elliott hadn't even fought back. He'd deserved what Jake had done, that and more. But now, things were different. Elliott was different. And Jake had to come to terms with the law of the land.

Still, Elliott knew that ultimately it wouldn't matter what the law said. Jake had fought fiercely for the Confederacy, though it was difficult to know what he believed, and he was still a formidable enemy. Whether or not Elliott was working within the law, he was bringing in immigrants who were a threat to Jake's way of life.

Dallas had long since stopped any pretense of reading her guidebook. She'd heard about range wars, the open warfare between ranchers, farmers, and sometimes sheepherders. Jamie's paper had reported the escalation of the feud. The man bringing in the immigrants seemed to be articulate and soft-spoken. Not, she decided, the kind of man who would be a fighter.

She could see him plainly through the center crack between the seats. Mr. Parnell was well-dressed, even a bit of a dandy. If she'd seen him at a Philadelphia social, she'd have thought him handsome. Tall, well-proportioned, polished, even; not the kind of polish that came with practice, like some of the gamblers she'd met, but the kind that came with breeding and family. Since the war between the North and the South she'd encountered many men like him, wandering from city to city.

As Mr. Parnell absently shuffled the deck of cards, Dallas could tell from the stiffness of his shoulders that despite his reasoned words of a few moments before, he was worried.

At that moment there was a screech of the wheels. The train locked its brakes and lurched, throwing Dallas forward into the seat in front of her. Her valise was torn from her hands and slid down the aisle into the gentleman's leg.

Immediately after the train had come to a groaning stop, the polished stranger was at her side, her valise in his hand, assisting her back into her seat.

"Are you all right, ma'am?"

"Ah, yes, thank you. What happened?"

"Probably some trouble on the track ahead. It happens frequently in these mountains. The boys will check it out and be back with a report. Are you sure you aren't hurt?"

"I'm fine, thank you, Mr. . . . ?"

"Parnell, Elliott Parnell, ma'am. And you are. . . ?"

She thought about not answering him for a moment, then decided that keeping her identity a secret would serve no useful purpose. It might, in fact, be

15

a way of getting advance information about the situation in Green Willow Creek before she arrived.

"I'm Dallas Banning, from Philadelphia." It had been several years since she'd actually lived in Philadelphia, but naturally she would not reveal the extent of her travels as an agent for Allan Pinkerton, who'd made use of her newspaper background as a cover for various assignments. At other times, she'd assumed the identity of an actress, a wife, once, even, a lady of the night.

"And your destination is . . . ?" the man asked.

"Green Willow Creek, Mr. Parnell."

"Green Willow Creek, Wyoming, is a long way from Philadelphia," Elliott observed softly. "Banning . . . You wouldn't be related to the Banning newspaper family, would you?

"Yes. James Banning, editor of the *Green Willow Gazette*, was my brother. Did you know him?"

"I did. I was the one who . . . found him."

Dallas was stunned. She hadn't known the name of the man who'd brought Jamie's body into town. Now she was face to face with him.

"I . . . I didn't know," she said in a tight voice. "I thank you for what you did."

"Your brother was a . . . dedicated man. His newspaper was responsible for bringing many new settlers to Wyoming, including me."

"Oh?"

"He, and others like him, wrote about the richness of the land and the opportunities it offered. Because of these stories, people are coming west."

"And you are bringing settlers?"

"Yes, I work with the land agent. The farmers will homestead the land and grow grain that we'll send back East."

"And you?"

"I'll be farming, too."

Dallas recalled the words of Jake's late-arriving ranch hand. "Mr. Silver's employees don't seem to think he'll like that very much."

"He won't."

It was back again, that odd tension in Mr. Parnell's body. His fingers, pinched white, curled around the handle of Dallas's valise.

The door of the car opened and one of the cowboys came in, stamping the snow from his boots and stopping at the potbellied stove in the rear of the car to warm his hands. "Brrrr!"

Mr. Parnell placed Dallas's case on the seat beside her and turned toward the man. "What's wrong?"

"Tree across the tracks. They're dragging it off now. We'll get under way again, soon as they clear away the snow behind it. Oughtn't to be more than a couple of hours late if we're lucky."

"It's really beginning to snow," Dallas observed, peering out the window at the swirling flakes. She wanted to ask about Jamie, to learn the details. But something held her back. "The snow is very beautiful, isn't it?"

"It's death," Mr. Parnell said starkly, "masquerading as something pure and clean."

A shiver ran through Dallas, a shiver not resulting entirely from the cold. "Are we in danger?"

"Of freezing to death? Always, when it snows. It comes on wings of white, covering everything in its path."

"You're something of a poet, sir."

"No. I was once; now I'm a farmer, or at least I'm about to make a new start at it. Now, if you'll excuse me, I have to check on my charges."

Elliott Parnell was right about one thing, Dallas realized later. Delays were common on the railroad, and there were several more before they finally pulled into Green Willow Creek the following

17

morning. The snow, meanwhile, had covered everything in its path. Dallas was hungrier and colder than she'd ever been in her life. Her feet felt as if they were asleep, and she stumbled as she exited the train and glanced about for assistance with her cases. But the cowboys had disappeared, and Mr. Parnell had gone to check on the immigrants. There was no one on the platform but Dallas and the exiting German immigrants, who seemed no more equipped for the cold than she. At least they could huddle together for warmth.

Fine. She could see buildings ahead. Dallas headed toward the stovepipe chimneys belching smoke into the gray-white sky. Smoke meant fire and warmth. Fire meant people. Behind her, the train would be pulling out soon, leaving Dallas Banning in the middle of the only street in a cattle town in the dead of winter with no one to turn to for help.

But she'd never needed help before; she'd manage without it now. She'd tracked bank robbers, thieves, and murderers, and not one had ever suspected that she was after him, until he was caught.

Now she hugged her small valise, gaining some reassurance from the knowledge that her derringer was inside. Pulling her cloak tighter to shut out the wind, she avoided the drifts by setting off down the center of the narrow street. There had to be a hotel. There were always hotels near rail stations. She'd find a place to stay, then get about her business.

The citizens of Green Willow Creek were about to meet another member of the Banning newspaper family. But this one had a greater mission than printing newspapers.

Dallas Banning was after a murderer, and Dallas always got her man.

Chapter 2

From inside the immigrants' car where he'd been called to assist an elderly woman, Elliott Parnell watched the raven-haired woman leaving the station. In her navy blue traveling habit and matching hat, she looked like a shadow against the snow.

Dallas Banning was a real beauty, and he had the feeling that she didn't even know it. There was an energy about her, a sense of purpose. Her face was open and honest, with dark eyes that sparkled and lips that were lush and naturally red.

He'd watched her on the train, coolly studying her guidebook and the countryside, and he'd sensed that beneath that calm exterior was something deeper. Without a word she'd staved off the other passengers, making it clear she didn't want to be disturbed. She had courage, all right. And if she really was James Banning's sister, she was walking out of a blizzard into a different kind of storm: the feud between the cattle ranchers and the farmers claiming the land to grow food.

Elliott would have made certain that she was taken care of, but herding the Germans from the train had to be his first concern. He must get them to the resettling building before the cattlemen knew they'd come, before Jake Silver learned that Elliott

19

Parnell was responsible for the new arrivals. He might have ignored Elliott's first trip to Green Willow Creek, but Elliott had the feeling that this one would be challenged.

Because tempers were already running high over the farmers moving onto range land, Lawson Pickens, the local banker who was the official contact between the community and the land speculators, had promised the townspeople that this was the last group. He'd played on their private needs by predicting more business for the merchants, convincing them to support their arrival. The support had been grudging, and it wouldn't take much to change people's minds.

Elliott had told Miss Banning that her brother's newspaper had written about the richness of the land; he hadn't told her that the stories might not have been founded in fact. Because the range grass grew waist high, eager land agents assured farmers that corn and pumpkins would do the same. Efforts by earlier settlers had proved that to be untrue. But Elliott had been assured by Lawson Pickens that the failures were the result of poor planning and no capital for supplies. The Germans, with their work habits and money, were expected to change that. Elliott hoped Lawson was right. But eastern newspapers were already reporting that there was trouble between the farmers and the ranchers.

Open warfare had not been declared between the two factions, but the *Gazette* had reported midnight cattle rustlings blamed on the farmers. The ranchers had retaliated by making secret raids on the farmers, destroying their homes and running off their stock. Elliott feared this group of immigrants might tip the scales. A range war was something Elliott didn't want to see.

Especially not a war commanded by Jake Silver.

At least the wind had dropped and there was a lull in the storm. The heavy snowfall had been an unpleasant surprise. It was already late May, and the spring thaw had begun. Then, out of the Sierra Nevadas, this storm had roared across the plains, as if it too were urging the farmers to go back.

As Elliott assisted the old woman from the car, he heard a shout and looked up in time to see a danger much closer to hand. A bunch of liquored-up cowboys were riding past the station, shooting guns into the air, bearing down on the startled Miss Banning caught by drifts in the middle of the street.

Elliott gave a yell and started toward her, but the riders were already too fast. He'd never get there in time.

He didn't have to.

From the general store, opposite where Dallas was standing, came a figure who grabbed her valise in one hand and scooped her up with the other, flung her over his shoulder, and stepped onto the wooden sidewalk beneath the roof over the entrance to the saloon.

Dallas let out a shocked cry as the horses thundered by. She might have been run over had it not been for the man's quick action. Now, hanging upside down, she felt her rescuer's hand cradling her thigh in much too familiar a manner.

"Sir, what are you doing?"

"Saving your life."

The man lifted her higher, then, as she started to slide, gave her bottom another tight squeeze. Being rescued was one thing, but this was out of line. Gratitude flew out of her mind as he groped her backside.

"Put me down, you . . . you . . . lecher!"

"Gladly!" He leaned forward, loosened his grip and let her slide to the sidewalk where she landed in a puddle of melted snow and ice. The valise followed with a thump.

"Well, you didn't have to try to break my leg!" Dallas scrambled to her feet, her embarrassment tempering her fear and turning it into anger.

"No, I could have let the horses do it!"

Dallas had never heard such cold dispassion in a voice. He wasn't flirting with her. He wasn't concerned about her injuries. She didn't know why he'd bothered to touch her so intimately. One minute he was there, and the next he had turned to walk away.

"Wait, please wait! I'm sorry to appear ungrateful. I was just startled."

As she scurried along behind him, all she could see was the hat covering his face and head, his heavy canvas duster, and boots with silver spurs set with turquoise. He wasn't stopping.

Dallas reached out and caught his arm. "Now, just a minute. Where I come from, a man at least gives a lady the chance to say a proper thank you. What kind of man are you?"

"I'm cold, I'm thirsty, and I'm ready for a woman. Are you volunteering?"

There was a snickering sound that ran through the room they'd entered. Dallas raised her head and glanced around. She wasn't the only woman in the saloon, but she was the only one wearing all her clothes.

Any other woman might have gasped. But Dallas suppressed her surprise. She didn't know the layout of the town yet, and until she did, she wouldn't take a chance of offending anyone, even these ladies of pleasure. "I'm afraid not. I'm a newspaperwoman, not a . . . an entertainer. Could you direct me to the hotel?"

He gave a dry laugh. "Hotel? There isn't one."

"Where do travelers stay?"

"Well there are rooms upstairs, and when it's not full, there's Lucy Jarrett's boarding house."

"Fine," Dallas said. "I'll take a room there."

"I doubt that." His words were sharp, clipped, yet very slow. There was a hint of the South about his speech. But it wasn't gentle and easy. Her rescuer had seen pain and absorbed it. It was a part of him and he radiated it with every word. If he'd ever been a gentleman, that day was gone, and Dallas knew she couldn't expect anything more than blunt truth from him.

This was her first test in Green Willow Creek, and she couldn't let him destroy her, not with half the town looking on. Drawing on every ounce of her control, she turned back to face the man who'd first rescued, but was now insulting, her.

He ripped his hat away, shaking off the glistening beads of melting snow that hung in the jet-black hair that touched his shoulders. He was frowning at her, his brow drawn into deep lines of displeasure; his lips, barely visible beneath a bushy mustache, pressed into a thin line.

His eyes, dark and deep, held her. She sensed danger and a hot intensity.

Where the man on the train seemed polished and well-mannered, her present adversary was anything but a gentleman. He was a man of steel who challenged with every glance. She shivered in response.

"Hello," a woman's voice intruded. "I'm Miranda. You must have come in on the train."

Dallas blinked, breaking the contact between her and her rescuer. With an effort, she turned to the woman.

"Ah, yes. I did. Dallas Banning." She started to hold out her hand, realized that she was clutching her valise, then lowered it. "I'm afraid I've made rather a mess of introducing myself to Green Willow Creek."

"Well, I don't know about what happened in the street, but following Jake in here might give your reputation a bit of a tarnish."

"Jake?" This was the Jake that Jamie had been worried about, the man the two cowboys had called hard.

"Why, yes," Miranda said, "I assumed you two knew each other?"

"Not likely," Jake growled and turned to the bar. "She's too skinny and her mouth is too big for my taste."

"Miss Banning?" Elliott Parnell rushed in from the street. "I saw what happened. Are you all right?"

Jake looked up, catching Dallas between him and the furious look he cast at Elliott Parnell.

Dallas didn't respond. The moment Jake had spotted Mr. Elliott, everything in the saloon had seemed to stop. All movement. All sound. For a long endless moment it seemed as if everyone in the room were frozen in place.

"Hello, Jake," Elliott Parnell said.

Jake Silver didn't return the greeting.

"Are you all right, Miss Banning?" Elliott asked again.

"Yes, Mr. Silver saved me from being run over. . . . I'm afraid I was in the street. . . . Did you get the immigrants unloaded?" Dallas was surprised to hear herself chattering nervously.

Jake finally spoke. "If she's with you and your sodbusters, Elliott, you'd better get her out of here."

Elliott took Dallas's arm protectively. "No, Jake. We simply came in on the same train."

"Now, just a minute, Mr. Silver," Dallas began.

She hadn't asked him to rescue her, and she didn't intend to be spoken to with such disrespect.

But Elliott Parnell didn't give her the chance. "Miss Banning is James Banning's sister."

"Oh? The troublemaking newspaper editor. Almost as bad as the Germans. I've got no use for either one. Take my advice, Miss Banning. Get on the next train back to wherever you came from."

"I don't need your advice, Mr. Silver."

"Suit yourself, but somebody didn't want your brother here, and my guess is that you won't be any more welcome!"

Dallas felt a shiver of pure anger ripple down her backbone. She might as well make her position known right now. She came to find out the truth and she wouldn't be threatened. "Mr. Silver—"

"Jake! Elliott!" Miranda interrupted, a warning in her voice. "Can't you see that Miss Banning is half-frozen? Men! You have to forgive them," she said, turning to Dallas. "At the risk of further staining your reputation, I'd be pleased to have you make use of my room to freshen up and get dry. That is if you don't mind being . . . here."

"I'd be most appreciative, Miss Miranda," Dallas said, following her golden-haired hostess to the stairs. "Perhaps you can suggest a place for me to stay."

"Perhaps. Though I'm afraid that the storm caught a lot of folks by surprise. Every room in town is full."

Dallas felt all the eyes in the room boring holes in her back. She didn't have to be told where she was and what was taking place beyond the doors on either side of the corridor. If being here ruined her reputation, so be it. She wasn't here to make friends anyway. Besides, a lead to Jamie's murderer was a lot more likely to come from these people than those who might be shocked by her actions.

For just a second she wondered what would have happened if Jake had marched straight up the stairs with her. Then she shook off the impossible picture that thought had created.

She wasn't here to be bedded.

She was here to kill a man.

She just had to find out which one.

Jake Silver watched the woman move up the stairs with Miranda. Like a maverick calf that insisted on going its own way, she was trouble. He had a bad feeling about her arrival, a feeling that had nothing to do with seeing her with Elliott.

Elliott had only been in Green Willow Creek for eight weeks when he accompanied the first group of immigrants. He'd come in July, when the plains were still thick with grass and the mountaintops in the distance were only capped with snow at the tips. When Jake learned that the section of land that was to be Elliott's touched his own, he'd tried again to buy it. Again, Lawson Pickens, the local banker, acting as financial officer for the speculator, had refused. Tersely, Jake had asked that the land be parceled out to one of the other farmers, any one of them.

Pickens had refused again. Elliott's land contained the only section of Green Willow Creek that didn't belong to Jake. The seller had allotted the land to Elliott with the promise that he'd share the water with the other farmers who might need it.

Exactly what Jake didn't want. Couldn't afford to allow. Refused to accept. Pickens promised that Elliott wouldn't interfere with the flow of the creek; it was written into the purchase agreement.

But Jake had learned about Elliott and trust.

There'd been a time when Elliott had risked his life to drag Jake out of the line of fire during the Battle of Shiloh. Jake had known what courage that took from a man who wasn't a fighter, and he'd rewarded Elliott by keeping *him* alive throughout the rest of the war. They'd formed a bond that had endured long after. There'd been a time when only a look would have sufficed between them—when Elliott would have known instinctively what Jake expected and would have done it without question.

But that time was gone. That trust had died in a mound of snow five years earlier.

Now all Jake could feel was anger, an anger so strong that it was all he could do not to take Elliott Parnell in his hands and finish the job he'd started in that cold cabin back in Kansas. He'd walked away then, leaving the job unfinished. But the killing instinct was still there, still alive, still tearing at him. He'd lived with it every day of his life since he'd lifted Sarah from the snow. Thrashing Elliott Parnell into a bloody pulp and feeding him to the cattle back on the Double J would still be easy.

But he couldn't kill him then and he couldn't do it now. Sarah made her choice and when she told Jake, he'd promised not to hurt Elliott. All that flashed through his mind now as he faced Elliott Parnell. Jake had made a promise, and even though the person he'd promised was dead, the promise was a bond.

Instead, Jake walked toward Elliott, stopped for a moment, then stepped around him and left the saloon.

A collective sigh of relief sounded as the doors to the saloon slammed behind him. Moments later, laughter and the clink of glasses resumed.

Only Elliott Parnell was left, standing in the middle of the floor, shaking with emotion. Five years ago he'd have followed Jake's suggestion to Dallas Banning and gotten back on the train. But he'd come a long way since Sarah's death. He'd been a coward once, a failure. And that failure had cost him what he loved most in life. Nobody knew that better than he.

Elliott hadn't expected Jake to walk away. From the first moment, he'd known that sooner or later they'd have to face each other. It was time Elliott confronted his demons and made peace with them, and that would start with Jake. But the confrontation would have to wait for another day. Now he had a group of cold, hungry people to care for.

The immigrants were his responsibility. He'd brought them here in return for a new stake for himself and their help in operating his own farm. During the year he'd worked with the government to bring immigrants into the new territories, he'd learned a great deal. It made sense that the land speculators would offer him a job. At first he'd refused, accepting only when they threw in free land as part of his salary. Now it was time to prove to himself that he could stand on his own. The first group of settlers should have already made a start on his house, and he had brought equipment to plant his crops.

If facing Jake Silver down was what it took to pull himself up, that's what Elliott would do. He didn't fool himself that he was the man Jake was, but he intended to stay.

"Welcome to Green Willow Creek, Miss Banning," Miranda was saying as they moved down the hallway.

"Please, call me Dallas."

"That sounds like a drifter's moniker, not a name for a lady."

"Dallas was my mother's maiden name. Her family came to this country from Scotland, so I suppose you could say they were drifters."

Miranda reached the end of the hall and opened the door, ushering Dallas into the kind of room that might have been found in the finest house in Philadelphia. The soft glow of lamps caught the finish of the satin bedcovers and made them shine. Fine rugs covered the rough wooden floor and a gilded mirror reflected the two women; one tall and dark, the other short and golden.

Dallas was struck speechless.

"Surprised?"

"Well, no," Dallas answered, then changed her answer to a more truthful one. "I mean yes. I didn't expect anything this grand out here."

"It's a far cry from the 'hell on wheels' I started with."

"Hell on wheels?"

"That's what they called the movable town that went along with the railroad. There was a cookhouse, a washhouse, bunkhouse, and— entertainment. It moved as the railroad did, but when I got here, I stayed, me and Dr. Horn. Jake was already here."

Dallas removed her bonnet and placed it on the bed. "And you—you like the work?"

Miranda laughed. "The saloon belongs to me. This is my home. Beyond these walls you won't see anything like it. Most of the houses around Green Willow Creek are pretty crude. Even Jake's adobe house is little more than bare walls."

That casual statement suggested that Miranda had been inside Jake's house. Dallas tried to hold back her curiosity but couldn't resist asking, "Jake's—wife? She must be as strong as he is."

Miranda's voice cooled and she gave Dallas a

sharp look. "Jake's wife? Jake lives alone. Other than Wu, that Chinese cook of his, the only people allowed inside his house are his top hands, and they're not welcome for long."

It was obvious that Miranda didn't welcome questions about Jake. "What about Mr. Parnell?"

"Don't know too much about him, except there's bad blood between him and Jake. Came here last summer with a group of farmers, got them set up, and left to get another group. So far as I know, he's living in that immigrant lodge, but I heard that he's building a log house on his land."

"I'll have to find some accommodations," Dallas said. "What about the shopkeepers? Where do they live?"

"Most of them live in the backs of their businesses, or upstairs. You can see what kind of weather we have. Doesn't happen often, but sometimes we're snowed in for days. People stay close to what's theirs."

Stay close? Where had Jamie lived? "Are there living quarters in the newspaper office?"

"Newspaper office?" Miranda gave her a disbelieving look. "Why yes, I believe there is a room James used for sleeping, but there's no kitchen and there's no fire laid and no wood burning. I'm afraid that the facilities won't be very comfortable."

"Could you find someone to build a fire? I'll be glad to pay for wood and his help."

Miranda added a log to the fire and poked the coals into new life. "Well, yes. I suppose. There's a boy who sweeps up for me. He lives in a room out back. He runs errands for the locals. In fact, he sold newspapers for your brother."

"In the meantime, I'll be pleased to accept your hospitality until a fire is lit. I am still chilled from my experience."

Miranda smiled, reached inside an ornate wardrobe, and pulled out a burgundy velvet robe lined with fur, laying it across the back of a brocade-covered chair.

"Take off those damp clothes and get into this. You can drape them over that chair by the fire. I'll go down and get you something hot to drink and some food."

Dallas took the robe and examined it. "Is this real fur?"

"That it is. Got it off a Russian prince."

"A Russian prince?"

"Yep. Duke Alexis Romanov. It happened back when they were building the railroad. He came along with some of those rich investors who wanted to go buffalo hunting, started in Omaha, and ended up here. They even brought their own private car."

"That must have been exciting."

"He was a handsome man, the young duke was, golden hair, side whiskers, and a downy mustache. He took a fancy to me and gave me this dressing gown. Said in Russia, all the women wear clothes like this in winter."

"It's very beautiful."

"Only one in the West. Lock the door behind me," Miranda instructed as she left.

Dallas heard the door close and moved closer to the fire. Miranda was right; she could use some food and something hot to drink. She was thoroughly chilled. The Wyoming wind had pierced her warmest cape as if it were made of gauze and her boots were soaking wet.

After locking the door, she removed her cape and her dress and slid her arms into the great sweeping sleeves of the fur-lined dressing gown. The garment was a deep, rich red, the finest velvet. The white fur lining extended beyond the inside, forming a cuff for the sleeves and a six-inch border of trim around the hem.

It was obvious that, other than her business, this robe might be Miranda's dearest possession. Dallas felt a humble sense of gratitude. She draped her dress over the chair, removed her boots and placed them by the fire, leaving her feet covered only by her cotton stockings. Then she saw the matching slippers peeking out from beneath the chair. White fur, with a red cord to draw them up close at the ankle.

Dallas glanced at herself in the mirror. She didn't often think about the way she looked. But dressed this way she felt like a czarina from some fairy tale. As warmth slowly returned to her limbs, she moved toward the heavily draped window and peeked out. Glass. In this rough little railroad town, Miranda had real glass in her window.

What on earth had made Jamie decide to settle in Green Willow Creek? There was never any doubt that he could publish his own newspaper. He didn't have to come out here to do it. All the Banning children had been trained as newspaper people, and their father's standards had been high. The others had taken their father's expectations in stride, but for Jamie, success had been elusive.

Maybe it was because Mother had been killed in a carriage accident when Jamie had been only a small boy. He'd missed the comfort of a mother's love, turning to Dallas instead. Perhaps his challenge was greater than that of the others because he was the youngest. Perhaps it was because Mr. Banning didn't know how to give him the nurturing he needed. No matter, Dallas knew deep in her heart that she might have changed what happened, and she hadn't.

But she'd find the answer; she swore that her

brother's killer would die. If that killer turned out to be Jake Silver, so be it.

Through the wavy pane of glass she could see below into the street. At that moment the wind died and she caught sight of a man on a horse riding slowly past, a man wearing a big hat and a heavy duster with a split in the back. The silver of his spurs caught a sliver of light spilling from the saloon, and for a moment he seemed to hesitate, turning his head toward the window.

Jake Silver.

The name fit the man who was already frosted with snow. The black horse snorted, his breath making a cloud of tiny ice crystals in the air.

Even from where she stood she could sense his tightly leashed anger.

Dallas quickly stepped back, though she doubted that he could see her. As if on signal, the horse moved off, picking its way through snow that swirled halfway up its legs. Jake was the key to the trouble, Jamie had said so. Now it was up to Dallas to find out what that meant.

Jake Silver, like the harshness of the Wyoming elements, might have been more dangerous than Jamie had anticipated. To Dallas, the storm was frightening, but no more so than the man in the street below who was challenging it. Others might have waited out the storm by staying in town, but not Jake Silver. He was leaving, and Dallas had no doubt he'd get wherever he was going.

It saddened Dallas to see how her gentle brother had been doomed from the start. He hadn't been tough enough to master the life out here. Perhaps she would not be either. But at least she had already made two friends: Elliott Parnell and Miranda. She appreciated Miranda's kindness and she intended to return the gesture.

And she was dressed in a red robe with cuffs and linings of fur, looking out into a world of white.

"It's death," Elliott had said, "masquerading as something pure and white."

Dallas shivered and turned toward the fire.

Outside the saloon, the snow had obliterated any sign of Jake. Elliott had to forget about Jake and get to the livery stable, where arrangements had been made to transport the new settlers waiting at the train station.

The local ranch workers hired on as drivers were ready, as were the wagons, but the weather forced the settlers to spend the night in the station. It was the next morning before Elliott and his homesteaders were finally loaded into the conveyances and heading for the building that would house them until they could claim their own land and start to build.

Until the snow stopped, Elliott would share the immigrant housing. During the months of dealing with the homesteaders, he'd learned respect for the sturdy men and their wives. They didn't complain, and they made do with whatever was available. Between their broken English and his poor German, they'd formed a bond of friendship that he hadn't expected.

By late afternoon they'd managed to reach the rough wooden structure that would be their home for the next months. Inside, earlier arrivals had built fires, prepared food, and waited to welcome the newcomers.

After unloading their goods and storing them in one of the outbuildings, the men, cold and wet, came gratefully to the fire. They offered Elliott and the drivers a place close to the heat before accepting bowls of hot, thick soup and settling down to eat.

Before they were half-finished, a commotion outside brought the farmers to the door.

A crude cart was being pulled by an ox, plodding through the snow. When it reached the bunkhouse, the driver stumbled to the ground and began to help the sobbing woman beside him to dismount. Instantly the farmers inside went to help bring her in, conversing angrily and too rapidly for Elliott to understand.

"What's happened?" Elliott asked and was rewarded with a rush of German, spoken too rapidly for him to understand.

Hans, one of the earlier immigrants, stepped up. "She says that the Devil of the Plains came, destroyed their house."

"He's at it again," one of the drivers said to another. "Looks like one way or another your farmers are going to get run out of the territory, Mr. Elliott. Too bad."

Elliott caught the exchange of laughter between the drivers but let it pass for the moment. "Devil of the Plains? What do you mean, ma'am?"

Hans answered. "They came in the night and tore down the house. Her husband tried to stop them, but he was killed by the Devil."

"In the middle of a snowstorm?"

"The Devil don't care. If he wanted to stomp on the soddie roof, he'd do it easy enough," the first driver offered. "Like Jake said, if you're where you don't belong, you have to expect trouble, and these people oughtn't to be here."

Elliott turned to the driver. "What's your name?"

"Folks call me Doak," he answered.

"Well, Doak, I'll give you two minutes to get your gear and get out," Elliot said, angrily reacting to the driver's attitude toward the settlers.

"Hey, what are you so put out about? Nobody's

going to mess with you. You're no foreigner. You're one of us!"

One of us? Not any longer. Elliott had done many things that he wasn't proud of, but he was trying hard to change that. "That's where you're wrong," he said. "I'm one of them, and they have a legal right to be here."

"Yeah? And who's going to enforce that legal right? The closest lawman is in Laramie, and he ain't likely to get involved in a fight between the cattlemen and these dirt farmers."

"One of your minutes is gone!" Elliott said, with more threat than he was capable of enforcing.

The drivers glanced around and saw the men inside the house forming a loose circle around the room. The farmers might not know what had been said, but they were ready to back up a tone of voice that they recognized.

The drivers weren't.

As they left, Elliott turned to the woman who'd been injured. He hadn't thought much about the people he was bringing in, other than what he could gain from them. But he'd seen too much pain and suffering, too many women who'd lost their loved ones. An anger grew out of the sorrow he'd carried around inside him, an anger that surprised him with its intensity.

Elliott Parnell realized that he'd just made another enemy in Green Willow Creek. And he knew that it wouldn't be the last.

Chapter 3

Doak found the old man camped out beneath a ledge at the base of the mountain near the crude corral they'd constructed. He slid from his horse. "You been out riding with the Devil?"

"None of your concern, boy! Give me your report."

Doak walked toward the fire. No point in letting the old man have everything his way. "You hear about that newspaper editor's sister coming in on the train?"

"I did."

"Wowee!"

"You get those Germans out to the settlement house?"

"Yep. You ought to see her. She's somp'um."

"Is that all you saw?"

"No. When I was at the settlement they brought in a woman. Seems one of the families got their house tore down and the man got killed. You know anything about that?"

"That's for me to know. And you not to talk about. Tell me about the woman. If she's anything like her brother, she could be trouble."

"Oh, she's trouble all right, man trouble. You just ought to see her. A real looker. Miss Dallas Banning ain't nothing like them girls at Miranda's. She's a sweet-smelling woman with silk dresses and gloves."

The old man forced himself to appear uninterested as he hunkered over the fire, squinting his eyes to shield them from the smoke. Too many years of keeping warm by smoky fires and too much strong drink had turned his eyes permanently red and his voice into a growl. He knew that Doak was loose-mouthed, and he'd cautioned him over and over about his careless remarks. They were too close to the end to let him mess anything up.

Doak used his hands to outline the woman's imaginary body. "Maybe I'll pay her a little visit, like I did her brother?"

The old man spat in the fire and listened to the sizzle the tobacco juice made as it fell in the flames. "Why?"

"Well, she's a real juicy-looking plum. Real class, like one of them singers in a traveling show. She don't belong out here. I could talk her into going back where she come from." The younger man didn't try to keep the suggestion of what he had in mind out of his voice.

"No, not yet. What I want you to do is get on back in the canyon and feed the stock before you go. The boss don't want to lose none of them steers. It took too long to get them."

Doak didn't know what they were up to, but he knew that rustling cattle was just a cover.

"How you planning on getting rid of them without Jake Silver finding out?"

"Oh, he'll find out and blame the farmers. By the time Silver starts his spring roundup, those farmers will have spooked the rest of his cows clean into the next state."

"Ah, Rejo, sometimes I think you been out here with these cattle too long."

"A man does what he has to do. Besides, I like cattle better than people."

Doak laughed. "Yeah? No wonder we found so many dead calves last spring. You'd rather have them than a woman."

The old man stood, all six feet five inches of him, leaning on his staff like some sheepherder instead of the flunky he was.

"Boy," he growled. "There's two things you don't talk about out here; a man's woman and his pecker. One takes care of the other and only God knows how he goes about it."

Doak thought about old Rejo's anger as he made his way back to the ranch where he worked. The old man thought Doak didn't know who they were working for, and that suited him fine. If Rejo wanted to rustle cattle from the ranchers and blame it on the Germans, that was okay. When Rejo was done following orders he'd have them in a range war, and that was when Doak intended to demand certain rewards for himself.

Doak would have the land Jake Silver claimed. Then he'd have control of the biggest water supply in the area. He wouldn't have to sell off his own private stock. They were hidden in a blind canyon, where he'd feed and water them until spring. Then he'd wait for the calves to come. By that time, he'd have a fresh supply of cattle with no brand to hide. And the cattlemen would blame Rejo, or they would if they ever figured out who was stealing from them. With land and water, and his own brand, he'd soon be able to buy him some silver spurs like Jake Silver wore. He'd decided to call his ranch the Double D. He liked the sound of that.

Doak thought about the German woman who had been brought to the resettlement center. He didn't know how he'd use that, but sooner or later he would. Taking on odd jobs at the livery stable now and then always provided information to someone willing to make a little money on the side. He hadn't been involved in tearing her house down, but no doubt Rejo had had a hand in it.

The old fool, staying out there in this weather. Sooner or later, Doak would be a rancher and not some hand hired to do all the dirty jobs. Until the war started, he'd stay where he could make money on the side. That was the beauty of being a cowhand—nobody knew what you did because the land was too big for you to be seen. Soon he'd decide what he'd do and when.

Starting with a call on Miss Dallas Banning.

No matter how fancy she was, any woman ready to be friendly with a woman like Miranda couldn't be too pure to appreciate Doak's special capacity for that kind of entertainment. Rejo was right. A man didn't talk about his pecker, he let it speak for itself.

She'd never be warm again. Dallas and Willie, the young boy Miranda had sent to prepare the fire, had spent two days cleaning the newspaper office and trying to make the upstairs room less drafty and more livable.

There was a potbellied stove in the office below, which did little more than take the chill from the air, and a small fireplace upstairs, which shared a chimney with the building next door.

Dallas walked to the stove and rubbed her hands together. They'd already burned all the broken furniture and old water-stained pulp paper. The intensity of the storm had begun to decrease, but had not yet fully abated. Only the railroad had a supply of coal to be used for fuel, and they refused to part with any of it.

Visitors to town were limited to riders and a few

brave men with ox-drawn sleds. There was no sign of another woman.

"Willie, where do you live?"

The red-haired, freckled-faced boy, not driven to stick with a job under the best of conditions, took the opportunity to stop working. Leaning on his broom, he answered, "Miss Miranda lets me stay in a room behind the saloon."

"What happened to your family?"

"Don't know. My pa left when they found gold up on Pike's Peak. My ma came here and stayed on for a while, working for Miss Miranda. Then one day she rode off with a man heading for a silver strike in Colorado and never come back."

"Oh, I'm sorry. I lost my mother, too, when I was eight years old. But I still had my father and my brothers." Dallas couldn't imagine any mother abandoning a child. She resolved to help Willie.

"Your brother James, he were a good man. Not too smart, but he didn't seem to know it."

Dallas lowered the box of type she'd collected from the floor where it had been scattered. "My brother *was* a good person. What makes you think he wasn't smart?"

"He should of kept his nose out of things that didn't concern him."

"But that's the purpose of a newspaper, to report the truth so that all may know."

"Yeah, and sometimes it gets you killed."

Dallas began to arrange the letters in order as she considered his statement. This was familiar work; she'd done it a thousand times in her father's newspaper office. Maybe Willie could help her.

"Didn't my brother have any friends here?"

"Friends? Don't know. Reckon he spent as much time with Jake Silver as anybody, Jake and Miss Miranda. But I don't know iffen you could call 'em friends. Jake and Mr. Banning used to do a lot of arguing when Jake would come to town."

"About what?"

"Jake wanted him to quit taking up for them farmers. Said if he didn't, he were going to take this place apart a board at a time."

Jake Silver. Everything revolved around Jake. She remembered his threat to her. Go home, he'd said. So he'd threatened James, too. But Jamie hadn't let it stop him from printing what he wanted to print. No wonder Jamie had considered Jake the key to the trouble.

"Surely Mr. Silver didn't mean that he'd harm James. That would be against the law."

Willie laughed. "Miss Banning, Jake's word is law here, or as much of one as we got, Jake and Mr. Pickens."

"Don't you have a sheriff?"

"Had one, but he got shot one night. Ain't nobody wanted the job since."

"Who shot him?"

"Don't know. Never found out."

Just like they'd never found Jamie's killer.

Dallas felt suddenly cold, and her stiff fingers refused to line up the letters.

She thought back to the conversation she'd had with Miranda the previous morning. At first when she'd asked about Jake, Miranda had cooled. Dallas had explained that she was interested in talking with people in authority who might know what happened to her brother. Miranda relaxed then and opened up. Jake had been here for five years, she explained. He'd claimed as much land as he could legally claim, then bought more from the railroad company. The cattle he'd driven up from Texas had multiplied and now numbered as many as ten thousand, grazing the open range. From the beginning, he'd managed to fight off the encroachment of the individual nesters who squatted on land and claimed it thereafter—until the railroad began to sell off land that the government had given to the investors.

That much Miranda told her. But nothing more. When asked about his strange reaction to Mr. Parnell, Miranda had professed not to know.

Maybe Willie would be more helpful.

"How long have the farmers and the cattlemen been feuding, Willie?"

"Long as I been here, but it's jist been in the last year that Mr. Parnell and them foreigners come in and bad things started happening."

"But surely there is enough land out here for everybody. I certainly haven't seen that many people in town."

"Oh, you'll see them soon enough when the thaw starts."

"Are there other cattlemen like Mr. Silver?"

"Not as big, but there's more. They jist don't have the water like Jake."

"Water?" That was something that Dallas hadn't heard about. From the amount of snow she'd seen, there ought to be enough water to float a schooner. But land used for farming had to be flat, and the only streams she'd seen had been in the mountains.

"Mr. Silver controls the water?"

"Green Willow Creek runs out of the mountain, across a corner of Mr. Parnell's land and straight through Jake's ranch. Since them farmers came they dip into it. It ain't dried up yet, but with more of 'em, there'll come a time when there ain't enough left for the other ranchers. Jake don't mind the cattle drinking, but them farmers want to siphon it off to grow cabbage."

"Have they tried to work out some kind of compromise?"

"That's what your brother tried to get them to do. There was some that said he might pull it off. Then he was killed."

"Do they said who did it?"

"Sure, the farmers say that Jake did it. Jake says that the farmers did it. Me? I think it was that Devil animal."

"What Devil animal?"

"The one Mr. Banning had been investigating. The one that rides the plains at night."

"Animal? Like a horse, or a wolf?"

"No ma'am. This is bigger, it's shaggy, and it blows poison at you if you get too close."

"You've seen it?"

"No, but there's them that has."

"And what makes you think that creature had anything to do with James?"

"He went out looking for it. Then he turned up on the road—dead. Mr. Parnell found him. The doc said he looked like he was scared to death and chewed-up, too."

Dallas knew that Jamie was found on the road outside of town, his body covered with bruises and lacerations. But she'd been told that it was a bullet that killed him and there'd certainly been no mention of any kind of animal. As for the idea that he looked scared, Dallas had no doubt that was true.

So was she.

"Willie, do you think that Miss Miranda would allow me to rent one of her rooms for a couple of days—just until we can get some fuel in here to heat this place?"

The shocked look on Willie's face was answer enough. "Miss Banning, that wouldn't be proper."

"But we've already burned everything here, except the table and the paper I'll need to print the *Gazette*. I don't think I can take another night without heat."

"Just let me ask around. If you're willing to pay, I'll find you something to burn, even if it's cow chips."

After his departure, Dallas was alone, listening to the wind moan outside the building. If the newspaper office hadn't been a corner building, it would have been better protected from the cold. If Jamie had been as good a builder as he'd been a newspaperman, the walls wouldn't have been so flimsy. If she'd come better prepared for the weather, she wouldn't be considering moving into a saloon.

Dallas allowed a rare sigh to escape. She would never have admitted it to her brothers, but she was having a mild case of second thoughts about having come alone. Never once had she been totally on her own as a detective—operative, she corrected herself, remembering Allan Pinkerton's preference for the term. She'd always worked with another staff member as a backup. This time she didn't even have the security of a police officer in town to fall back on.

Except, as Willie had pointed out, Jake Silver.

Hardly a reassuring thought, considering he was one of the major suspects—the only suspect, until she was able to get out and ask questions of someone other than fourteen-year-old Willie. It was obvious that Willie viewed Jake as bigger than one of Ned Buntline's dime novel heroes.

Well, she allowed herself to admit honestly, he was big. And he was physically the kind of man a novelist might write about. Even now, as she shivered before the stove, her detective's curiosity was piqued by the memory of slate-blue eyes and silver spurs.

* * *

Jake Silver swore and tossed his half-smoked cigar into the fireplace. First Parnell returned with more immigrants. Now there was a woman, a maverick who was determined to make her own way even if it meant freezing to death.

"Well, let her. She isn't any more my responsibility than that fool brother of hers."

"Yes sir, Mr. Jake," Willie said and turned to go. Jake had been his last hope, the only one with a large enough wood supply to share.

"No, wait." Jake stepped into the hallway and barked, "Wu! Pack up some blankets and some supplies."

"Yes, Mr. Jake. You going cow driving?"

"No, I'm going to town. And don't ask questions, you nosy old woman."

"Not old, Mr. Jake. And Wu not a woman. Wu not like you calling him woman. If you pay Wu lots of money, Wu will have his own woman soon."

The arguments between Wu and Jake rose and fell with the moment, Wu always planning to send for a Chinese bride from his home province, and Jake always giving orders that Wu ignored unless it suited him to obey.

Jake didn't know much about Wu, not even his age. He'd rescued the Chinese man when he'd been caught in a tunnel of snow while working for the railroad and left for dead by the crew boss. Wu had made a reluctant houseboy and cook, at first threatening daily to return to his country where he could marry and have children to care for him in his old age. Of late, his threat had turned into sending for a wife to come here.

Behind Wu's disdain and Jake's short temper was a sense of family that neither would ever admit to. But Jake did understand Wu's loneliness. The empty feeling was always there, just below the surface, tarnishing everything with its grayness. Maybe he'd take a ride over to Abilene and look around for a woman for Wu among the Chinese who'd stayed on after the railroad had been finished. And there was always San Francisco. For some time, Jake had felt an urge to see the Pacific Ocean. Once this business with the farmers was settled, he might just take a train ride west.

The farmers. That brought him back to Elliott Parnell, and the pain in his gut. Jake had avoided Elliott the last time he was in Willow Creek. Elliott stirred up memories that Jake had closed off five years ago.

Memories of Sarah.

Sarah laughing in that infectious way, looking at you as if she could see straight into your soul. She was soft and gentle, making a man feel good about himself and the world. Like Jake's mother, Sarah made a man believe he could accomplish anything.

Until Elliott let her die.

Jake had lost everything he'd ever loved—his home, his mother, his hope for a future—as if his loving it had in some way destroyed it. By leaving Sarah to die alone, Elliott became the symbol of all Jake's losses. Jake couldn't forgive him.

Dear, gentle Sarah was nothing like that fool woman who'd almost gotten herself run down by horses. Dallas Banning. What kind of name was that, anyway? What kind of woman got on a train alone and rode halfway across a country to—do what? He had no idea why she was here. But he sensed she was trouble. Unbranded. A maverick.

It would serve her right if he let her freeze to death.

"What about it, you Chinese heathen? Have you got the supplies ready?"

"Mr. Jake, I not heathen. I belong to the Celestial body of heaven. You the sinner!"

Wu slammed two baskets down on the desk Jake was pacing around. "Blankets in hall closet. You want wood? Cut it yourself. Wu not slave!"

Jake started to curse, called back the words and shook his head in approval. "You're right, Wu. Thank you. There will be a star in your Celestial crown."

Wu was right. Jake would hitch up the sled and take her a load of wood. He blamed himself for not knowing that James Banning had been in danger. Keeping his sister safe would be Jake's penance, even if she was the most infuriating woman he'd ever met.

Chapter 4

Dallas heard someone open the door to the newspaper office. "Did you bring what I need?" she asked as she backed out from under the table where she was searching for an errant exclamation point.

"Well, now, that depends, little lady."

Dallas raised up and turned around. The two men standing in the door were strangers, smiling, weathered men who didn't look like they'd come to pay for a newspaper subscription.

"I'm sorry," she said, edging her way to the valise that contained her derringer. "I was expecting Willie, with a load of fuel."

"Oh, we're loaded," the second man said, "and this looks like just the place to get rid of our—" he chuckled "—our load."

Slowly, a step at a time, they were coming closer. Dallas sidled closer to her gun.

"I've been trying for two days to get this place warm," she chattered. "Wouldn't you be more comfortable if you closed the door?" She smiled and reached behind her to unsnap her case. "Then we can discuss your—problem."

One man looked at the other and let out a chortle of disbelief. "Whooee, did I tell you this was a sweet-smelling woman, or not?"

"You did, Doak. You sure 'nuff did."

Dallas slid her hand inside the valise and closed her fingers around the handle of her gun, bringing it slowly out, confident now that she could slow them down, if not stop them entirely.

The man called Doak moved toward the door while the other man moved toward her, a wide grin revealing the loss of a tooth and a tobacco stain at the corner of his mouth.

"Well now, little lady. Let's me and you get down to business here."

She waited until Doak had turned back and started toward her. With both men clearly in her sights she brought her arm around to the front of her body, her gun extended.

"I think not, boys. The newspaper office isn't open for official business yet. Anyone entering without permission will be considered an intruder and shot."

"What the hell?"

Doak made a move toward her, just as she fired. The first man slumped to his knees and let out a scream. She hadn't intended to hit him. Then he sat back on his heels and she saw that his collapse was from fear, not injury.

At that moment the door crashed open and Jake Silver stepped inside, his gun drawn, the expression on his face a dare to the most stouthearted. "I wouldn't make any sudden moves, boys," he said.

"Now, wait a minute." Doak began retreating toward the door. "Don't get bent out of joint, Jake."

"No, we didn't mean no harm," the man on the floor said, coming to his feet. "We just come to see . . . to see—"

"—if the lady needed any help," Doak finished.

"And I appreciate your concern," Dallas said, "but I can look after myself." She lowered her gun and took in a quick breath of relief. Her gun carried two shots, but she had wasted one as a means of getting their attention. She'd never shot anyone, though she was convinced that she could if she had to. Thank goodness someone had come to the rescue.

Even if that someone was, once again, Jake Silver.

"Miss Banning?" Willie, his arms full of dark blankets, came skidding in the door. "You all right?"

"Of course I'm all right," Dallas snapped. "I'm accustomed to taking care of myself."

"You have a gun?" Willie watched as Dallas replaced her derringer in her valise.

"I do. And as you heard, it's loaded. Did you bring the wood?"

"Jake—I mean, Mr. Silver brought it, in his sled." Willie deposited his goods on the table.

"Since these boys here came to help," Jake added dryly, "I think Miss Banning would appreciate them bringing in the wood. Wouldn't you, Miss Banning?"

The two cowboys didn't wait for her answer. With Willie helping, the wood and several baskets were unloaded in record time. Jake didn't move. He paid little attention to the men, focusing on Dallas instead.

"Thank you, gentlemen," she said as they brought in the final load. "I didn't realize what you had in mind, or I wouldn't have been so—unfriendly."

Under Jake's watchful eye, they accepted her thanks and exited the building in record time.

Shortly thereafter, Willie, conscious of the odd tension building between Jake Silver and Miss Banning, excused himself. "I guess I'll be getting along now, Miss Banning. Here's your money. Mr. Silver wouldn't take none."

"Thank you, Willie. I'll expect you in the morning."

"Yes, ma'am."

Then they were alone. Jake Silver glanced around at the newly swept room, noting the lack of furniture and the lack of warmth. The woman might be one of the Bannings of Philadelphia, but she was apparently made of tough stuff.

Jake didn't understand a woman like Dallas Banning. He'd brought her wood and blankets, but he had the feeling that if he hadn't, she'd have taken an ax to the hills and cut down her own tree.

Dallas had gathered her hair severely back with a large handkerchief, allowing it to tumble down her back. Beneath the kerchief there were escaping tendrils that curled stubbornly around her oval face. He'd been wrong about its color; it wasn't black. In the watery light from the overhead lamp he could see that it was a rich, warm brown. Her wide mouth, now trembling in stern disapproval, was surprisingly rosy. Whether the color came from her emotional reaction to his intervention or something else, he didn't know.

"Willie was right. This place is cold, Miss Banning. Where's your bed?"

"I beg your pardon?"

"Your bed. Wu, my—cook, sent blankets."

"Oh, of course. I thought . . ." Her voice trailed off in confusion.

"I know what you thought. But believe me, if that's what I wanted, I wouldn't need a bed to get it."

He stopped, slowly dropping the blankets, his expression was one, not of displeasure, but of stern challenge. His gray eyes were like mirrors, reflecting the light, never allowing another's gaze to penetrate to the inner truth.

"I'm not certain why Willie went to you."

"Because I'm the only one who can help you."

He stood, leaning indolently against the table, his back resting on the drum of the printer, his arms folded against his chest, watching her for a long moment.

"Thank you," she snapped, in a voice so tight that even she wouldn't have recognized herself, "you've helped me. Now what are you waiting for?"

"The last time we met you told me that where you came from a man allowed a lady to apologize. I'm waiting."

There was no smile on his lips, what she could see of them beneath the mustache, but the hint of it in his voice was just enough to change the anger of her reply to a more polite one.

"I'm sorry if I seem ungrateful, Mr. Silver. It's just that I really am accustomed to taking care of myself and, somehow, you seem to have been appointed my guardian angel."

The silver in his eyes turned opaque black, as if darkness had descended in the newspaper office.

"I'm no guardian angel, Miss Banning. I lost my angel wings long ago." He turned to go.

"Wait, Mr. Silver. I'd like to talk to you about James."

He seemed to wrestle with her request for a moment. Finally he turned back and removed his hat.

"James didn't belong out here, Miss Banning."

"Neither do I. But a hard life didn't kill him, a bullet did."

"That's true. But if a bullet hadn't, the isolation would have. He was too eager for approval. That's hard to come by when you're determined to print the truth. It bothered him, for he liked people too much."

"That's a family characteristic."

"Then you wouldn't like it much on a Wyoming ranch. Sometimes weeks pass without seeing a soul. Out here, people are too busy staying alive to worry about anybody else."

Jake didn't like the defensive way she made him feel. Why didn't he just get the hell out and head down to Miranda's? Instead he picked up some of the small pieces of wood from the pile and turned his attention to the stove.

"I think Wu sent bread and meat and—who knows what else," he said as he fed some of the splinters of dry kindling into the coals. As they began to flare up, he added lengths of wood, carefully spacing them to allow the fire to draw properly.

Dallas watched him, conscious of the sound his spurs made in the silence as he worked. Drawn by the warmth, she moved closer, then hesitated as she considered whether it was the fire or the man that drew her.

"What I'd really like," she confessed as she held her hands out to the stove, "is a cup of hot tea. Do you suppose Wu put tea in the picnic basket?"

"Does a Chinaman wear a queue?" He rose and turned back to the table storing the baskets, picked up the larger one and brought it closer to the stove.

"Is there a smaller table?"

She glanced up at the loft. "There was. I burned it last night in desperation."

"There is a loft fireplace?"

"Yes."

"If you expect to sleep up there tonight, I'd better start a real fire." He gathered up an armful of kindling and wood, then climbed the stairs to the second floor.

Dallas didn't want to consider what Jake Silver might think about the crude sleeping arrangements she had made upstairs. There was a corn husk mattress that she'd dragged to the fireplace for the first night, her valise, and her trunk. Nothing else.

Moments later she'd opened the basket to find a teapot, a tin container of tea leaves, an iron cooking vessel, and two loaves of bread that, though cold, still smelled fresh-baked. Real food and tea.

Quickly she filled the teapot with water and placed it on the eye of the stove. By the time she'd checked the second basket containing meat, cheese, and cans of fruit, she heard the sound of Jake returning. He was carrying her trunk, which he placed near the table.

"Our table," he explained.

"Chairs?"

"Don't need them." He spread one of the blankets on the floor adjacent to the stove and the trunk.

"Oh, a picnic. Do you often have picnics in the middle of a blizzard?"

Jake pulled the rolls of paper on which James used to print his newspaper close to the stove. Then he draped them and the print table with the other blankets, enclosing the picnic area in a tent around the stove.

"No. I don't have picnics anymore. Picnics are for women and dreamers, like . . . like James."

"Tell me what happened to my brother."

"Didn't you get a letter from Lawson Pickens?"

"Oh yes, your banker wrote a very kind letter. I'll admit I expected to hear from the marshal or perhaps even your minister. I didn't."

"We don't have a marshal and the only preacher in town is Mr. Bowker, the undertaker, and he's no real man of God."

"I see. Mr. Pickens explained that James's body was found outside of Green Willow Creek. He'd been killed. Nobody knew why. He said Jamie was a good man and, so far as anyone knew, had no enemies. They surmised that his death was an attempted robbery. Was it?"

"I doubt it," Jake answered.

At least he had the integrity to give her an honest answer. "Why?"

"His money was still in his pocket. That pretty well rules out an attempted robbery."

"So, why was he killed?"

"Somebody wanted him dead."

"Why?"

"He was stirring up trouble with that newspaper of his."

"What kind of trouble?"

"The kind of thing an outsider wouldn't understand."

But Dallas couldn't let that pass.

"Did you disagree with my brother, Mr. Silver?"

"Often and loudly."

"Did you kill Jamie?"

There was a long pause. "No, but I could have. He wouldn't be the first man I've killed."

Dallas believed him.

He had killed men and probably worse. She didn't know why, but for now, she was willing to take that answer at face value. Pressing Jake Silver would only irritate him, and nothing would be gained by that. She'd try a different tack.

"There seems to be one school of thought that thinks there might be a connection between Jamie's death and his attempt to bring the disagreement between the farmers and the cattlemen to an end."

"Could be."

"And then, of course, there's Willie, who believes it was the Devil of the Plains that killed him."

56

Jake let out a dry, unsmiling laugh. "Devil of the Plains?"

"Yes, though he seemed to have a bit of a problem trying to figure out how he changed from spitting poison to spitting bullets."

"Your brother was shot, Miss Banning, and he was beaten, but it wasn't a poison-spitting monster who did it."

"Beaten? I wasn't told that."

"There was no point in telling you."

Dallas could hardly speak, she was so stunned. "Didn't you think we deserved to have all the facts?"

"It wasn't my decision. Now why don't you see about serving what Wu sent."

To cover her pain, she checked the teapot with shaking fingers. When the water boiled, she added the leaves and inhaled the fragrant Oriental odor. With a knife she discovered rolled up in a napkin with other utensils, she sliced the bread and cut pieces of cheese. Laying them out on their table, she turned to find Jake scowling at her.

"Something wrong, Mr. Silver?"

Something wrong? Oh, yes, maverick. Something is very wrong. All this is wrong. Being here with you when you've just lost someone you loved. Jake had done all this before, shared a meal with a woman who'd lost a loved one, let himself be drawn into her pain, take on her cause. He never should have come here. He'd known it, and still he'd come. "I want a drink of something other than that green water Wu calls tea."

"He must have known that," Dallas said, lifting a bottle from the basket. "My guess is that this is some kind of whiskey."

"Damn Chinaman . . . Always stays one step ahead of me." Jake took the flask, his rapid movement catching Dallas by surprise. She felt the touch of his bare fingers grazing hers and jerked away, almost upending the bottle.

"Careful, Miss Banning. Depriving a man of what he needs is dangerous."

"Why do you keep talking like that, making suggestive comments like some crude cattleman? Where are you from, anyway?"

Jake took a long pull on the bottle and leaned back against the table. "From? Let's just say, most recently from hell. And I am a crude cattleman, Miss Banning. Don't ever fool yourself that I'm anything else."

Dallas chose not to argue. "I may not be a westerner," she said instead, "but I'm a fairly keen observer of men. You haven't always been out here. My guess is that you're originally from somewhere in the South; that there was a time when you drank tea from china cups."

She poured tea into one of the small cups Wu had provided, adding a dollop of honey, and took a sip, allowing the hot sweet taste of it to slide down her throat.

Jake took a sip of whiskey, then looked down at the bottle he was holding. "Hell knows no geographic boundaries, Miss Banning. The South, too, was one of its unwelcome hosts."

Jake didn't like the warm feeling that came with the whiskey. He didn't like the way this woman asked too many questions.

He drew himself to his feet, recapped the bottle, and handed it back to Dallas. "You'd better keep this whiskey. You might need it—for medicinal purposes, if not for entertaining."

Jake pulled on his hat and his gloves.

"I bid you good afternoon, Miss Banning. Think about what I suggested. Catch the next train back to

Philadelphia. Wyoming is too wild a place for a woman like you, and I might not always be around to keep you safe."

"I won't expect you to, Mr. Silver. And I think you ought to know that I like Wyoming wild."

By the next morning, the melted snow puddled across the street like a small, shallow lake. Wagons and ox-drawn carts, their wheels mired up to the axle, came into town in a steady line. Short of joining them, Dallas Banning was forced to wait for the sun to dry up the mud.

"People," Dallas said, as she watched from her window, and was surprised at the joy she felt at their appearance. Some of them she identified as members of the German immigrant community. Others looked like any other American farmer and his wife. Children, risking the displeasure of their parents, raced down the wooden sidewalks like wild Indians on a rampage.

The quiet was gone. Like an old bear waking from hibernation, the world was coming back to life. Dallas made a mental list of what she had to do. First order of business was replenishing the supplies necessary to print the paper. The telegraph office would send her order, and her father would see that it was filled and shipped. He'd also send copies of his newspapers so that she could reprint the news out here.

She'd discovered old copies of the *Gazette* stored in a wooden box. Dallas intended to read them all, searching for clues.

Then she would visit the local bank to arrange for funds to be transferred and to introduce herself to the man who'd written to her about Jamie. Like any banker in a newly settled area, Lawson Pickens wore the mantle of power. As the financial agent between Mr. Parnell's immigrants and the land company responsible for locating them here, he was an especially important figure.

Then she would call on Miranda, who'd been kind to her, with an invitation to come to tea, followed by a visit to the general store, where she'd select a thank-you gift for Wu, Mr. Silver's cook.

She looked around, satisfied with the work she and Willie had accomplished now that the building was warm enough to move around in.

Willie had rounded up scraps of tin and lumber, which they'd used to seal up the cracks in the building. They'd lined the walls with drapes made of assorted fabrics from the general store. She wouldn't want to invite the mayor of Philadelphia for tea, but they'd managed to create a warmer, interesting interior. Still, leaving the newspaper office was an adventure she'd put off until the sun came out.

She ought to get the printing press in order, but the mechanics of the machine had never been her field of interest. In her father's plant, the printer was as big as half a room. But the one Jamie had used was a smaller, hand-operated model. At least the paper fed itself into the press, otherwise she'd be forced to stand for hours in order to put out one weekly issue. For now, until her supplies were ordered, the press could wait.

For now she was looking forward to accomplishing her errands.

With any luck, she might find out in the process what was happening with Mr. Parnell's farmers, or she might find someone willing to talk about Jamie.

Or Jake Silver.

Chapter 5

Elliott Parnell stood on the porch of the settlement house, staring out across the plains. Life seemed to have come full circle for him. He'd left his plantation home, proudly accepting his commission to serve under Confederate General P.G.T. Beauregard, who was attacking the Yankee major occupying Fort Sumter, outside of Charleston.

Elliott had been such a fool. As a plantation owner's younger son, he'd never inherit the land, so there'd been no point in learning to be a farmer. Instead he had dreamed of distinguishing himself as a soldier. But he was no better soldier than he was a farmer.

Then Jake had taken him under his wing. When Jake said they'd go west after the war and build a ranch, he'd followed willingly. But they'd both fallen in love with Sarah, and Jake had left, leaving Elliott with a wife and the land they'd planted. Without Jake, he'd lost his direction. Soon he'd reverted to the only life he knew, that of a plantation owner. Plantation owners didn't do the work; they had it done.

One by one, their hands had left, unable to follow directions that were contradicted from one day to the next. Sarah, too, had called him a failure. And she'd been right. Without Jake, he was nothing.

It hadn't all been his fault. He couldn't make it rain. And he couldn't make the crops grow, or the cattle stay within the boundaries of their land. He couldn't fight the bandits who came, drove the cattle away, and stole their other stock. But he could have stopped pretending. He could have faced the truth earlier, and taken Sarah away before it was too late.

But he'd been too proud.

Sarah.

The memory of Jake holding Sarah's lifeless body as he walked through the snow had haunted him for five years. After burying Sarah, Elliott had ridden away from their farm. For the next two years, he had wandered. He could recall little of that time now. Not until he awoke in a Mexican jail, dead broke and stinking of cheap whiskey.

After that, in a rage of frustration, he signed on with a gang of the outlaws who'd robbed and driven settlers out of Texas. The old, gentle, incapable Elliott died, and a tough, bitter man emerged. Then one day, during a raid, he was faced with a dying, pregnant woman. He buried her, then dropped his gun and rode away.

The old Elliott had destroyed Sarah, and he'd almost destroyed himself. The new Elliott was neither a gentle southerner nor a hardened outlaw. He was still finding out what he'd become. The only thing he knew was that Sarah should have married Jake. He'd known that at the time. She loved them both. And she was destroying the relationship between the two men. It was Jake she loved the way a woman loves a man. But it was Elliott who'd needed her, who'd played on her gentleness and cried when she couldn't feel for him what he felt for her.

Sarah couldn't take tears. She felt that she'd turned her back on the husband who'd died along the trail. After that she couldn't hurt anything or anybody. Jake could survive without her. Elliott couldn't. She'd chosen Elliott and Jake had left them.

She never told him in so many words that she regretted her choice. But he heard her cry sometimes at night. And he saw her watch the horizons endlessly. And that knowledge had eaten away at him until he'd finally faced the truth.

Without Jake, Sarah was half the woman she once was.

Without Jake, he was nothing.

Now he and Jake were in the same place again. And this time they were enemies. Jake was the successful rancher, and Elliott was starting over as a farmer who would encroach on land Jake believed ought to be left free. This time Elliott had to make it. He had to prove to Jake that he was a man. More important, he had to prove it to himself.

The first group of settlers had been there nine months. Now it was time to see what they'd done through the winter. Elliott climbed on a borrowed horse and, accompanied by Hans Dornier, the local blacksmith who'd been one of the first to give up his land and move back to the settlement house, rode out to see what they had accomplished.

It wasn't much. Elliott would never have found his way without Hans. He'd never have been able to talk to the immigrants had it not been for Hans, who had learned some English during the time he'd been in this country.

As they rode along, Elliott pulled his collar closer to his chin. The air was still cold, even though the sun was bright in a cloudless blue sky that went on forever. "Why didn't you choose to farm, Hans?"

"I built house. While you gone, they came in night and burn it—the monster."

"Monster?"

"The Devil from the hills. I don't build back. He leaves me alone now."

"Did you see him, this Devil?"

"No. I only hear. My wife hurt bad. When she died, I come here and build forge."

Elliott hadn't known that Hans lost his wife. He lived alone now, working his blacksmith's shop by day and living in the settlement building at night. Elliott wasn't certain that was all Hans knew, but that was all he was going to say.

The wind fell and for a time the day was pleasant. The sudden thaw had turned the range into a creek bottom, soggy and unsteady, turning their excursion into a much longer trip than it might have been.

Only a few families had constructed sod houses. There was no wood to be had, and cutting strips of thick, matted topsoil was hard work. Hans explained that the houses continually sprinkled dust in the heat and, when it rained or when the snow melted, the inside was as wet as the outside. Still, they were warm and they were private. After three days in the settlement house, Elliott could appreciate privacy.

"How about the planting, Hans? Did your friends get any ground prepared before winter?"

"Nein, or little," he answered. "The ground makes dull plows and much work for me. Maybe now, that ground is soft, it will welcome the seed."

Elliott knew that the grasses grew halfway up a man's leg. He still wasn't convinced that corn and potatoes would flourish but if range grass grew, so might oats—if the thick mat of roots could be pierced. And he already had agreements with buyers in Chicago to take their crops. "How many families are ready to plant now?"

"Eight or perhaps less. Some grow weary and talk of leaving the land."

"Why? They've already invested their money and time in coming here." Elliott shaded his eyes against the glare of the bright sunlight. In the far distance lay purple mountains in the west. In the other direction, there was open land as far as he could see, except for one thin wisp of smoke curling toward the sky.

"They have little money left for food and supplies. They are afraid, and there are some who would buy the land."

"But they came here to farm their own land."

"Yes."

The first sod house had come as no surprise to Elliott. He'd seen a few when they'd originally come west. Kansas had been sparsely populated then, but never as bare as this Wyoming territory. The farmer came to the door in answer to Hans's call.

Elliott waited in the background, watching the children playing about the doorway like mice, curious, but afraid to come out. Afraid, or cold. From the looks of them, they hadn't eaten too well, and their arms had outgrown their sleeves. He was beginning to understand that the task he was undertaking was much larger than he'd anticipated.

"I've returned with more of your countrymen. And I'll be here now, to help you," Elliott explained, through Hans. "If you have problems, you come to me and we'll work to settle them."

The farmer glared at Elliott, spat on the ground, and turned back inside.

"He doesn't trust you," Hans explained. "He was told that this was the land of plenty. He's very disappointed."

Elliott didn't want to admit that he, too, was disappointed. This was a formidable land. And they had formidable enemies in the claiming of the land. Jake, the other ranchers, and now this monster, whatever the hell that was. Perhaps it was some kind of rogue buffalo. They were almost gone now. And Elliott had seen none on his journeys through the new territory.

The only bright spot in all this hopelessness so far was Miss Banning. "I see smoke, Hans, in the distance near the mountains. Is that one of our settlers?"

"No, maybe bad men who come with Devil in the night."

"Devil? I'm sorry, Hans. I can't believe in a Devil who comes down from the hills. I can't believe you do."

Hans lowered his eyes, then, as if he was shoring up his courage, jutted his chin forward. "I didn't see him, but I heard him. His cry is from the belly of hell."

"Somebody must have seen him. What does he look like?"

"Those who have seen say only that he is as big as a building; that he is evil and angry. He kills."

That was as much as Elliott could get out of the man. Hans was ready to get back to the safety of his shop. And the heat, too, Elliott suspected. Elliott found it interesting that Hans had learned to utilize the same kind of oily sod that the wagon trains used to grease their axles. This sod caught fire easily and burned hot, allowing the blacksmith to bend and work with the iron pieces he'd brought to the prairie. With sod and charcoal, he'd learned to survive.

Halfway back to the settlement, Elliott peeled off and headed toward town. It was time he had a little talk with Lawson Pickens. The surveyor's marks had been obliterated and would have to be replaced. And Elliott was anxious to visit the piece that belonged to him. He'd been so rushed on his first trip that he'd hardly spent any time on his own land. He'd been a failure as a farmer five years ago. But he'd learned a lot since then, and he was anxious to do it right this time.

The road into Green Willow Creek was a quagmire of mud and ruts. Wagon wheels had churned up the mud and melted snow so that even Elliott's horse was forced into a slow walk. There were people on the crude sidewalks, women with shopping baskets, men leaning lazily against the buildings watching, and horses tied to the rails in front of the businesses.

Elliott rode by the newspaper office, noticing the lamplight shining through the clean glass window. But there was no sign of Miss Banning. He'd stop at the bank, then he might have a meal with Mrs. Jarrett at the boarding house before he headed back to the settlement.

Bank of Green Willow Creek, the sign read. Elliott reined in his horse, studied the mud, and decided there was little choice. Either he rode the horse into the bank or he walked through the mud to get there. He slid to the ground, hooked the horse's reins over the rail, and sloshed to the sidewalk. As he reached for the knob, the door opened and a woman stepped forward, almost bumping into him before she raised her gaze to meet his.

"Mr. Parnell. How nice to see you."

"Miss Banning. The pleasure is all mine." And it was. She was wearing that same navy blue traveling dress with its matching cape and blue hat. Over her arm she had slipped a shopping basket that was empty yet.

In the sunlight he could see the liveliness of her expression, the brightness of her eyes. Like a lovely light in some dark place, she lit up the sidewalk with her energy. "Are you settling in?" he asked.

"Oh, yes. And you?" She stepped away from the bank, vacating the doorway. Elliott followed, forgetting his mission for the moment. As she moved down the sidewalk, Elliott fell in beside her.

"Well, that's difficult to say. Dealing with families who are living in such close quarters is—"

"A challenge? So is being snowbound without supplies."

"I'm sure you're right. At least the settlement house had been stocked with provisions, and many of the original settlers are still there to help the newcomers."

Something about the way Mr. Parnell said "still there" gave Dallas pause. "Is there a problem with their settlement?"

"Only the elements and a bit of disappointment in the wilderness. But that will change once the snow melts and the range turns green."

"A man with a positive attitude. I like that, Mr. Parnell."

And Dallas did like his confidence. An easy smile and good manners went a long way, she decided, at least they did when they were genuine. She was still a bit uncomfortable over her meeting with Mr. Pickens. He'd been gracious, but he'd held her hand a second too long. When he'd assisted her to a chair before his desk, he'd stood behind her, holding the chairback while he leaned forward to talk to her. She could still feel his breath against her cheek.

Now she put that behind her, remembering the story Willie had passed on about the destruction of one of the immigrant's houses.

"I heard that you had a bit of trouble. A settler's house was destroyed."

"Yes, that's true."

"Do you know who did it?"

"No. And it isn't the first time that's happened. It seems that the farmers aren't welcomed with open arms."

"What do you intend to do about it?"

"I don't know. That's why I'm here, to talk with Pickens. You were leaving the bank; did you meet our banker?" he asked, making conversation that might extend their chance meeting and change the conversation to a topic less threatening.

"I did. He seems . . . very helpful."

"He's a man who fills a lot of shoes. He's the unofficial mayor, the financial liaison for the land company, and he takes care of our money."

"Yes, he's the one who wrote to me about Jamie."

"Your brother. Of course, I'm sorry. His loss must make this journey very difficult. How long will you be staying?"

She stopped and glared at him in surprise. "Staying? Permanently, Mr. Parnell. Or, at least until I learn what happened to my brother."

Permanently? He liked the sound of that. Somehow his arrival in a town where he, too, was unwelcome was softened by her presence. She was a connection to civilization that he very much needed.

"I'm sorry, Miss Banning. I didn't understand. I thought you were here to settle his business."

"Yes, but there's still the newspaper," she answered and turned to move off down the sidewalk again. "I intend to publish it, just as Jamie did."

"You do?" Elliott knew his surprised reaction was wrong as quickly as he caught sight of the narrowing of her full mouth. Though he was pleased that she was staying, he didn't know how to respond to her admission that she was looking for answers to what happened to her brother. He was already learning that there was an underlying dark element in the community. He wasn't sure how safe any stranger would be, especially a woman.

Before he could repair the damage he'd done, she'd squared her shoulders and moved away. "Now, if you'll excuse me, I have to get to the general store. I must pick up some supplies."

Without hurrying along beside her like some adoring puppy, he couldn't go any farther. "Damn!" He'd made her angry. Of course she could probably put out the paper herself. She was a Banning, and even a drifter knew that other than Horace Greeley, the Bannings were the most powerful newspaper people in the country.

He considered inviting her to have lunch at Miss Lucy's boarding house, then changed his mind. She probably wouldn't welcome the intrusion. He turned and headed back toward the bank. He might as well talk to Lawson about what had happened at the settlement.

"It isn't the first time it's happened since you've been gone, Parnell," Lawson Pickens said. "Unfortunately, there are some who've become outspoken about running the settlers out."

"But why? For the most part, they're hard workers. They keep to themselves, and some of them do have their own money to spend with the local merchants."

"You know the answer to that. It's barbed wire. The ranchers are afraid that they'll fence off their land and the cattle won't be able to graze."

Elliott shook his head. "They very well might, to protect the grain from the cattle, but there's enough land for both."

"For now, maybe. But the cows will be injured on the wire and sometimes the fence will cut them off from open land. But that's not the worst."

"I'm afraid to ask. What?"

"Water. There isn't enough rain to grow crops and there isn't enough water to irrigate."

"What about Green Willow Creek? I was told that it was a good source of water."

"Unfortunately, except for a section of the creek that runs across the top corner of your section of land, the creek belongs to Jake Silver."

"I wish you'd assigned that section to someone else, Pickens. Jake and I don't get on very well, and that could make any negotiation difficult."

Lawson Pickens smiled. "Yes. I got the idea that you and Silver knew each other. What happened?"

"We had a difference of opinion, years ago. Nothing that should affect this." Elliott had no intention of making their past known. Whatever problems he and Jake had couldn't be allowed to spill over into the other problems that were brewing.

"Well, your land borders Silver's land, the creek, the mountains and the settlers' land. Your piece is the key section, Elliott."

Elliott was beginning to get a bad feeling. He'd been surprised to find that Jake was the largest cattle rancher in the territory. They hadn't crossed paths on his first trip, and he'd hoped that any meeting might be avoided until he had things under control. He'd done little more than select a site for the house he was building. Now he was learning that he was to be Jake's neighbor. Not only that, but he would control a section of the creek that Jake depended on for his cattle, the creek that was the only source of water for the farmers. He looked at the odd smile on Pickens's face and let out a measured breath.

"Why me?"

"It had to go to one of the homesteaders, and you're the only man who can be depended on to share the water."

Elliott didn't respond. He had no answer. He felt sick.

"I saw you with Miss Banning," Lawson Pickens said, changing the subject. "She's quite lovely, isn't she? Foolish, but lovely."

"Foolish?"

"Of course. She can't publish that newspaper. The citizens won't support a ladies' gazette, and after her brother's futile efforts, she can't hope to accomplish anything more."

"You sound as if you hope she doesn't."

"On the contrary. It's to all our best interests to have any disagreements settled quickly. The more business that comes to Green Willow Creek, the more money in all our bank accounts."

They agreed that the surveyor would return and replace any missing markers as soon as possible so that the farmers could begin claiming their plots and planting them.

"By the way," Elliott said as the banker followed him out the door, "what do you know about the Devil of the Plains?"

The banker laughed. "That's the product of someone's imagination. You know how those old miners were. They made up all kinds of stories to keep people away from the mountains where they'd staked their claims. The monster was just the latest one."

"Then there are no actual reports of the creature?"

"Only from a few crazy farmers and a drifter or two who'd had too much rotgut whiskey."

Elliott accepted the explanation, but an uneasy feeling accompanied him down the street. Maybe it was just a story, but there were apparently plenty of people who believed it.

The town of Green Willow Creek was still crude, but it was surprisingly complete. A doctor's office, a dressmaker's shop, a general store, the newspaper office, and the livery stable lined one side of the street. On the other side lay the bank, the boarding house, and the saloon. At every establishment he tipped his hat to the proprietors who were visible. In return he received either a furtive look or a nervous smile. He couldn't decide if his unease came from the stony countenance of the citizens or the story about the monster.

In any case, he cut his visit short and returned to the settlement. He hadn't expected it to be easy, but creating a new life was turning out to be a more emotional wrench than he'd anticipated—not like it had been the first time he came west. The confidence, the warm camaraderie of the three of them against the world was missing. Time had changed everything. Nothing would ever be the same.

Chapter 6

Pete, Jake's late-arriving ranch hand, found the Indian woman, half-frozen, near an outcropping of rock the hands called Bitter Butte. His first thought was that the Devil had killed her and dragged her back to his lair.

The woman was wearing a white leather dress embroidered with shells and precious stones—a ceremonial dress, Pete decided. He decided too that there was more to her being there than simply being lost in the snow. Indians weren't strangers in Green Willow Creek, but they were mostly old women who came to trade for food or men in search of liquor.

This one wasn't young, in her thirties probably, but she was still a fine-looking woman, almost regal in her bearing. And he discovered, when he tried to lift her from the rock where she was sitting, that she wasn't injured, only suffering from exposure. She stared at him stonily, then after a sigh of resignation allowed him to lift her to his horse and ride away from the rocks.

"Do you understand English?"

At first she didn't answer, then, she nodded. "I swore an oath to let Mother Earth decide my fate. She sent you."

"Who are you?" Pete asked.

"I'm called Shadow."

"What are you doing out here with no blanket?"

She could only answer him truthfully, "Waiting for death, or life. Whichever is to be."

"Where are your people?"

"Dead. All dead. Killed by the Devil of the Plains. I never believed in bad spirits. I was wrong."

"So why come out here?"

"To seek him out, to offer myself to the Devil."

"Ah, come on, lady. There's no Devil. That's just some miner's half-baked story to keep you out of these hills."

"I didn't see him, but I heard him," she protested, her expression evidence that she was still remembering the experience. "He had a cry that would make the dead walk. He brought his spirits with him, but it was the beast who trod over my uncle and my brother."

"Where are they?"

"I buried them. Then I came here to wait for answers from the Mother Earth."

Pete shivered. The woman sat stoically behind him, not holding on, using only her knees to keep herself erect. What was Jake going to say?

He was still wondering that when he found himself standing in the middle of the hallway trying to explain his actions to Jake Silver.

"She was just sitting there, in the snow, like she was waiting for someone to come along and give her a ride."

"What did she say?"

"That her name is Shadow and that she was waiting for Mother Earth to decide her fate, or something like that."

"Are you hurt, ma'am?" Jake asked.

"No."

Jake studied her carefully. The odd silver-gray streaks in the woman's hair were a common characteristic, identifying her as a member of the Mandan Indian tribe who'd come to the territory originally from the land around the Minnesota River. They'd mixed with the early traders. She spoke English. It was likely that she'd attended some of the missionary schools.

"She said her uncle and her brother were killed by the Devil of the Plains," Pete explained. "She has no family."

"So you brought her here." Jake didn't know why he was making such a fuss. She wasn't the first stray he'd taken in, but she was the first woman—since Sarah.

"Should I have left her?" Pete asked. "She didn't even have a blanket."

I wish to hell you had. That was what he wanted to say. "Probably," was what he said. "But you didn't. Now we have her."

"Not for long, I'd bet," Pete said. "I don't think Wu will welcome her to the big house and the men—well, a woman in the bunkhouse just wouldn't work."

Jake glanced back at the woman. "What did you expect to accomplish out there in the snow, ma'am?"

"I was waiting for answers. I accept the answer that came. I will stay with this man who brought me."

Jake bit back a smile. The woman spoke more than a little English and she apparently knew a good thing when she found it.

"No way, Jake," Pete protested. "I got me a girl in town. Irene's pretty sweet on me. She wouldn't like this, not one bit."

"All right, then," the woman said, swaying a bit

76

as she tried to stand straight before her captor. "Perhaps I was wrong. I will go."

Jake frowned. The woman was still half-frozen and they were arguing about her fate as if she were a stray animal. He couldn't turn her away. He never sent anyone who was needy away. He knew what it meant to be rejected. Jake decided to turn her over to Wu until he could decide what to do with her.

"No, the Double J has enough room for one more. Pete, take her to the kitchen and tell Wu to find her some dry clothing. We'll talk about what to do next after she's warmed up."

"Come along, ma'am," Pete said. "Wu is our cook. He'll look after you."

"Wu?" she questioned. "What kind of name is Wu?"

"He's a Chinese. From China." Pete glanced at the woman's hair and added, "He don't wear those funny clothes anymore, but he wears his hair in a braid, like your warriors."

Jake watched the woman as she followed Pete to the kitchen. An idea was forming itself in Jake's mind. For months Wu had been threatening to send to the old country for a wife. . . .

It didn't take long for him to hear Wu's opinion of the matter.

A singsong chattering of Chinese words turned sharp and grew louder. Even from where he was standing, Jake could hear Wu's displeasure and his footsteps. Wu was headed toward the parlor. Jake decided a trip to the barn was in order. He ducked out the front door. He'd check on the horses. His move didn't fool Wu. He didn't reach the barn before the Chinaman fell in behind him.

"Mr. Jake, why send woman to Wu's kitchen?"

"But Wu, you wanted a wife. Looks like Mother Earth sent you one."

"Wife? Wife? Wu pick own wife, must come from House of Golden Sun. Not pick some wild woman with great white teeth. She say she stay. She not leave. She sleep in kitchen by fire." Clearly shaken by the encounter, he was rubbing his hand.

"What happened? She bite you?"

"She say next time I tell her what to do she use a knife and cut off Wu's queue. You get her out of Wu's kitchen, Mr. Jake, or Wu put powder of the horn in your food and turn you into a toad."

Jake bit back a laugh. The thought of the Indian woman threatening Wu with a knife was just what Wu deserved. Good for Shadow. A few hours in the cold didn't stop her from defending herself. She might speak English and conduct herself like a lady, but she was full of spirit.

Jake's thoughts went to the woman back in town, where they'd been more often than he wanted to admit. Dallas Banning wasn't a savage, but her instinct to survive was equally strong. She'd fired her gun at her attackers without hesitation, and, Jake was certain, deliberately missed. He wondered what she would have done if her action hadn't stopped their advance. Or if he hadn't arrived.

For a moment his lips relaxed into a half-smile. He wouldn't want to be the one to find out. She'd bite, and kick, and probably do great bodily damage before she'd allow herself to be subdued.

Wyoming was the place for her. It was as wild as she was; the first territory to give women the right to vote. From what he'd seen of Miss Dallas Banning, she'd probably decide to run for sheriff and go after the Devil of the Plains by herself.

"Something wrong, Mr. Jake?"

Wu had stopped complaining and was watching Jake curiously, waiting for an explanation for his employer's odd expression.

"No!" Jake snapped. He was behaving as foolishly as the ranch hands who went to town and caught sight of Miranda for the first time.

It had been too long since he'd allowed himself to think about a woman like Dallas, a woman with family and breeding, a woman with fire and determination. He avoided dwelling on the past, remembering a time when life had been good and full of promise. Now life was simply something he got through, one day at a time. If he didn't expect anything, he wouldn't be disappointed.

He was Jake Silver, owner of the Double J cattle ranch, and that's all he wanted to be. His father, the plantation owner, wouldn't have thought much of Jake's accomplishment in the West, for he never thought much of Jake. He had never wanted Jake. His father's rejection was the first for Jake Silver, but it hadn't been the last.

"You were in her situation once, Wu, and I didn't turn you away. Look after her, she's alone."

"Today I take care. But Mr. Jake find place for woman?"

Jake nodded and watched Wu leave the barn, crossing paths with Pete, who'd come into the barn.

"Where you heading, Jake?"

"I think I'll ride out to check the creek. All this runoff is going to flood it."

"Want some company?"

"No. Just keep an eye out here. No telling who'll come looking for Wu's bride."

"Anybody comes and I'll give her back," Pete promised warily.

"Let Wu handle it."

"I'm not sure he can. That woman might be a savage, but she's calm and she's cold."

"Don't underestimate Wu," Jake warmed. "He's been with me for a long time, and he's probably lonely. Maybe having someone to deal with personally will be good for him. Besides, I'm thinking those two will be a good match for each other."

"I wouldn't want to take bets on whether he'd win," Pete said uneasily.

Jake thought about the expression on the Indian woman's face. "Neither would I. In the meantime, I think Wu's going to have his hands full."

"Yeah? Well there's more to Wu than most people think. I've seen him in his room burning those candles, sitting so still that you'd think he was dead."

"I'm not surprised," Jake admitted. "Wu's never talked about his life before he came to California to build the railroad, but I think that, back in China, he might have been someone special."

"Why would he have come here?"

"Same way a lot of our men went to China. He could have been separated from his people somehow, maybe even shanghaied."

Pete looked at Jake with astonishment in his eyes. It was clear that the idea of the slim, serious man from China being more than just a laborer would never have occurred to any of the hands.

Jake gave a whistle that brought Blackjack into the barn to be saddled.

As Jake mounted the horse and rode out of the barn, his ranch hand was silent. Jake decided he'd said too much. Why had he sent that woman to Wu, anyhow? Some women were trouble. A man knew it the first time he saw them, knew it but still couldn't steer clear. And once a woman put her mark on a man, he couldn't get her out of his mind no matter how hard he tried.

Dallas Banning was a woman like that, and he wasn't sure why. She definitely wasn't the kind of woman who needed a man to take care of her. There was no weakness in her, no sweet need that reached out and touched a man. Maybe it was her eyes that bothered him—vivid hazel eyes that seemed to come at him in the silence. Dark hazel eyes and a set of wide lips that brooked no nonsense.

She was strong-minded, a challenge. He'd seen her as a maverick, and he'd always refused to allow a maverick calf to get away from the herd. It was a matter of pride, pride and control. It might take him half a day to change the calf's mind, but eventually Jake won.

It wasn't, he told himself, the who or the what. It was winning. Winning was everything to Jake.

He never intended to lose again.

The snow was almost gone, revealing the churned-up ground and the trail of hoof marks leading away from the main herd. Jake studied the range. The signs indicated that the horses had been shod, so their riders weren't Indians. And they weren't taking the steers to safety. They were being separated out and moved toward the mountains.

Rustlers!

For months he'd been losing cows. Only a few at a time. Only what would be needed to feed a family, or start a small herd for a farmer who wanted to grow more than cabbages. But that, coupled with the loss of public grazing land, could become a problem.

"Damn!" Jake wasn't the only cattleman being affected by this kind of thievery. It hadn't started until those farmers had come in. Now it was becoming an everyday affair. And his fellow ranchers were threatening to take action. There'd already been several incidents with the settlers—houses set afire or pulled down, crops disrupted by stampedes. The farmers weren't normally fighters, but they'd invested their savings in their new lives and sooner or later they'd retaliate, and he wouldn't blame them.

The last thing Jake wanted was this kind of vigilante revenge. So far he'd been able to suppress it by refusing to give his support. But with the influx of new Germans it would be harder to keep things under control.

The building of the railroad had been both a blessing and a curse. The same train that carried his cows to market now brought in the farmers. It hadn't been so bad until that fool back east had invented barbed wire. Until then, the cows could just push the wire fences down. Now, they'd be hurt. And even that wouldn't stop them when they'd eaten all the grass where they were. They'd push through the fences to get to food; to get to the farmer's crops; to be shot.

Jake swore and glanced at the sky. The afternoon was almost gone. The range wasn't a friendly place at night. He didn't want to take the chance of being caught out on the plains alone with rustlers in the area. He'd have to turn back for now. The trail would still be there tomorrow, providing the creek didn't continue to spill over its banks.

Either they had too much water or not enough. Sooner or later someone would figure a way to harness the runoff. Too bad the inventor of barbed wire hadn't tackled that problem. The melting snow fed the thick roots of the plains grasses that formed a mat that kept the melting snow from reaching down below its roots. When the runoff became more than it could absorb, the matting let the water collect like a shallow lake across its surface. So much water now, so little when the snows were gone.

Jake turned his horse back to the ranch. Everything had seemed simple when he came to the new territory. There'd been no railroad, no farmers, no newspaper editors. He'd had no long-term plans, no great ambition to become a wealthy land owner. Then the vast empty plains had been invaded by people. Elliott Parnell had come back into his life. And now there was this Dallas Banning.

Jake was riding into the barnyard when he heard Wu.

Wu was sitting on his basket. He was wearing his two prized possessions: a woven cone-shaped straw hat and a blue embroidered robe, the clothing he wore only on special occasions.

"What are you doing, Wu?"

"I wait for sled to take Wu to town."

"Why?"

"I find job there."

"Job? Doing what?"

"Being very good cook at leaving house."

"That's boarding house, and why would you want to do that?"

"Wu know you not happy with his cook."

"I'm very happy with your cooking, Wu. Why would you think otherwise?"

"You bring woman to take over Wu's kitchen."

"Take over?"

"You see."

Jake walked through the hallway, crossed the back porch and entered the little building that contained Wu's kitchen, his living quarters, and a storage room. The Indian woman was stirring the pot cooking over the open fire. She was wearing one of Jake's shirts and Wu's apron.

Jake choked back a rare laugh. Wu'd been shut out of his kitchen by a woman half his size. "Where'd she get my shirt, Wu?"

"I give. You say get her dry. I dry."

"And your apron?"

"She say she earn food. She cook. Wu say he cook. She not listen."

"Wu, you're going to have to let her know who the boss is here. Otherwise, she'll have you doing tricks and waiting on her."

"Wu tell her, but she not listen."

"Maybe you need to get her attention."

"Get attention? How?"

There was something about the way the woman stood that told Jake she wasn't entirely oblivious to Wu's dilemma. In fact, Jake had the feeling that she was baiting Wu and testing him. Obviously, she'd made up her mind to stay, otherwise she'd have been long gone.

Maybe she'd been turned out of her tribe. Maybe she'd left on her own—a pilgrimage. Whatever her reason, she'd decided to stay here. It was Wu who needed to decide where he stood.

Taking a calculated risk, Jake walked across to the woman, caught her by the shoulder to protect her from the fall, then shielded his action as he pushed her to the floor. "Listen, woman, I don't allow anybody in my house who doesn't follow orders. If you won't listen to Wu, maybe you'll listen to me."

After a moment she allowed fear to wrinkle her brows and reflect from her eyes. She slid away from Jake, looking beseechingly at Wu, who couldn't begin to control his surprise.

"Mr. Jake. Why you hit woman?"

"She's just a woman who needs to learn her place!" Jake said, biting back a smile. "Maybe another lick would help her do it. Hand me a piece of that cut wood."

"No! Mr. Jake not hit Wu's—Wu's helper." Wu planted himself between Jake and the woman, holding himself to the full measure of his short stature.

"What does Wu's helper have to say about that?" Jake asked.

The woman came slowly to her feet and put her hand on Wu's arm. She lowered her eyes and whispered. "It isn't necessary that you get hurt because of me, Wu. I'll go."

"No, missy. You not go, Wu forgive."

"Thank you," she said lowering her eyes.

Jake stepped back. "Make up your minds. I don't like my household upset. I don't care who cooks and who cleans. I just don't want problems."

"There will be no problems, Mr. Silver," the woman said. "I'd thought to die, but the Mother Earth does not wish it so. We will work together. I thank you for allowing me sanctuary. You should know that no one will come for me. There are no more members of my family left. I have nowhere I wish to go."

"You have home now, missy," Wu said quietly. Then added, as if he were ashamed of his emotion, "Now, stop wasting time and see to Mr. Jake's food. You sleep in kitchen."

"I will sleep in the storeroom."

"No. No. Wu say kitchen. You cook, and clean. Wu teach."

"I know more about cooking than you, you bossy man."

"Wu not bossy. Wu belong to Celestial body, House of the Sun."

Jake left them arguing fiercely. His decree that they should get along was forgotten in their attempt to override the other's wishes. Wu might regret taking up for the woman. Wu, he thought, might well find himself wishing that she'd never been found. And yet beneath the bickering there was a hint of respect—and interest.

Later, when Jake stood at the window looking out

into the moonlit night, he thought about how easily and how quickly a man's life was changed by a woman.

He wondered how Wu would handle this new interruption in his life. He wondered what Dallas Banning was doing in town. He wondered what the next weeks would bring. He wondered what he would do about the new immigrants.

And Elliott Parnell.

Dallas came down the stairs. She was carrying her heavy cape and bonnet, but she was wearing a bright yellow dress. Willie let out an appreciative greeting. Though it was Sunday, he'd reported in at the regular time. She'd let him build up the fire, then prepare their morning pot of tea.

"Willie, tell me about the woman who was brought to the settlement house, the one whose husband was killed."

"Don't know much, Miss Banning. Her name was Greta something or other. And they say the Devil pulled down her house and stomped on her husband. He looked like somebody beat him."

Greta something or other. Greta had actually seen whoever had killed her husband. She'd be able to give some kind of description. At least that was a place to start looking for James's murderer.

Dallas had received a telegram from her father that her printing materials were en route. She'd spent the last week buying supplies from the general store and arranging them in the newspaper office. With Willie's help, they were turning it into an official office and reasonably comfortable living quarters. Her sleeping loft was hung with Jake Silver's saddle blankets, which closed off the drafts. And her mattress had fresh stuffing and a new cover.

Downstairs she'd set up shelves for James's favorite books and a few of her own. There were canned goods and a few bulk food supplies. All she had to do now was find someone to do her laundry and arrange to take one meal a day at the boarding house. And since today was Sunday, this would be a good day to begin.

Dallas smoothed the wrinkles from her best church dress and took a final look around the room. "Will you be attending Sunday services, Willie?"

Willie's shocked look, followed by the side-to-side shake of his head, answered her question.

"Why not? Would Miss Miranda object?"

"Eh, no ma'am. I reckon the townsfolk wouldn't appreciate me being there."

"Nonsense. I'd be pleased to have you escort me." Dallas herself was not the most loyal of churchgoers. Often she'd found herself playing a role that prohibited attendance at church. Here, however, establishing herself in the community was essential to her mission. And today was the day she intended to overcome the curious glances and suspicious frowns of the townspeople.

The bright sunshine since the storm had turned the muddy street through Green Willow Creek into a rutted, dried-out thoroughfare. Dallas imagined it would become a corridor of dust when the heat of summer came. This morning, the sidewalks and the street were filled with people all headed to the small building at the edge of town.

"You going to wear that?" Willie asked, studying the yellow dress and jacket.

"Well, yes. I thought it would be cheery after the bad times."

"Yess'um, but the women 'round here, they don't have no dresses like that, I mean, not 'cept Miranda."

"Oh, I see." And she did. The dress might cheer

her up, but it would call attention to the dreariness of the lives of the other women. And after her rather spectacular entrance that first day, it was important that Dallas fit in with the citizens. Quickly, she retired to her sleeping loft and pulled on her dark blue traveling gown, still rumpled from the trip.

Not exactly suitable for attending church in Philadelphia, but for the Wyoming Territory, she hoped that she'd blend in.

Willie elected to stay behind in the newspaper office. He'd think about church—next Sunday. Dallas decided it had more to do with clothing than reluctance and made a mental note to buy some clothes for the freckle-faced boy who was obviously growing at a rapid rate. She'd buy everyday clothing and an extra set to be kept at the newspaper office for Sunday.

A short time later she was picking her way across the open area around the building that served as a church on Sunday. Though it had originally been built as a schoolhouse, according to Lawson Pickens, a teacher had never been hired. It now stood in as a meeting place when not needed as a church—and occasionally as a jail.

There were only a few wagons beside the building; most people came on foot. As Dallas made her way into the building, a hush fell over the scattering of people inside.

"Good morning, Miss Banning, welcome." Mr. Bowker, a rather sallow-faced man wearing a black suit came forward. *The undertaker.* Dallas bit back a smile. She'd met the man inside the general store where he was buying nails "for the coffin I'm building," he'd explained. Lately, he'd tried to keep one ready, "because of the trouble."

He was also a carpenter; Jake had already said he doubled as the minister. She was learning that in the

West, people were forced to fill more than one need. The banker was a collection agent. The doctor treated people and animals and pulled teeth on the side. Miranda ran a saloon that offered rooms, food, and certain kinds of entertainment.

What the city of Green Willow Creek didn't have was an officer of the law.

Dallas took a seat on the aisle. "Thank you, Mr. Bowker. I'm looking forward to the service."

She was barely seated when there was another entry. This time the silence was accompanied by shocked expressions. Dallas turned to see what had caused such consternation.

The immigrants. There were a man, two women, and several poorly clad children. This time, nobody offered any welcome. Nobody made room on the benches. Nobody spoke. Finally, Dallas stood and held out her hand. "Please, come and sit with me," she said, sliding down the bench so that the only other occupant was forced to make room.

With timid smiles the immigrants came forward and sat down, with one woman falling to her knees, bowing her head, and whispering words that would have been recognized in any language as a plea. Then, looking up, she seemed to freeze where she knelt.

Dallas leaned forward and took her hand, pulling her up to the bench. The woman allowed herself to be assisted and continued to hold Dallas's hand as Mr. Bowker began reciting a passage of Scripture. Never once did the woman take her eyes from the front of the church.

Ignoring the furtive glances of the churchgoers, Dallas concentrated on the rather disjointed sermon delivered by the undertaker. When the members stood for the final hymn, she stood as well, along with the immigrants, who merely hummed the melody.

Afterward, the German farmers filed out of the church as quickly as they'd entered. Dallas turned and went after them.

"Wait!"

The group came to a halt by their wagon.

"Miss Banning," Mr. Bowker called out and hurried after her. "We're pleased that you could join us."

"Yes, indeed," Lawson Pickens said, moving up beside Dallas. "I didn't know you knew any of the farmers. Hello, Adolph."

The farmer merely nodded and turned his gaze to the heavy work boots he was wearing.

"I don't," she said. "But I'm very pleased to meet you." She held out her hand to the immigrant, who stared at it for a moment, then shook it formally. "I just thought you seemed uncomfortable. And as a newcomer myself, I know how that feels."

"Nonsense, I can't imagine you not fitting in anywhere," a round, wren-brown little woman said, pushing her way between the two men. "Seeing somebody new in this place is a real pleasure. You're welcome, all of you. I'm Lucy Jarrett."

Dallas smiled. "I'm so pleased to meet you. As a matter of fact, I was going to take a chance that you'd allow me to share your midday meal."

"I don't cook on the Lord's day," she said. "You're welcome to share what's left from yesterday, but it'll be cold."

"Miss Banning," Lawson Pickens interjected, "I'd hoped that you'd join my wife and me for dinner. She sent me to find you and issue the invitation in person."

"But I . . ." Dallas looked helplessly at Lucy. A cold meal wasn't what she had in mind, but neither was sharing a dinner table with Lawson Pickens. She's already met Mrs. Pickens, and the woman was such a timid soul that Dallas found herself wanting to pat her on the head.

"Thank you, Mr. Pickens, but I think I'd like to ride out to the settlement house. Mr. Parnell invited me, and this is such a nice afternoon for a drive. Perhaps another time."

Leaving him standing openmouthed behind her, Dallas reclaimed the startled immigrant woman's hand and began moving toward the wagon. "Do you think there is someone who could bring me back later?"

"Ja, ja, we bringen," the man said, and began assisting the women into the wagon; first Dallas, who was given the seat beside the driver, then the other two women, who sat on stools in the back.

"My name is Dallas Banning," she said.

"Adolph Schmahl," the driver said. "And wife, Lena, and friend, Greta Bittner."

Greta was the woman whose hand Dallas had held. Greta was the woman whose husband had been killed. Now Dallas understood. She'd come to church to pray. Greta, staring off into the distance, didn't acknowledge the introduction.

"Did you know my brother, James, the newspaperman?"

"Ja. We know James. He visit. He write good about us."

Greta spoke softly, "James wrote about my man. He say we can make things right if work with him. He was wrong. They killed him, those cattlemen. Now they've killed my Wilhelm."

"Did you see the monster, Mrs. Bittner, the Devil of the Plains?"

"The monster was a messenger from the devil, but it was the men who killed."

Dallas tried to ask her more questions, but the woman lapsed into silence. Adolph explained that nobody had been able to get a description of the creature, for Greta was convinced that it was the devil in animal form. "Dr. Horn says that she doesn't want to remember," Adolph said sadly. "She's blocked it out of her mind."

They were moving steadily away from town and across the plains. Dallas studied the open range ahead of the two mules and shaded her eyes with her palm. In the distance she could see a tall structure. It was moving.

"You have a windmill?" She couldn't contain her astonishment.

"Ja. It's the only way you can get water if you don't live on the creek. The well isn't deep, but there is water, for now. It took all our money."

They were almost at the house when three men came, riding as if they were being chased by the devil, shooting pistols wildly in the air.

Adolph tried to draw the mules to a stop as the men came closer. But the sound of the gunfire frightened the animals and they began to run.

"Stop it!" Dallas called out. "Stop firing those guns! You'll hurt someone."

"We want our cattle back, you thieving foreigners. And we're going to get them!"

"Nein! Nein! We have no cattle!" Adolph was yelling, trying desperately to control the mules.

Dallas didn't know whether the wheel hit a pothole, or one of the shots hit a mule, but suddenly the wagon was taking a crazy angle and careening to its side.

The two women in the back were flung out. Dallas and Adolph were jerked forward and the wagon turned over, catching the driver beneath the wheel.

Moments later Dallas heard sobbing and a groan.

She pulled herself to her feet and turned toward the riders who'd drawn up their steeds.

"What are you trying to do?" she screamed, "kill us?"

The men looked at each other in surprise.

"You're that newspaperwoman?"

"And you're one of those men who work for Jake Silver."

"I can't believe it," one of the other riders said, "you're an American."

"You're right. I'm an American. And if I had my gun I'd arrest you all. What's the meaning of this?"

"We're just trying to stop the cattle rustling. These people are stealing us blind. First the water, now the cattle."

There was another moan.

Dallas turned her attention to Adolph, who was caught under the wheel. Both women were trying to right the wagon.

"I want you to get down and help get this wagon off this man's body, immediately," Dallas said to the man she recognized as the gambler called Slim.

"Yes, ma'am," he said and climbed from his horse. Soon the three men had the wagon upright again and were placing the man in the back. If Dallas were any judge, Adolph had a broken leg. She was torn between seeing that he got proper care and confronting Jake Silver with what his men had done.

"Just get me to the settlement house, ma'am," Adolph said, his face pale, but strong. "Mr. Parnell will see to my leg."

Dallas was an accomplished rider, but getting Adolph to the settlement house involved driving a team of mules, which Dallas had never done. Greta had lapsed into another terrified silence, and Lena was in no condition to drive anything.

Though she knew the answer, Dallas needed to make certain. "Who do you men work for?"

"Jake Silver," Slim answered.

"And what are you doing out here?"

"We've been into town and we're just on our way home," one of the riders answered.

"And does Mr. Silver know what you're doing out here?"

There was a furtive look about the men as they looked at each other. "He just told us to keep a look out for the thieves. But everybody knows who's doing the stealing. It never happened until these people got here."

"Well, these people haven't been out stealing anything. They've been to church, which is where you'd better go and ask forgiveness for your sins."

"Yes, ma'am," Slim's young associate said. "Can we do anything else for you?"

"You can. You can drive this wagon back to the settlement house. I'll take your horse. I want to have a little talk with Mr. Silver."

"You want my horse?"

"I do. And I want it now!"

The boy handed her the reins and stood by to assist her into the saddle. Her dress didn't allow room for straddling the animal, and a cowboy's saddle wasn't meant for riding sidesaddle. Dallas studied the situation for a moment, shimmied her skirt up her legs enough that she could step into the boy's hands, then vaulted onto the horse cowboy style.

"Now, Slim, take me to Jake Silver and be quick about it."

Chapter 7

After almost an hour, the cowboy called Slim led them to the banks of a fast-moving shallow creek, bordered by a barrier of bare-limbed trees.

"Is this Green Willow Creek?" Dallas asked.

Slim nodded.

"And these are willow trees?"

"Yep." He glanced at Dallas, his gaze fastening on her exposed legs. Caught by her stern expression, he frowned and looked across the creek, giving her the impression that he might decide to abandon her here and head for the mountains in the distance. The second man following behind cleared his throat nervously.

"Don't try it," she warned. "I think you're already in enough trouble with Jake Silver without making it worse."

Her guide took in a deep, resigned breath and headed down the creek to a more open area, where he started across.

Dallas followed, eyeing the creek with interest. It didn't seem like much. If this was the major water supply for the area, she could see where there could be big trouble. Even now, as the snow was melting, it wasn't imposing. She decided the shape of the stream was something like a flat tongue, nudging at the banks like a recalcitrant child making a mocking gesture.

The recent heavy snowmelt had made the river run over its banks before retreating and darting swiftly across the plains, leaving a scattering of snow lilies and wild buttercups along its path. The calendar had said that it was spring, but it would be summer before all the snow was gone.

Following Slim's horse, Dallas's less surefooted animal picked his way across the cold creek, splashing water on Dallas's legs, wetting the ruffles on her underwear. Unconsciously she raised her skirt, then realized how the sight of her bare legs was disconcerting the cowboys. She gave up any hope of staying dry and rearranged her skirt. The horse seemed to tiptoe across like a barefoot boy determined to wade before the sun had warmed the earth. Rocks caught the current, causing frothy horseshoe-shaped eddies as the water parted and swirled about the obstacle.

"I thought Green Willow Creek would be bigger," Dallas said.

"Sometimes it gets down to where it's half what you see now." Slim's horse picked up his gait into a trot, as if he knew he was almost home.

In the distance she could see the ranch house. After what Miranda had said, it came as a surprise. The walls were built of adobe bricks, in the style of a Mexican hacienda. Miranda's observation that it was little more than bare walls might be accurate compared to her Victorian bedroom. To Dallas, the pure, clear lines of the Spanish house with its stark, simple facade was impressive, like the man who lived there. Circling the whitewashed building was a low white picket fence, along which bare vines spread like the veins of a leaf.

"Roses," Dallas whispered. Out here in the middle of nothing but brown land and blue sky, there would be roses in the summer. Mr. Silver had planted roses. She was surprised. But then everything about Jack Silver surprised her.

As they drew nearer the house, the front door opened and a familiar lean, dark figure stepped outside. He waited, perfectly still.

They rode into the courtyard and reined the horses to a stop. The cowboy from the train, the one called Pete, walked up to stand beside Jake. Neither man spoke. Jake focused on her face, allowed his gaze to drift down to the hiked-up skirt, revealing the ruffles on her pantalettes and her shapely stocking-encased legs.

"I didn't expect company," Jake said. There was a forboding look about him. He needed a shave, and his hair looked as if he'd been threading his fingers through it. His shirt was only half-buttoned.

Dallas threw her leg over the horse and slid to the ground, tugging her skirt back to its proper place.

"I was on my way to share a meal with the farmers at the settlement house. Your men stampeded the wagon I was riding in and broke my host's leg."

"Is that true?" Only a slight flicker of Jake's eyes indicated that he was addressing the two cowboys.

"Yes," Slim began, "but we didn't mean to hurt the man. We just thought those immigrants needed a lesson. I mean, after we lost those new calves and their mamas right out of the holding pen—"

"So you did spook their mules?"

"Yes, but we didn't know that Miss Banning—"

"Get down to the bunkhouse," Jake snapped. "and wait for Pete. He'll be bringing you your wages."

"Wages? You mean we're fired?"

"That's exactly what I mean. And I'll expect a contribution to the injured man from each of you."

Dallas hadn't known exactly what to expect of Jake Silver, but she'd had an idea his action would be swift and nonretractable. "I hope you don't intend to fire the boy I sent with the wagon," she said. "I don't think he was in on what happened."

"You took his horse?"

"Yes, while he drove the injured man back to the settlement."

"I'll think about it." He handed Dallas's reins to Pete. "Pay them off, Pete, up to the minute. Come inside, Miss Banning," Jake said solemnly. "Wait in the parlor while I have Wu set another place for dinner."

Before she could protest she found herself alone in a parlor that was sparsely but elegantly furnished. There was a low sofa of bright red and a few colorful large pillows arranged before a cold fireplace. The only wall ornament was a painting of a woman with soft blonde hair and blue eyes.

Moments passed as she continued to wait by the door. It suddenly occurred to her that she had left herself without means to get back to town. She wondered if she'd been hasty in demanding an audience with Jake Silver. After all, what reason did she have to believe he wasn't the mastermind behind the attack on the settlers?

When he returned, she decided to take control of the situation.

"Thank you, Mr. Silver, but I won't join you for a meal. What I would like is to ask you some questions."

"Why?"

"I'm a newspaperman, Mr. Silver, like my brother."

"You're not much like your brother, except for your tendency to stick your nose into other people's business. Do you plan to publish the paper?"

"Certainly, as soon as my supplies arrive."

"I suppose this means that you intend to continue to fan the flames of the dispute."

"Absolutely not. I intend to present the truth, nothing more, nothing less."

"Surely you don't consider that as a means to negotiate peace?"

"I don't know, Mr. Silver. Did Jamie?"

"He did. Even managed to arrange a few shouting matches between a couple of farmers and ranchers."

"Well, I didn't come here for that. I'm only interested in finding my brother's killer. In the meantime, I intend to print the truth, just as he did."

"I'm not sure it matters what you print," he said in a low voice, then, as if he'd made a decision, turned toward the back of the house. "All right, come into the dining room. I'll consider your questions. This is my houseman, Wu."

A Chinese man with a long queue met them in the hallway, giving Dallas an open smile and a solemn bow.

"Welcome to venerable House of Silver, Missy."

"I'm pleased to meet you Wu. Thank you for sending the food baskets."

"Stop bowing, Wu," Jake snapped. "And bring her some food."

The room into which both men were leading Dallas contained only a table and chairs and a blazing fire. An intricately woven Indian blanket hung on one wall; two sconces on either side of the doorway and a many-branched silver candleholder on the table were filled with fat white lighted candles.

Everything was silver and white, except for the orange in the blanket, the rag rug before the fire, and the blue-hot coals in the cone-shaped fireplace. Dallas wanted to shield her eyes from the brightness. Though the wind outside was still cold, the warmth of the room was almost overwhelming.

"Would you care to remove your cape?" Jake asked, as he pulled out the heavy dark chair and waited for her to sit.

"No. As I mentioned before, I'm not here to eat. In fact, I ought to get back to town soon. It gets dark so early."

"Fine. Sit and watch while I eat. Wu doesn't allow me to let my food get cold. He may look slender, but I wouldn't recommend crossing him."

Dallas figured that crossing Wu was much less dangerous than crossing Jake Silver. And then she was sitting. Jake's hands were on her shoulders, untying and removing her cape. Wu took the cape and disappeared though the curved doorway into another room.

She swallowed the lump in her throat and forced herself to speak calmly. "Perhaps I could do with a cup of Wu's tea."

Jake moved away from her chair, taking the empty one at the end of the table. Almost instantly, Wu reappeared bearing a tray with a teapot and cup. Wu was followed by an Indian woman with long dark hair streaked with gray. She placed a bowl filled with steaming soup before Dallas.

"Just tea, please." Dallas didn't know why she was being so difficult. Simply smelling the wonderful soup made her mouth water.

"Wu's soup is very good," the woman said in a polished voice that caught Dallas by surprise. "I recommend it."

"You work here?" Dallas's question slipped out.

"Yes, I work for Mr. Silver, as does Wu."

"Close mouth, Shadow woman," Wu instructed. "Mr. Jake deal with his woman."

"I am not Mr. Jake's woman!" Dallas snapped,

her temper beginning to frazzle at the edges. "I'm not anybody's woman. And I'm getting tired—"

Her stomach growled.

Jake laughed. "Sometimes our bodies speak louder than our words."

Dallas cut her eyes back to Jake. The room was instantly rife with tension. Jake was no longer laughing. "Now listen, Jake Silver. I only came here for answers and that's all I will accept!"

"Of course. But you'll wait until I'm ready to talk and I won't be ready until we've finished *our* meal."

He turned to his soup and began to eat slowly and quietly, ignoring her.

Dallas sat stiffly. She would have stared her opponent down, except that Jake wasn't looking at her. Instead she could only gaze at the amber luster from the fire falling across the side of his face and shoulder, reinforcing the suggestion of heat. His dark hair was pulled back and tied with a leather thong. His white shirt, still open at the neck, was in stark contrast to the dark trousers, which were tucked into thigh-high shiny boots. Like some Spanish conquistador he sat at the end of the table, master of all he surveyed. He touched his linen napkin to his upper lip and along his mustache, then dropped it carelessly on the table beside his glass. He leaned back and watched as Wu removed the bowl. Now that he was finished with his soup, he was surveying her.

Dallas glanced at her bowl. The soup was tempting. Perhaps it would serve her purpose to eat it. He had promised to talk once the meal was over.

She tried a spoonful of the soup. "Delicious," she said before she could stop herself.

The firelight was reflecting in his dark eyes. He was so lithe, so tense, like a leopard still and waiting for his prey. She had never before encountered a man like Jake Silver. From that first moment in the saloon when she looked into Jake Silver's eyes, she'd recognized the ice, felt the contradiction of the fire within that drove him.

"When did you first meet Jamie?"

"Last December, after he bought the *Gazette* he came out to interview me."

"So he was here before the trouble started?"

"No, there was trouble then, from the first settlers. Elliott didn't have anything to do with them. They rebelled against the false promises made by greedy land speculators."

"What happened to those settlers?"

"There weren't nearly as many, and they didn't stay long when they found out the land wasn't what they'd been promised. There were incidents, even then, but the real trouble didn't start until the next July, when Elliott Parnell brought in the German immigrants."

"That suggests that someone else other than the Germans might be behind the attacks, doesn't it?"

Jake frowned. That thought had crossed his mind frequently. But there'd been no pattern, and nobody had been hurt. A few missing cattle here and there could be signed off to change and the Indians. "That's what your brother said."

"What else did he say?"

"That Elliott seemed to be a good man and that I should meet with him."

"Why didn't you?"

"Your brother was killed and Elliott left town almost immediately."

A sudden horrifying thought crossed Dallas's mind. "You don't think the two are connected, do you?"

"I doubt it. Elliott might be a coward, but he wouldn't kill an innocent like your brother. No, Lawson Pickens said it had something to do with equipment for the settlement. Then his next group was delayed while they waited for a boat carrying some of the settlers straight from Germany. I'd hoped they'd given up the idea of coming."

"What did you and Jamie argue about?" she asked softly.

"About freedom and responsibility and how a man must choose his course of action."

Dallas could imagine her brother in such philosophical debates. They'd certainly had enough of them through the years. Jamie had been the only one with whom Dallas could discuss her dreams and thoughts.

And Jamie had matched her strong views, often playing devil's advocate just for the sake of argument.

"Which side were you on?"

"The side of the West and the men who first came here."

"Do you mean the Indians?"

Jake pursed his lips and glanced down at his plate. She was quick, this sister of James Banning. She didn't talk like a woman. She wasn't soft and agreeable. There was an energy about her that challenged and invigorated him.

"No, though of course, you're right. At least as right as any of us can be. This land belonged to the Indians, but we're here now and there's no turning back civilization. I suppose it's a matter of survival of the fittest."

He looked toward the fire and Dallas knew that he was remembering some other time, some other war.

"Do you know who killed Jamie?" Dallas asked.

When he turned his eyes back to Dallas, there was great sadness and pain in their dark depths. "No, and if I did, what would it matter? You couldn't bring him back."

Wu served thin slices of beef and rice. Dallas no longer demured. She ate the food, relishing its delicately seasoned flavor. After the woman brought and cleared away coffee and a sweet pudding, Jake turned his chair to the fire and invited Dallas to do the same.

"Are you really going to fire the men who caused the accident?"

"They've already been fired."

"Isn't that a bit extreme, given the reports I'd had that the ranchers are trying to get rid of the immigrants?"

"Get rid of them, yes. But my men know that I don't allow them to harass anything, cattle, people or—immigrants."

"The last time I heard, immigrants were people."

"The last time—you set great store by the last time, don't you, Miss Banning. Me, I try to put the last time behind me. It makes life easier."

"Do you think that Slim and his friends are responsible for the other attacks on the immigrants?"

"No, I don't." He lit a thin dark cigar, leaned back in his chair, and crossed his legs at the ankle.

"Then who?"

"I haven't been able to find out. I've been too busy trying to find out who is rustling my cattle."

Rustling his cattle? She stood and walked toward the fire, trying to settle the nervous tension that seemed to be growing as the fire dwindled. "You really are losing cattle? How can you tell, with all the snow and the storm?"

"You always lose a few. But these rustlers do their stealing the easy way. They take cattle we have rounded up and brought to safety."

"And you think the immigrants are doing the rustling?"

"I do. It didn't start until they arrived."

"But appearances can be deceiving," she argued.

"Like a woman coming to call with her skirts hiked up around her waist?"

Dallas blushed. "I'm sorry. I didn't have time to worry about convention. Pulling it up was the only way I could ride the da—horse without falling off."

Jake bit back a chuckle. He'd been surprised to see a woman riding like a man. But what he'd been unable to forget were the black stockings and the legs that hugged the horse's body, legs that were strong enough to hold a man between them.

Jake swore and pitched the half-smoked cigar into the fire as he stood. "Come, I'll take you back to town before it gets dark."

"That isn't necessary," she said, recognizing the end of a conversation that had turned surprisingly pleasant in spite of the rise and fall of unaccountable tension. "Just allow me to borrow a horse. I'll have Willie return it."

"Riding out on the plains alone isn't safe for a woman, even in the daytime." He stood opposite her, close to the fire, close to her as he said, "After the sun goes down, anything could happen."

Dallas's breath seemed to rush from her lungs. "Like what?"

"You could meet the Devil of the Plains."

"I could." The silence lengthened, broken only by the sputtering of the fire. "Maybe," she whispered in a voice that was so low he had to lean forward to hear. "Maybe I already have."

He hadn't known he was going to kiss her. The heat that flared up was like a prairie fire, sudden and fierce. His need was a burning demand that he claim her lips with his.

What stunned him was the instant response.

With a little gasp she melted against him, surrendering in that moment to a need as great as his own. In the next moment she stiffened, and he understood that she was as surprised as he.

Then her arms went around him and he was pulling her into his embrace. A deep shiver started somewhere about his knees and shimmied upward. He closed his eyes and reached for control. He had none.

Beneath the onslaught of emotions into which she'd been flung, Dallas felt as if she were on fire. She was lost in the taste of him, of the cigar he'd been smoking, his after-dinner brandy, his tongue that invaded and ran knowingly around her mouth.

Confusion and fear finally loosened the power that held her. Desperately she pulled away and forced her arms to release their clasp around his neck.

"I'm sorry, Mr. Silver. I didn't intend anything like that to happen."

"You didn't make it happen, Miss Banning."

"No, but I didn't stop it."

"No, you didn't."

But she had. If she hadn't drawn back, he would have stretched her out on the rag rug before the fire and lifted that petticoat. He'd have peeled down those black stockings and felt those long legs clasped around his body.

She must have called out, for she heard Wu answer.

"Yes, missy, you ready for cape. I get."

And then she was sitting in a small carriage, her knees covered with a blanket that protected her from the cold but did nothing to shield her from the touch of Jake Silver's thigh. In unspoken agreement they rode in silence, across a black night, hung with a spattering of icy stars and a sliver of a moon.

"It's very beautiful, here," she finally said.

"Beauty is deceiving. It can kill."

"That's what Mr. Parnell said—about the snow. That it was beautiful death."

Jake felt a wrenching in his heart. He'd almost done something very wrong tonight. He'd allowed his feelings to overpower him. He'd almost lost control.

Over a woman he didn't even like.

Jake was beginning to understand that Dallas was a danger far greater than the immigrants, than prairie fires, than snowstorms.

When they reached Green Willow Creek, Jake drove the carriage to the newspaper office. Before he could assist her, Dallas had helped herself down to the ground. She started inside, paused, and turned back.

"Mr. Silver, I wonder if you would check on Adolph, the man with the broken leg."

"It's already being done. Wu sent one of the hands for the doctor when you first arrived."

That's what he'd done when he left the room. And she'd thought he simply went to pay off the two fired hands. Once again she'd misjudged Jake Silver.

"You take your responsibilities seriously," she said.

"I do. Including you. Don't strike out without a proper guard again, Miss Banning. If you want to come calling, send Willie to tell me."

"I wasn't alone, Mr. Silver. I was with Adolph and Lena, and Greta Bittner, the woman whose house was pulled down. I should have been safe. I hope, if you find that your men were guilty of the deed, that you'll accept the responsibility for repairing the house."

"There are some things that can't be repaired, Miss Banning. The sooner you learn that, the safer you'll be. Go back home, Dallas." His voice softened as he added, "I can't promise to keep you safe."

Chapter 8

Dallas let herself into the newspaper office, locked the door and leaned against it.

He couldn't keep her safe? She hadn't asked him to keep her safe. She could look after herself. At least she always had—until tonight. Tonight was— well, she couldn't explain what had happened tonight. She'd flirted with her brother's friends, joined them in their wild escapades, even experimented with kisses before, more than once, but only with men she'd been sure she could control. And the kisses had been, by comparison, chaste, passionless encounters.

Her father had tried to rein in her high spirits, but without any real hope of success. Mrs. Banning's death when Jamie was only a baby had left Dallas to be raised by a series of housekeepers, each determined to take the devil out of her and turn her into a lady.

They'd all failed. They failed first and foremost because Dallas's father and older brothers didn't really want her to be some simpering young woman who batted her eyelashes and played foolish courting games. She was their equal. They liked her and she liked them. It was as simple as that. And she took care of Jamie, relieving them of the responsibility for doing so and the guilt that they hadn't.

From the time she could tag along, she'd followed her father to the newspaper, learning along with her older brothers. When they went away to get a higher education, Dallas followed. It was poor Jamie who always got left behind. And it was Jamie who came to Wyoming and lost his life trying to prove himself.

Though most women were not expected to accomplish more than making a good match, Dallas had been trained to think for herself. When she met Allan Pinkerton, she knew she had found an outlet for her imagination that was worthy of her efforts.

Before long she had moved to Boston and become the operative inside a bank who discovered which employee tipped off the bank robbers. She attended balls to look for jewel thieves. And once she'd become the companion to a sick man who was dying before his time, only to learn that his wife had been feeding him poison.

But nothing had prepared Dallas Banning for Jake Silver's kisses.

Dallas had always been honest with herself. She'd been in dangerous territory this afternoon and she couldn't allow herself to be in that kind of situation again—not with a man Jamie hadn't trusted.

A man she couldn't trust.

A man with fire in his touch and ice in his eyes.

Dallas had a job to do in Green Willow Creek, and she couldn't allow anything to get in the way. Clearly she must avoid being alone with Jake Silver again.

In an attempt to learn more about her brother's enemies, Dallas routinely took her meals at Lucy

Jarrett's boarding house, where she shared a table with many of the unmarried businessmen in town. Over the new few days, Dr. Horn confirmed that he'd set Wilhelm's leg, at Jake Silver's expense. The gossip was that Jake had even sent his own man out to look after the stock and do any chores that might otherwise go undone while the immigrant was unable to move about. Jake's paying the bill hadn't surprised her. His sending a man out to help had.

Still, at the end of a week she was no closer to finding answers than she had been when she arrived. She hadn't found anyone who admitted to seeing Jamie that day except the livery stable owner and Elliott Parnell, who'd found his body.

One afternoon Dallas called on Miranda, who was on her way to pick up a gown from Irene, the local dressmaker. Miranda suggested that Dallas come along. Dallas readily agreed. She enjoyed Miranda's company, staring down any of the women she encountered who gave her a look of disapproval. The businessmen in town made certain that she was accepted by their wives. Having seen the kind of newspaper Jamie printed, they decided early on not to chance offending a Banning.

Dallas liked Irene immediately.

" 'Course, you'll also need a real party dress," Miranda said, "for the spring dance. Irene is wonderful with a needle."

"Spring dance?" Dallas questioned.

"Oh, yes, next week," Irene explained. "These winters get pretty long. Once the snow melts and the temperature gets warmer, we hold a dance in Miranda's saloon."

"Not saloon, restaurant," Miranda corrected haughtily, as she mimicked the expression of a lady—lifted eyebrows and affected disdain. "What it is for the rest of the year, my dear, is what it is, but," she smiled and dropped a curtsy, "the night of the dance, it's a fine restaurant. Otherwise the ladies won't come and I won't be allowed to take part. That's why Irene is making me a new dress. I may have to pretend, but I still like to shake them up."

Dallas looked at the red dress and decided that the vibrant color would shake up more than the women. What happened if some of Miranda's regular customers turned up unexpectedly, looking for a room and entertainment? "Does everyone come to the dance?" she asked.

"Everybody in the territory close enough to town comes in. The ladies see to that."

"Even Mr. Silver?" Dallas's question popped out before she could stop it.

Irene looked up, an expression of surprise on her face. "Sometimes Jake comes, but not always. He's pretty much a loner. But Pete, he's one of Mr. Silver's ranch hands, Pete and the other hands always come."

Dallas surmised from the glow in Irene's eyes that if Pete came, it was probably to see Irene.

"Jake's not much on socializing," Miranda said, "he avoids crowds."

"This shade of green would be lovely on you. What about it, Miss Banning?" Irene asked. "Miss Banning?"

"I'm sorry, what did you say?" Dallas felt a flush on her cheeks and she quickly gathered a swatch of the fabric in her hand to cover her confusion.

"I said," Irene repeated, "this emerald-green satin would be so perfect on you."

Dallas was halfway to refusing when she caught a glimpse of the expression on Miranda's face. It said plainly that Miranda recognized Dallas's interest in

Jake, and that while it didn't make her happy, she was resigned to the truth. Knowing Miranda, Dallas was equally certain that she didn't intend to forego her campaign for Jake's attention.

Desperately Dallas forced her attention to the fabric Irene was holding. The color was spectacular. She didn't know what kind of party dresses the women of Green Willow Creek wore, but she'd have a better chance of fitting into her new community if she allowed Irene to make a dress rather than wearing one of her Philadelphia gowns.

"What about the immigrants?" Dallas asked.

Miranda slipped off her dress and handed it back to the dressmaker. "I don't know. They weren't here last year."

Irene took the red dress and draped it across a chair. "Oh, there were a few nesters, but they didn't come into town. And they're all gone now anyway."

"That seems wrong," Dallas protested. "The immigrants have had such a hard time. They need some sunshine as much as the rest of us. I think I'll speak to Mr. Pickens about inviting them. I could make up some kind of flyer."

Miranda stepped back into her own dress. "I doubt that they will come. A couple of old-time farmers have been invited, but Elliott probably won't want to set up a direct confrontation with the ranchers just yet. You see what happened at Sunday services."

Elliott. Miranda was on a first-name basis with both Jake and Elliott. Dallas didn't know why that bothered her. So far as she'd been able to ascertain, neither man visited Miranda professionally. Perhaps she was jealous of the easy friendship Miranda had with the two men.

Dallas was growing frustrated in her search for

Jamie's killer. Her attempts to ferret out information about the murderer were bringing one blank stare after another. Everybody had liked Jamie. Nobody could suggest any reason why anybody would kill him. The only person he had ever had any words with was Jake Silver.

A party might prove to be a golden opportunity to get some answers. All she'd really learned so far was that Jamie had been trying to negotiate a settlement between the farmers and the cattle ranchers. He'd even talked a few men into agreeing to meet to talk about the problem. But the meetings had turned into shouting matches.

"All right," she agreed, making a mental note to stop by the bank and withdraw funds from the generous amount of money her father had dispatched. "I'll have the green fabric. What do I need to do?"

"Not a thing, Miss Banning," Irene said.

"Please, Irene, call me Dallas."

"Of course, Miss—Dallas. And if you'll trust me to do it, let me surprise you."

A bit reluctantly, Dallas agreed to being surprised, left a deposit for the gown, and agreed to return for a fitting in five days.

While Dallas's dress was being made, she sent Willie to Mr. Lewis's store for new clothing for him to wear to the dance and an extra set of everyday clothing to be kept at the newspaper so that he'd always have something clean. Cleanliness was a requirement that Willie would have to come to terms with.

Willie had a quick mind, and now that he could see the potential, he was eager to get the paper going. As her official full-time assistant, he was learning how to set the type and ink the presses. Soon the supplies would arrive, and she'd be ready to think about writing the stories.

"Willie, I don't mean to sound moralistic, but how on earth did the town ever come together to have their dance at Miranda's saloon?"

"Oh, they didn't mean to. The first year it was planned for the schoolhouse. But a storm come up and blew the roof off and nobody could get back home. The only place big enough for everybody to take shelter was Miss Miranda's."

"And they went there?"

"Well, it was only to wait out the storm. But it took two days. They didn't have nowhere to sleep and no food to eat. Miss Miranda just finally come right out and said, 'You all just pretend that this is the finest restaurant in New York City. You've come here to eat and I'm your hostess.'

"She fed 'em and give 'em blankets. When she run out of both she sweet-talked Mr. Lewis into getting more from the general store. She was willing to pay extra, and me and him done it. She didn't charge them people a thing. After that, they just kept on pretending."

Dallas shook her head in disbelief. She'd never pretended in her life. If she felt a certain way, she acted on it, unless it compromised her job in some way. Her job. She'd never expected to be publishing a newspaper. Her job had been with a detective agency, and she'd loved her work. Loved it so much that she'd allowed herself to get carried away with her own importance.

She'd known that Jamie needed her to help him stand up to their brothers, had always depended on her. But she'd had a chance to do something few women ever had, become a Pinkerton detective, and she'd left Jamie behind. She knew that he was determined to find a way to show the others that he was as smart and as self-sufficient as they. She'd told him to wait. She'd let him think that she was coming home; that they'd be a team. But she'd delayed returning and Jamie had gotten tired of waiting.

If she could get the printing press to cooperate she'd be able to do something to make it up to him. So far it stubbornly refused to do so. Dallas was reasonably competent with firearms, horses, and competition. But mechanics eluded her. She couldn't get the press to work. And none of the offers of help came from people who knew anything about machines. She was about ready to admit defeat and suffer further delay while she sent for one of her father's printers to help, when Willie came up with a suggestion.

"Why don't you ask at the settlement house? There's a man out there who runs a blacksmith's shop. He repairs farm equipment. Maybe he'd know what to do."

Dallas thought for a moment about Jake's advice that she not venture out of town alone and promptly disregarded it. She wanted to check on Adolph and Lena Schmahl. This would give her a chance to do both. Besides, she had her derringer. She could look after herself, if she went prepared to do so. Still, bringing Willie along wouldn't be a bad idea.

The next morning, while Willie rented a buggy for their visit, Dallas bought a sack of flour from the store and two loaves of fresh-baked bread from Lucy Jarrett as a gift for the Schmahls. She placed her derringer in her handbag, then met Willie at the livery stable.

"Willie," Dallas asked when they had left Green Willow behind, "where was my brother's body found?"

"About two miles out, along this road. That's what Mr. Parnell said."

"Did they say Jamie might have been to the settlement house?"

Willie shrugged his shoulders. "Maybe. But he could have been most anywhere. There's a fork in the road just beyond. One road goes to settlement and the other heads off toward the mountains."

"Show me, please, where he was found."

The spot, when they arrived, was no different from any other part of the road. It wasn't like being in the city. Willie was right; Jamie could have come from anywhere.

"What about his horse, Willie?"

"Never found it. Wasn't his, anyway. He rented it from the livery the morning he rode out. It was a big piebald with white ears. One of Wally's favorites."

"You mean he rented the horse and lost it? I thought a horse always returned to the barn."

"This one didn't."

"What about the cost of the animal?"

"Reckon old Wally was just glad *he* weren't the one riding it when the Devil of the Plains attacked.

"Willie! My brother was shot to death."

"That never did make no sense. Everybody knows that creature got ahold of him. Mr. Banning never even used his gun."

"My brother didn't even own a gun, at least not before he came out here."

"Don't know about back East, ma'am, but out here, he had one. I seen it. It was a Colt. I think Dr. Horn still has it. They thought maybe it was the gun that killed your brother."

"Was it?"

"No, wrong kind of bullet."

So, it wasn't an accident. Dallas made a mental note to reclaim the Colt from Dr. Horn. Her derringer was fine, but it was useless as a real weapon. A Colt was a better idea if she anticipated trouble. She intended to talk to the doctor about what kind of bullet killed Jamie. And she wanted a better description of the other injuries.

There was also the problem of the horse. It could have been stolen, or it could have bolted and be halfway to California by now. In any case, she'd arrange to pay old Wally for his loss.

But Dallas couldn't stay focused on her brother's death this morning. The morning was still cold. Her breath was visible in the air. With a bright sun warming the morning and the plains rolling endlessly in undulating waves of brown grass, her spirits lifted. Beyond the sea of brown were the stark Black Hills to the right and the majestic, snow-frosted mountain in the distance ahead.

"Somebody told me that the Devil of the Plains lives in the mountains, Willie. Which ones?"

"They say he roams between Bitter Butte and the section of the Green Mountains that juts out like a pointing finger."

"Who says?"

"Don't know. The Indians, maybe."

"What Indians? I haven't seen an Indian in town."

"Not many of them left. But there's a few braves who attack the settlers and the wagon trains passing through. They're just hungry since the buffalo are all gone."

Dallas shook her head. Indians, farmers, ranchers, and the Devil of the Plains. She'd never worked on a case with so many suspects. "Consentrate on the ones who stand to gain," Mr. Pinkerton always said.

Except for murders motivated by pure rage, he'd always been right. But crimes of passion were usually easier to solve because the criminals were more likely to make mistakes. Unfortunately, she didn't think that Jamie's death was a crime of passion. It had been premeditated.

The temperature climbed steadily as they drove. In a matter of days, the world had gone from icy white to watery browns and new, pale greens. There were bare spots where the grass was sparse, areas were prairie animals lived. Dallas watched furry brown prairie dogs play in the sunlight, darting back to the safety of their burrows as the buggy approached.

By the time they reached the settlement, Dallas had removed her cape and bonnet, turning her face to the sun. Her dark hair had slipped from the bun in which she'd fixed it, curling softly around her square face. There was something about this land that appealed to her. It seemed to understand and feed some wild, secret part of her that she'd never known was there. If she could sing, Dallas might have. Instead, she hummed along with the turn of the wheels.

The immigrants' housing came into view in the distance. It looked like a rough, brown cigar box with chimneys spaced two across the front, two on the back and one on each end.

Behind the building Willie called a bunkhouse were several smaller structures, a barn perhaps, and farther away, a building that belched black smoke into the air much like Dallas would have expected Indian smoke signals to appear.

As the buggy reached the door, two women stepped out, one holding a rifle, the other holding a large knife.

"Hello," Dallas said brightly. "I'm looking for Mr. Parnell. Is he here?"

"Ja. Ja. Parnell," one woman said, nodding her head.

The woman with the rifle didn't lower it.

Dallas looked helplessly at Willie, then started to climb down from the buggy.

"Nein!" the rifle bearer snapped, leveling the rifle at Dallas. Dallas sat back down, wishing that she'd studied German instead of Latin in college.

A man wearing a leather apron stepped around the corner of the building, his hand held out in disapproval. "Nein, Greta. Good morning, miss. You seek Mr. Parnell? Follow me."

They found Elliott behind the barn, overseeing the assembly of what appeared to be a mechanical plow with multiple shaves.

"Miss Banning!" Elliott dropped the tool he was holding and came forward, wiping his hand on his trousers before offering it in greeting. "What brings you out here?"

Gone was the black frock coat and the brocade vest that Dallas had attributed to Elliott the gambler. This man was a farmer, sleeves rolled up, face colored from the sun.

"I came to inquire about hiring one of your men to do a job for me."

Willie had walked over to the piece of equipment and was examining it curiously, leaving Dallas to broach her request in private.

"What kind of job?"

"I've been told that one of your immigrants is very good with machinery, and I need help."

"What kind of help, Miss Banning?"

"One half of my printing press seems frozen in place. I've done everything to free it from its restriction. If you have someone who could look at it, I'd be glad to pay."

"Well, I don't know. They don't go into town often." Elliott turned to the man wearing the leather apron. "This is Hans Dornier, Miss Banning. He's our blacksmith and expert on machinery. Hans, Miss Banning has a job for you, if you're interested."

"A job? In town?"

"Yes," Dallas responded, "I have a printing press that seems to be frozen in place. I wondered if you'd see what you could do?"

Hans looked questioningly at Elliott. When Elliott nodded his approval, Hans's face broke into a smile. "Ja! Ja! Tomorrow. I come to town tomorrow, for work."

"Thank you, I appreciate your taking time away from your work. Now, Mr. Parnell, if you'll direct us, I'd like to call on the Schmahls. Do you think it would be all right?"

Elliott looked from the machinery to Dallas and back again. "Of course," he finally said. "I'll be happy to drive you."

"That won't be necessary. Willie and I will go, if you'll give us directions."

"Well . . ."

Clearly, Elliott wasn't comfortable with that idea, but it was equally clear that he needed to work on the plow. He gave Willie the directions.

A short time later they were following a newly made trail away from the settlement house toward the mountains in the distance.

"Miss Banning," Willie said after they'd been driving for half an hour, "how long are we going to be gone? I'm getting pretty hungry."

Dallas smiled and lifted one of the two baskets

she'd placed beneath her feet. "Then let's stop and eat. This looks like a pretty spot."

Willie was ready and a few moments later Dallas opened the basket where Miss Lucy had packed bread and meat. A jug of cold coffee and a chunk of cheese completed their meal. Absorbed in the food, neither noticed the group of riders approaching until the leader let out a bloodcurdling cry.

"Lordy, Miss Banning. They're Indians, Cheyenne. Three of 'em, and we ain't even got a gun."

"Oh yes, we have," Dallas said, patting the pocket of her jacket. "But when you're outnumbered, sometimes it's better to find other ways to thwart trouble."

She glanced at Willie, his freckles blood-red against his white face, and reached inside the other basket. "Lean down, Willie."

"What?"

"Put your head down, now!"

Willie complied. Dallas dashed flour on his face, then brushed away the excess from his shirt collar. "Wipe your brows and lips. Hurry."

By that time a very pale-skinned, freckled boy was facing the Indian who'd ridden up to the wagon.

"Stay back!" Dallas said sternly. "This boy has the spotted disease." She gestured wildly at Willie's freckles. "If you come close, you'll die!" Ducking her head, she said in a low voice, "Moan, Willie. Look sick and point to your face."

Willie enthusiastically complied.

The three Indians spoke among themselves, looking longingly at Dallas and gesturing at Willie. At last they backed away, turned, and let out war cries that made Dallas swallow what little breath she had left.

"It worked, Willie. They thought your freckles were measles."

"Lordy, Lordy, Miss Banning. You're some smart lady. Suppose they hadn't believed you?"

Dallas drew her gun from her pocket. "Then we'd have been in trouble. My derringer only has two shots."

Chapter 9

"Miss Banning did what?" Jake Silver stared at Elliott Parnell in disbelief.

"She staved off a Cheyenne attack by convincing them that Willie had the measles."

"What in hell was she doing on the prairie without an escort?"

"I tried to stop her. But telling Dallas Banning she can't do something is like telling the snow to stop."

Jake swallowed his anger. He never thought of snow that he didn't think of Sarah; that he didn't feel such pain that he couldn't breathe. Now, the man who'd been responsible for old nightmares was standing before him—the man he'd promised Sarah not to kill.

"I came here, Jake, because I think we need to talk."

"Get on your horse and go, Elliott. I have nothing to say to you."

"But I have something to say to you. I know you don't want to talk about Sarah, and I won't. But I do want to talk about Dallas Banning."

Jake narrowed his gaze, allowing himself to look squarely at Elliott Parnell. The man who'd saved his life ten years earlier was gone. The once open and gentle face was lined and weary. The smile that had once come so freely was gone forever. Elliott had changed. He wasn't asking. He wasn't apologizing.

Jake waited. He wouldn't agree to talk. He didn't want to forgive Elliott. Forgiving Elliott was forgetting, and he wasn't ready for that. "What in hell could we have to say?"

"I want to know if you're interested in her?"

"Why?"

"Because I think I am. And I don't want to compete with you over a woman again, not like it was with Sarah."

Jake swore. "Never mention Sarah's name again, Elliott. Get out of Green Willow Creek. Pack up your farmers and move them on. Somebody is going to get hurt, but it won't have anything to do with Dallas Banning—unless she brings it on herself."

"I can't, Jake. They've invested their life savings. I don't have a choice. I have to see this through."

"So be it," Jake said, and turned his back on Elliott, leaving him standing in the foyer.

When he heard Elliott leave, Jake let out a deep sigh and walked toward the fire, reaching blindly with one hand for the fireplace. He bowed his head, leaning it against his arm, and closed his eyes as the heat flamed his face.

God, would it never end? The pain. The loss. The anger.

Anger was the power that generated movement, that fueled his actions, that kept him alive.

Elliott was here in Green Willow Creek, forcing him to think about people and loss and death. And this time he might not be able to walk away, for there was nobody else to stop the bloodshed that was bound to happen. The other ranchers were already secretly organizing a vigilance committee, bent on driving the farmers out.

The farmers led by Elliott.

Jake might want Elliott dead, but not that way.

"Mr. Jake?" Wu was standing beside the table. Jake hadn't heard him come in. But, with Wu's soft cloth shoes, Jake was often unaware of his presence until he spoke.

"Damn it, Wu. Don't sneak up on me like that!"

"Not sneak, Mr. Jake."

"What do you want?"

"Wu ask question?"

"So long as you don't expect an answer. I'm fresh out of answers."

"Pete talk in kitchen, about spring dance. Wu think Shadow woman is sad. Wu think about taking her to dance."

It took Jake a moment to assimilate Wu's question. "You want to take the Indian woman to the dance? Why?"

"She once very proud woman. She think people steal land from her family and send monster to kill them. She not proud woman now. Wu want Shadow to feel dignity again. All persons need to be proud."

In that moment Jake had some insight into the pain Wu must have felt coming to this land, either willingly or otherwise, and being subjected to ridicule and pain. Perhaps giving Shadow back some of her pride was his way of reclaiming his own.

"She say she have no more family, she belong this one. She learn to be lady now. Wu think that Shadow already a lady. Wu take lady to dance."

"Wu, with the temper of the town running as high as it is, I don't know that she would be safe."

"But Wu ask you go. You make safe. People not make trouble if Jake Silver there. We only watch from Miss Miranda's inside porch."

Inside porch? Miranda's balcony. That could work.

Still, the townspeople, the ranchers, Elliott

Parnell, and Dallas Banning. Now Wu and Shadow. Jake couldn't think of a more explosive mix. It was a disaster primed to happen. Somebody would get hurt, and Jake didn't want it to be Wu. He'd gotten attached to the feisty Chinaman.

Wu ought to be able to go to the dance. From the beginning, this territory of Wyoming was settled in a different way from the earlier states. Equality for all its people had been the goal. They'd even given women the right to vote and hold office. If Wu and Shadow wanted to be equal, he'd do what he could to make it happen.

"Why the hell not, Wu? How much gunpowder can an Indian and a Chinaman explode?"

"Thank you, Mr. Jake. Wu have Shadow make Mr. Jake special meal. And, and . . ."

"What else, you sly old crook?"

"Wu not know how ask, but . . . but . . . Mr. Jake teach Wu dance?"

Jake didn't think he laughed. But Wu later swore that he had. At Wu's cry of dismay, Shadow charged from the back of the house with an iron skillet in her hand to take on Wu's attacker.

Wu had to restrain her. Wu's woman, as everyone had begun to call her, was a wildcat. Jake smiled. He didn't know about dancing, but she was the kind of woman who would warm a man's bed, if she and Wu were ever to make a match of their relationship—a real spitfire, she was.

A spitfire like Dallas Banning, who'd shot at her attackers in her newspaper office, who'd forced his hands to admit to being responsible for breaking one of the immigrant's legs. Now she'd warded off an Indian attack. She was a damned fool. Jake decided that Wu could have a woman like that if he wanted her. Not Jake. Dallas Banning was the last woman on earth he'd want, even if she did set his pulse racing. Desire only blinded a man and made him do foolish things.

Like kiss a woman he didn't like.

Like spend his time remembering her response, her touch, the feel of her against him.

Elliott wanted her; let Elliott have her.

Dallas was no lady. She was an out-of-control rebel, and in the last ten years Jake had learned to avoid what he couldn't control.

Soon after sunup, Dallas heard a knock on the front door of the newspaper office.

After sliding her arms into her wrapper, she brushed back her hair and went to open the door.

"Mr. Dornier? I didn't expect you so early. I don't even have a fire going down here yet."

The German stood outside the door, his hat in his hand.

"Sorry, Miss Banning," Elliott Parnell said, coming to stand beside the blacksmith. "But we have a great deal to do, now that the ground is thawing."

"I'm sorry. Of course, come in." She stepped back, pulling the ties to her wrapper tighter. "Willie always banks the coals down here, I'll just add some more wood."

"Nein, Hans make fire."

Dallas closed the door behind the two men and watched as her lamps were lit and the fire in the stove quickly rekindled into a blaze.

"This newspaper machine," Hans finally said. "Show me."

Dallas directed him to the small hand press and demonstrated how it seemed frozen in place.

"I'll just get dressed," she finally ventured, "while you look at it. Then I'll make tea."

"Miss Banning," Elliott said, catching her arm as

she started up the stairs, "why not let me walk you down to Miss Lucy's for a proper breakfast?"

"Ah, no. Thank you, but I keep a few supplies here in the storeroom. If you'll get some water from the barrel—"

He was holding her arm, standing close to her, his face a study in conflict.

"What's wrong, Mr. Parnell?"

"Please, couldn't you call me Elliott?"

"I . . . I suppose. What's wrong, Elliott?"

"I have something to ask you, and I feel like such a fool."

"Nonsense. Ask me."

"I'm afraid you'll refuse. If you don't wish to accept, please know that I'll accept your decision."

"Elliott, if you don't ask your question I'm not going to get dressed and have my morning tea. If I have to wait much longer for my tea, I'll definitely refuse."

"Will you allow me to escort you to the dance?"

Dallas was taken aback. She'd already decided to attend the dance. She was to go for her final fitting on her dress the next morning. She'd even allowed herself a certain amount of anticipation. But an escort? She hadn't anticipated that. She wasn't even certain what the protocol was in this case. Perhaps she would be better accepted by the community with an escort. In any case, she didn't want to hurt Elliott. What harm could it do to accept his invitation?

"I'd like that, Elliott. Thank you for asking me."

Elliott smiled in relief, and dropped her arm. "I didn't think you'd accept."

"Why not?"

"I thought I sensed something the other day, something between you and Jake. I don't want to compete with Jake."

"What nonsense! Of course there isn't anything between Jake Silver and me. He's Miranda's friend, and even if he weren't, he's not the kind of man a woman ought to care about. He's obviously a rogue."

Dallas didn't know whether she was trying to convince Elliott or herself. Judging from Elliott's expression, he didn't believe her, but he was gentleman enough not to argue.

"Sometimes," he said softly, "a woman can't control who she loves and maybe it's better if she doesn't try. The consequences can be disastrous."

Dallas was only too well aware of that. "What time will you be picking me up, Elliott?"

"About eight o'clock? I thought we'd have supper first."

"That sounds very nice. Now, let me dress and see to our tea."

By the time Dallas had dressed and arranged her hair, the smell of tea wafted up to her sleeping loft. Elliott had made it.

By midmorning, Hans had freed the frozen arm of the press and had it clanking merrily. Elliott didn't mention the dance again, and kept his distance from Dallas as if he was afraid she'd change her mind.

It wasn't until she'd paid Hans and they'd left her office that she understood Elliott's reluctance over Hans making the trip to town. There on the opposite side of the street was a line of cowboys leaning against the rail.

They allowed Elliott and Hans to climb into the wagon before the first gun was fired. Dallas didn't know what was about to happen, but she wasn't about to let the blacksmith get killed because he'd come to help her. Without a thought she opened her door, marched out into the street and put her hands on her hips.

"You men stop that! Right now! Or I'll write an editorial for my newspaper that will bring the U.S. marshal so fast you won't be able to say Devil of the Plains."

Elliott climbed down from the wagon and strode back to stand beside Dallas. His hand rested on his weapon.

"You heard me," Dallas snapped, daring them to disagree. "I'll start making a list of your names if you don't get back inside."

Glancing at each other uncertainly, the men finally reholstered their guns and filed back into the saloon.

"Thanks, Elliott," Dallas said, dusting off her hands as if she'd plunged them into the flour barrel.

"Dallas, what are we going to do with you? You just can't keep taking on the world. You're going to get hurt and we might not always be there to protect you."

" 'We?' Who do you mean by 'we'?"

Elliott shrugged off her question. But in his heart he knew the answer. Just as before, it was him and Jake.

On her way for her fitting the next morning, Dallas stopped in to call on Dr. Horn.

"Do come in, Miss Banning. Are you feeling unwell?"

Dr. Horn looked more like a farmer than Elliott did. He had a thick shock of white hair and wore a scrubby worn pair of brown worsted trousers held up by suspenders.

"No, I'm feeling very well. I stopped by to inquire about my brother's gun. I understand he owned a Colt that you have in your possession."

"Yes, a Colt .38. I still have it here somewhere."

"I'd like to ask you some questions about that, if you don't mind."

"I never intended to keep it," he said, as if he thought Dallas was accusing him of stealing the gun.

She hastened to set him at ease. "I never thought that. As you know, Dr. Horn, I came here to find out who killed my brother. I'm a newspaper reporter. I know about guns and medical reports. I understand there were other wounds?"

Dr. Horn studied Dallas for a moment until he seemed satisfied with the idea that a woman could do what was considered to be a man's job.

"Yes, there were wounds, hoof marks. He lay on the road after he was shot. It isn't unusual for a wild animal to disturb a body."

"So close to town?"

"We often have wild animals take a stroll down main street, Miss Banning. Just last fall there was an elk—"

"I'm sure you do," Dallas interrupted, "but do you have an opinion as to the kind of animal that made the wounds?"

Now the doctor look uncomfortable. "No, I can't say that I do. They were . . . rather unusual. But I can assure you that your brother was killed by a bullet."

"Were you able to determine what kind of gun fired the bullet?"

"A Colt .45, and they're a dime a dozen out here."

"Is there anything else you can tell me, Dr. Horn, that might help me learn who killed my brother?"

"No. I'm truly sorry."

"Can you think of anybody who might want to harm Jamie?"

"No, ma'am. Your brother might be as pesky as a horsefly, but he was fair. Outside the problems between the ranchers and the farmers, the only thing he made any enemies over was the school."

"What school? I haven't heard anything about a school."

"That was the problem. The schoolhouse was built, but nobody ever got around to hiring a teacher. He thought the children ought to have lessons. He even gave a few of them books so they could practice their reading."

That sounded like Jamie. He would have given away his last dime if a child needed it. All the more reason for the citizens to be more helpful in locating his killer. His death made less and less sense.

"I'll take Jamie's weapon with me, if you don't mind, Dr. Horn," Dallas said as she took her leave of the doctor.

"Certainly. But be careful. These pistols can be very dangerous if you don't know how to use them."

Dallas smiled and took her leave. There was no reason to let him know just how qualified she was to shoot the weapon.

Dallas returned to her office and hid Jamie's gun under her mattress before she met Miranda at the dressmaker's shop.

Now she was studying herself in Irene's looking glass. She'd expected the fitting to be a chore, but the dress was stunning. The emerald color brought out the green flecks in her eyes and set off her skin beautifully. She'd never considered herself attractive, never cared that she wasn't. But this dress could change all that.

"It's lovely," Miranda agreed. "You've outdone yourself, Irene. All we need now is to get Dallas's hair out of that bun. Will you allow me to dress your hair, Dallas?"

"I'm afraid that my hair defies restraint. Unless I bind it, it becomes a frizzy mess."

"Nonsense, you have beautiful hair. It makes me want to be a brunette."

Dallas turned slowly to study her blond friend. "Why? In that red dress, there won't be a man in the place who can keep his eyes off you."

"And there won't be a woman either. Wearing red before the prominent citizens of Green Willow Creek will be like wearing red at the bullfights in Spain."

"What's wrong with wearing red to a bullfight?" Irene asked breathlessly.

"Well, I've never been, but the Russian duke told me about going to a bullfight. They wave a red rag at the bull to make him charge."

Dallas smiled. "And I'm thinking that's what you're doing. Are you trying to attract anybody special?"

"Oh, yes. He's special all right. But he doesn't want to be attracted."

All the way back to her office, Dallas thought about what Miranda had said. Dallas decided that Jake was probably attracted to Miranda, all right, but he was the kind of man who wouldn't show it. Still, he was a man and she didn't think even he would be able to resist Miranda in red. Her warm feelings about the way she looked in her green dress vanished as she walked.

The printing supplies arrived by train. Knowing of her connections back East, and assuming that the newspapers would be sent back to interested parties there, Mr. Pickens, the banker, Mr. Lewis, the operator of the general store, and Mr. Bowker, the carpenter/undertaker/preacher, stopped in to inquire about advertising in the paper. Now, with ink, new paper, chemicals, and type—and the promise of income—Dallas Banning was ready to put out a paper.

All Dallas needed to print her first issue of the *Willow Creek Gazette* was a lead story. She got it the next day when a rancher and one of his riders brought in the body of one of his cowboys, wrapped in a blanket and draped across a horse.

Dallas immediately requested that she be allowed to view the examination so that she could write the story for her paper. Dr. Horn refused, but after a great deal of heated discussion, he allowed Dallas to wait in his office within listening distance of the room where he examined the body. The rancher called attention to the hoof marks that had trampled the body to death. "What did it, Doc?" he asked.

"I don't know," the doctor answered. "The hooves are much too big for horses or cows."

"What about an ox?"

"Well, maybe. I've never seen one leave a print like that. But I don't have another answer."

"The Devil of the Plains," the rider said. "The creature has to belong to one of them farmers. That's where Cappy was riding when it got 'im, along the butte between the mountains and those foreigners. They done it!"

"Now wait a minute," Dallas said, stepping into the examining room. "You don't know that they're involved."

"Have to be," the ranch owner said. "The rustling didn't start till they come here. Now they're killing my men. We've got to put a stop to it."

"My brother was killed," Dallas said, "and I don't think it had anything to do with the farmers."

The range hand scoffed. "Yeah, that's because you're after one of them. Heard you rode out to see Parnell and that he come calling on you."

"Don't be ridiculous. I rode out to see Jake Silver, too. He brought me wood. Does that mean I'm after him?"

The man shuffled his feet, reluctant to give in. "Maybe. Maybe not. But them farmers are behind this, as sure as there's a God. And somebody's gonna have to do something about it."

Dallas went back to her office. She had her lead story, but she wasn't happy about it. A news story now could make trouble. With the threat of retaliation hanging in the air, she didn't want to think about what might happen at the dance. And the dance was tomorrow night.

The month of May had hurried through its last days, giving sunshine and warmth that brought wildflowers to the banks along Green Willow Creek and flocks of birds that stopped off on their way north. The second Saturday of June, the day of the dance, dawned bright and clear.

Dallas, drawing her shawl about her shoulders, started up the sidewalk to Irene's shop. The dress was done. Irene had even fashioned a confection of ribbon and lace for Dallas's hair.

"I appreciate the ribbon, but I'll never be able to get anything like that to stay in my hair. My hair's too fine, like wispy feathers. If it weren't down to my waist I'd never be able to tie it down."

"Don't worry. Miranda will fix it. She's very good at dressing hair."

Miranda. Dallas wished she hadn't agreed to allow Miranda to put some fashion in her hairstyle. She was perfectly satisfied with the way she looked, and if Jake Silver didn't appreciate her appearance, so be it. He might not even show up, and she certainly wasn't trying to attract him anyway. Elliott Parnell was her escort for the evening.

Dallas had given Willie the day off. Miranda needed him to clean the saloon and pin up the decorations. On her return from the dressmaker's, Dallas worked on her story, with little satisfaction. What was wrong? She had the event and the details, and she knew that any one of her brothers would have whipped the facts into a tight little article that would be read with indignation.

And that might be the problem. Indignation. Her story could push the ranchers into action. Did she want to do that? She still didn't know what kind of animal killed the ranch hand, but she was fairly sure it wasn't an ox, and she didn't believe Hans or any of the others would have murdered anybody.

"So? What kind of newspaper woman are you, Dallas Banning? Crimes have been committed and you don't think anyone is guilty?"

But that wasn't the truth either. The trouble was, she didn't want anyone to be guilty. Jake had had enough hurt and pain in his life. She could see it in his eyes. And Elliott? Elliott was a man who needed something, or somebody to care about him. But he would never hurt anyone to make that happen. His kindnesses in dealing with the immigrants proved that.

That afternoon Dallas heated water on the woodstove and filled a basin in which she washed her hair. Next she poured hot water into the elongated tin tub she'd bought from the general store. She smiled, remembering Willie's embarrassment when she asked him to carry it from the store to the newspaper office.

After carefully locking the doors and closing the drapes to cover the window, she crawled into the tub, first submerging her head to rinse the soap from her hair. Afterward she allowed herself a good soak that lasted much longer than the heat in the water.

Shivering, she left the tub and sat by the fire to dry her hair. She'd empty the tub in the morning. The time was growing late when she began to dress, pulling on her lace undergarments, her silk stockings, and fine dancing slippers. Then, at last, she slipped her arms into the dress. There was only one problem—the buttons. She couldn't reach those in the middle of her back. No matter, she'd worry about that when she got to Miranda's. Miranda would dress her hair, then Dallas would return to the office to wait for Elliott.

Covering her hair with a scarf, Dallas threw a short white velvet cape around her shoulders and slipped out into the late afternoon. The saloon sign had been covered and a hastily printed handwritten sheet of newsprint read: *Miranda's Fine Restaurant*.

Dallas gave an amused laugh and hurried inside. There were stairs beside the front door, leading to a balcony that circled the large room. Woven garlands of greenery hung in loops along the balcony rail. Ribbons and lace were tied on the oil lamps, and tablecloths covered the tables. The piano player and two fiddlers were tuning up at the far side of the room. But the most astonishing change was the red length of fabric that turned the bar into a food counter. Already there was a punch bowl and glasses and a tray covered with a white cloth. Miranda's contribution to the food. Dallas suddenly realized that she should have brought something.

Quickly she moved up the steps, meeting Willie at the top. "Miss Miranda said for you to wait in her room. She'll be up in a minute."

Dallas hurried along the corridor to the door at

the end and went inside. Evidence of Miranda's dressing was obvious. Colored silk stockings, petticoats, and wrappers lay on the bed. The dressing table was spattered with powder, and dried flower petals made the room smell like midsummer.

Dallas sat on Miranda's stool and removed her cape and her scarf. She laid the ribbon and lace headpiece Irene had fashioned on the table and ran her fingers through the riot of dark hair that fell across her face, her shoulders and down her back. It was still a bit damp from the washing, making the possibility of control even more unlikely.

Brushing it out only made it fly into a cloud of fine black lace. Combing it out one strand at a time was the only answer. The neckline of her gown gave her little freedom of movement to work with her hair. Finally she unfastened the top button and allowed the dress to slide low on her arms, catching only at the peaks of her breasts.

There was a brusque knock on the door. It opened immediately, leaving Dallas no time to pull the dress back in place. She glanced into the mirror, expecting to see Miranda's pert face.

Instead, the face she saw was that of Jake Silver.

"Miss Banning!" he said, in a low, hoarse voice.

"Mr. Silver." The face reflected was so sharp and hard that Dallas let out an involuntary gasp and tugged at her dress.

He leaned indolently against the doorframe. The upper part of his face was in the shadows, but she could see his mocking smile. He stood there for a long minute, then deliberately closed the door behind him and walked over to where she was sitting. "I didn't expect to find you here."

His voice came so softly that she almost didn't hear it. "I'm sure you didn't. I'm sorry if you're disappointed."

"Disappointed? Now why would you think that? You're a very beautiful woman."

There was no concealing her surprise, nor the blush that spread across her face. "You're mocking me, Mr. Silver."

"I never mock a woman, Miss Banning, and I never lie to one. You'll always know where you stand with me."

Dallas wished the light from the lamp weren't so bright. She wished she hadn't come here. She wished she weren't going to the dance with Elliott Parnell. Jake Silver was no gentleman engaging in a genteel flirtation. She didn't have a backup Pinkerton agent hovering in the background, ready to come to her aid. She was on her own, and she was in big trouble.

"Is there something I can do for you?" she asked, then thought about what she'd said and cringed. Of course he came to Miranda's room expecting something.

His smile widened and he narrowed his eyes as he appeared to examine her intently. "Are you considering changing your profession, darling?"

Dallas started, catching her dress as it started to slide back down. She lifted her eyes to meet his challenge. He was teasing her, challenging her as her brothers always did, and she found herself responding just as sharply. "Would you pay for my services if I did?"

Their gazes melded in the mirror, held together like two pieces of hot wax. A current ran between them, too powerful to ignore, too intense to break. His reflection was surrounded by the silver glow of one of the lamps.

Jake had come to Miranda to tell her that Wu and Shadow would be attending the party. Wu had sent into town for a dress. It had been far too large, but

Shadow had taken it up and adapted it to her petite figure. She'd braided her hair with ribbons and curled it on her head like a crown. She was lovely. But she was still an Indian, and Wu was still a Chinaman. And Jake wanted to make sure Miranda was prepared.

Looking at Dallas Banning, all thoughts of Shadow and Wu were driven from Jake's mind by the rapid rise and fall of Dallas's breasts. A moment ago the dress had fallen so low that he could see the dark circle that surrounded her nipples.

Now her hair caught his attention. It was beautiful in the lamplight. As she combed, little sparks of fire seemed to shimmer beneath her touch. "Well?" she prompted, waiting for his reply.

He chuckled. "Are you expensive?"

"Very. In fact," she added with what she hoped was a warning, "I don't think you could afford my price."

"Try me."

"I might, if you have something to offer that I want."

The air between them was as fraught with electricity as her hair. The suggestive words had come unbidden, teasing and curling around her tongue, words that might have been written for a play on a New York stage.

She stared at him in the mirror and knew that he was as caught up in the moment as she. Dallas stood and pulled the dress back to its proper place, while she reached behind her for the buttons.

"You were looking for Miranda?"

"I was."

"Well, I'll just get out so you can do—whatever it is you came to do."

The buttons still eluded her.

"Damn!"

"Tsk! Tsk! What language for a lady," he said.

"I'm no lady."

"That's a lady's dress, a rather daring lady. What's wrong with it that you have to hold it together?"

"The buttons. I can't reach them," she answered with irritation.

"Buttons are a speciality of mine. Please, Miss Banning, allow me."

Jake laid his hands on her shoulders, allowed them to slide down to the opening at the back. Excruciatingly slowly, he began to button her dress.

Meeting her eyes in the mirror, Jake Silver touched her bare skin as if he were a cat marking its territory by rubbing its cheek across the edge of a rug.

"You look lovely this evening, Miss Banning."

"As do you, Mr. Silver."

He did. There was no denying that the man was an icy study in black and silver, a man who knew his power to magnetize and who made full use of that power.

Like a wild animal caught in the sight of a wolf, Dallas stared. She was burning up. She was freezing to death. He was drawing her into his circle of power, and she was reaching for a place both forbidden and eternally tempting. Dallas had never been one to avoid danger, but this temptation was new and alluring. She'd always heard that women were drawn to dangerous men, but this was her first experience with the heady rush of feelings instigated by a true rogue.

As Jake slid the final button in place, he felt Dallas swaying against his hands. He moved his hands lower, clasping her waist as he leaned forward, touching her hair with his face.

"You smell like flowers," he said, "expensive flowers. The kind a man would bring a woman."

"Oh, Jake," she whispered, staring at him with eyes that were curiously innocent. Jake knew that he should pull away, but he'd done the noble thing once in his life, and he'd regretted it every day since. He wasn't sure he could do it again. He hadn't expected to feel this kind of desire for Dallas Banning. The loneliness must be getting to him.

"Jake, don't do this."

Dallas would never know what might have happened then, for the door opened again, admitting a stunned Miranda, followed by Shadow.

"Oh, I'm sorry. I didn't mean to interrupt," Miranda said.

Dallas jerked away. "Don't be silly. You didn't interrupt. Jake—Mr. Silver was only fastening my dress. I can't reach the buttons."

"I see," Miranda said, unable to hold back the frost from her voice, "and Mr. Silver's certainly had enough experience to help, though his experience generally comes from unbuttoning a woman's gown."

All present decided it would be best to ignore this statement. Dallas turned her face away from the mirror to focus her attention on the Indian woman who looked ready to take flight at any moment.

"Hello. I'm so very glad that you came to the dance. I'm Dallas."

"Shadow," the woman answered. "Wu wanted me to come here. He thinks that Miss Miranda will be my . . . my . . ."

"Friend," Jake supplied the word. "That's why I'm here, also, Miranda, to ask you to take Shadow under your wing. Otherwise I *wouldn't* have come."

Miranda cut a sharp eye from Jake to Dallas. "Of course," she said, "I'll be happy to. Did you bring the ribbons for your hair, Dallas?"

Dallas nodded and sat back down. Some of the

closeness she'd shared with Miranda had vanished. Dallas glanced at Shadow, sympathizing with her uncertainty at being here. To some extent, she shared Shadow's plight. "Here, Miranda, on the table."

Jake glanced once more at Dallas, then backed lazily toward the door. "I'll be going then, ladies. Until the dance?"

"Yes, of course," Miranda answered coolly. Shadow only nodded. Dallas didn't trust herself to speak.

Jake hadn't intended to stay, but he wouldn't let Dallas off so easily. At the risk of further angering Miranda, he couldn't resist one last challenge to Dallas. "When you decide the price, Dallas, let me know. You'd be surprised what a man is willing to pay."

Dallas half rose from the stool. Then Jake was gone. The door slamming behind him like the sound of a gavel hitting the desk of a judge. The gauntlet had been flung.

Chapter 10

Jake stood outside the saloon, leaning against one of the posts that held up the roof. He smoked a cigar and watched the dancers inside.

It had been an unexpected pleasure to come face to face with Dallas Banning, alone, her dress hanging about her breasts, an inviting glow in her eyes. Even now his pulse quickened at the memory of her brazen words, and he wondered about her past.

After that intimate episode in Miranda's bedroom, he'd stayed in the saloon, finding himself a secluded corner of the bar where he could watch the stairs. He'd downed too many drinks, refusing to think about what he was waiting for.

After the look in Miranda's eyes, Jake wouldn't have been surprised to see a bald Dallas descend the stairs. Miranda wasn't one to hide her feelings, nor to fail to act on them. Perhaps because he understood that fierce honesty, he'd avoided accepting what Miranda had offered. For Jake had come to Green Willow five years ago empty inside. All emotion and feeling had died long ago, died or been smothered. Even Miranda couldn't rekindle it.

When at last Dallas pushed open the swing doors and stopped on the sidewalk, he was stunned by what he saw. He watched as she walked back to the newspaper office. He hadn't considered Dallas particularly beautiful. Bold, yes. Vibrant, impetuous, passionate, but not beautiful. He'd been wrong.

A newspaperwoman who charged into a gathering of angry cowboys was a fool, and a fool ought not to be a temptress wearing a green satin gown that displayed her bosom to the world. She was asking for a different kind of trouble.

Jake pushed away his glass and reached for the bottle instead. "Hell, why should I care who she shows off to? The devil take her." He felt better for a moment, then considered what he'd said. She'd probably take off looking for that devil any day now, just like her brother.

During the rest of the afternoon, an unusually large number of people began to gather for the event: ranchers, townspeople, and cowboys. Here and there, he spotted new faces he hadn't seen before—outsiders, brought in by the vigilance committee newly formed by the ranchers. He'd known that was in the works, but they'd kept it quiet, knowing that he hadn't approved.

The winter had been long and hard. They'd all lost cattle to the cold, then more to the storm. Never before had so many cattle strayed so far. Rounding up and branding the new calves would be long and hard this spring. The ranchers deserved a little fun before the hot weather came.

As did Wu. Jake had shown him the back steps where he could join Shadow and watch the party in private. Jake had invited them to join him at his table, but Wu decided it would be more prudent to keep his distance for now. He didn't want to cause any trouble.

Perhaps Wu was right. Having Elliott there was bad enough; at least his group of farmers had stayed away.

Through the window, Jake watched Elliott enter the saloon-turned-resturant with Dallas. He hadn't expected that. He hadn't expected the quick fury that rushed through him, either. In her white cape and green dress she looked like the Carolina belles of his youth. And like moths to a candle the residents were drawn to her, both those she knew and those anxious to make her acquaintance. The husbands shook her hand, and elbowed their wives to force them to speak. With a word or two, or a quick hug, she made each of the women accept her presence.

Moment later Dallas unwrapped her offering for the refreshment table, revealing a box of imported chocolates, which she placed on the counter. From her drawstring purse she brought out hard candies, which she handed to the children sitting along the walls and under the tables. Before the first tune was played, she'd won the hearts of everyone there, except Miranda, who still seemed piqued.

Jake was curious to see how this meeting between the two would go. He didn't know how she did it, but moments later Miranda and Dallas hugged, and Miranda was adroitly transferred into Elliott's arms to begin the dancing.

Jake gave a chuckle of admiration. Miranda and Elliott were whirling around the floor, Miranda's head flung back in laughter. Dallas soon followed, partnered by Mr. Bowker, whose face was as red as Miranda's dress. Dallas had turned what could have been a cat fight into a tribute to Miranda and Elliott by letting them open the dance.

Well done, darling, he thought. You elevated the two least appreciated people here to a place of importance. He watched for a long time, listening as the musicians gave a spirited rendition of "Turkey in the Straw," followed by a waltz. He wasn't needed here. Jake left the saloon, mounted his horse and started back to the ranch, satisfied that Wu and Shadow were in good hands.

At the edge of town he spotted the strange wagon coming toward Green Willow Creek. Immigrants, heading for the dance. He hadn't expected that and knew that probably the townsfolk hadn't either. Jake groaned. He ought to just keep riding, let them work it out on their own. Elliott was there. He was the one who'd brought the farmers to Wyoming. Let him keep the peace.

Hell, Elliott couldn't look after himself. He'd turn the town into a battlefield and somebody could get hurt.

Somebody.

Blackjack responded instantly as Jake pulled on the reins, turning him back toward town and urging him into a gallop. Jake dismounted, looped the reins over the rail and reclaimed his place by the window.

He couldn't see Dallas for a moment. Then he found her. She was on the balcony, pulling Wu out into full view, asking him to dance. At least they were in the position to dance; Wu's right hand was resting hesitantly on Dallas's back, his left one clasped tightly by Dallas. With an encouraging smile Dallas was forcing Wu to move to the music.

He should have known Dallas would never let Wu hide in the shadows, not after she'd sent a stick-pin to Wu as a thank-you gift. Dallas would dance with the devil if he'd come to the party.

She'd probably have danced with Jake, if he'd stayed inside. The thought sobered him.

Beyond the swinging doors he heard snatches of conversation between Mrs. Pickens and another woman he couldn't see.

"Effie, would you look at her," the second

woman said, "she's actually dancing with that Chinaman."

"What can you expect from a woman who intends to operate a newspaper, like a man!" Effie Pickens said with disdain.

"I didn't notice you hanging back when Mr. Pickens was greeting her."

"But Louise, you know Mr. Pickens expects me to be the official hostess for the town. If it were up to me . . ."

"Yes, Effie, I know you wouldn't have done it on your own, but would you look at that dress, green satin, cut practically down to her—"

"Oh, dear! And Mr. Pickens actually wants her to come to dinner. I suppose I'll have to do it, since she has so much money in his bank."

Louise sighed in a show of resigned understanding. "Well, I don't intend to have anything to do with her. I don't understand why Jake Silver helped her. He certainly didn't get along with her brother."

"And he actually allowed his cook and that Indian woman to come here. I don't know what this town is coming to."

Jake wanted to confront the two women, to defend Dallas and Wu. But it wasn't worth the effort. Besides, he was too sober. Defiantly he took another pull from the bottle he was still holding in his free hand, then set it down and moved through the swinging doors. Wu's bringing Shadow to the dance wasn't a good idea, but he'd be damned if he'd let those two witches cause trouble.

Up the stairs he marched, oblivious to the startled frowns of the party goers. Past Wu and Dallas, he moved in that lazy deliberate way he had of walking. "Miss Shadow," he said, as he bowed to the Indian woman, "would you care to dance?"

A surprised Shadow glanced at Dallas and Wu,

then back again, before breaking into a full smile and nodding her head in agreement.

Moments later they were moving around the balcony, giving way to Wu and Dallas when they met. Shadow had a natural grace that quickly made itself known. Jake heard the sounds of muted conversation in the room below, but he didn't acknowledge any of it. Then suddenly there was a hush and the music came to a stop.

"Who said you could come to the dance?" an angry male voice said.

Dallas moved toward the rail and peered over.

Standing in the doorway were two men and two women. Farmers, she judged from their dress. Standing opposite the newcomers was the same rancher who had brought his dead cowhand into town.

"I did," Elliott Parnell said, stepping between the farmers and the rancher. "I was told that everyone was invited to the dance."

"Everyone but those fence-building sodbusters!" another rancher said, and came to stand by the first.

Jake joined Dallas at the rail. He'd taken her arm protectively, and she'd instinctively leaned against him. At that moment Elliott Parnell looked up and caught sight of Jake and Dallas. Jake, his old friend, his old enemy, was also his new enemy. Not only was he one of the ranchers who was trying to keep the farmers out, but he was standing with his arm around the woman Elliott wanted.

"I don't think so," Elliott said quietly. "These people are residents of Green Willow Creek, just like you. So long as the members of the community are invited to the dance, they have a right to be here, too."

Jake cringed. Leave it to Parnell to be softhearted. He could have just kept quiet, or sent the farmers home. There was a time he'd have been too scared to speak up. The man had changed.

"Get away from them outsiders, Parnell," one of the newcomers said. "You don't want to get hurt."

Elliott spread his legs as if to say he was standing his ground. "You forget, gentlemen, I'm an outsider, too."

"And so am I." Dallas pulled away from Jake and marched down the stairs to join Elliott. "Do you intend to hurt women?"

"Damn!" Jake swore out loud. She was doing it again, a maverick going her own way. And as a matter of honor, Jake went after her, unhurriedly, but with that dangerous air that forced people to stand back. "I don't think we want to start anything in front of the women, do we?"

"Not unless it's with us women," Miranda said, stepping up and slipping her arm around the rancher doing most of the talking. "Let 'em in, Walsh. I've been waiting for you to invite me to dance all night. I think this is our tune."

She nodded to the man playing the piano and put her arm around the rancher's neck, smiling at him until his confusion dissipated the moment. Moments later the dancing had resumed, leaving Dallas, Jake, and Elliott standing together at the door with the farmers and their wives.

"Do come in," Dallas said to the two women, holding out her hand in welcome.

"Nein, we go," one of the farmers said. "We not come where we not wanted."

"A little late for that," Jake muttered under his breath, "but probably a good idea."

"I don't think so," Elliott argued, standing firm. "They have a right to be here."

Dallas heard angry comments of disagreement die in the sudden tension between Jake and Elliott.

"Maybe Jake's right," Dallas said. "Maybe it's too soon."

Elliott glanced around and saw the men slowly moving back against the wall and toward the front door. Miranda might think she'd stopped the confrontation, but she'd only delayed it.

"Maybe you're right, Jake, but then you usually are, aren't you? I regret I won't be able to see you home, Miss Banning. I'd better get these folks back to the settlement."

"Don't worry, Elliott," Dallas said, "I'll walk myself. Just get your people home safely."

Elliott and the settlers left, followed by Wu and Shadow.

After a dance with Dr. Horn, during which she asked several questions that produced no new information, Dallas decided that any chance she might have had to learn anything at the dance about Jamie's death had vanished in the confrontation. Elliott had gone. Jake apparently had left with Wu and Shadow, leaving Miranda's spirits dragging.

Dallas begged off a dance invitation from Mr. Pickens. After finding her cape on the table in the corner, she slipped quietly through the doors and into the night.

The stars were as bright as the diamonds on the tiara Mrs. Vanderbilt once wore to a ball Dallas had attended. Allan Pinkerton had sent Dallas there to see that the jewels weren't stolen, and she'd been successful.

Walking along the wooden sidewalk, she let out a deep sigh. That time seemed so long ago. She'd left behind her friends at the agency. She'd received only one communication from her father, a telegram that read: "Get the job done and get back here where you belong."

But Dallas didn't know where she belonged.

Not with the agency any more. That all changed when Allan Pinkerton had the stroke.

Not back in Philadelphia, attending fancy balls and leaving calling cards in silver dishes on tables in the hallways of houses she didn't want to visit in the first place.

That life wasn't like this wild new territory of Wyoming. The people here might not always be right, but they stood up for what they believed. They'd even given women equality. If Dallas weren't involved in her own crusade, she might even consider applying for the job of sheriff here in Willow Creek. Once she'd found Jamie's killer, she might just do that. That would show her father that she was serious about making her way in life without his help.

Of course there was the matter of Elliott and Jake. And the conflicting emotions she felt about both men. Jake had made it plain that he had no need for a woman, other than the obvious. He'd even offered to pay for her services.

Dallas smiled at that wicked thought. Miranda's entertainers didn't have to make personal choices. They gave themselves to a man because their livelihood demanded it. What made other women succumb to a man's charms? And they did, she'd seen ample evidence of it in her work. Granted, most of them were married; that made taking a lover so much easier. But that wasn't always the case. There were some women who never married and many of them always had a man at their side. Of course that was in the city, where certain alliances were accepted. Out here, nothing would go unnoticed.

She was so deep in her thoughts that she didn't realize for a time that she wasn't alone. Then she heard footsteps behind her. Steady, paced, in cadence with her own. Stopping, she turned around, facing the shadowy figure trailing her.

"Yes? Did you want something?"

"Yep, I reckon I do. You owe me, Miss Banning."

It was the man who'd forced his way into her newspaper office that night, the man called Doak. "Just what do I owe you?"

"For unloading a sleigh full of wood. For causing me to lose my job."

He came closer. Dallas thought about her derringer and remembered that she'd left it back in her office. She'd considered bringing it, but there was nowhere she could conceal it on her person. It hadn't mattered, for she had expected to be with Elliott. And she'd come to expect Jake's presence if she were in danger.

Instead she would have to defend herself alone.

"I'm sorry you lost your job, but you brought that on yourself. Still, if you feel that you are owed money for unloading the wood, come with me to my office and I'll pay you."

"No you won't!"

Jake Silver stepped out from the shadows between two buildings.

"Jake—" the man Dallas recognized as Doak was clearly startled. "Jake, I didn't mean nothing. I was just at the dance, and I didn't think it was safe for Miss Banning to walk home alone."

Jake dropped his cigar onto the sidewalk, trailing a scattering of fire in the darkness. He ground it out with the tip of his boot and laid his hand on the gun he'd strapped on since he left the dance.

"Now, wait a minute. I ain't armed. You can't fire on an unarmed man."

"I can," Jake said in a deadly voice, "and I might if the town weren't ready to blow up anyway."

"Then I'll just be leaving," Doak said, backing

slowly away, until he reached the corner of the building and took off into the darkness.

"Once again, Mr. Silver," Dallas said, "you've come to my rescue."

"Seems so."

She turned and started down the sidewalk, hesitating until she heard the sound of boots behind her. Neither she nor Jake spoke, walking in a quiet so thick that even the music seemed muted, as if it were miles away.

"Thank you—Jake."

"You're going to get yourself killed, Dallas, just like your brother."

"Maybe. But I'm not going to back down."

"What kind of person are you, to constantly tempt fate?"

"The same kind of person who takes in Chinamen and Indians. Who rescues stray women and buttons their dresses. Or was that unbuttons?"

They'd reached the newspaper office.

Dallas took her key from her string purse and inserted it into the lock. When she heard it click she turned back and looked up at Jake.

"Would you care to come in for a cup of tea? Or I still have the whiskey that Wu sent—for medicinal purposes—if you need medical attention."

"I need attention all right, but I've already tried whiskey and it didn't help."

"What do you need?" Her voice was hoarse and whispery. For she knew what he needed, knew because she needed the same.

"I should walk away from you, Dallas Banning."

"Yes, you should."

"Damn it to hell, why do you continue to torment me?"

She shook her head. She couldn't speak. She

couldn't tell him to go, nor could she back into the newspaper office and leave him outside in the dark.

He lowered his head. She could smell the whiskey, feel the heat of his breath on her hair. It wasn't unpleasant, or perhaps it was and she was so caught up in the moment that she didn't notice. His lips were only a heartbeat away from touching hers.

Even in the darkness she could see his stern frown, the tortured expression in slate-gray eyes that bored into her with daggers of ice.

And then ice turned into fire and she was in his arms, lifting herself to meet his kiss. Dallas would have gasped from the heat if her mouth hadn't been filled with his tongue, if his hands hadn't been lifting her up against him, into the male part of him that throbbed between them.

The groan she heard was his. The tingling she felt in her nipples increased from the friction of his brocade vest as he ground his body against her, pushing her hard against the door at her back. One hand left her bottom and moved up, tangling itself in her hair, pulling the pins from the careful arrangement Miranda had made, holding her so that he could pull his lips away and move down her neck.

As if she had no control over her body she moved her head, allowing him full access to her throat and lower. Fingertips left her hair and followed the path of his lips and suddenly there was no more fabric between his mouth and her breasts.

Her body was exposed, but there was no cold. His mouth captured one nipple and seared it with fire. The other breast was caught in his hand, filling his palm.

Dear God, what was happening to her? Every part of her was being assaulted with waves of heat, and she was powerless to resist. Then, suddenly, the door opened and they were falling backward into the office.

The hard floor jolted her, taking her breath away. Jake was sprawled over her, pressing against her, trying to catch himself with his hands. That motion only made his lower body press harder against her, exerting pressure against that part of her that burned with wild anticipation.

"Well, darling," Jake said, lifting himself with his elbows, "this isn't the best place for this kind of thing, is it, but if you've settled on a price, I'm willing."

Dallas gasped. All pleasure drained from her body, leaving only a case of acute embarrassment and a lingering frustration that she chose to ignore.

"Get off me this minute, you rogue. You're drunk!"

"That I am, ma'am. What's your excuse?"

"I was . . . I am . . . I don't know," she said softly. "And I don't believe your excuse, either."

"Believe it, darling," Jake said, coming to his feet and pulling her up with him. "Because you don't want to know the truth. The next time, I won't stop."

And he was gone, leaving her bruised and shaken in the dark. "The next time," she whispered, "I don't think I can stop you."

Chapter 11

It was the whiskey, Jake told himself as he rode back toward the Double J. He would never have kissed the woman again if he hadn't had too much to drink.

The whiskey and the buttons.

That damned dress.

Jake pulled off his glove and rubbed his thumb against the pads of his fingers for a moment. He could still feel the texture of her hair, that mass of dark silk he'd tangled between his fingers. And flowers. The fragrance of flowers was still there. He carried it with him, on his chest, his mustache, his fingertips.

The fragrance of Dallas Banning.

His gut tightened as he felt himself respond to the thought of her. She was fast becoming an obsession, and he had to find a way to deal with that. The focus of his life had to be the cattle he'd round up and ship to market. Then he'd leave Pete in charge and take a trip to California, to see the Pacific Ocean. He'd cross the mountains and put this part of his life behind him.

This vast country, like his past, had become divided into compartments, like stalls in a barn; the place where he'd lived before the war was sealed off now, only a memory. Then there was the section containing the ranch he and Elliott and Sarah had carved out of the Kansas wilderness, the section he'd abandoned first when Sarah chose Elliott, then forever when Jake had discovered Sarah's body. Now he was thinking of leaving Wyoming and moving on once more.

But once he reached the ocean, he would run out of land. There was no place he could go to leave his memories behind. Distance was no answer. A man could put his life back together again just so many times. He didn't know if he could do it again. He hadn't even succeeded this time. God knew, he'd tried. But he'd only carried Sarah with him. Now he was replacing Sarah with new memories. And he didn't want to do that.

There was no room in his life for sentiment, for recalling warm summer days when Sarah had walked across the fields, bringing a midday meal to him and Elliott as they plowed. There was no place for softness. Softness killed, physically and sometimes emotionally. That was worse. The body would, given the time, heal itself. The mind played tricks and punished.

After Sarah, he'd sworn that no woman would ever get inside his gut and squeeze the life out of him.

When Sarah died, she took all that was left of the man once known as Captain Jacob Silver, officer of the proud army of the Confederacy. The Confederacy wasn't proud any more, and Jacob had put the past behind him. Damn it, he'd thought he had.

Until Elliott had brought the farmers to Wyoming.

And Dallas.

Dallas Banning had come and he couldn't seem to stop her from making a place in his mind.

Dallas. Even the name was brash, a step-out-of-the-way-I'm-coming-in kind of name for a woman who did just that. She'd been magnificent at the dance, standing down any attempt to harm the farmers, without flinching. He was certain she'd been just as determined when she'd come between the blacksmith and those cowboys. And the Indians. Most women would have hidden in the wagon, screaming in fear. Not Dallas.

She, too, was a woman with compartments in her past. He didn't know the entire story, but it made no sense for her to come out here, alone, determined to find her brother's killer. Women didn't do that, not even in 1874. There was a fire about her that burned deep inside, that drove her to take on the impossible. He didn't know what fueled it, but he could identify its presence.

Once he'd had that burning drive. His fire had died.

But Dallas's still burned.

Unlike his methods of distancing himself from life, she grabbed it by the throat and said, "pay up." She'd quickly made a place for herself in Green Willow Creek, carving out her own space in this vast, wide-open land. Even Miranda, who considered her a rival, liked her. Lawson Pickens liked her, or her money. Lucy Jarrett liked her, therefore ensuring a place of acceptance for her with the wives, and now Wu was her newest champion.

And damn it all to hell, he liked her.

Jake rode a few lengths more, then reined his horse in and started back to town. He'd rid himself of his need for Dallas by visiting Miranda. She'd made it clear that she expected him. Her invitation had always been there, though he'd never taken advantage of it. Until now.

Miranda had been angry to discover him in her

room with Dallas, his hands on her shoulders, his desire obvious, even to her. He still didn't know how in the hell that had happened. For a moment, when he'd seen Dallas sitting there, he'd thought she was waiting for him, and he'd reacted instinctively.

But she wasn't there for him. Not Dallas. It was Miranda, who offered herself, who didn't ask for anything, who'd seen in the beginning that he had nothing to give. Miranda had been angry that he'd been with Dallas, and he didn't blame her. He'd go back and use that anger, turning anger into passion that would wipe out the picture of Dallas with her hair flying and her breasts bare.

"Ho! Blackjack!" He pulled on the reins, stopping their forward progress, then cursed and turned the confused horse back toward the ranch again. Taking Miranda when he wanted Dallas would be wrong. He should have shoved Dallas's dress up and plunged himself inside her right there on the floor of the newspaper office. She'd have been willing. Hell, she wanted it as much as he. She hadn't slapped his face, or pushed his hands away. She'd leaned against him, opening her mouth and taking his tongue inside, returning every move he made.

Before he'd asked her to name her price.

"Damn it to hell, Blackjack. Let's ride, boy, fast—like the Devil of the Plains."

As if the horse understood, he charged across the plains, through the night like a strong, hot wind.

When they arrived at the ranch, Jake removed Blackjack's saddle and wiped the black horse down, rewarding him with a pail of oats before turning him into the corral. Jake started back to the big house, passing Wu's little building, catching the sound of laughter and low voices from inside.

Jake didn't think Wu and Shadow were arguing now. Jake paused, listening to the soft sounds of conversation. Maybe Wu had finally found his woman.

Jake's gut twisted even tighter.

He'd sleep another night alone.

But tonight it wasn't by choice.

"I told you to stay out of Green Willow Creek, boy!"

Doak squatted uneasily beside the fire. How'd the old man find out he'd been to the dance?

"Why? Just 'cause I lost my job with Jake Silver don't mean I have to hide out up here in these mountains."

"No, but if you let anybody follow you out here, you're gonna ruin what I've been working on for the last five years. You got that, boy?"

"Rejo, I'm not a boy. And it's time you stopped calling me one. I been driving cows since I was ten years old."

"And it's been that long since you learned anything."

"Go soak your head in that pool of ice water in the rocks, you old fool."

"Go feed Devil."

"Not me. I ain't going nowhere close to that creature. He don't like me."

"He ain't friends with nobody. But that don't mean we ain't gonna feed him. Now get to it. He's already earned his oats, and he's gonna do more. It won't be long now before we're all gonna be rich. A rich man don't have to answer to nobody, even the law."

"And what you gonna do with all your wealth, Rejo?

"I'm going to claim something I gave up long ago."

*   *   *

Elliott watched the wagons pull behind the fence. He'd expected Lawson Pickens to intervene between the farmers and the ranchers at the dance. He hadn't. Some land agent he was. Of course it wasn't the farmers he was interested in, it was just the sale of the land and the money in his bank.

Even if it meant only a short walk down the sidewalk, leaving Dallas to get home alone had been hard for Elliott. But he was responsible for the immigrants, even if Pickens shunned his job. Elliott had been expecting some of the men to come after them.

He'd seen men like these newcomers before, ridden with men just like them, and worse, after Sarah died. They loved killing and hired themselves out to whichever group paid the most. Between jobs they had robbed the men who had hired them.

They were trouble, and he didn't have any idea how to stop them. His farmers weren't fighters. Not only did they not have the weapons, they were forbidden by the government to take up arms. Maybe it would pay him to send for some outside help, just in case. He could hire a couple of men to patrol the boundaries of the farmland, just to let the ranchers know that they couldn't be run over.

But did he want to make that move? What kind of retaliation would he invite? He was there to protect the farmers, see that they were successful in their efforts. A large food broker in Chicago had already offered to buy their produce.

Elliott turned his horse away from the settlement house and started toward his own land. Because most of his efforts had been directed toward getting the farmers settled, they'd made little progress on building his house. But tonight he felt like sleeping under his own roof, even if home consisted only of four walls and a dirt floor.

He'd demonstrated how to use the new plow by tilling his own piece of land. Even with the steam-driven machine it was harder than he'd ever imagined. With Hans working alongside of him, and Adolph directing their efforts from the wagon, they managed to get the first field torn up. He had a new planting device. A pouch containing seed was attached to his waist. From the pouch a line ran down beside his leg. All he had to do was walk along the row. When he planted his foot it automatically released seeds. The ground was dry enough to plow, but still damp enough from the melting snow for the seeds to sprout quickly.

Adolph had shaken his head at the idea of the planter, but Hans had immediately seen the potential for a much larger application of the idea for use with the mechanical plow.

Come late summer, Elliott's land would be chest-high in corn and oats. He'd wanted wheat, but Adolph had insisted on oats. Oats for horses and cows in a land where cows were more important than men. Time would tell if he was right.

Time would also tell about Dallas Banning. No matter how much Elliott tried to convince himself that Dallas was available, he knew deep down that he was only fooling himself. She'd been beautiful tonight. And so had Miranda. Dallas, with dark hair and hazel eyes, dressed in green, and Miranda, with her mass of blond curls and happy smile, vibrant in red. Two women who wanted Jake.

Elliott admired Miranda. She'd lived a hard life to get where she was. And she made the town accept her. Equality was the word here; though it was a lie, both socially and morally, the residents gave lip service to the idea. Where else in the world could a saloon owner mix with the ladies of the town on an equal footing? Miranda outshone the wives and they knew it. So did the men. But he'd known tonight as she danced with him that she was watching for Jake. Still, she'd had a bright smile for Elliott and just for a moment he'd felt an unexpected stirring of response.

He hadn't expected Jake to side with him tonight against the ranchers. But he should have. No matter what Jake might think personally, he never simply followed the herd. He made up his own mind and followed his conscience. Always had, even during the war, even when it meant disobeying his commanding officer. He was the same way on the range. If one calf strayed, he'd dog it until he brought it back, often risking his own life. Just as he once had for Elliott. And Sarah.

Jake Silver would take an unpopular stand if the cause was just. He'd almost lost his life at the Battle of Shiloh doing just that. But the coming confrontation between the ranchers and the farmers was a stand not even Jake could make.

Only Elliott knew that rolls of the new barbed wire were on the way. Jake would understand what that meant, the end of free range for his cattle. But without the wire, the farmers's crops would be trampled by the cattle before they had a chance to grow.

The barbed wire would surely trigger a range war unless Elliott could work out a compromise. Maybe he could talk to Miss Banning. She could write some stories for her newspaper explaining the situation.

Like her brother had attempted to do.

Before he'd been killed.

Dallas spent her days getting the equipment ready to print her paper. She read her father's newspapers for stories she could reprint in the *Gazette*. Like Jamie, she knew that these people were starved for information about the East, and she'd print all the news, even the items that might appeal only to the more educated.

She could have printed the *Gazette* at any time, but she kept delaying, making up one page, then tearing it down and starting again. Sometimes she thought it was the memory of Jake's kisses that was interfering with her concentration. But the truth was that printing the first issue would be an acknowledgement that Jamie was really gone. And she couldn't bring herself to face that yet.

Meanwhile, she heard from Willie that more and more strangers were arriving in town. Mr. Pickens reassured her that drifters normally came to Green Willow Creek this time of year to round up the cattle. But Dallas wasn't convinced that all was right in this town.

Every night when Willie went back to Miranda's, she locked the downstairs door, lit her oil lamp and read Jamie's newspapers. The first few issues were fairly routine: weddings, funerals, late national news reprinted. There was a small story about a new patent being issued to a Joseph F. Glidden of Illinois for an improved barbed wire. There was another about a book called *Twenty Thousand Leagues Under the Sea*, by French writer Jules Verne. Dallas smiled, wondering how many of the residents of Wyoming cared about such a book. But Jamie wouldn't have let that stop him from printing the information.

Jamie had arrived in Green Willow Creek in December of 1872, nine months before the financial panic of 1873, triggered by the failure of the brokerage firm that had been financing construction of the Northern Pacific Railroad. In July of 1873, the first group of immigrants had arrived in Willow Creek.

The Crédit Mobilier, the group of men who'd financed the building of the Union Pacific Railroad, sold land to a speculator who appointed Mr. Pickens as his financial agent and Elliott Parnell as the man to deal with the settlers. Through Mr. Pickens's efforts, the settlement house was built to house the farmers while their land was being surveyed and private dwellings were being constructed.

In a series of articles, Jamie wrote about the settlers who, filled with false information, expected to grow cabbages and turnips as big as washtubs. They had been promised hogs and sheep eventually. At least, that was the plan advertised by the land speculators, who stood to make a great deal of money.

When the initial sales to settlers were disappointing, the land was then offered to immigrants who were lured west by the glowing, exaggerated tales of crop success.

From the first Jamie had questioned the claims of the land speculator. The *Gazette*'s reports on the failure of the first settlers confirmed Jamie's reservations. The land grew range grass abundantly, but little else.

Elliott had said that newspaper stories had brought the immigrants to Green Willow Creek. Maybe that was true in the beginning, but after only a few months, Jamie's stories changed. The truth was, the crops were never what they'd been advertised to be. And Jamie reported the truth.

The headlines told the story.

First Group of Settlers Abandon Land.

Small Ranchers Join Forces to Fight Future Settlement.

In 1873 the paper announced the expected July arrival of the first small party of German farmers—and their representative, Elliott Parnell.

In August came the first recorded retaliation. *German Family's House Destroyed by Vandals.* The ranchers claimed the house was destroyed by a common prairie fire. Elliott protested the claim. That story was followed by *Local Rancher Promises Revenge for Wanton Deaths of Cattle*.

Elliott Parnell's arrival had seemed to accelerate the feud. Thereafter, one incident followed another: missing and dead cattle, sod homes destroyed before completion, and fences pulled down. One by one, families either abandoned their land or sold it to one of the ranchers. But even Dallas could see there was a limit to the amount of debt the ranchers could absorb.

It was in September, two weeks before Jamie's death, that Dallas found the first mention of the Devil of the Plains. A farmer and his young son had been run down by what the child described as a poison-spitting monster that sounded like a devil from hell.

Jamie apparently was fascinated with the monster and interviewed several citizens who recalled earlier stories about the Devil, starting with an old prospector a year ago who told of seeing the Devil in the mountains. But Jamie's story said this was the first time anybody had been injured by the creature. Afterward, the Devil appeared regularly, taking out his rage on both the ranchers and the farmers.

Then Jamie was killed and the newspaper articles stopped.

Dallas refolded the last newspaper and started to replace it in the box when she noticed a tablet. The penciled writing was faded, but she took the tablet to the window, studying the document.

> *... seems clear that there is a person behind the appearance of the Devil of the Plains. Two people stand to gain—which one? Enemies—Need to find monster ...*

Perhaps the scribbles were the beginning of an article, or a letter, or maybe he was just recording his thoughts. At any rate, Dallas had a starting point. Jamie was convinced that one of two men stood to gain from the disturbances and the two men were enemies.

Jake Silver and Elliott Parnell.

The next day Elliott brought in the battered body of an immigrant who had been attacked and killed in the night. The farmers at the settlement had given chase to the monster and the riders who accompanied him, losing them just beyond Bitter Butte when storm clouds covered the moon and left them in darkness.

"What did the Devil look like?" Dallas questioned Elliott when he came by the newspaper office.

"Who knows? The family was so hysterical that I got descriptions from a fifty-foot hairy-legged ape to an oversized wog with clubbed feet."

"What's a wog?"

"You never had anyone tell you that if you didn't behave, the wog would come in the night and strike you with his great red forked tongue?"

Dallas laughed grimly. "I did not. Did you?"

"Of course. My nurse raised me on stories of the wog and the snake. They were here when the first immigrants came to the new land. The Indians passed the stories on to the settlers, who used them appropriately to discipline their children."

"Did you ever see one?"

"Every night in my dreams. It looked like a strange dog, or a wolf, with a large head, big pointed ears and long front legs. Its back legs were shorter and it had a tail that made a loud swishing sound when it wagged."

"And that's what you think killed those men?"

"No," Elliott said wearily, "I don't. I think it's something, and I think it's controlled by real men on real horses. I just can't figure out what, and I'd better soon. Some of the farmers have already gone, and others are leaving."

"Oh, Elliott, I'm so sorry. Will you lose your land if they go?"

"No, my land is mine, but I need these farmers. I need their knowledge and their expertise. I intend to succeed this time—no matter what."

Long after Elliott left, transporting the carpenter, who would act as both undertaker and minister, Dallas thought about what he'd said. The Devil of the Plains had now transformed into a wog. Clearly someone had to get to the bottom of this story, and who better than a newspaper reporter and former Pinkerton agent?

Dallas Banning was about to go monster-hunting.

Chapter 12

Dallas decided to make her own arrangements with the livery stable. Explaining her plan to Willie could expose it to Jake Silver, and that was the last thing she wanted to do.

Telling Willie that she was not feeling well, she sent him home early and told him to take the next day off from work. Then she went down to the general store for supplies.

Before dawn the next morning Dallas rented two horses from the livery stable. Wearing Willie's spare pair of trousers and shirt and Jamie's jacket and hat, she left Green Willow Creek. On the second horse she'd packed her supplies. She carried Jamie's Colt .38, a bedroll, a iron skillet, coffeepot, and food supplies. The store owner had been told the supplies were for Greta, the widow of the immigrant who was killed. The livery stable operator had been told that she and Willie were going to visit Jake. By the time they found out otherwise, she'd be gone.

When the sun came up, Dallas was far out of town and heading for Bitter Butte and the section of the Green Mountains that jutted out like a finger. With the freedom of Willie's trousers she could ride efficiently and with better control of the horse that had proven to be a bit more frisky than she'd been led to expect.

The mountains were farther away than they appeared, as was Bitter Butte, a wind-smooth pinnacle of rock that looked like an upside down red-brown funnel.

Having traveled to the settlement house and the adjoining farms, and to the Double J beyond, Dallas felt confident enough that she could find the place she was looking for. Her goal was to locate the site where the monster was known to have been seen.

Once she'd found out more about this monster, she would have a way to get the attention of the warring factions before someone else was hurt. Killing cattle and destroying houses was bad enough, but executing people went too far. So far the death toll included two Indians, two ranchers, one immigrant, and Jamie. And she had a feeling that the worst was yet to come.

It was late afternoon when Dallas finally reached the other side of Bitter Butte. Up close it was a much larger section of rock than she'd imagined, and she'd spent an inordinate amount of time picking her way around it, stopping every few minutes to search for hoofprints. But the ground was too rocky. There were no prints.

Worse still, as the sun dropped, the wind came up, a cold wind that whipped across the open prairie, found the corridor between the butte and the foot of the mountains, and streaked through. It came in gusts so strong that it nearly dislodged her hat. She'd better stop and make camp, she decided, before it got too dark to see. She'd hoped to find a stream, or a pool of water for the horses, but there'd been none.

Finally she chose a spot that was shielded by two sections of rock. After securing the horses, she unloaded her supplies and gathered enough scrub brush and dry grass to start a fire. She would need more to ward off stray animals through the night, so after securing her supplies high by hanging them from a rope looped across a rock, she started off toward the mountain.

Long before she reached the outcropping of rocks she realized that once again she'd misjudged the distance. The sun, already behind the snow-capped peaks, fell lower, and the purple shadows turned into the gray of twilight. She would have to make do with what she could find to burn, else risk retracing her steps in total darkness.

She turned and started back. Suddenly she smelled the smoke. It seemed to be coming from her right. Someone nearby had a campfire. Someone?

Some Pinkerton agent she was—she'd left her gun back at her camp.

Carefully she walked toward the crisp, clean smell of smoke. The silence was eerie. Behind her, cut in half by the spindle of Bitter Butte, was the moon, low in the sky yet, but bright, very bright.

Finally she reached the protective section of rock and leaned against it. There was no way of knowing whether the campfire builder was just on the other side or farther up in the canyon. Allowing her breathing to slow, she slid through a crack in the rocks and peered into the darkness.

Two men were hunched close to the fire, eating from tin plates. They were talking in a low murmur, too low to be understood. Who were they? And why were they hiding out here? Of course they could be ranch hands, shielding themselves from the desert breeze, but she didn't think so. For one thing, the camp did not look new. The grass was beaten down and the pile of ashes was sizable. She could see no sign of saddles. Either they were on foot or the horses were stabled out of sight of the fire. But Dallas had learned enough about the West to know that no cowboy would stable his horse out of reach in an emergency.

If only she could hear what they were saying. Dallas inched closer, hovering against the rocks, dashing from one outcropping to another.

Then she heard it, a low grumbling, wheezing noise and the answering bellow of unease from a cow. What was it? The noise continued, growing louder, though remaining guttural and unfamiliar.

"Better go see about him," an older man said.

"Not me. He's crazy. Only a Devil would bite the hand that feeds him." That voice was younger and sounded vaguely familiar.

Dallas held her breath to hear better. The noise went on, as did the sound of milling around by more than one cow, and finally, the neigh of a horse. There had to be a corral of some kind beyond the campfire. But heaven only knew what these two men had penned up there.

And then she knew. The monster. The Devil of the Plains. It had to be. But what kind of monster? In the darkness her foot slipped on a rock, and she heard the rock roll down and clash with another.

"Hey, Rejo, did you hear something?"

Dallas froze. She didn't want to be discovered until she saw what was in the darkness ahead.

"Yep. Must be one of those coyotes. Been hearing them for a night or two. They come sniffing around, but they don't get close to us. That thing back there scares even them."

Coyotes? In the rocks? That was all she needed, to come face to face with a wild animal. Then she shook her head, throwing off the idea. Here she was tracking a Devil that spat poison, killed people, and ate their flesh, and she was worried that she might meet a coyote.

After a few minutes the two men resumed their arguing. Finally the older man stood and moved away from the fire into the shadows. Apparently he'd decided to feed the creature himself. There was movement and a sound that Dallas couldn't identify. Then the younger man rose and walked away from the fire, directly toward the spot where she was hiding.

She stood immobile. It was black dark now, in the area along the rocks. Without light from the moon, she doubted that he could see his hand in front of his face. But what was he doing?

Then she understood as she heard the sound of water bouncing off the rocks. The man was relieving himself, and he was doing it close enough that it practically spattered on her boots.

Please, let him hurry. Let him go away before I explode. Just as she thought she couldn't hold her breath any longer she heard the older man return.

"All right, Doak, I've done the feeding. I'm going to turn in. You keep a watch, in case the boss sends for us."

Doak? The hand that Jake had fired? The one who'd come to the newspaper to collect for damages he considered she'd caused him? Dallas let out her breath, just as he let out a sigh of relief, then turned back toward the fire.

"I wouldn't be surprised if he does send for us. He's got the ranchers stirred up. Now it's time to get after them foreigners. I like that, they're scared to death of the creature."

The ranch hand settled down on a rock and pulled out his gun, checking it, and leaning back against the cliff. Why would he sit way back here, away from the fire? That didn't make any sense.

Once the sun went down the prairie got very cold. Dallas was wearing a thick shirt and a jacket, but she'd already begun to shiver. Doak had to be cold. She leaned against the rock, absorbing the remaining heat left by a day of sun.

Now what, Dallas? You're here. You can't leave and you can't get past Doak. She was likely to become even more miserable before the night was over. Then what would she do? As soon as the sun came up, they'd see her. And if they didn't, they'd find her camp.

Soon she heard the unmistakable sound of snoring. The man called Rejo was asleep. That was when Doak stood quietly and moved about halfway to the fire, carrying a blanket he'd evidently brought with him. Moments later he was bedded down and covered.

So much for security, Dallas thought, allowing a smile to chase away her fear. In the silence she could hear the guttural mumbling of the creature they had penned up. Now she heard Doak's snores join Rejo's.

Carefully, Dallas stepped out away from the rock. The moon hadn't risen above the cliff surrounding the canyon. It was important that she move quickly while it was still pitch-black. She could cross the open area and avoid the potential of more rock slides waking the sleepers. Soon she'd worked her way around the campfire and into the canyon. It was too dark to see, but she could hear and smell the corral.

Cows, yes, a number of cows. And horses; how many, she couldn't decide. And the creature, whatever it was, was moving back and forth in great thumping steps. It was chewing loudly and breathing like some machine. And there was something else, a sound of trickling water.

Dallas stood still, listening until she decided where the water was. She was thirsty and hungry. Unless she was going to eat with the creature, she'd stay that way. But water she could have, if it wasn't inside the pen.

The night sky was velvet-black, spattered with tiny glass stars that gave no illumination, but turned the sky festive with faraway lights. She'd have to find the water by touch and sound. Holding out her hands to make certain that she didn't walk into a fence, she made her way toward the trickle of the water.

Moments later she touched rock, wet rock, rock being splattered by water dropping on more rocks below. She knelt down and found the stream of water that rushed from a tiny crack in the rocks. She removed her hat and filled it with water. After drinking, she replaced the hat on her head. At that moment she heard the sound of heavy steps coming toward her, and the steps didn't belong to anything human. Before she could move away, something cold and wet touched her cheek and expelled hot, fetid breath.

"Get back!"

She didn't mean to scream, but she couldn't hold it back. In the next seconds the cattle, the horses and the unidentified creature began trampling the fence and stampeding out of the canyon.

"What the—?"

"Doak, catch the horses!"

The campfire was scattered beneath the animals' hooves. Doak and Rejo disappeared into the center of the stampede.

Even in the confusion, Dallas tried to see what kind of creature she'd frightened. But it was swallowed up in a cloud of dust in the darkness, and all she knew was that it was big and tall and smelled terrible.

What was it and what was it doing out here? And to whom did it belong?

Dallas hugged the side of the canyon until the dust finally settled. She was alone, without being any closer to knowing who was responsible for the damage done by the monster than before. Doak and his partner had been forced to go after their horses and their killing creature, but they might come back.

As she worked her way out of the canyon, she allowed herself to think about the men. Doak was the cowboy that Jake said he had fired. But had he? That could have been for her benefit. He was out here, near Jake's land, keeping watch on the Devil of the Plains. For Jake?

No. That didn't feel right.

Still, she couldn't see either of these men being connected with Elliott Parnell, either.

Just as Jamie had said, two men stood to gain.

At least Dallas had one piece of the puzzle, confirmation of the monster and connection to its keeper. Experience suggested that once a plan started to unravel, the rest would follow. She'd just get back to Green Willow Creek and print her story about the monster. That ought to stir Jamie's killer up a bit.

But getting back to Green Willow Creek would be harder than she'd planned. When she finally got back to her campsite, she saw that her horses were gone. They had probably been spooked by the stampede.

She didn't dare light her fire for fear the men would return and find her. And she didn't dare lower her rope holding the food, for moonlight flooded the rock she'd tied it over. If the men were watching, she'd be seen. Miserably cold, Dallas found a small opening in the rocks, crawled in and covered herself with the bedroll. She'd start back at first light. By keeping Bitter Butte behind her, she'd find her way.

Oh Jake, my unwilling guardian angel, where are you when I need you?

Morning would be a long time in coming.

The walk back to Green Willow Creek would be even longer.

She wondered what Willie would do when he couldn't find her. Would he come looking for her? What if the two rustlers found her first?

For that's what she'd convinced herself they were. Rustlers, independent businessmen who'd found a way to make money by using some creature from hell as a cover.

But why kill the ranch hands? And why kill the Indians?

And what would they do to her come morning?

All morning Jake had stayed close to the house. He'd slept only lightly the night before, finally rising to pace the room, staring out the window. What had started as a vague unease had grown by the minute until at last he dressed and left the house.

By midmorning, he'd been to the barn and ridden out to the campsite where his men were preparing to search for new calves and begin the branding process. He was looking for trouble.

Expecting trouble.

But everything there was normal.

The creek was flowing smoothly, no evidence that anybody had tampered with it or that the flow was slowing. He glanced at the sky. Maybe another freak storm was coming. Maybe there was a prairie fire burning out there somewhere, heading toward them. Maybe there really was a monster and it was headed toward the Double J. He studied the horizon.

Nothing.

Still, something was wrong, very wrong.

He'd lived by his instincts too long to ignore them. And this morning he knew something was about to happen. He'd ridden back to the house for lunch when he heard the commotion.

"Mr. Jake! Mr. Jake!" Wu hurried across the yard from the barn where he'd driven his wagon filled with supplies after his monthly trip to town.

"What's wrong, Wu?"

"Miss Banning. Miss Banning's gone."

The news hit him in the gut.

Dallas. Dallas was in trouble. Jake met Wu halfway, his long legs eating up the yards in three steps. "What do you mean, she's gone?"

"Willie say she left town yesterday. Say she come here to see Mr. Jake. She not come. Nobody see her since."

Jake swore. "Who was with her?"

"Nobody. She tell Willie she sick, go home. Then she rent two horses and leave very early, before town awake."

Two horses? That indicated a long journey or a pack animal. Jake swore again. "Where's Willie?"

"He's gone to tell Mr. Parnell. He say they look there. You look here."

Pete was already saddling the horses. But there was too much territory, too many mountains for four men to cover when they didn't have any idea where she'd gone. Or why.

"Go ring the dinner bell, Wu. Call the men and tell them to start looking. I'll head toward Elliott to plan our search, then cut back toward Bitter Butte."

Shadow hurried across from the kitchen, pulling a

coat over her bare arms and cramming a hat on her braided hair. "I'll come too."

"No!" Wu said. "You stay here."

"Wu, I know this land better than anyone. Miss Banning is our friend. I must help."

The fear on Wu's face didn't vanish, but he nodded his acceptance and turned back toward the large dinner bell mounted outside the kitchen. The sound of the bell carried across the open plains and, as Jake heard it bellowing, he was glad he'd allowed Wu to put it up. For the first time it didn't recall unhappy times when his father summoned the hands home from the fields. For the first time he welcomed its thundering peal.

Where would she have gone? And why?

He's avoided going into town since the night of the dance. Though he'd paced the floor and made a huge dent in his whiskey supply, he'd stayed away. The only outsiders he'd seen had been the ranchers who'd come to tell him about their meeting. They'd reported more missing cattle and shown him the poster calling for a protest meeting they wanted printed up and asked for his approval.

He'd refused. That kind of rabble-rousing meeting would only generate more trouble, and he wanted no part of it. He'd fought for a cause he believed in once and lost. He'd soon learned that it wouldn't have made much difference if his side had won. In a war, nobody won.

He'd thought he was through with killing.

He was wrong. He'd done what was right once and he'd let Sarah die. Now Dallas was in danger. If anybody harmed Dallas, Jake would kill him. Without a thought. Without regret.

Silently Shadow rode along beside him, searching, scanning the sky and the horizon. A lone hawk circled above, then flew away as if frightened. Jake sensed that Shadow, too, was worried about what was out there. She didn't have to say so.

"Do you think she's dead?" Jake finally asked.

"Do you, Jake?"

In the crisis of the moment, they'd become equals; each dropping any pretense that Jake didn't care about Dallas.

"Look inside your mind," Shadow said. "If the feeling is true, the Great Spirit will let you see."

He started to protest, then stopped. He recalled the unease that had kept him from sleep and forced him to ride his boundaries. He turned it inward, closing out the urgency of the moment. And gradually the picture came. There was a sense of movement, of flight, the feel of wind on his face. Not definite forms, only a melding of the senses. As if he were looking down from some faraway place.

There was anxiety below. There was fear. There was pain.

But there was life.

Finally he straightened up and urged Blackjack into a faster pace. "She's alive, but she's in danger."

Chapter 13

Elliott had sent for all the men with horses or mules. They were gathering in front of the settlement house when Jake rode up. It surprised Jake that he was glad to see Elliott. He noticed the new sense of ease with which his old friend wore his gun.

"Any sign of her, Jake?" Willie asked anxiously.

"None. I thought I told you not to let her go out alone."

"I didn't know she was going. I shoulda known," he admitted miserably, "what with her telling me that I could have the day off. She don't ever take a day off. I'm sorry, Jake."

Jake forced himself to be more rational than he felt. "I'd hoped you or some of your people might have seen her, Elliott."

"No," Elliott answered wearily, "at least not any of the men here. Any idea where she's gone?"

"None." As least none that Jake wanted to give voice to, though an idea was forming in the back of his mind.

"What are your plans, Captain Silver? My men are ready to follow your orders."

Elliott was automatically deferring to Jake's leadership, just as he'd always done. Neither man voiced their past relationship, but both knew that they were temporarily a team again—for Dallas's sake.

Starting at the railroad in town, the settlers' land lay like a half-moon curving around his own land and ended with Elliott's piece at the source of Green Willow Creek. Jake divided the map of the territory into chunks, assigning two men to each section. "Fire three shots if you see any sign of her. The sound will carry, and we'll converge on your position."

The women handed out small parcels of food and canteens filled with water. Their fear lay unvoiced, but they knew that the search might be long.

As the men rode away, Jake lingered, holding Blackjack to a nervous dance. His eyes met those of Elliott, and the look that passed between them was fraught with meaning.

Then they turned in opposite directions, each riding off into the afternoon, each carrying the memory of Sarah in his heart.

Dallas doggedly put one foot in front of the other. The sun was inching toward the Green Mountains behind her. She stopped to take a precious sip of water. Her canteen was nearly empty. Surely she wouldn't die of thirst out here. This wasn't a desert. This was a grass-filled plain, sodden with melting snow only a short time past.

Only a few weeks ago she'd stepped off the Union Pacific train heading for California and almost been run down by some rowdy cowboys. Only a few weeks later she'd been kissed by a man and felt the violent longings of desire sweep over her. Now she was lost, alone, and a long way from where she ought to be.

A great brown bird flew overhead, swooping down in front of her and flying away again. A hawk, catching some prey Dallas had scared up with her trek through the grass. The bird seemed to follow her, dipping close to the earth, then soaring into the sky again.

Sticking to her plan of keeping Bitter Butte at her back, Dallas glanced behind her. With no visible trail to follow, she needed a constant point of reference. On foot, she was too short to be able to see any sign of civilization, even supposing she'd managed to get close to any.

The butte was still there, exactly where it was the last time she'd looked. The bedroll was growing heavier and heavier in her arms. She would never have believed that the temperature would shoot so high so quickly, but she felt perspiration rolling down her face, and the jacket she was wearing was unbearably hot.

Still, she hesitated about removing it. She couldn't carry it, her food supplies, and the bedroll. And she didn't know how long it would take her to get back to town on foot. As long as she had her supplies, she could survive without her horse.

Recapping her canteen, she lifted the bedroll and started off again. The hawk continued to keep her company. By late afternoon she checked her landmarks again. The butte hadn't moved, and neither did it look any farther away.

Allowing herself a small sob of frustration, she slid to the ground and leaned back against her bedroll. She wasn't going to get home before dark. She wasn't even going to get to one of the immigrants' sod houses before nightfall. For hours she'd searched the horizon for a sign of smoke, though it would be just as likely to belong to the rustlers. At this point, she'd be willing to take a chance on talking her way past the rustlers.

Again the hawk dived to the ground. She lay,

watching its graceful wings against a sky that was gradually losing its light. At least, when the sun set, she wouldn't die of heat exhaustion.

"No, idiot, you'll freeze to death if the creature doesn't come back for you first." Wearily, Dallas started to get up, then hesitated.

What was that singing sound?

Not the Devil of the Plains. He didn't sing. He growled. But this wasn't exactly singing, it was more like a rapid rattle, like a gourd made into a baby's toy, like a—

Snake.

Dallas froze, but she was too late. Through the thick fabric of Willie's trousers, she felt a sting on her thigh. She'd been bitten by a rattlesnake!

The rustling grass told her the snake had moved on. Panic-stricken, she tried to recall what to do about snakebites. Somehow she knew one should cut into the wound and suck out the poison, then apply a tourniquet.

But she had no knife and she would have a hard time reaching the spot to do any sucking. She couldn't even cut a hole in the trousers. Shaking, she hoisted herself to her feet and untied the cord holding the pants up. On her thigh were two small red spots, only two. And one was more of a scratch.

Gathering all her courage, she took the flesh in her hands and squeezed as hard as she could, for as long as she could. The spots bled, but not a lot. She doubted that what she'd done had helped much. She ripped a strip from her bedroll and tied it around her thigh as tightly as she could. Then she refastened her trousers. All she could do now was find help as quickly as possible. Leaving behind her supplies and the bedroll she started across the plains.

The sky darkened. Time blurred, and as the moon rose she realized that the butte was no longer be-

hind her, but over her right shoulder. She hazily realized that she was no longer heading toward Willow Creek or the immigrants.

She was heading toward the Double J.

In her confusion she glanced up. Overhead, a
hawk make a silhouette against the moon. "Hawks
don't fly at night," Dallas whispered and shivered as
it flew away into darkness.

Her strength seemed to desert her along with the
bird. "Jake," she whispered and collapsed. "I need
you, Jake."

In the distance a coyote howled.

The hawk returned, hovering overhead.

In another canyon near the point where Willow
Creek surged out of the rocks and headed toward
the Double J, the Devil of the Plains heard the coyote, paused for a moment, then went back to grazing on tree leaves and new grass that grew by the
creek.

On the range, Jake felt a sharp pain that cut
through him. His insides suddenly felt as if they'd
been sliced into silvers of glass. There was pain.

"What's wrong?" Shadow asked.

"She's hurt."

"Where?"

"Close, but damn it to hell, I don't know where!"

Shadow brought her horse to a stop. She sat, listening, allowing the night to close around her.
"Jake, where was she going?"

"I'm not certain, but I suspect she was looking for
the Devil."

"Why?"

"Because that's what her brother did."

"And where did he go?"

"Nobody knows."

"Who killed her brother?"

Jake let out a deep ragged sigh. "I don't know,

Shadow. I really don't know. I don't understand any of this. I don't even believe there is a Devil."

"But there is."

He looked up in surprise. "You saw it?"

"I didn't exactly see it. I heard it. But it didn't kill my uncle and brother. The men riding with it did. They just forced the monster to ride them down, to crush them under its big feet. They didn't want us there, in the canyon."

"Why didn't it kill you?"

"I was above them, on the mountain behind some rocks. They didn't know I was there."

"And you didn't tell anyone?"

"My people have long believed in the Devil. They thought that he was a bad spirit sent to punish them. The others left, joined other tribes. We were the only ones who stayed. I was to go into the mountain to ask Mother Earth to protect us. They waited below. Two men came. They killed my uncle and my brother. I heard the monster and I hid. After that, it didn't seem to matter any more."

"Where did you hear this Devil?"

"At the base of the Green Mountains, where the mountain points its finger."

"Finger? Yes, I know the place, near the source of Green Willow Creek. There's a canyon there." Jake wheeled Blackjack around and cut a path away from his section of land toward Bitter Butte. Shadow followed. She too felt the urgency. In reassurance, she touched the bag of herbs she'd brought along and urged her horse to keep up.

Jake felt Dallas's pain. And it led him to where she was.

If she hadn't cried out, he would have missed her and not found her until morning. Dismounting before Blackjack came to a full stop, Jake stumbled and fell to the ground beside the dark form.

He wasn't even certain it was Dallas until he pulled the hat from her head. Flowers. He knew, for he recognized the smell of flowers and that mass of dark hair that spilled across the ground.

"Dallas! Dallas! What's wrong?"

He knew she was alive because he felt her body heat. But why didn't she answer? Then he discovered her tourniquet.

"Is she still breathing, Mr. Jake?"

They were employer and employee again. "Yes, but she's burning up with fever. I think she's been bitten by a snake."

"Get her back to the ranch, quick."

"Yes." Jake lifted her to his horse, balancing her across his saddle until he could mount and gather her in his arms. He fired his gun three times, then rode as he'd never ridden before.

Wu opened the door and, assessing the situation, danced ahead to pull back the covers of Jake's bed. Moments later, Shadow had removed the tourniquet and ripped away Dallas's trousers, revealing the tiny wounds.

"Snakebite," she said. "Only one fang caught her; the other is just a scratch. But one is enough. The flesh already swells."

"We can't let her die," Jake said.

Wu left the room, reappearing with a pan of boiling water. "Go away, Mr. Jake," he said. "We take care of Mr. Jake's woman."

"She's not my—" he started to say, then broke off. She was his woman. Not that he wanted her or any other woman.

But for now, this night, she was his and he was responsible for her. Jake closed his eyes and clenched his hands. Death was there, but he wouldn't let it take Dallas. There had to be a way to save her.

The dinner bell was being rung. Nobody was supposed to ring that bell except Wu, he thought, then realized how foolish the thought was. Then the bell stopped, and he heard a commotion in the yard. He walked to the window and looked out. It was Elliott and Willie. Pete and the other hands were gathering.

"Look after her, Shadow," Jake said and left the room.

"We heard the shots," Pete said outside. "What happened?"

"Snakebite." Jake's voice was clipped and cold. "Sometime today, I think."

Elliott swore. "How bad?"

Jake shook his head. With no one to cut the wound and suck the venom out, the poison had gone straight into her bloodstream. Then she'd walked on the leg, trying to get to him.

"She's still alive," he answered.

"What was she doing out there, Jake?"

"My guess is that she was looking for the monster."

By this time there were eight men present. The others listened uneasily, each man thinking that it might be their woman. Each man having faced the dangers of the life they'd chosen. Each man afraid.

"This Indian woman, Wu's woman," Elliott said quietly, "can she help?"

"I don't know. She's trying."

"Well, it looks like this time it's up to you, Jake. I hope you do better than I did."

Jake's response was cold, and deadly, not directed at Elliott, but himself. "I intend to."

Willie sniffed and covered it with a cough. "Any sign of her horses?"

Jake shook his head. "No. She'd apparently been

wandering on foot for a while. Willie, what in hell was she thinking of?"

"It was that Devil of the Plains," Willie answered. "That's all she talked about. The trouble is, everybody is afraid of the monster. Nobody has looked for it. Maybe she thought if she found the Devil, she'd solve all our problems."

Wu stuck his head out the window overhead. "Mr. Jake, you come here, please."

Jake took the stairs three at a time, reaching his room before Wu had closed the window. "What's wrong?"

"She talks about the monster."

Dallas was tossing back and forth, holding up her hands as if to ward off something, or someone. "No! Stop! Stop, you ugly beast!"

Jake walked to the bed and stood, looking down on her. He didn't dare touch her, or he'd be holding her in his arms. "You're all right now, Dallas," he said softly. "Try to rest."

"Jake?" She raised up, searching for him, then, catching sight of him, she fell back to the bed, whispering almost under her breath. "Jake . . . Elliott . . . please help me."

Jake knew she was delirious, but he wished her voice didn't sound so final. He wished he didn't feel her pain. He wished the hurt he was absorbing came only from the snakebite, not from her soul.

Elliott and the others finally left. They had to get back to their families and their duties. Shadow made up foul-smelling concoctions that she rubbed on the cut she'd made in Dallas's leg while Wu brewed liquids that they forced Dallas to swallow. Dr. Horn came and said that they'd done everything that could be done. Finally, at midnight, Jake came back into the bedroom.

"Go to bed, Shadow, I'll take over."

"There's nothing else to be done," the Indian woman said. "We keep her comfortable, and we wait."

"Fine. I'll keep her comfortable, and I'll wait." His voice was firm, and Shadow, flexing the muscles in her shoulders, stood and nodded.

"Keep wiping her face with a wet cloth," she instructed and, holding up a clay cup, added, "get as much of this liquid down as you can. We'll know by morning."

Jake lowered the flame in the lamp and pulled his chair close to the bed. For a time he did nothing but watch Dallas. She was restless, thrashing back and forth as if she was in great distress. He wiped the perspiration from her brow, wrung out the cloth, and wiped it again. But he felt such pain that he could scarcely touch her.

Pain had become a part of him, filling up all the spaces in his inner self that weren't occupied with the daily business of survival. It was more than simply empathy with Dallas; it was pain for all the suffering he'd seen.

She groaned and shifted her position beneath the muslin sheet, catching it with her knee and pulling it lower.

Shadow had dressed Dallas in one of his linen shirts, leaving it open at the top. When she'd twisted her body she'd opened the shirt, exposing one pearl-colored breast. Her body was more wiry, thinner than Sarah's had been. He'd never watched Sarah when she slept, but he had seen her bathing in the creek, scooping handfuls of water and sloshing them over her lush body.

He'd thought then that she knew he was watching, that she'd turned herself seductively around and around in the moonlight, all for his benefit. But he'd never mentioned it, and later he'd cursed himself because he'd never acted on the invitation. He hadn't, but Elliott had. Jake would never know whether he blamed Elliott for weakening or himself for refusing what he was afraid to take.

Now he reached forward, intent on closing the shirt. Just as he touched the fabric, Dallas's hand reached out and caught his arm. With surprising strength born of fever, she pulled herself up from the bed and leaned against him.

"Help me, Jake," she pleaded. "I'm so hot. It hurts."

Her eyes opened, hazel eyes flecked with gold that seemed agitated and wild. "So hot," she said over and over again. "My leg's on fire! Stop the pain!"

With a growl of fury, Jake stood, sweeping Dallas and her sheet into his arms. He started down the stairs, pushing past a startled Shadow as she inquired what he was doing, and walked into the yard. Minutes later he was at the bank of Green Willow Creek. He sought the deepest part, the part dug out for his own personal bathing, and walked into the water, submerging both him and Dallas into its icy current.

After an initial struggle, Dallas relaxed against him, sliding her arms weakly around his neck and resting her cheek against his chest. She let out a sigh of relief and pressed against him. In no time the icy water had lowered her temperature, and her breathing had evened out into a deep, restful sleep.

He didn't know whether he'd helped or done her harm, but as he walked back toward the house he felt a great weight fall away. In the distance the coyotes howled. The moon dropped beyond the highest peaks of the Sierra Nevada, and the night grew quiet.

Up the stairs he carried her, removing the soggy

shirt and laying her on the bed. Now she was beginning to shiver. Jake thought for a moment, stripped off his wet clothing, crawled in beside her and drew her close. There was an instant awareness as two bodies touched. Then, little by little, warmth returned to her body and she relaxed.

This time, being close to her was not sexual to Jake; it didn't drive him mad with desire as her touch had done before. He simply held her, willing his strength into her, trying to absorb her weakness into him. Through the darkest part of the night until the sun began to cast faint fingers in the east, he continued to hold her.

Dallas slept on, and finally, Jake also slept.

Later in the morning, when Shadow slipped into the room to check on her patient, she found Dallas in Jake's arms. Her color was good and her breathing slow and even. Jake looked at peace. She'd never seen that expression on his face before.

Quietly she backed out of the room and went back to the kitchen.

"Jake's woman?" Wu asked. "Is she all right?"

"They're both all right—for now."

When Dallas opened her eyes, the sun was high in the sky. Shadow was sitting quietly beside the bed.

"Shadow? Is that you?"

"Yes, Dallas. It's me."

"How did I get here?"

"Jake found you."

To Dallas, everything seemed hazy, as if she were walking through a cool fog that shifted as she moved. "Jake found me? How?"

"He said you called out to him."

"I don't remember." But she did, in some half-formed way she seemed to recall lying on the prairie grass. There was great pain and she was very hot.

"There was a hawk," she whispered through lips so dry that she could hardly speak.

"Ahh, a hawk. That's how you sent the message, how he knew where to go. Take a little water." Shadow lifted Dallas's head and held a cup filled with cool water to her lips. She took a sip, then another.

"Water. Yes, I remember water. Cold water."

"Yes," Shadow agreed. Learning that Jake had taken Dallas to the creek and plunged both of them into the cold stream wouldn't make sense to Dallas now. It didn't really make sense to Shadow, but Jake had known instinctively what to do, just as he'd known where to search. And he'd comforted her in the way a man reassured a woman.

"Let me look at your leg, Dallas."

"My leg?"

"Yes, you were bitten. Do you remember a snake?"

She remembered. At least she remembered the sound of its rattlers, then the pain. It was coming back.

"The Devil!" she said and sat up, groaned and fell back to the bed, gritting her teeth for a long minute before she spoke again. "I saw it, Shadow. I saw the Devil of the Plains."

"I know, you told me."

"I did?"

"You've done a lot of talking, Dallas, mostly about Jamie."

"Jamie was my brother. I loved him dearly. He and I were a team. Then I went away and left him. If I hadn't gone away he might not have died."

"We can never know the future, Dallas. Your brother had his own destiny to face."

There was a long, quiet minute.

"Jamie saw him too. I know he did." Dallas said,

sudden anxiety bringing a frown to her face. "You have to help me, Shadow, I have to tell . . ."

Shadow helped raise Dallas's head, holding a cup of liquid to her lips. "Not yet, Dallas Banning. From now on you are Jake's woman. And you must think wisely before you speak."

Dallas swallowed a few mouthfuls of the bitter liquid, then sank back to her pillow. "Why?" She was suddenly so tired. Her eyes closed, but still she heard Shadow's answer.

"There might be some who do not wish you to speak the truth. You could be harmed."

"Like Jamie." She tried to stay awake, but consciousness slid away into a deep, cottony sleep that hushed her speech and stilled her thoughts.

Like Jamie.

Chapter 14

Moonlight spilled through the window, casting a silver glow on the floor around the bed. Dallas had been awake for a while, just watching Jake. He had a whiskey glass in one hand and a lighted cigar in the other. Like some night predator stalking his quarry, he stood motionless, staring out the window into the night.

There was an unexpected vulnerability about him. From the first moment she'd laid eyes on Jake Silver, he'd seemed indomitable. Now, a black shadow in the moonlight, he looked almost lost, and she wanted to comfort him.

She'd tried to fight the attraction she'd felt for him, but it hadn't lessened. At every turn he'd been there for her despite his claims that she meant nothing to him. Now he'd saved her life again and she was through pretending that he meant nothing to her.

She must have made a sound, for he turned. "How are you feeling?"

"I feel strange—as if I'm floating," she said. "Was I run over by the Devil of the Plains?"

"Don't joke! You're lucky you weren't."

She shuddered. "You don't know how true that is."

"You saw it, didn't you?" He pulled a straight chair to her bed, straddled it, and sat down, leaning his arms over the back.

"Not exactly. But I did find the canyon where they had penned him up."

"They?" His voice tightened and he leaned forward.

"Two men."

"Did you recognize them?"

She wondered whether the tension in his voice was from fear or concern. The woman in her wanted to tell Jake that she had recognized one of the rustlers, but the detective in her stopped her. "No. They were just rustlers."

"Rustlers? Why would you think that?"

"Because they penned the monster up with a small herd of stolen cows. At least, I assume they were stolen."

Jake considered what she'd said. Rustlers? Maybe. All the ranchers had reported losses, and he had his suspicions that the thieves weren't the farmers, but that didn't explain the monster.

"Did they see you?"

"No, but they heard me. I'm afraid I screamed when the creature charged past me. But they still might not have known if I hadn't gotten myself bitten by a snake and had half the territory out looking for me. I'm sure they've figured out it was me."

Jake knew she was right. She'd have to stay here, where he could protect her until he got to the bottom of the Devil of the Plains story. Keeping her ought to be easy; with her injury she was a week away from walking on her own.

"Where was the monster, Dallas?"

"In a blind canyon just beyond Bitter Butte."

"Are you going to tell me what the monster is?"

"I would if I knew. Do you?"

Jake cut a sharp glance to her face. Then, taking a long sip of the whiskey, he swirled it around his mouth and swallowed it. "No. Why should I? I've never seen it."

She believed him. Just as she'd believed him when he'd said that he didn't lie.

"I didn't see it either. It was dark. All I know is that it is big and has bad breath."

Jake let out a deep laugh. "Bad breath?"

"It breathed on me. It was as close to me as you are, but it scared me so badly that I guess I closed my eyes. Then it was swallowed up with the cattle as they broke out of their pen and disappeared into the darkness." Dallas cleared her throat and tried to turn on her side. Excruciating pain racked her body from her foot to her rib cage. "Oh!"

"What's wrong?" Jake stood up, flipped the cigar into the pan filled with water beside the bed, and set his glass on the table.

"It feels like the monster stepped on my leg."

"Can I do something for you? Another pillow?" he asked, fussing unnaturally with her covers.

"Yes, there is one thing you can do," Dallas said, releasing a pent-up breath, then pursing her lips in private amusement. "I'd like a glass of that whiskey you're drinking."

He let out a relaxed laugh, one that came from some place deep within, the kind of laugh she'd never heard from him, the laugh of a man who was expressing genuine pleasure.

"Well, darling, if you want a good stiff belt of whiskey, I'll be happy to provide it." He left the room, returning shortly with a bottle and a second glass, which he filled with the amber liquid.

Dallas started to take the glass, then thought better of trying to drink while she was lying down. She raised herself on her hands with the idea of scooting back against the headboard of the bed. That was when she found out how weak she was and how painful it was to make a movement of any kind.

"Hold on, maverick," he said, "let me help you."

After setting her glass on the table, he placed one hand under each arm and lifted her easily to a sitting position. Then he stacked pillows behind her head. "How's that?"

"Better," she admitted, accepting the glass and sipping it slowly. "What was that you called me?"

He thought a moment. He'd become so accustomed to thinking of her as a maverick that it had just slipped out. "Maverick. That's a cow or a calf that is unbranded. I prefer to think of them as wild ones, free spirits with minds of their own."

"And you think that's what I am?" she asked.

"You're unmarried, aren't you?"

"I am."

"And you certainly have a mind of your own," he observed.

She took a quick hot breath, snared by the intensity of his gaze. "You didn't say that I'm wild."

"Are you?"

"My brothers have called me that."

"Brothers?" he questioned. He'd known about Jamie, of course, but he'd sensed that she was a loner, like him. It came as a surprise to learn she had other brothers.

"Yes, three older brothers and a father, back in Philadelphia." She licked her lips, tasting the whiskey as she asked, "Does that bother you?"

"No. Not unless they have some objections to my rescuing you and bringing you here."

"Why would they?"

Jake swirled the amber liquid around in his glass, then said in a dangerously low voice, "I don't know. They might consider this a bit intimate."

Dallas felt the warmth of the whiskey spread through her—the whiskey and something else.

In spite of the fact that he was a loner, with a Stay Away sign engraved on his spirit, he seemed to have the uncanny ability to draw her close. The medicine Shadow had given her had not only dulled her pain, it had freed her emotions, and she responded with every inch of her being to the thought of being intimate with Jake Silver.

"I don't know why they'd think that," she said softly. "We haven't been intimate, have we?"

"Not physically—yet."

She took another sip of the whiskey, welcoming the heat that fanned out from her stomach, relaxing nerve endings coiled into knots, relaxing too her normal rein on her thoughts. "That's good," she heard herself saying. "I wouldn't want to miss the experience."

"I wouldn't want you to miss it either."

Dallas slid down into the pillows, her eyelids growing heavy in spite of her best attempt to hold them open. She didn't want to sleep again. With his laugh, Jake had opened up to her, and she didn't want to lose the ground she'd gained. She had to keep him talking, not for her, for Jamie.

"Is this your bed?"

"Yes."

"It looks like you, strong, with purpose."

She was so lovely, in his bed, so delightfully uninhibited in her movements. Subconsciously Jake knew it had to be the combination of the medication and the whiskey, but her honesty still tightened his throat.

"Where will you sleep? she asked, "if I'm in your bed?"

"There's another room across the hall."

Dallas shivered. He was so close, and this bed

was so big and lonely. She drained her glass and held it out for a refill.

"More. I'd like more, Jake Silver who stands in the moonlight like a ghost. Are you a ghost, Jake?"

"I think sometimes that I am, doomed to wander the earth." He took the glass. "I don't think you need any more whiskey, darling," he said with a tenderness that she couldn't miss.

"You are not only a silver shade, but you believe yourself to be a very wise man, Jake Silver. But you can't know what I need. Not even my father knew."

"What do you need, maverick?" He sat down on the bed beside her, brushing her hair away from her face.

She yawned and smiled. "I feel like a little girl. Did your father ever sit on the side of your bed and give you a good-night kiss?"

"No, but my mother did. Every night. Is that what you want, Dallas Banning?"

"Yes." She said and realized that was exactly what she wanted, the good-night kiss she never got, the reassurance she gave to her little brother when she was as much in need as he. "Yes, Jake, kiss me, please."

Her lips were soft and warm. He tasted the whiskey as her tongue hesitantly played with his. Once more he felt her innocence and wondered at the need he felt to protect her. A woman he called maverick because of her aggressive nature was, here in his arms, a little girl who was asking for something he wasn't certain he could give. Before the kiss grew into something he wouldn't be able to stop, he pulled away.

She sighed in disappointment. "Didn't you want to kiss me, Jake?"

"Yes, I wanted very much to kiss you. But it isn't smart of you to let me."

She opened her eyes and frowned, reaching out with her fingertips to touch his chest. Her eyes widened as he shivered at her touch. Then she smiled. "I don't think you always know that much about being smart, Jake. I don't think you know what you need."

Oh, he knew what he needed, all right. If he hadn't, his body would have told him. Another minute of holding her, of feeling her firm breasts pressed against him, and she would have known, too. But she'd gone to sleep, leaving him with a need that was more than just physical. There was an emotional need here that made him want to comfort and share.

With her dark hair spread like lace over the white covers of the goose feather pillows, she looked like one of those portraits in the art galleries he'd visited in the East. Her eyes were closed in sleep, her cheeks still rosy against the alabaster skin, one graceful arm behind her head, the other resting gently on the sheet where it had fallen when she loosened her grip on the whiskey glass.

"She's still very weak, Mr. Jake. You ought not to be giving her whiskey on an empty stomach," Shadow said, standing in the darkness behind him.

"Whiskey has been known to ease many a man's pain."

"And cause it as well. Go to bed, Mr. Jake. I'll stay for a while."

Shadow was right. He needed to get away. He needed to feel the darkness of the night around him and let the crisp, cool wind blow away his thoughts.

He started out the door, stopped, picked up the bottle and took one last look at the sleeping woman before he left the room.

Maverick! He'd brought her back to the herd. She didn't look so determined now. She looked defenseless. That bothered him more than the fury she usually greeted him with. He should get out of her life and leave her alone.

To the barn he went, carrying the bottle with him. Minutes later he was astride Blackjack, riding through the night. It was times like this when he missed Elliott's friendship—what they'd been to each other—before Sarah had chosen Elliott.

Jake let Blackjack have his head. They rode toward Bitter Butte, then beyond, until they came to what had once been a fenced-in area up a ravine. By that time the clouds had covered the moon and the rain had begun to fall. Any chance of following the trail of the escaping herd and the monster would be obliterated by the rain.

Still he tried. He cut straight across toward the creek, which was filling with water once more. But the rain was falling so hard that he couldn't see. Finally he gave up and started back to the Double J.

When he returned, Wu was lighting a fire in the parlor.

"Any change, Wu?"

"Not yet, Mr. Jake. About same. But don't worry. Jake's woman will be fine."

"I wish you'd stop calling her my woman. It isn't that way, Wu."

"Old Chinese belief say when a life is saved, that life belongs to the one who saves it. You saved Miss Dallas's life, Mr. Jake. She belongs to you."

"I'm not from China." Jake took off his wet hat and duster, dropping them on the floor. "Bring me some coffee, Wu, and a bottle of whiskey."

"Coffee, yes. Whiskey, no. Shadow say no more whiskey for Mr. Jake."

"Wu! I said coffee and whiskey. On second thought, forget the coffee!"

* * *

The morning sky was a bright, cloudless blue. Miranda held an umbrella over her head and shaded her eyes as she looked up at Elliott, who was nailing rough planks across the roof of his house. "Wu sent word this morning that Dallas is doing fine. I didn't know if he'd think to tell you."

"No, he didn't." Elliott hadn't expected Jake to send a report on the state of Dallas's health. He'd said he'd take care of her, and he had. Jake always did what he set out to do.

He never lied, either, except perhaps to himself. Elliott thought that Jake was more interested in Miss Dallas Banning than he would admit.

While Elliot wasn't surprised that Jake hadn't stopped by, he was astonished that Miranda had. So far as he knew, she rarely left Green Willow Creek; certainly she'd never journeyed to the settlements. But here she was, smiling at him as if they were old friends and she expected him to help her down and bid her welcome.

He did exactly that, catching a glimpse of a basket in the foot of the wagon.

"That wouldn't be food, would it?" he asked as he swung her to the ground.

"Yes, it would. I was afraid I'd arrive at mealtime and you'd feel obligated to invite me to stay. I didn't want to embarrass you."

"Well, you would have. I rarely eat in the middle of the day. Once I leave the settlement house, I don't return until time for the evening meal."

He didn't explain that he felt driven to succeed— not for his father's sake or Jake's, or for Sarah's, but for his own. This time his land and the crops he intended to grow were the future, his future.

Miranda was thoughtful, too, as she looked up at Elliott. The man looking down at her was a very different man from the one who'd escorted Dallas to the dance. This man was dressed in a rough blue shirt and denim work pants tucked in worn black knee-high leather boots. From his back pocket hung a handkerchief, streaked with dirt.

He was sweaty and very male, and he didn't apologize for his appearance. She liked him even more for that.

The walls of Elliott's house were up, along with half of the roof—a roof that was plain and uneven but a real roof, not sod like most of the others.

"Will you join me for lunch, Mr. Parnell?"

"I'd be delighted, Miss Miranda."

He lifted the basket from the wagon, gallantly offered Miranda his arm, and escorted her across the yard away from the house. There were no trees for shade, no cool flowing spring in which they might dangle their feet. Instead, Miranda took a tablecloth from inside the basket and spread it across the greening prairie grass.

"Please sit down, Elliott." She unwrapped bread and cheese and meat. Then she uncorked a bottle and poured wine into two glasses.

"Wine?" he asked. "Wine, for a picnic?"

"When you own a saloon, you drink wine on a picnic," Miranda retorted. She took a big gulp of the liquid and began to choke. "Sorry," she managed to say, "I guess I'm not used to such fine wine and fine company. Truth is, I'm not used to picnics. Men don't usually share a tablecloth with me."

"They don't know what they're missing." He lifted his glass in a toast, touching it to hers, then smiled broadly.

After they had enjoyed a pleasant meal, Miranda stood and turned toward the mountain.

"I like Wyoming. I like the open plains and the mountains. The Indians believe that the spirits live up there. That the mountains are sacred. I think that I like knowing that they are looking down on us."

Elliott came to stand beside her. "Sometimes I believe that, too. If you look at them when it's storming, there's a power there. But I like the open spaces, too. They make a man feel free."

Miranda turned back toward Elliott, a quick breeze catching her blond hair and tugging at it. She caught her breath and her eyes widened, as if she'd just realized something.

"You know Jake from before, don't you?" she asked.

"Yes, did he tell you?"

"No, Jake doesn't talk about his past. But I could sense the strong tension between you."

"Jake's a very strong man."

She took a step closer, casually touching his shirt. "So, I think, are you, Elliott Parnell. Why are you out here, in this wilderness? What kind of man are you, really?"

"I'm a farmer, Miranda. That's all, a simple farmer."

"You may be a farmer now, but there's nothing simple about you. Will you ... will you come to town to visit me?"

"You mean to the saloon, as a—"

"Customer?" Her eyelashes fluttered closed. "If that's what you want, Elliott. That's the business I'm in, pleasing men. I think I'd like to please you."

"Why?" Elliott said in a voice more angry than he intended. "You're an intelligent and beautiful woman. Why offer your body to me?"

"What else have I to offer?"

"Friendship. Friendship is what a man needs from someone he cares about."

Her eyelids fluttered. "Cares about?"

It was obvious that this idea was new to Miranda.

"Have you ever been married, Miranda?"

"No. I've seen what marriage does to a woman, turns her into a drudge and takes her smiles away."

"Some women like being married, having children."

"You've been married, haven't you, Elliott?"

"Yes, once. A long time ago. She died."

She reached out and put her hand on his face in a gesture of comfort. "I'm sorry."

Jake took her hand and held it for a long time, watching as she dropped her gaze in uncertainty.

"I'd be pleased to come into town, Miranda. Perhaps I could escort you to dinner at Mrs. Jarrett's on Friday evening?"

"To dinner? In public?"

"Unless there's somewhere else you'd like to go."

"Oh, no. I mean there is nowhere else. I mean I'd like to go. Are you sure?"

He took her chin in his hand and smiled, gently touching his lips to hers. "I'm very sure."

Back at the wagon, when he attempted to assist her aboard, she hesitated, chewed on her lip for a minute, then blurted out the truth.

"Thank you, Elliott, but there's another reason I'm here. I felt sorry for your farmers the other night. I know how it feels to be left out. They should have been invited in. If it had been up to me, well . . ."

"I understand, Miranda. I'll tell them."

"And that's not all. I thought you ought to know that some of the ranchers were in my saloon talking. They're scared, really scared. They've already brought in some gunfighters to run you out and they've organized a Vigilance Committee. I'm afraid that your people are in danger."

Elliott's expression turned grim.

He saddled his horse. "I'm going to escort you back to town, Miranda."

"You don't have to do that. Everybody around here knows me. They won't harm me."

"After what happened to Dallas, I'm not sure anybody is safe."

Lawson Pickens eyed Jake warily. "How's Miss Banning?"

"She's going to be all right. But that isn't what I've come about. Lawson, I'm worried about all this monster business," Jake said.

"No more than I, my boy. What I can't figure is what in tarnation the thing is."

"Neither can I. I'm not even sure there is a monster. It might be pure hysteria. Like the Salem witches."

Jake studied the map of the territory behind Lawson's desk. Except for Elliott's tag of land that extended well into the Green Mountains, a line could almost be drawn down the middle of the valley.

The ranchers' land ran along the mountain range and curved gently around the settlers'. Lawson hadn't marked the trouble spots, but it was clear that the monster had avoided the town.

Lawson Pickens absently wound his pocket watch. "What do you think we ought to do?"

"Me? I don't know. That's your job."

"Don't be a fool, Jake. I'm only a banker. My duties as land agent are complete. All the land has been allotted. The immigrants are your responsibility. From here on out, all I do is collect their payments and deposit them to the account of the seller, for a small fee, of course."

"For my money, Pickens, that makes you still involved. I don't want the farmers here, but I don't trust Elliott's ability to look after them."

209

Lawson raised his gaze, uneasily. "Just what would you expect *me* to do?"

"Send for the territory marshal. Appoint a sheriff. Something."

"But I'm not a city official."

"You're the nearest thing to a mayor we have. If you don't do something, at least get the other merchants to appropriate some funds and I'll send for someone to help keep the peace."

"Oh? And who would you send for?"

"There are numerous gunfighters for hire. If you put out the word that they're coming, that might put a stop to a range war."

Lawson Pickens stared at Jake in shock. "I'll talk to some of the city fathers, Jake. Feel them out. I'm sure we can do something."

"Good, let me know." Jake stood. It was late. He'd ridden into town to put some distance between him and Dallas. Now he found himself hurrying back.

Lawson Pickens rubbed his forehead and narrowed his lips. The last thing he wanted in Green Willow Creek was more gunfighters. He'd talk to the other merchants. But he knew in the end they'd leave it up to him. And that was the way he wanted it. But Jake was right about one thing—everybody needed to know that things were getting out of hand.

"Rejo, did you hear it?" Doak asked as he herded two of the recaptured cows back toward the corral.

"Hear what?" Rejo, nudging the now-docile creature inside, closed the bar, imprisoning three of the runaways.

Doak climbed down from the piebald horse he'd run down and said hesitantly, "It sounded like a woman's scream. I—I even thought I saw her."

"You eating loco weed? There ain't no woman out here."

"No, and I ain't been drinking neither."

"Then you must have been dreaming. A fine guard you are."

"I wasn't asleep," Doak protested, then added defensively, "I guess it was one of those coyotes." He glared at the monster, now munching range grass. "I still don't know how you caught him, Rejo."

He stayed well out of the way of the long-necked animal. More than once the Devil had let out a roar of anger and lunged for Doak's arm. His teeth were sharp and pointed, like those of some wild cat. And his eyes, big and dark, were windows of the hate he had for his captors.

"I didn't. He feels comfortable with the cows. Where they go, he goes. I'm just worried about watering them. I don't relish herding them down to the creek every day. Without water it'll be harder to keep them hidden. You go into town and tell the boss that we need some barrels and a couple of mules."

"Now wait just a minute. You don't think I'm going to haul water for all those cows and that creature, do you?"

"Yes, I do. And you'd best be getting about it, else you'll be the one leading the Devil to the creek, on a rope."

Doak swore. He'd go to town, all right. It had been too long since he'd had a proper drink and a conversation with a lady.

On second thought, maybe conversation wasn't necessary. Neither was the drink. He'd just concentrate on the lady and forget all the rest. Tomorrow was soon enough to worry about barrels.

Several times on the way into town Doak stopped and listened. He had the feeling that there was someone out there, following him, but he couldn't see anyone. It was all this Devil spirit business. He was getting spooked, imagining that animal was trailing him.

But it wasn't the Devil that caught Doak just above his ear and hurled him unconscious to the ground, it was a bullet, a .45-caliber bullet. Rejo climbed off his horse and checked to make certain that Doak was dead. Then, using a long stick to encourage him, he made the animal walk back and forth across Doak's body. Rejo reholstered his pistol, climbed back on his horse and checked the location to make sure this was the same place that the newspaperman had been found. He hated to lose Doak's help, but he didn't have a choice.

A small boy, hurrying back from a hunting trip that had taken him farther from home than he was supposed to go, heard a strange, guttural grumble and saw a tall, shadowy figure loping off into the darkness. With his heart in his throat he tore out for home, stumbling over Doak's mutilated body in the road.

When he regained his senses enough to repeat his tale to the men in the saloon, they agreed with Lawson Pickens; it was time to appoint a sheriff to keep law and order in Green Willow Creek. They put it to a vote and, in a surprise move, elected Elliott Parnell to the position.

Lawson watched the men leave the saloon to recover the latest body. Elliott was a good choice. He would do the job that Lawson Pickens wanted. All Lawson had to do was convince Elliott of the need and Jake of the wisdom.

He smiled and went home to Miss Effie. Tonight he had a little something to celebrate, and he liked to do his celebrating during the first part of the week. It gave Effie and him plenty of time for sin before Sunday services.

They never missed Sunday services. It wouldn't have been proper. Though, he reasoned, with Bowker conducting the services, one never knew whether or not God listened. Sooner or later they'd get a real preacher.

Until then, sinning was so enjoyable.

He only wished that Effie weren't quite so submissive. If only she'd be aggressive once in a while.

Chapter 15

The room in which Dallas was spending her conva-
lescence obviously belonged to Jake. There was no
furniture except the bed, an armoire, and a straight
chair. The fireplace was small but efficient, and it
smoldered throughout the cold night.

Stark white walls with no adornment.

Efficient, simple, nothing frivolous. Everything
with a purpose.

Just like the man who occupied the room. The
man who had vanished since the night they'd drunk
straight whiskey and shared a good-night kiss.

Wu and Shadow took turns sitting with Dallas. It
was Wu's turn now. He was telling her stories about
building the railroad. He'd come to this country to
make his fortune, return to China, and take a wife.
But his family had died of a fever while he was
away, and there's been no reason to return to China.

"I'm so sorry, Wu. That must have been hard,
making a life in a new country that was so different
from your own."

"Yes, Miss Dallas, but Mr. Jake found me and
now he's my family."

"Found you?"

"Yes. The last winter we work on the railroad,
snows come and never stop. It cover our houses and

we not able to get to mountain where we blast. We build tunnels to go from sleeping place to work, never see sky."

"Oh, my goodness. That must have been awful."

"One day, very bad. Tunnel fall in. Many men killed. The rail bosses quit looking for workers, but not Mr. Jake. He hear about people buried and bring men to dig. Found Wu. Wu's life belong to Mr. Jake now."

"That makes you sound like a slave, Wu."

"No, not slave!" he said angrily, "Family. Like you, Miss Dallas. Mr. Jake save you, your life belong to him now."

Dallas started to argue that her life belonged to her and her alone, then lapsed into silence. She could never explain the high price she'd paid for that freedom and how precious it was to her.

For days, Shadow changed the dressing on Dallas's leg, dosed her with bitter liquids, and brought her food. At the end of the week, Willie even came for a visit, bringing a package of clothing from Miranda.

To Dallas's surprise, Miranda's parcel contained the Russian dressing gown with the fur trim. It now lay across the foot of the bed. She couldn't decide what the gift of the dressing gown meant. Was it simply concern or something else? She didn't feel comfortable about wearing it until Shadow handed her Miranda's note.

> *Elliott and I actually had dinner at Lucy Jarrett's boarding house. What do you think about that, Dallas? Get well soon. Don't let Jake drive you crazy.*
>
> Miranda

A smile touched Dallas's lips. She'd never had women friends before, and now she seemed to have two: Miranda and Shadow. But Jake remained conspicuously absent. And she missed him. If she was a member of his family now, he had a strange way of making her feel welcome.

Dallas had never been inactive for so long in her life. She was going crazy. The pain had diminished, and she'd grown strong enough to sit up alone; now she was determined to stand.

It was midafternoon when Dallas heard horses approaching, several horses, at the front of the house. They came to a stop, and the low murmur of conversation turned into an obvious disagreement.

Determined to know what was happening, Dallas slipped her feet to the floor and stood, putting all her weight on her good leg. She tried hopping and found that the jarring set off spasms of pain greater than those that occurred when she limped.

Gritting her teeth, she forced herself to take the few steps to the window. Cracking the shutters, she peered into the yard below. Outside the picket fence were six cowboys, mounted on horses, talking to Jake and Pete.

"The man worked for you. We thought you ought to know." The man directly in front of Jake apparently was the leader.

"Are you certain it was Doak?"

"No doubt. His face was all messed up, but it was him."

"Yeah," another man added, "in the same spot as that newspaperman who got himself killed. It was downright spooky."

From a third rancher, she heard, "I tell you, Jake, we've got to put a stop to this right now. We're all missing more cattle, and one of Fred's hands has disappeared."

"Yeah," the second rider spoke up, "it's those farmers. We all know it, Jake, and as the largest rancher in the area, it's time you took a stand with us."

The first man waved off the others who'd all started talking at once. "There's something else you don't know, Jake. The townsfolk have appointed themselves a sheriff."

"Oh? Who?" Jake was surprised. He hadn't expected action so soon. He couldn't imagine who they'd coerced into taking the job. Sheriffs in the West didn't last too long, and the pay was so low that they couldn't survive unless they had another job.

"Elliott Parnell."

That surprised Jake. The Elliott he'd known could never have handled the job as sheriff. And why would Elliott agree to take the job? Unless the ranchers were right and the farmers were responsible for the missing cattle and the deaths being attributed to the Devil of the Plains. Appointing the farmers' spokesman as sheriff would certainly go a long way toward protecting the criminals.

Jake realized logically that he should have been suspicious when Elliott turned up in cahoots with the speculator who bought land from the railroad stockholders and sold it to the immigrants. Jake suspected that the land being sold was poor growing land with little water supply. But somewhere lingered the memory of the gentle man Elliott had once been.

"I'm not certain about this," Jake said, "but I'll attend your next meeting and listen to your plans."

The men visibly relaxed and began talking among themselves. As far as they were concerned, they were a unit now, joined in a common effort. Their first order of business was to issue an ultimatum to the farmers: stop the rustling and killing, or they'd be forced to retaliate.

"No," Dallas whispered. Issuing ultimatums wouldn't bring the trouble to a stop. If Jake and Elliott could get past the animosity between them, they could defuse the situation. She didn't want the trouble to escalate. She didn't want to think about death and mutilated bodies. She'd talk to Jake again. If Jake refused to listen, she'd have a talk with Elliott, explain to him what she saw at the camp, suggest the possibility of outside rustlers. Both Jake and Elliott were reasonable men; they'd keep trouble from breaking out.

Sure, and President Lincoln stopped the War Between the States. Now two other equally determined adversaries were on a collision course and it was going to take more than Dallas's suggestions to stop it. Jamie, who had both men's ears, hadn't been successful. What Dallas had to do first was talk to Jake. Though she was in his bedroom, it was obviously that he'd been avoiding her. That had to stop. Nothing could be accomplished by dodging an issue.

If Jake wouldn't come to Dallas, she would go to him, with a little help from Shadow.

When Shadow came later in the afternoon to check on Dallas, she brought up her plan. "I want to go downstairs for dinner, Shadow, and I want you to help me do it."

"But Dallas, your leg is still swollen. You aren't ready to walk yet."

"I'm not hiking up Pike's Peak, Shadow, just going down a few steps. If you won't help me, I'll do it by myself. I need to talk to Jake."

Shadow gave Dallas a puzzled look, then relaxed her lips into a smile. "Of course I'll help. If you promise not to overtire yourself. It's only been a week since I opened the wound."

"But you admitted that it wasn't a full bite. Only

one fang penetrated. The other was more of a graze. I'll be fine."

"All right, if you insist."

Dallas sank back into her pillows. "I insist. I think I'll take a nap now and have my bath later. I'll wear my chemise instead of one of Jake's shirts."

It was late afternoon when Shadow brought the bathwater and Dallas's freshly laundered petticoat and chemise. After her bath she donned the under-garments and slipped on the velvet robe. Shadow combed her hair and tied it back with a white rib-bon.

"I can't decide whether I look like a Russian cza-rina or a dance-hall girl, Shadow. I can't imagine what Mr. Silver will think."

"Mr. Jake will see your spirit is true. White rib-bon in hair for purity of heart, yes. White is also for courage, and when Mr. Jake sees you at his dining table, you will need it."

Dallas suspected that Shadow was right.

She was sure of it when Jake, who was already seated at the table, looked up and saw Dallas being escorted by Wu and Shadow.

"What in hell are you doing, Dallas?"

"Joining my host for dinner."

"You're supposed to be in bed."

"You haven't been back to visit me."

Jake didn't rise. He didn't come to Wu and Shad-ow's assistance. He simply glowered at Dallas, dar-ing her to move, then leaned back in his chair in quiet fury when she reached the chair and sat down. Silence ensued until Wu and Shadow left the room.

"No, I've been busy," he finally said.

"You look like you haven't been getting much rest," she said, taking in the drawn look about his eyes.

"I haven't."

"Perhaps it's time you returned to your own bed."

"Are you suggesting that we share it?"

"Certainly not. I have no intention of sharing a bed with you."

"Oh? Then what would you call what we did the first night you were here?"

Dallas gasped. This wasn't going the way she'd planned.

"We shared a bed?"

"Not *a* bed, *my* bed, and you curled yourself around me like a vine attaching itself to a fence post."

"Did you, I mean did we . . ."

"No," he said dryly. "I told you once before; when we do, you'll know."

Wu came in, bringing a tray holding two bowls of steaming soup. "Chicken with rice, Mr. Jake, keep body up."

"Just what I need, Wu," Jake said with a scowl. He was already up, and Wu's soup didn't have a thing to do with it. As a matter of truth, he'd ridden poor Blackjack every night until the horse was exhausted, trying to sap his physical need for Dallas. Nothing had helped.

Now the object of that desire was seated across from him, wearing a fur-trimmed robe that made her look like an old-world courtesan. Though she was covered, his imagination supplied a most vivid mental picture of what might be hidden beneath.

Dallas didn't know what she was doing, tempting him physically with her body and mentally with her quick wit and conversation. He took a spoonful of soup. But maybe this was good, seeing her here on neutral ground. He'd needed to talk with her for days, but he just hadn't trusted himself to do it in the bedroom.

After several minutes during which she sipped

daintily from her soup spoon, she licked her lips, exposing the tongue that had explored his mouth so eagerly when he'd kissed her the night of the dance.

"Doak's been killed, Dallas."

"Doak, the man who used to work for you?"

"Yes, they found him in almost the same spot where your brother was killed."

"Did anybody see it happen?"

"No. A boy who'd been hunting came along just afterward. He claimed he saw the Devil flying away, a black shadow, with wings."

"Doak was killed by the monster?"

"He was shot and then trampled by your wild beast. I've been looking for it everywhere, but I haven't been able to find it. You did, and you don't even know this country."

"I stumbled on it by accident, Jake, but I can't believe that nobody in Green Willow has actually seen the monster. Somebody has to have some knowledge of its whereabouts."

"Maybe that's because the people who've come in contact with it are dead."

"Except Greta Bittner, and she won't let herself remember."

Wu removed the soup bowls and replaced them with plates of beefsteak and potatoes. "Missy Dallas, you rather have rice?"

"No thanks, Wu, the soup was excellent. I doubt I'll be able to eat all this. All I want now is something liquid."

Jake let out an approving chortle. "Good idea. Wu, bring the whiskey."

Wu went to the kitchen and returned carrying a teapot and cups. "No strong spirits, Mr. Jake. Wu bring hot tea, read leaves."

"Forget the tea leaves, Wu. If you want to tell the future, bring us a deck of cards with our whiskey."

"Not nice, Mr. Jake. Not nice make fun of Wu. Wu read leaves and tell. You wait."

For several minutes, Jake cut up and ate a large portion of the thick steak, then pushed his plate away and pulled out a thin black cigar. He stood and walked over to the fireplace, took a splinter of wood and lit it from the fire, then touched it to the end of his cigar.

"All right, Dallas, what really brought you down here tonight? I know you're not strong enough to do this, so you must have something up your sleeve."

"I wanted to see you."

"Well, darling, I don't think that's very smart, but have your fill."

"No, I mean . . ." It wasn't going to be easy. Jake Silver would never be easy.

"Don't misunderstand this, Jake; what I want is for you to arrange a meeting with Elliott and the farmers, to negotiate a settlement of the problems between you."

"That's not what you really want."

"It is what I want, what everyone wants," she said, ignoring his implication.

"Maverick, you sound like your brother. What makes you think I have the power to do any negotiating about anything? What makes you think I even care?"

"You care, Jake. You cover it up with indifference, but you care. And you are the power in Green Willow, Jake. You and, now, Elliott. And I think that you and Elliott can work together to settle the trouble."

"Elliott and I were a team once, Dallas, but not now, not ever again. Go back to Philadelphia, Dallas. This isn't your problem."

"Jamie's death made it my problem." She stood,

desperate to find a way to reach him, ready to beg, if necessary.

"Please, Jake. I'm asking you," she said softly.

He lifted his eyebrows in surprise, revealing for a split second the hunger in his eyes before he hooded them again. "You overestimate your charms, darling."

She moved toward him. "I don't think so, Jake. You asked me once to name my price."

Feeling suddenly weak, she leaned for support against the mantel over the fireplace.

"And have you?" he asked in a voice so tight and low that she could barely hear. "Have you settled on a price?"

"I'm ready to negotiate, but you'd better hurry. Jake, I've never fainted in my life, but I think I'm going to, now."

She felt her body turn into honey and slide untidily to the floor. The room blurred for a moment, as she felt strong arms clasp her and lift her up, pulling her up against a chest that was as hard as stone. The whirling stopped.

"What in hell do you think you're doing, Dallas? You're no saloon girl selling her favors to a man."

Jake's slate-gray eyes caught the light of the fire and shimmered, like frost on granite. Beneath the anger there was a hint of fear.

"Would you buy them, Jake?" Her throat tightened as she felt the wild flutter-beat of her breathing. If Jake weren't holding her, she'd surely be disintegrating into a million pieces, like some comet hurtling through the heavens. Hot. Cold. Weak. Strong. All those feelings chased each other in waves of changing emotions.

"I'd buy them," he growled. "You damn well know I would."

She slipped her hand into the open collar of his

shirt and felt the pounding of his heart, like a train roaring down the mountain, heading for the dark unknown.

"Why have you stayed away from my room, Jake?"

"I haven't. I've watched you for hours as you slept."

That admission surprised her. "But not while I was awake. Why?"

"Because I wouldn't be able to keep myself from—"

She raised her face. "From what?"

Her cheeks were flushed a delicate pink. Her dark eyes were even darker, her pupils wide now in the shadows, giving her a look of wonder. She was panting slightly, her lips parted so that he could see perfectly shaped white teeth and the tongue that had driven him to a state of madness.

The clasp at the neck of her velvet robe had come unfastened and allowed one side to fall away, exposing the delicate lawn of her chemise. The shape of her breast was clearly outlined, as was the button nipple that peaked saucily beneath the fabric.

Jake felt as if he were going to explode. His body was straining to free itself, and he knew it would take little to erode the last trace of reason.

Then she smiled and moved her hand from his chest up to his neck, drawing his face down to her own.

"Dallas," he whispered, then again, "Dallas . . ." He was drowning in the heated frenzy of her eyes. The quick little pants of her breath were like bellows stoking coals that were already molten, into flames.

Dallas was shaking. Every segment of her body felt as if it were a writhing mass of heat, of unformed but demanding need. She wanted—she couldn't quite put words to what she wanted. There was nothing but feeling and yearning.

"Please, Jake. Please . . ."

"Please what?"

"Kiss me, Jake. Just one simple kiss." She was past caring what was proper and what was not. Never in her life had she held back when she wanted something, and she wanted Jake Silver.

"Nothing about you is simple, Dallas. I know it, and still I can't refuse."

And then he put his mouth on hers and kissed her, and all the pent-up heat and shimmering waves of pleasure came together beneath their lips in sweet agony. Jake plundered and tasted, claimed and released, and through it all, Dallas felt as if she were being burned alive. The hand supporting her hips found its way beneath the voluminous expanse of fabric, caressing her bottom as intimately as he had that first day.

The other hand, around her back and beneath her arm, found the side of her breast and fanned the fires that raged beneath her skin, building to a sweet yearning that forced her to accept the truth. Any bargaining she was doing was for herself, not for Jamie nor to settle any dispute. This was between her and Jake, between the man who'd saved her life and was now destroying it with fiery heat.

She raised her hands to push him away, to give herself a moment of respite while she gathered her scattered senses. Instead, her hands found the back of his neck and drew his lips back to hers, opening her mouth, taking the tongue inside. And he was using his mouth to invade her, searching, searing in such a powerful way that she felt herself melt against him. She wanted more. She wanted it never to stop.

Then suddenly they were sitting in Jake's chair

and she felt the pulsating insistence of his maleness against her body. She let out a gasp of surprise that Jake immediately caught with his mouth as he pressed her head back against his arm so that he could reach her neck.

Moments later the ties to her chemise were open and those lips were playing across her breasts in such maddening slowness that Dallas felt herself lifting her body to reach his mouth.

Yes. This was what she wanted, what she'd been waiting for. Forward? Aggressive? She'd always been that, but it had been on someone else's behalf. Tonight was for her. She'd be whatever it took to have this man. Tomorrow she'd face the consequences. But tonight she'd know what it meant to be a woman.

"Oh, Jake," she whispered. "Oh, Jake. Jake. Jake, please." Over and over, she repeated his name, as if she were caught in some spell that she knew would ultimately destroy her but from which she couldn't get free.

"What are you asking, darling?"

"I want . . . I want . . ."

"So do I," he said. He caught her bottom and pressed her against him, over and over, registering her tremors of response. Sometime during their kisses his shirt had been tugged from his trousers and lay open, allowing her breasts to press against his bare chest. In another moment he'd be inside her, making love to her as he'd never loved a woman, not even Sarah.

Sarah! That thought and Wu's voice stopped him.

"Mr. Jake!"

Wu stood in the doorway, his eyes wide in shock. Behind him Shadow peered over his shoulder, her own expression less readable yet more intense.

"Go away, Wu!" Dallas said weakly. "I'm all right."

"Yes," Jake said, "she . . . she almost fainted. I'll take her back to bed."

Shadow stepped into the room. "Shall I assist?"

"No," Dallas snapped, burrowing closer to Jake to conceal the extent of her nudity. "I'll be fine. Thank you."

Lifting her once again in his arms, Jake left the room and made his way up the stairs, eternally grateful for the voluminous skirts that had, only moments ago, been a deterrent.

Downstairs, Wu examined the tea leaves left in the bottom of Dallas's cup.

"It was meant to be, Shadow."

"I didn't have to look in a cup to know that, Wu. What's wrong with them being together?"

"I don't know. But I see trouble coming and I not know how to stop it."

Shadow smiled. This terribly kind, gentle man, who gave so much to those he cared about, had no idea how much he'd come to mean to her. When Jake teased Wu about his woman, Wu blushed and turned away. But more and more often she'd felt his eyes watching her when he thought she wasn't aware. And she'd responded. As an Indian she'd had to learn about so many kinds of people, Wu was simply another.

Life among her people had been more simple. Had one of the men of her tribe desired her, he would have made it known and she would have responded according to her desire. But Wu was too proper, too bound by his own customs. Ever since the night of the dance, they'd practiced the dance steps they'd learned after supper. Shadow had shared some of her tribal traditions and the dances that portrayed their history.

Wu had absorbed this new culture and told her about his homeland, about his wise father who'd lived to a very old age, about his sister who married a Mandarin merchant and moved to the city, and finally about the woman he'd planned to marry and who'd died of a fever brought to his land by the very same men who'd kidnapped Wu and forced him into a Chinese labor camp.

Everything Shadow learned about Wu made her respect him more. She knew that Wu would never believe she found him attractive. His proud nature and appearance gave him a mysterious look that fascinated her. He was like one of the spirit gods. Taller than most Chinese, he was lean and strong, and his long dark hair was intriguing. For he too, like the men of her tribe, braided his hair into a pigtail that was a measure of his manhood.

That braid only increased her interest.

When she came to the Double J, she'd left her people and taken on a new life. As a woman she longed to know a man, and she'd learned to care for Wu. She knew that if more were to happen, she would have to initiate it, for to Wu she was as unapproachable as Jake Silver had been until he met Dallas Banning. Dallas who knew what she wanted and went after it.

Listening to the silence overhead, Shadow came to a decision. "Come with me, Wu. Sometimes the trouble between a man and a woman is better resolved without talk."

Wu looked at Shadow in surprise. "But what about Mr. Jake?"

Shadow blew out the lamp and took Wu's hand. "Wu, let Jake worry about his own woman. Tonight, you deal with yours."

Chapter 16

Upstairs, Jake let out a deep breath and held Dallas for another moment while he gathered his composure. What in hell was he doing sweeping her up in his arms and taking her to his room? He ought to slam her down in that bed and get out before he did something foolish. He even took a step toward the bed. Then she began to shake and stopped him from leaving.

This situation had never happened before. It was obvious that she was in distress, crying, he'd guess. He'd frightened her, allowing her to see the real man. He couldn't blame her, but he'd thought she was different. He didn't even have a handkerchief.

The shaking turned into sobs. Sobs? No the woman wasn't crying. She was laughing. She was hysterical. Jake put her down and pushed her away so that he could see her face.

"What in hell?"

"Oh, Jake. Your expression was priceless. I'll admit this is all new to me, but surely you've been caught in flagrante delicto before?"

She moved even farther away, crossing her arms across her chest, gasping for breath as she laughed.

Jake swore. "You find all this amusing? You throw yourself at me, welcome my attentions knowing that the servants are in the room next door, and you find my response amusing?"

"I threw myself at you? Yes I did. But Jake, look at yourself and tell me what's reaching for who— uh, whom?"

Jake swore again and turned his back. Hell, he'd wanted a woman before, but never so bad that her laughter couldn't shrivel that desire up and kill it. He put his hand on himself, trying to adjust his trousers so that his problem would be less obvious. But Dallas wasn't having any of that. As if his need for her had freed her inhibitions, she moved around in front of him.

"This is all new to me, Jake. But you'll have to explain. If I do this to you, why hide it? You've seen me, or a good part of me. My nipples hurt and my body feels as if it's on fire. You did that with your kisses, and you've seen the results. I think it's only fair that I be allowed the same rights." She reached out and slid her hand inside his trousers, gathering his hardness into her hand.

"What are you doing?" he asked, unable to hide the shock in his voice.

"Am I not supposed to talk about this? I'm sorry if I embarrass you, but I've never been with a man. My brothers never talked about it, and unfortunately I don't have any lady friends willing to share their bedroom adventures with me. I really want to understand."

The maverick was charging into quicksand and dragging him right along with her. "I can promise you that all this is new to me as well," Jake said, trying to regain control of the situation.

He tried to move away from hands that were playing a maddening game with his lower body. Tried and found that he'd moved forward instead.

"I've seen Jamie, hundreds of times as a baby, but never like this."

"Have you never been on a farm?" He was growling.

"No. And I never had a pet. I take it this is normal for the male of all species." She ran her fingers around the length of his shaft, then ventured off into the body hair beside. "I didn't know the hair would be so thick and soft. It's like your mustache."

"Don't do that, Dallas. I'm very near losing control. You don't know what that means. Please."

The "please" got through to her. She let him go, stood back and studied him carefully. "You're right. I don't know what that means. I'm twenty-five years old, Jake. A single, untouched maiden. I never thought to have a lover; there were more important goals in my life. I'm not particularly pretty. I'm far too outspoken. Truth is, I never expected a man to want me. Your desire comes as a great surprise to me. And I find that I rather like it."

If he'd been stunned by her wild response to his kisses, he was speechless now. This was no ordinary conversation between a man and a woman, not even a married man and woman. She was frank, honest, outrageous, and from the looks of her nipples, still as aroused as he.

"What are you saying, Dallas?"

"I'm saying that I know what I'm asking. I'm awake now and I don't want you to stop."

"I thought you came downstairs to negotiate."

"I did. I thought that you could bring an end to the trouble that's about to explode. I still do."

"Are you still negotiating?"

"I think I am. But there's a difference I hadn't counted on. Before, I was negotiating for Jamie. This is for me."

She let her velvet robe and her petticoat and chemise fall to the floor. She was standing before the fire, her body outlined in orange flames that seemed to intensify with every breath she took. She held out her arms.

All he could think about as he looked into her eyes was that he wanted to accept her challenge. All the cold, lonely years disappeared as she waited. He wanted to tell her that she was making a mistake, that she deserved better, that he'd hurt her. But even more, he wanted to bury himself inside her and let her warmth envelop him.

Slowly he unfastened the last button of his shirt and the buttons of his trousers, and, stepping out of all his clothes at once, went straight into her arms.

If Dallas had expected ruthlessness, she was surprised. From the moment Jake lifted her in his arms and carried her to his bed, he became gentle and tender, touching her with his lips, his hands, even his toes and the sides of his feet; he left his mark on every inch of her.

"You are so beautiful, my little maverick. So strong, yet so soft, so giving."

She felt beauty blossom inside her as Jake painted her skin with sunshine, moonlight, and fire. Had anyone else spouted such foolish words she wouldn't have believed them, but Jake was wickedly honest, and she found herself returning his movements and his words.

"Jake, is this what happens between a man and a woman?"

"Not always," he murmured, kissing his way across her breasts, teasing them with his tongue, taking them inside his hot mouth as if he were a suckling babe. He was constantly moving, sliding his strong body back and forth, seeking the moist place between her legs and driving her mad with that part of him impatient to find the source of her longing.

Her hands caught his head, threading her fingertips through his hair, holding him close as she bucked and wiggled beneath him. His lips left her stomach and traveled lower, his mustache brushing her skin with strokes of fire.

Dallas trembled. She was hot. She was cold. She was on the verge of flying apart and disappearing into the fire. She pulled her legs together, straining every muscle in her body to hold back the tide that threatened to erupt.

Now he was pressing himself down, between her legs, using his male part as a wedge, and she felt the tightly wound muscles and nerves in his back and arms tremble even more than she was shaking.

"Please, maverick," he was saying. "Open up to me. Let me inside you. I want you! I need you! I . . ."

She kissed him, and opened her legs, arching herself up to meet him, and all the gentleness was gone. In a storm of fire he plunged inside her, causing pain, causing a roiling sensation of nerve endings that seemed to surround him and hold him inside her in a ball of fire. When he attempted to pull back she moved with him, clasping him even tighter.

He groaned.

She swallowed his moans and knew for that moment, just before the convulsion began, that this was meant to be. Every outrageous thing she'd done in her life had been preparing her for this night, for loving Jake Silver.

Then it happened. He started to jerk, and the tide she'd been so desperately holding let go, drowning her in such powerful tremors that she thought the bed had shifted.

Long moments later, when her body stopped moving and her mind reassembled itself in some kind of weak semblance of order, she knew that she'd experienced something that was very rare.

She wanted to speak, but she didn't know what to say. She wanted to put her arms around him, to feel his skin, to know that she was not alone in this incredible aftermath of sensation. The moonlight flowed through the window. The coals from the fire still cast a glow. Moonlight met firelight and converged on Jake Silver's back.

They were still joined. She could feel him big and tight. As if he knew what she was thinking, there was a light movement and he started to pull out, started, and stopped. He lifted himself slightly and looked down at her.

"Did I hurt you?"

"No, did I hurt it—you?"

He laughed softly as he felt himself begin to push back inside. Even swimming in his body fluid she was still tight, holding on to him with every muscle. He had the odd thought that she was kissing him inside, doing wonderful things to his body that she shouldn't do.

"Ah, yes, you hurt so good. It's been so long, maverick, I couldn't hold back. It's always hard the first time."

"It doesn't get hard the second?"

He laughed. "It's already hard again, or maybe it still is. I can't be sure. But I think we ought to stop now, Dallas."

"I don't, Jake. I never want to stop."

Once more Jake found himself giving in. Instead of leading, he was being led. Instead of pulling away, he was plunging inside her body, reveling in her wild abandon, loving every moment of her pleasure.

Morning found them entangled in the bedclothes,

in each other's arms. Dallas was his. He was the first man to love her, and there would never be another. Jake didn't vocalize his thoughts, they were just there, in his mind, in his heart.

He would have seen the danger if he'd been thinking clearly, but loving Dallas had pushed all rational thought from his head, and all restraint from his body. He'd never been so tired nor felt so good.

He'd made love to her over and over again, concerned that she'd be sore, tender, yet unable to stop himself. And she'd never held back. In one night they'd touched, kissed, loved every part of each other, become lost in a sea of sensation that blotted out every other thing in the world. At sunup he gave her one last kiss and let himself slip away into the first real sleep he'd had in months.

His body sighed in contentment. The shell around his emotions had been pierced, and the chamber around his heart had, just for one night, been filled with loving Dallas.

As dawn broke across the mountaintops, Dallas looked down at the man whose head was planted against her breast. She'd never expected anything like they'd shared. The night was precious, and somehow she knew that the day would spoil what the night had nurtured.

She touched Jake's hair and sighed.

It was so soft, so different from the man. Why did it have to be Jake Silver who had touched her life with such wonder? He might give her a night, maybe more, but never a lifetime. What would happen now?

Answers remained elusive. She didn't know. Maybe she wasn't supposed to understand. Shadow had said that Jake saved her life, therefore she belonged to him.

She knew that, but she wasn't sure Jake would.

Maybe it would be better if she let him figure that out for himself.

Dallas slid from the bed and dressed quickly in the calico dress Miranda had sent. Lovingly she folded the Russian dressing gown to be returned to Miranda.

With a sigh she let herself out of the room and walked gingerly down the stairs. A puzzled Pete hitched up the carriage, and before the town was fully awake, Dallas was back in Green Willow Creek. But she'd left something behind, something that would never be hers again, unless Jake brought it back.

She'd left her heart.

Pete helped Dallas from the carriage and into her newspaper office. As if he'd known she was coming, Willie was waiting with the fire burning and water ready for tea. Miranda was the first of a steady stream of people who came to call. She didn't come alone.

"Hello, Dallas." Miranda's escort was Elliott, who cast a worried look at Dallas, then, satisfied that she was in fact recovering from her ordeal, turned his frown into a smile. "People were worried to death about you—until they heard Jake was looking after you."

"Please, come in, both of you." Dallas, seated in a padded chair by the stove, smiled and waved them in. "Willie, get Miranda and Elliott a cup of tea."

"Are you sure you ought to be out of bed?" Miranda asked. "Maybe you shouldn't be alone. I'll be glad to offer you a room at my place."

"I'm fine, both of you, really I am. Shadow and Dr. Horn made sure of that."

"Why on earth did you ride out alone?" Elliott finally spoke up.

"Someone had to get to the bottom of this problem," she said. "Do sit down and tell me what has happened while I was gone. I feel as if I have been away for months instead of days."

Dallas couldn't help but notice that Miranda and Elliott were casting secret looks at each other as they made every effort not to sit too close or appear more than just friendly to each other. There had been a time when Dallas wouldn't have recognized the signs of their interest, but no longer.

They were involved with each other, more than involved, if Dallas was any judge. But they were worried about her reaction to this development. Why? Then it hit her. Dallas had been Elliott's partner for the dance, and Miranda wasn't certain that Dallas wasn't still interested in him. In less than a week everything had changed. Dallas concealed a secret smile. Only a short time ago it was she who'd been worried about Miranda's interest in Jake.

As if Miranda sensed Dallas's observation and didn't quite know what to say, the blond beauty hurried to assist Willie in pouring the tea. Even her demeanor had changed. Wearing a simple day dress of dark green, Miranda had covered her golden hair with a matching green bonnet adorned with a saucy yellow flower. She might have been any well-dressed young matron out for a social call. It appeared that her red dress had been retired, if the protective look in Elliott's eyes was any indication of his feelings in the matter.

Dallas studied the tea tray and considered how best to relieve their concerns. "Elliott, would you like—?" She was about to say cream, but a quick glance told her that the hot drink had already been prepared to his liking. Miranda looked up, ready to hand it to him, and caught sight of the smile on Dallas's pursed lips.

"Oh, Elliott has . . . has joined me for tea several times while you've been away. I hope you don't mind."

"Mind? Why ever should I mind? I'm just pleased it's tea you're drinking. I fear that many more days as an invalid under Jake's—" she stopped, thought a minute and said, "—private care and instead of tea, I'd either be howling at the moon or be drinking whiskey—straight."

"Under Jake's private care? I see," Miranda said. The two visitors looked at each other, and relaxed.

"I don't," Dallas said, letting out a long, pent-up breath. "And that's why I came home—to think."

Miranda looked puzzled. "About drinking whiskey?"

"No," Dallas answered, "about Jake Silver."

Elliott stood and came to stand beside Dallas. "Jake is a man who rarely commits himself, Dallas, but once he does, he doesn't give up, unless you let him down. But I guess you already know that, don't you?"

"I'm learning about Jake's determination, all right. But what I don't understand is his attitude about this range war."

"That's simple, Dallas," Elliott observed. "A man like Jake doesn't like change. He doesn't relinquish control easily. This is his land and he'll fight to keep it, but he'll do it alone."

"Dallas, is everything all right?" Miranda asked.

"Of course; why would you think otherwise?"

Miranda frowned. "I find it hard to believe that Jake let you go. It isn't like him to let Pete drive you."

"He doesn't know I'm gone. He probably does now, but I left while he was—still asleep."

Elliott frowned. "But Jake is always up before the sun, unless he's—"

Miranda and Elliott glanced at each other. Miranda nodded. "I think we'd better go, Elliott. My guess is that Jake is probably on his way and I don't think we want to be here when he arrives."

Miranda drained her cup and came to her feet. "I'll have your meals sent down," she promised. "And Willie will be here day and night, if you need him."

Dallas shook her head. "Nonsense, I'm fine. Maybe you'd better take Willie with you. I'd like to be alone for a while." Dallas didn't believe that Jake would come, but she didn't want Willie caught up in the crossfire if he did.

"Is there anything I can do for you?" Elliott asked.

"No, you'd better go. As the newly elected sheriff you might have to subdue Jake if he's too angry with me, and I don't know how easy that job will be."

"I wasn't exactly elected. It was Dr. Horn's idea to appoint me. Do you really want me to arrest Jake?"

Dallas laughed. That was the last thing she wanted to be responsible for. Having Elliott arrest Jake would be like a meeting between David and Goliath, and she wasn't sure how good Elliott was with a sling.

"No, at least not yet. But I would like to know about Doak, the cowboy who was killed. Jake said his body was found in the same place where Jamie was murdered."

"Yes," Elliott agreed, "that's true. He'd been shot and mauled, just like the others."

"And nobody saw the monster?"

"Only a terrified boy who is convinced that the Devil sprouted wings and flew away."

"Do you think you can find the Devil, Elliott?" Dallas leaned her head against the back of her chair.

"Haven't found him so far. I'm beginning to wonder if the boy isn't right. Maybe he has wings."

Miranda stood up, took their cups and handed them to Willie, who was hovering like a wet nurse behind Dallas. Before she left, she whispered in Dallas's ear.

"Did you wear the robe?"

Dallas smiled. "I did. Thank you. Why didn't you send a nightdress?"

"I thought you might not need one."

"I didn't."

Miranda and Elliott left, with Willie following behind. Dallas closed her eyes and waited.

It was Dr. Horn who came by next, reminding Dallas how lucky she was to have survived a rattlesnake bite and confirming that the most recent crime was a duplicate of Jamie's murder.

"What kind of gun was used?"

The doctor frowned. "I never saw a woman so curious about death and killing."

"I told you, I'm a reporter."

"It was the same kind of gun that killed your brother."

When he found out why she'd gone out alone, he reprimanded her, offering to accompany her if she got any more fool ideas. He cautioned her to rest and promised to keep her informed about any other information that might pertain to Jamie's death. He left shaking his head in wonder that she actually wanted to view the next body, if there was one.

Lawson Pickens was next. "Folks are thinking twice about being away from home after dark. I hope you'll refrain from riding out alone."

But it was Lucy Jarrett who seemed to see the situation most clearly. She brought a dried apple cobbler because "It's Jake's favorite," and confided that she was "delighted that Jake is finally taking interest in a girl."

"But Jake isn't interested in me," Dallas protested. "He was just kind enough to look after me. I mean Shadow, Wu's woman, did the medical work. Jake just gave me his bed."

Dallas knew she was blushing. She couldn't seem to stop the flush of heat from sweeping across her face. "I mean he had another bed. There were two," she stammered, only making everything worse.

Lucy patted her hand and smiled. "Don't fret, Dallas, there's nothing wrong with you staying out at Jake's place. I imagine half the single women in town would offer their arm to a snake if it would get them that kind of attention. Don't squander the opportunity, girl. Go after him."

"But I wouldn't know how. I mean Jake isn't interested in me, any more than any other woman."

"Oh no? Then why is he skulking around outside the back of your building?"

"Outside this building?"

"Yep. Has been since before Lawson Pickens happened by. Seems he's waiting until the rush of well-wishers is over. Never knew him to stand back before." In a loud voice she called out, "Guess I'll be going now, Jake."

"Good," Jake bellowed as he pushed open the door with a clatter. "Dallas, what the hell do you think you're doing?"

Lucy Jarrett picked up her basket and cape. "About to share a dried apple pie with you, if you don't scare her to death, Jake." Lucy pulled the blinds, pausing to offer an explanation to the man in the doorway. "Not enough pie to go around,

Jake. Looks like the key's in the door. You'd better lock it behind me."

Dallas watched as Jake pulled the door firmly closed and heard the lock click into place, then he turned to face Dallas. She hadn't known how she'd meet the anger she knew would come. Coolly? With chagrin?

The answer was neither. She took one look at Jake and knew that he was covering his confusion with consternation, his concern with bluster, and his need to see her with pure fury.

"I didn't know whether or not you'd come," she said.

"You realize that you almost got Pete fired."

"Why would you do such a rotten thing?"

His eyes were simmering, his mustache vibrating as he ground his teeth together. "I didn't. But I came damned close. Why'd you leave?"

"You needed your bed back. And I thought I'd give you time to think about what happened."

"I damned sure didn't need to find it empty."

"Oh? What's that supposed to mean? What did last night mean to you, Jake?"

"How the hell do I know? Do we have to talk about it?"

"I do. I need to know where I'm going and why."

"You knew where you were going last night when you took my pants off."

"No, you're wrong. I didn't. At least I didn't know how it would be. I don't think I can deal with that for long and walk away, Jake. It's too powerful."

"Then don't walk away."

"Oh? And what do you think your friends and neighbors would say about me moving in? Even Wyoming is too civilized to allow two people to openly live in sin."

"Too damned civilized."

He hadn't moved. He was still standing just inside the doorway.

"Come and sit down, Jake. I'll serve you some pie."

"Where's Willie?"

"I sent him to Miranda's. He won't be back until tomorrow."

"Why would you do that? Why, Dallas?" Jake slowed his speech and allowed himself to fill his eyes with her. But it wasn't his eyes that ached, it was his chest—his heart. He hadn't wanted to find her, to care for her, to need her. But when he'd opened his eyes and found her gone, he'd felt as if he'd been robbed.

Finding his horse already saddled in the barn had told him that Pete had expected him to follow. They'd crossed paths just outside of Green Willow, with Pete lifting his hand in salute as Jake galloped by.

Jake hadn't planned what he would do, except tell Dallas what he thought of her taking off without his knowing. He'd ridden behind the building, intending to slip in without being seen. But there were visitors, one after the other. Just when he thought it was his turn, another person appeared.

Jake became grumpier by the moment, and hungrier and harder. That seemed to be a permanent state for him now. He'd had too little sleep and too much whiskey for days. He didn't even know what he was doing here. If Dallas had wanted to stay on at the Double J he'd have been uncomfortable, but he had been the one to bring her to his home. But they'd made love and she'd left and that bothered him in a way he hadn't expected.

While he waited, he'd watched half of Green Willow Creek come and go. Dr. Horn left about midafternoon and Jake made up his mind to go in. At that moment he looked up, saw Lucy Jarrett, and ducked back behind the building once more. "Damned busybodies!"

Finally, when it looked as if Lucy was going to spend the day, Jake gave up and rounded the building. He'd just tell her that he had business to discuss with Dallas. He'd make it clear to Dallas that she'd done a foolish thing driving back from his ranch without him, considering what had been happening. When he'd heard Lucy's invitation and realizing that she'd seen him, his frustration erupted. He shoved the door open.

He had the odd sense that all this had happened before. He'd come into town with a load of wood and a basket of food. This time the food was in his saddlebags, and the fire was already burning brightly in the woodstove.

The last time he'd come she'd been grateful. This time she was looking at him with a half-smile on her lips and mischief in her eyes.

"What are you smiling at?" His voice was little more than a low growl.

"You, Jake Silver. Why are you frowning?"

"I . . . I told Willie not to leave you alone. I'll skin him alive."

"Would you like me to send for him? He could join us for tea."

"No! And I don't want any tea. Wu sent you some food."

"Oh? Where is it?"

"On Blackjack, outside, in back, in the saddlebags where Shadow put it."

"Would you like to bring it in?"

"Not on your life. If I open that door the undertaker and Mrs. Pickens will be there. They must be the only ones who haven't come to call. Why don't you have a back door, anyway?"

"Why, Jake! I think you're jealous."

"I am not jealous. I'm worried. When I take someone into my care, I expect them to cooperate with my efforts to keep them safe. I didn't tell you that you could leave."

"And I didn't ask."

"Of course not; Dallas Banning doesn't ask. She's a rebel. She simply acts. No matter what the consequences."

"Oh, Jake, darling. You've kept me safe from the first. And you've fought every moment of it. I simply gave you a chance to take back control of your ranch and—your life."

"Like hell. You stopped any chance of that when you took off like some thief in the night."

"It was broad daylight, and I didn't steal anything."

"You didn't have to," he whispered. "Somewhere between the whiskey drinking and taking your virginity, I think I gave it to you."

"Gave me what, Jake?"

But he couldn't tell her, not yet, the feeling was too tenuous, too new, too uncertain. "A damn fine roll in the hay, maverick, and I don't think I'm finished with you yet."

Dallas stood up and smiled. "Then do you think you could shut up and kiss me?"

He could, and did.

When Mr. Lewis, the store owner, came by later, he took one look at the drawn curtains and decided to call another time. Miss Banning was probably worn out and resting.

Chapter 17

In the canyon, beyond Bitter Butte, the Devil of the Plains was munching on dried range grass and grumbling heavily.

"Hurry up, you mangy critter. We aren't done yet," Rejo said. "There's a sod house that has to come down, and a few Germans who haven't yet learned that their place isn't here. And maybe, a reward for Rejo, if we do a good job. A big reward."

The moon rose, bouncing like a butter-colored ball from behind the mountain. The light it cast fell on the railroad town of Green Willow Creek, where Jake and Dallas lay on a simple mattress in the newspaper office as if it were a royal bed. They lay in the darkness talking, each being careful not to speak words that gave promise to tomorrow.

The now was all either would admit to, all either would believe in; it was more than either of them ever dreamed of finding.

In another bed, just down the street, the satin hangings of Miranda's Victorian bedroom made a picture-book setting for a golden-haired woman who was learning that belonging had come easier than she'd ever thought possible. It came with loving a man who didn't care about a person's past,

only about the future that both were learning to believe in.

On the prairie a torch was hurled onto the oily
sod roof of one of the farmers. The sod caught fire
with a roar. The family barely got out before the
walls were engulfed. The next victim of the night
was a rancher whose smokehouse went up in
flames.

Only the coyotes heard the furious roar of the
Devil of the Plains as it belched forth its displeasure
and loped across the plains with its loathsome
keeper.

The rancher watched the last of his hams turned
into charcoal and resolved to join in the fight
against the farmers, no matter what Jake Silver
thought. The farmer and his wife made it back to
the settlement house, where they decided to hand
the deed to their property over to Lawson Pickens
and go back East.

Dallas and Jake shared the apple pie at midnight.
It was still dark when he left, the issue of where
their relationship would lead postponed for another
time.

For nearly a week, Jake combed the valley looking for the monster during the day and came back
to Dallas at night. He always slipped away before
daylight, leaving Dallas more confused about her future and more in love than she'd ever thought possible.

Being with Jake in her loft at night was like a fan-
tasy that only disappeared in the light of day. She
didn't know how many of the townspeople had seen
Jake, but she caught the secret smiles of the men
and the tucked frowns of their wives. Dallas felt
pleasantly tired, though worried. Loving Jake was
too easy and too necessary. She'd never understood

how a woman could lose herself in a man until now. It would be easy to forget about Jamie's murder and the newspaper.

Easy, when she was with Jake.

Impossible when she was out of his arms.

Somehow the situation had to be settled. The body and the intellect were powerful enemies, both claiming her focus, both declaring war on her peace of mind.

When the news arrived about another immigrant's house burning, Elliott called a meeting of the city officials who had appointed him to the job as sheriff. He wanted a firm show of support for him to do whatever was necessary to put a stop to the lawlessness. The town meeting was set for the following night at Miranda's place. If all went well there, he'd schedule separate meetings with the ranchers and farmers, then bring them all together.

Dallas put out a special edition of the *Gazette*. The headline read: *Immigrants Homeless as Sod House Is Torched*. A second line, smaller, but still set off in the heading, proclaimed *Vicious Attacks on Citizens Escalate*.

This time there was no holding back. Dallas's news articles were barely more than editorials recounting all the deaths attributed to the Devil of the Plains and discounting the monster theory as a malicious prank by some person or persons unknown to deliberately accelerate the friction between the farmers and the ranchers. But she stopped short of admitting that she'd seen the monster, for in reality, she'd never gotten a good look at the creature.

This issue of the *Gazette* was printed on both sides of the paper. On the back Dallas added an article about the capture of Nez Percé Indian Chief Joseph, who was charged with a desperation attack on the whites in Idaho. She reprinted an article from her father's paper that protested cruelty to animals, particularly livestock being shipped to market by rail. She wondered what the people of Green Willow Creek would do with the Devil of the Plains.

Willie said that many of the farmers had plowed their land and already some of the crops were sprouting in the rows. But they were worried about cattle overrunning the fields and the increased attacks by the Devil of the Plains. The ranchers were worried too, for the range grass was greening and only now were they learning how many of their cattle had not survived the winter.

The morning of the merchants' meeting with Elliott, trouble struck again. A number of cattle were found slaughtered and left to rot on the plains. Once more the soft ground was heavily imprinted by the mystery hoofprints. And worse, a rancher had been killed.

This time there was no holding back the anger of the cattlemen. During the afternoon, one of the smaller ranchers appeared in Dallas's newspaper office.

"Morning, ma'am," he said. "Could you print up fifty copies of this notice for us? And I want it run in your paper, too."

"Certainly. May I see it?"

He handed Dallas a sheet of tablet paper, such as might be used for making lists.

Dallas took the paper, read it, and felt her heart twist.

ATTENTION RANCHERS AND OTHER
INTERESTED PARTIES!
There will be a general meeting on Friday night next, at the schoolhouse. The subject will be how to get rid of the Germans. 7 o'clock. Come.
                    Signed
                    The Vigilance Committee

"You aren't serious about this, are you?"

"Dead serious, ma'am."

"But don't you see? This will lead to bloodshed."

"Blood's already been shed, Miss Banning. The man who was killed had a wife."

"You mean like the German who was killed or the families who have been burned out? And of course there's Adolph Schmahl, who still can't walk on his leg. Not to mention the crops that have been destroyed. What about the sheriff's meeting? Why don't you give him a chance?"

The man did have the decency to lower his gaze. "I can't be concerned about them, Miss Banning. This is a rough life out here, and I have to think about my wife and family. I could be next. And we can't forget, the sheriff is one of them. Will you print my notice?"

"Does Jake Silver know about this?"

"I reckon he does. He's a rancher. Only difference, he don't have a family. But he has cattle and he's lost as many as the rest of us."

"I'm sorry," Dallas said. "I can't print these flyers. That would be taking responsibility for the meeting. But I will print your notice in the newspaper. As a newspaper editor, I have no choice."

"Thank you, ma'am. When will the newspaper be out?"

"It won't be out until Monday, and I'll tell you now that along with the advertisement I intend to run a strong editorial protesting such action."

For a moment the rancher was taken aback. "Not until Monday? Five days?"

"That's right. I've used up my ink and I'm waiting for more," she lied.

"Never mind. The ranchers's meeting *will* be Friday. I'll ride to every ranch and tell them myself.

Too bad you're on the side of those foreigners, just like your brother."

The man's words, "just like your brother," echoed through her mind. She had to find a way to get to the bottom of the attacks on the Germans. She knew that Jake couldn't be involved. And it seemed unlikely that the ranchers could do this kind of thing without his getting wind of it. The first thing she'd do was attend Elliott's meeting this evening with the city officials and merchants. She was one of the town businesspeople. She was entitled to attend. Then she'd cover the ranchers' meeting—for the paper.

Apparently she was the only one who felt she should be there, for a stunned silence fell over the merchants that night when she stepped into Miranda's saloon.

"Miss Banning," Lawson Pickens said, hurrying to her side. "Is there something wrong?"

"Of course, else why have this meeting? Please, don't let me stop you. I'll just sit here with Mr. Bowker." She sat down beside the startled undertaker and unfastened her cape.

"Well, I mean ... this is highly irregular," Mr. Pickens said. "We don't generally welcome the women."

"The territory of Wyoming has given Miss Banning the right to hold elected office, gentlemen," Elliott Parnell said, redirecting the attention of the men to the front. "You know she could run for my job."

"And win," Miranda added smugly. "Get on with it, Lawson, she has a business here, just like me."

The banker glanced helplessly around the room and nodded. "Fine, get on with it, Elliott. What is it that you want?"

Dallas allowed her gaze to wander about the room. All the major players were there, plus a few men she didn't recognize and one very lean figure sitting at a table in the corner. She didn't need light to recognize the profile. For the last two nights she'd learned every inch of it in the light, in the dark and with her eyes closed.

"Jake," she whispered, and wondered why a rancher was sitting in on this meeting. The vigilance committee wasn't meeting until Friday. Her racing pulse began to settle down, and her confidence rose. With Jake and Elliott both here, something good could be accomplished.

"Yeah, get on with it, Parnell," another man echoed. "What do you want?"

"I want to know that the businessmen in Green Willow Creek understand exactly what could happen here."

"Sure," one of the men Dallas didn't recognize said, "as sheriff you're going to run those dirt farmers out of the territory. Why else do you think we appointed you to the job?"

"Then you're going to be disappointed. I'm both a farmer and the sheriff. As sheriff I'm going to find a way to settle the disturbances. What I want from you is assurance that you'll support me in finding those who are guilty and bringing them to justice, no matter who they are."

"Alone?" The amused voice belonged to Jake.

"I hope not," Elliott answered. "My plan is to ask the businessmen to appoint a deputy and the ranchers to appoint a deputy."

"That sounds fair," Miranda agreed. "Seems to me that Mr. Pickens would be a good choice. After all, he's the one who started it."

Dallas wanted to smile. The least likely man in

the room was probably Lawson Pickens. He probably didn't know how to use a gun.

"I most certainly did not. The Union Pacific Railroad financiers are responsible. They're the ones who sold off the land to speculators. I only agreed to handle the financial interests. You can't blame this mess on me."

"Of course I can, Lawson," Miranda shot back. "I remember when they first came out here. I know who played up to those diamond-studded crooks, who tried to find a way to weasel into their pockets. Men talk. Men tell things in here."

Dallas listened to the low rumble of conversation that threatened to turn into something nasty. Having the various factions fighting among themselves wouldn't solve anything.

"Blame isn't the point, Mr. Pickens," Dallas said crisply, "solutions are! I don't think anybody wants a confrontation between the ranchers and the farmers."

The group of men might have allowed Miranda to speak out, but Dallas was still an outsider. They all turned to look at her, uniting once more in their displeasure.

"You're right, Miss Banning," Lawson Pickens said, "of course I am concerned about a confrontation, but I don't see any way to head it off. I accepted the appointment as financial agent, but I've discharged my duties, and except for collecting the payments for the land company, my position has come to an end. I'm not qualified to be a deputy. I don't even ride a horse well. I think you ought to appoint Lewis."

"My question is," Dallas went on quietly, "why would the farmers destroy their own houses and crops? I can't believe they'd murder their own."

"But these ranchers were here long before the

farmers came," the store owner, Lewis, argued. "We didn't have cattle rustled and killed then."

"That's the beauty of the story about the Devil of the Plains," Jake observed dryly. "That lets everybody off the hook."

Dallas felt the tension rise. She gave Jake a quick look and continued her argument. "Mr. Pickens, you brought those people here. And all the merchants benefit from their business. It's up to all of you to help find a way to allow them to live unmolested."

Lawson squirmed, fingering his shirt collar as if it were too tight. "I've been thinking about that, Miss Banning. I'm not entirely unfeeling. As a matter of fact, I'm prepared to find buyers for their land. Of course the price won't be as high as what they spent, but they will have funds to locate somewhere else."

Elliott took a step toward Lawson Pickens. "I suppose you'd handle the sales?"

Dallas was beginning to get a very bad feeling about the direction that the meeting was taking.

Lawson nodded at Elliott. "Of course; after all, it's the Christian thing to do."

"Christian, be damned!" Elliott said. "You're just taking advantage of them in another way. This is what you had in mind all along when you had me appointed sheriff. You want the farmers to leave. And I'm supposed to do your dirty work for you."

"Elliott, congratulations. You're getting smarter." Jake stood and ambled slowly toward the front.

Lawson Pickens looked surprised. "Jake, how can *you* say that? After all, the evidence points to their being in the wrong over this cattle rustling as well as murdering the ranch hands."

"And who's guilty of harming the farmers? The

way I see it," Elliott said, "is that all we have here is speculation. We need evidence."

"The evidence," Mr. Bowker said quietly, "is that the killer was the Devil of the Plains. What we need to do is get a search party together and find the monster. I don't know anything about being a deputy, but I'll certainly help search for the Devil."

All the men began to agree. "I say we put together a posse," one said. Another added, "Jake and some of his boys can come. How do you want to do it?" a third voice asked.

Elliott Parnell unrolled Lawson Pickens's map of the territory and the merchants crowded around.

Dallas turned to Dr. Horn.

"If we did find the monster, what would that prove?" she asked.

"Maybe nothing," the doctor answered. "Tempers are too high."

"But if it doesn't belong to either side," she argued, "we could prove that neither side is responsible for the trouble."

"I think it's too late for that," Jake said. "Let them get up a posse to look for the monster. It'll keep them busy."

Dr. Horn disagreed. "You'd better think about letting them organize, Jake. There's more trouble you don't even know about."

Dallas felt Jake's hand on her arm, as if to shield her from what she was about to hear. "What more could there be, Dr. Horn?"

"Spence, down at the telegraph office, confided in me earlier, Miss Banning. He said that our sheriff has cabled back East for some private law officers."

Dallas gasped and turned toward Elliott. "Private law officers? You mean like Pinkertons?"

"No, I mean like gunfighters."

Dallas gulped. Everybody in the East had heard

about gunfighters and range wars. Dime novels had been written about them. People in law enforcement knew that these were the toughest men in the West. Now Dallas knew she had to do something, before the ranchers meeting on Friday—five days.

"So—our sheriff is hiring his own deputies," Jake commented dryly. "Looks like Elliott has learned to play rough."

"Will you go with them, Jake?" Dallas asked.

"I don't think so. Looking for the Devil will keep them occupied while I figure out what's really going on."

"If nobody else can get to the root of all this, how do you expect to do so?" Dallas asked.

"Through logic. Most criminals are lazy and stupid. I only need one of those to lead me to the mastermind."

"Perhaps," Dr. Horn agreed, more than a little worried. "May I see you home, Miss Banning?" he asked, studying Jake's hand on Dallas's arm.

"No, I have something I need to do, but thank you anyway." Dallas turned her attention back to Elliott, who was making certain that all the men understood the plan.

Jake tightened his grip on Dallas's arm. "And what would that be, Madam newspaperwoman?"

"I need to find out what time we're going to leave in the morning."

"Damn it to hell!" Jake's voice rose above the din, quieting everyone. "You don't think you're going to join this group of idiots, do you?"

"Lower your voice, Jake," Miranda said in amusement. "People are beginning to stare."

"Let them!" Jake tightened his grip on Dallas's arm, forcing her away from the tables and out the door. Miranda walked alongside, giving the impression that Dallas's exit was of her own accord. At the sidewalk she gave Dallas a quick hug, whispering in her ear, "Looks like Jake hasn't been getting much sleep lately. He seems a little tired."

On the street, Dallas stumbled and felt Jake's arm slip around her waist. He was practically carrying her as they walked back toward the newspaper office.

"I read your editorials," he said.

"Did you approve?"

"Does it matter?"

"I think it does," she said. "I want to be fair."

"That's what your brother said."

"Was he?" she asked.

"Yes, but others weren't, and it got him killed." Jake tried the door, found it locked, and held out his hand.

Dallas handed him the key and watched as he opened the door and stepped inside, listening for a moment before allowing her to enter. Moments later the drapes were drawn and Jake was propped against the worktable, staring at Dallas.

"Do you know where the Devil of the Plains is, Jake?"

"I knew where he was, but not where he is. He's constantly being moved. But, even if I knew, I wouldn't tell you. You'd just get yourself killed."

Dallas dropped her gaze to the floor. "So you intend to see justice done single-handedly?"

"Not me, darling," he lied, "I'm no crusader. All I want is to protect what's mine. Every man for himself."

"But what about the farmers? You sent one of your men to help Adolph. You don't like what's happening to them, I know it."

"No, I don't," he admitted. "But they're Elliott's responsibility. Let him take it. I'll do what I can on my own. I don't want you to go to any more meetings. Something could turn ugly."

"You still don't understand, Jake. I make my own decisions."

"Not this time. God knows I never wanted you, but I won't allow anything to happen to you. Stay here."

He'd come to a decision during Elliott's meeting. He'd have to find the person behind the trouble, not Elliott. But the less Dallas knew, the safer she'd be.

Dallas wished that he'd pull her into his arms and say it was because he needed her to be safe, needed her in his empty bed, wanted her beside him.

But he'd never do that.

And she'd never allow him to make choices for her.

"Will you stay with me?" she asked.

"Do you want me to?"

She lowered the flame in the lamp and unbuttoned her cape. "Yes, I suppose I do."

He closed his eyes so that he wouldn't see the unvoiced questions in her eyes, and kissed her. Dallas was the one good thing in a life that had gone wrong.

They undressed each other, slowly, gently, turning sweet, cherishing kisses into deep, commanding ones. Dallas squeezed her eyes shut to hold back the tears. It felt so good to hold Jake and be held. If nothing else in her world was right, this was.

She sighed and leaned against his strong, hard body. Always when they were in each other's arms, the unsettled questions were pushed aside. Each knew that they'd have to be faced, tomorrow or next week. Greedily they took the moment and stretched it into long hours that lasted through the night.

As he'd done for over a week, Blackjack found his

way back to the Double J carrying Jake, who dozed with his eyes wide open.

As Jake flung himself across his bed he cursed his weakness. He knew that he'd have to let her go. But he couldn't, not yet.

Chapter 18

While the posse was searching for the monster, Dallas, with Willie as her traveling companion, spent all the daylight hours riding from one small ranch to the next, pleading with the wives to influence their husbands to find a way to stop the impending confrontation. Her pleas were met with suspicious resistance.

The search party's results were no better. The ranks began to shrink as the men had to get back to their own lives. They might have lost their zeal, but Dallas didn't.

Jake didn't come back. At first she was glad, for she didn't want to have to defend her actions. But that didn't stop her from reaching out for him during the night only to encounter the cold empty space beside her. Of course she wasn't surprised when Willie told her that Jake hadn't joined Elliott's posse, either.

"Did the men expect him to?"

"Can't say, but they didn't much like it. Said they'd have a better chance of finding the Devil if Jake would come along."

Every day Elliott and his men went out again to search. Dallas and Willie rode out, too, appealing to the farmers' wives. Dallas made the same suggestion to them that she'd made to the ranchers' wives. They had even less success here.

Then something happened that escalated the situation.

She and Willie were almost finished; only two farms were left. The first belonged to Greta, the widow who was valiantly trying to plant her land alone, the second to Adolph and Lena.

Long before they reached Greta's farm, Dallas heard the gunfire. "Willie, hurry!" He flicked the reins against the backside of the horse and brought it to a fast trot. The gunfire continued.

Dallas, her heart pounding in her throat, pulled Jamie's Colt revolver from beneath the seat and checked the chambers to confirm that it was ready to fire. Then she saw the smoke.

"Hurry, Willie, something's burning."

"Miss Dallas, I don't know about this. I think we ought to go for Jake. He's not going to like you being out here with people firing at each other."

"Faster, Willie. Jake Silver doesn't tell me what to do, and as long as you work for me, neither do you."

By this time, the sod house in the distance was blazing. Dallas pointed the revolver at the sky and fired two shots, which caught the attention of three men on horseback who were riding around the house. One shouted at the others and motioned toward the approaching carriage. Then all three whirled around, surrounding the tall, gangly animal churning up a cloud of dust and dirt.

"Look, Miss Dallas," Willie yelled, "it's the Devil. But it's too dusty, I can't get a good look at him. Don't get too close!"

But it wasn't the Devil that drew Dallas's and, finally, Willie's attention. It was the sod house. By the time Dallas and Willie reached it, the dried grass squares with which it had been constructed were completely ablaze.

"Greta!" Dallas called out. "Greta, it's me, Dallas Banning. Come out!"

But there was no response. Dallas slid from the carriage, covered her head and face with her cape, and started toward the house.

"No, Miss Banning, you can't go in there!"

"But Greta's in there." She stopped at the water barrel beside the house and stuck her entire head into the water, soaking her shawl and hair. Then, as the water ran down her neck and shoulders, she took a running leap and broke down the door.

Inside there were smoke and heat and sparks of fire falling like dust motes through the air. Too much smoke and heat. Dallas couldn't see anything. After a moment she had to let out the breath she was holding. As her lungs filled with the thick, hot air, she choked. The roof and one wall began to collapse.

At the last minute she raced out into the clean air, coughing so badly that she couldn't breathe. Willie began to yell. It took her a few minutes to realize what he was saying. Dear God, she was on fire! Her dress was blazing around the hem. At that moment Willie charged into her, knocking her to the ground, where he covered her with the carriage blanket, smothering the flames.

Later, as they made their way back to town with Greta's charred body, Dallas knew that settling the range war now was beyond negotiation, beyond rational talk. Too many deaths and too much damage had taken place. Elliott and the men from town had gone searching for the monster, but the monster wasn't the enemy. The enemy was the human mastermind of this evil plan. The women she'd spoken with for the last two days were beginning to believe the Devil was some kind of ghost creature. Nothing Dallas could say would change their minds.

As Dr. Horn took Greta's body inside, Dallas begged him to intervene. "Somebody has to do something. I've tried, but I'm an outsider and they won't listen to me."

"They didn't listen to your brother, either. This kind of war addresses a man's purpose for being, Dallas. At heart all men are warriors."

She'd never felt so defeated.

"I'm sorry, Dallas," Dr. Horn said, "but there's nothing anybody can do. It's been that way since the beginning of time, fighting over the possession of land. Think about it. A good example is the Peloponnesian Wars, one of the shorter ones. It still lasted almost thirty years. The good citizens of Sparta and Athens fought each other for so long they forgot what they were fighting for. This may not be as grand, but it's the same thing. And I don't think this war is going to be any easier to settle."

Miranda accompanied Dallas back to the newspaper office.

"Call if off for now, Dallas. Come back to the saloon with me and I'll prepare you a bath to wash all that soot from your face. Then we'll treat your burns."

"Burns?" Her own injury had been forgotten in the aftermath of Greta's death. But Miranda was right. Her eyes burned. Her clothing was a singed mass of burned calico, and her ankles were stinging like she'd been in an ant bed.

"Thanks, Miranda, but I'll manage. I have some thinking to do. Oh, and get your dressing gown. It's over there on the stairs."

Miranda picked up the Russian dressing gown and draped it over her arm. "Now come along," she said briskly. "I'm not leaving you here to manage alone. If you need to think, we'll do it together."

Half an hour later found Dallas submerged in a tub that was almost as large as the water storage tank outside the newspaper office. The water was warm and relaxing, and she leaned her head back against the tub as Miranda hustled around trying to make Dallas comfortable.

The Russian velvet robe with the fur trim was lying across the painted screen behind which the tub was secluded. "I want you to know how touched I was by you sending me your robe, Miranda," Dallas said. "I know how much it means to you."

"Friends mean a lot, too," Miranda said, pulling a stool close by the tub and sitting down. "Now, what do we need to think about?"

"How to stop the war."

"There's no way, Dallas. When grown men get an itch to fight, sometimes it don't matter a hoot in hell what they're fighting for. Each of 'em thinks they're right and you're not gonna change their minds. It's always been like that."

"That's what Dr. Horn said. "History has recorded wars lasting for a hundred years. Plays have been written about them."

"Really? And you've seen them?"

"No, but I read some of them. There was one Greek playwright who wrote about the Peloponnesian War. They fought for nearly thirty years."

"La! Without stopping?"

"Oh, they took time off every now and then to come home, make love to their wives, refill their money belts, and take off again."

"Seems like they'd have all died or gone broke."

"They almost did."

"How'd you learn all that?" Miranda asked, in awe of her friend's depth of knowledge.

"Along with my brothers, I read all the classics."

"Like Jamie. He was always trying to get Willie to read those books he sent back East for. Said we'd learn from the past. All I ever learned from the past was how to get out of the way of a drunk. Come to think about it, guess that was a good thing, considering I run a saloon."

Dallas looked at her friend. "Your father?"

"No. He was a good man, weak, but good. Believe it or not, the drunk in my family was my mother."

That shocked Dallas. Not many women had access to alcohol, and fewer fell to its addiction. "Are they still alive?"

"Nope. My father worked in a dive, back in St. Louis, on the waterfront. My mother was the cook. She'd been drinking all day. One night I refused to get more whiskey for her, and she took after me with a knife. My father tried to stop her and they killed each other with the same knife."

"How awful for you."

"Oh, I didn't know it then. I lit out, hid on a train of workers heading for the new railroad site out West. It was years later when I found out what happened." She got a pensive expression on her face. "That's why I don't drink. I guess I am afraid that history will repeat itself."

"Sometimes we do learn something, I guess." But Dallas wasn't getting anywhere with finding any solutions in the past. She hadn't even been able to save Greta. She let out a sigh.

"Do they hurt?" Miranda asked.

"What?"

"Your burns?"

"Oh, no, I mean yes, I suppose they do."

"Then get out of the tub and let me see what we

have. Dr. Horn went out to one of the ranches, but I sent for Shadow to bring her bag of herbs."

That information roused Dallas. She stood and allowed Miranda to drape a towel around her, then draw her to her bed.

"Jake knows what happened?"

"Probably. I expect him to come busting through that door any minute. You'd better get in bed."

"Oh, I can't take your bed, Miranda. I'll just go back to the newspaper office. Besides, he won't come to your room. He wouldn't want to take a chance on meeting Elliott. I mean—"

Miranda grinned. "You mean that we haven't done a very good job of keeping our . . . friendship a secret?"

"Not very."

"Neither have you, Dallas. If you're going to hide Jake's horse behind your building, you're going to have to build a back door and a stable."

"That obvious, huh?"

"If you know what to look for," Miranda admitted. "But I don't think you have to worry about Elliott. This trouble has kept him pretty busy. He's taking his official duties as sheriff seriously. He's staying close to the farmers, especially since he hasn't been able to get the ranchers to agree to meet with him."

"Jake could make it happen," Dallas said wearily, "if he'd just do it."

Miranda came restlessly to her feet. "I'm worried, Dallas. I don't think that Elliott can stop a range war without Jake's help. It's going to happen, and he could be hurt."

Miranda turned to the window and stared out into the street. "Can you believe it, me falling in love with a farmer? Elliott deserves somebody better. He's going to be an important man, Dallas.

What will people say about him if he's involved with a saloon girl? Elliott says he doesn't care what kind of woman I've been. But now, with this trouble getting worse, I'm scared."

Dallas dropped the towel and slipped her arms into the velvet robe. Her mind was desperately trying to find answers that would preserve Miranda's future without destroying her own.

"There's something else you ought to know, Dallas. The barbed wire is here."

"Barbed wire?" Dallas shook her head as she tried to arrange the robe so that it didn't touch the tender places on her ankles and her wrists. "How do you know?"

"The train brought several large rolls of it this morning. It's waiting at the station for Elliott's farmers to pick it up. Oh, Dallas, the ranchers will never allow it. Even Jake might believe the farmers have a right to farm, but he'll never let them close his cattle off from the grass on the range."

Jake. Barbed wire. The potential for real fighting galvanized Dallas. Miranda was right. The ranchers would never allow that. She had to try one last time. And this time, she'd start with Jake.

"Send Willie to bring me some clothes. I'll go and talk to Jake. I'll tell him. He must be convinced that this has to stop."

There was a knock on the door. Miranda opened it, admitting Shadow, who came quickly to Dallas's side. "Willie said you're hurt."

"It's nothing really, just a few burns."

"The foreign woman was killed?" Shadow pushed back the robe's sleeves and examined Dallas's hands.

"Yes, she's dead. I tried, but I couldn't save her."

"Like my family, it was not meant to be." From the pouch she carried, Shadow took ointment and gently rubbed it on Dallas's injured hands and ankles.

"Help me, Shadow. I have to get to the Double J and talk to Jake."

"Mr. Silver isn't there. He has gone to the meeting."

"What meeting?"

"The ranchers heard about the barbed wire and moved up the meeting. It's at the schoolhouse—tonight."

"Then help me to dress. I'll go there."

"I'll go with you," Miranda decided.

"Shadow also go."

Moments later the three women were on the walkway, heading for the schoolhouse, each desperate to keep their men alive.

Spence from the telegraph office was there, up front. Elliott, Jake, Pete, even Wu, along with several other ranchers and a group of well-armed men that Dallas would have recognized as gunfighters even if she'd never been a Pinkerton operative.

"We're too late," Miranda whispered as they walked into the schoolhouse just as Elliott removed his badge and held it out to Jake.

"My first obligation is to the farmers. I brought them here and I'll protect them. If it means taking their side against your ranchers, I'll have to resign. It's in your hands now, Jake," he said. "I won't fight you."

"I have no interest in being the sheriff, Elliott. And you can't back away when the war gets rough. The West will change when farmers string up wire, and I don't like change. But I don't like people dying, either."

Elliott shook his head. "You can't stand alone any longer, Jake. You have to pick a side."

For a long time Jake simply stood and looked at Elliott. "I swore to put an end to killing when I took off my uniform. Elliott, I don't ask anybody to settle my trouble, and I won't become involved in yours."

"Times change, Jake, and so do our priorities."

"But not our honor, Elliott. You took an oath to keep the peace, just as I once promised not to kill you. If you take back your promise, I will have to take back mine. Is that what you want?"

"Elliott!" Miranda ran toward the front of the room. Elliott held out his hand to stop her and shook his head.

"No, Miranda. Go back to the saloon. This is no place for you. You could get hurt."

"I won't leave you, Elliott. You can't ask me to. I won't. Give them back the badge. Let them have this land. We'll move farther west, buy more. I'll help you raise cabbages if that's what you want, but I'm not leaving you." She slipped her arm around his waist and faced Jake defiantly.

Jake turned, allowing his gaze to fall on Dallas. He waited. Dallas didn't move. She stood in the doorway looking at Jake, a Jake whose body had turned to ice and whose eyes had turned to steel. He didn't tell her to go home; he knew that she wouldn't. He didn't even speak; there was no need. Everything about her said clearly that this could be the end of anything between them.

"Don't do this, Jake," she finally said.

"You have a choice, Dallas. You can always go home. I can't."

"There is always a choice."

Jake's gaze didn't waver. "And you've made yours."

He knew she was disappointed in his position. He'd hoped she'd understand why he had to look as if he was taking sides. Someone was working very hard to set up just such a confrontation. Until Jake figured out who stood to gain, he'd let them think they'd succeeded.

He hadn't expected Dallas's disappointment to bother him, but it did.

He was only now learning that when a man and a woman loved each other, one became the other's strength and faith in the future. If faith was absent, the heart was empty.

Allowing Dallas to turn and walk away was the hardest thing Jake had ever done.

By day the farmers strung the barbed wire. By night the Devil of the Plains tore the wire down and churned up the freshly plowed rows.

By day the ranchers rounded up the calves for branding. By night the Devil of the Plains stole them away from their pens.

Where the Germans might have been amenable to some kind of peaceful settlement before, the men now began to arm themselves, guarding their homes and families while they waited for outside help to arrive.

Dallas, sick at heart, watched Miranda return to her saloon, where Elliott visited secretly at night. She knew that Shadow and Wu were together, for Pete passed on the story of Shadow's pursuit of the Chinaman to Irene when he came to town. The temperature rose. The range grass grew, and the crops that weren't torn up by the Devil began to die. But Jake didn't come back to her bed, and her heart was sore with grief.

The two gunfighters Elliott sent for arrived. Tensions flared. Days passed when no new planting was done, no new branding took place. Everything in Green Willow slowed down, including the water in the creek now that the runoff was over. Except for Dallas's newspapers. She printed a new one every day, which everybody read and nobody agreed with.

Trading at the general store came to a stop. Church services were canceled temporarily. Lawson Pickens began to get frantic messages from the land speculator, threatening to send someone else in to collect the payments due. Tensions rose. Something had to happen.

Something did.

Wu got shot.

Dallas couldn't believe that Wu had been hurt. "How did it happen, Willie? Who would harm Wu?"

"He went off by hisself and bought a pig. He was bringing it home when somebody took a shot at him."

"A pig?"

"Yes'm. A pig. He had it tied in the back of the wagon. It was still there when the horse got back to the ranch."

"And Wu, how is he?"

"Don't know yet. Jake sent Pete to get Dr. Horn. All Pete said was that Wu got shot in the head."

Dallas was stunned. The ranchers and the farmers, she could understand, but Jamie and now Wu? It made no sense. Neither man was a threat to anybody. "Was there any sign of the . . . the Devil of the Plains?"

"Not this time. Least not that anybody knows."

"Go fetch us a wagon, Willie. We're going to the Double J."

"I don't know if Jake would like you riding out by yourself. Specially not after this. You know what he said."

Dallas turned and gave Willie a look that said clear enough what she thought about that.

Willie tried to argue. "But you see what happened to Wu. Don't go, Miss Banning. Please?"

Dallas could see that Willie was scared. Never before had he questioned their forays on the prairie. But this had shaken him. It had shaken Dallas, too. If someone had tried to murder Wu without blaming it on the monster, she had a good idea who it was. One of the gunfighters.

And the frightening thing was that the killer could have been hired by either side.

By the time Willie had rented the wagon Miranda had heard the news and come running. "I don't like it, Dallas. The men in the saloon don't care anything about Wu, but they're talking about arming themselves and taking action against the farmers—against Elliott."

Dallas knew that Miranda needed reassurance. So did she. "Surely they don't think Elliott had anything to do with Wu's being shot. It had to be an accident of some kind, somebody hunting maybe."

But Miranda wouldn't be comforted. "Even Effie Pickens stopped me on the way over here, and she only speaks to me once a year, at the spring dance. Lawson is talking about sending her back East to stay with her sister. Maybe even sending for federal marshals. He's got her scared to death."

"Calm down, Miranda. I'm going out to talk to Jake," Dallas said.

Wu was sitting up in his own bed, chattering angrily, as Shadow fussed with a bandage around his head.

"Woman stop! Wu not want hair cut away. Wu's pigtail a measure of his manhood. Now Wu not same."

"You're alive, Wu!" Shadow snapped. "And if you don't stop talking, your hair isn't the only thing I'm going to cut off."

Jake chuckled. Wu looked stunned. And Dr. Horn shook his head in amusement as he looked up and caught sight of Dallas standing in the doorway with Willie behind.

Jake hadn't turned, but she could tell the moment he became aware of her presence from the tension in his stance. And for a moment she allowed herself to drink in the sight of him. After being with her every night, he'd suddenly stopped coming. A few days without him had been too long. Just seeing him set her pulse racing. She was afraid that Dr. Horn could read her thoughts in her face.

"Is Wu all right?" she asked the doctor as he gathered up his bag and prepared to leave.

"He's fine, Miss Banning. Lucky he's alive. Bullet just creased his skull. He fell back in the wagon and knocked himself out."

"Hello, Wu," she said, and came to stand by the bed. "Who did this to you?"

"Wu not know, for sure. Only know somebody follow Wu from settlement."

"Somebody?" Jake moved closer to the bed. "You never mentioned that before. Who was it?"

"Wu not see, only hear."

"What did you hear, Wu?" Dallas asked.

"Man whistle."

Dallas frowned. "You mean like a song?"

"Not song, signal. Like he calling animal. Then animal answer and horse ride fast. Wu drive wagon fast, too, before Devil of Plains catch him."

"Animal, Wu?" Jake questioned. "You think the whistler was calling the Devil and the Devil answered."

"No. Animal that answer is coyote. Wu hear coyotes many times. Devil much big monster. Different."

"But you were shot, Wu," Jake argued. "Not mauled, like the others. Could we be dealing with a different killer?"

"Devil of the Plains out there. Wu smell, but not see him. Not hear him. He evil spirit that comes on silent feet. Try to keep Wu from bringing pig."

Jake didn't know what to make of Wu's story about the whistle and the answer of the coyote. But with Dallas sitting there, he'd revealed enough. She'd probably mount a campaign to find a whistler and put herself in danger.

"About that pig, Wu," Jake said dryly, "were you planning a barbecue?"

"No cook pig. Pig present. Pig not shot?" Wu asked anxiously, then winced and leaned back against the head of his bed.

Jake shook his head. "The pig is safe, you old heathen. Get some rest, and tomorrow I want to hear why you took such a fool chance."

"Not heathen, Mr. Jake. Wu honorable man. Pig part of ancient ceremony."

Shadow, sitting quietly on the bed beside Wu, reached out and touched his lips with her fingertips. "Just rest now, Wu."

Wu looked at Shadow and smiled. "Pig is token of affection for wife to be."

Jake smiled. "Wife to be?"

Wu placed his hand on Shadow's. "Pig for you, Shadow woman."

"For me? Why?"

"Old Chinese custom. Groom present honorable wife with pig."

"And what does honorable wife give husband?"

But Wu didn't answer. He was asleep.

Chapter 19

Dallas and Jake followed Dr. Horn back into the main house and down the center hallway.

"He was lucky, Jake," the doctor said. "Whoever fired that shot meant business."

"I know. What do you think about his hearing somebody whistle?"

"Probably the wind," Dr. Horn said, passing the story off as being unimportant. "He was scared, heard the coyotes howling at the moon and put the two together. I'm more interested in the shooting. Who in God's name would want to hurt Wu?"

"Maybe," Dallas suggested, "it was meant to be a warning to you, Jake,"

Dr. Horn nodded his agreement. "She's right, Jake. I'd be careful if I were you. With all those gunfighters around, this situation could turn into a full-scale war."

"I know."

"Miss Banning, would you and Willie like to ride back with me?" Dr. Horn asked.

Dallas shook her head. "Take Willie. I want to stay and talk with Jake."

"I'll see her back to town," Jake said reluctantly, clasping Dr. Horn's shoulder. "Thanks for coming."

"Any time, Jake. Though Shadow seems to know

as much about healing as I do. Maybe I ought to take her on as a partner."

"Good night, Miss Banning," Willie said, and climbed into the buggy with the doctor.

After they left, Jake made his way to the parlor, not bothering to close the door behind them. There was no one to hear the dressing-down he was about to give Dallas Banning.

"All right, maverick, what are you doing out here?"

"Just what I said. I came to talk to you."

"About what?" he snapped and walked to the window, turning his back on her.

Dallas sighed. She'd hoped for a different reaction. But he wasn't going to make this easy. When had he ever been easy to deal with?

Only when they were making love and he allowed his mask of ice to slip temporarily. Her plan to discuss the situation without emotion vanished the moment she saw him turn away.

Dallas moved forward, slid her arms around his waist and pressed her face against his strong back. "Don't do this, Jake. Don't you understand? That might have been you who was shot instead of Wu. We have to talk about us, Jake, but we have to stop the trouble first."

She felt him flex his muscles as if he were trying to lift off a weight pressing down on his shoulders. "You shouldn't have come here, Dallas. This isn't your concern."

"You're wrong. My brother's murder brought me here, but now there's you. There is something between us, Jake Silver, and you can't just ignore it. I had to come to you. I've missed you."

He twisted out of her arms and turned to face her. "You expected our little secret trysts to go on forever?" His voice was bitter, catching her by surprise.

"They weren't even secret. Everybody in the valley knew that Jake Silver was sneaking in under the cover of darkness to see the newspaperwoman. Secrets always end up hurting someone, Dallas."

"I wasn't expecting it to last forever. But I did expect you to let me know if you were tired of me."

He turned back to a table by the window. "I should have," he said, pouring himself a generous measure of whiskey and taking a long swig. He didn't know how long he could keep from touching her if he stayed that close.

"Join me in a little whiskey, maverick?"

"I don't think so, Jake."

He wished she wouldn't look at him with such trust. It was dangerous for a woman to let her heart show so plainly. A lie he could deal with. Trust was hard.

Dallas straightened her shoulders. She could see there was a two-day growth of whiskers on his face. He looked as if he hadn't slept, and she was sure he had lost weight. He could push her away, but that wasn't what he wanted, and it wasn't what she wanted either.

What she wanted was more than just secret meetings. What she wanted was a man who was strong enough to admit he needed her.

"What," she finally asked, "do you intend to do about Wu?"

He drained his glass and refilled it. "I intend to find out who shot at him. Then I'm probably going to kill him."

Something inside Dallas recoiled. "Then someone who cares about his killer will kill you. Don't you think this has gone far enough?

Jake risked a quick look at Dallas and instantly regretted it. She was so stoic, so determined, standing there like Joan of Arc, ready to be burned at the stake. God, he cared about her. And because he did, he had to keep her believing that they were through.

"I think it's gone too far," he said quietly. "I don't think there's any stopping it."

"Have you tried?"

"I've tried." He didn't tell her how many miles he'd ridden, searching for the monster, talking to the ranchers. He and Dr. Horn had discussed all the possible hiding places, and neither of them had come up with any answers.

"And you don't want my help."

The silence that followed spoke louder than words.

"I guess I'm wasting my time talking to you, then," she said. "I'll go."

"Yes. Go back to Philadelphia, maverick. I don't want you . . . ," his voice broke slightly, "I don't want you to die, too."

"I have a last request."

"Make it!"

"Kiss me good-bye, Jake."

"Don't make this so damned hard, Dallas."

She took the glass from his hand, took a seductive sip, then set it on the table. Turning her shoulder toward him, she raised her gaze, challenging him with a deliberately provocative look. "Just kiss me, Jake. Then—if you tell me to, I'll go."

He groaned and jerked her close, sinking his chin in her hair, feeling her melt against him as her body was caught up in a shiver of need.

His lips found hers, found, claimed, and ravished. And he was lost. Night after night, he'd fought this need, fought the urge to ride the plains and come to her. Without her beside him, the nights had stretched into a blackness that seemed to go on forever.

But she was here, in his arms, and he couldn't

think of anything but the feel and taste of her. Even now, facing unknown disaster, all he could concentrate on was the unleashed passion of her love.

Love?

Was that what this was?

To Jake, love was the priceless treasuring of beauty and gentleness, the kind of life his mother had deserved—not this avalanche of desire. Not this completeness of spirit when they touched. Not this promise of tomorrow that sang in his soul when he held her in his arms.

Like heat lightning on the plains he felt the exploding power race through their bodies. Like a man drunk on the smoke of the opium pipe, Jake Silver lost the strength to resist.

In the middle of the afternoon he pulled Dallas to her feet and dragged her up the stairs to his bedroom. No more secrets in the darkness. Moments later they tore off each other's clothing and stood drinking in the sight of each other in the sunlight.

Jake's senses were heightened to the point of no return. They stood so close that he breathed in every pant of air she released. Every glance was a firing of that white-hot core of heat that burned between his legs. He was hard. He hurt with the pain of knowing that she could bring him to this state and that she knew his weakness. Yet he could not turn away.

"Why did you stop coming to me, Jake?"

"Because I was afraid that if I didn't, I'd be lost forever. Does that make you happy, to learn that you've enslaved me?"

"No more than you've enslaved me," she whispered. "And you're not lost, Jake. I found you and I don't intend to let you go."

"But you must, maverick. You don't understand." *Every thing I love is destroyed.* But the thought was lost as Jake put his arms around Dallas, lifting her so that her legs slid around his waist. Shifting her, he moved her back and forth against his shaft, sucking in quick panting breaths of air that seemed to evaporate in the heat of his lungs. He was burning. He was smothering.

Then he was pushing her away from his body and positioning her so that she took him inside, her legs fastening tight around his waist.

She was hot and wet.

He was hard and ready.

"I didn't want this to happen, Dallas," he whispered as he began to move.

"Why not? It's wonderful. It's like being one person, instead of two." She tightened her legs around him. "Love me, Jake!"

And then he, too, was lost in a wash of heat. They fell together onto the bed. Hot skin fanned flames higher in skin that was already at the boiling point. Endearments were whispered and sighs matched moans as together they were incinerated by the storm of heat like sagebrush caught up in a prairie fire.

"I don't ever want to stop, Jake."

"You're driving me crazy, maverick."

He dragged his mouth across her nipples, licking, following the curve along the valley between her breasts. He threaded his fingers through hers and held her captive beneath him.

Dallas panted, lunging to meet his mouth, helpless to do more than twist her body wildly beneath him. Tremors of fire rippled through her, intensifying as he thrust inside her. Then abruptly, he brought his body to a stillness that was more exciting than his movement.

"Don't stop, Jake," she pleaded. "Don't stop."

And then he plunged deep inside her and they were both riding the wave of fire, feeding the flame.

When it finally catapulted into fiery release, they arched against each other in one long, shuddering explosion.

Afterward, she sobbed, stunned by the intensity of what they'd shared.

They lay, still joined, for a long, breathless moment. Then Jake eased himself from her. Still holding one hand, he turned away, hating to break the connection of their bodies.

"And now it's over again," she said in a stiff voice, a voice that was barely holding back the tears.

Jake took a deep breath. He couldn't continue to take what she was offering with no promises in return. It was up to him to protect her, and the only way he could be certain of that was to separate her from what he was about to do.

Jake had to find the person behind the trouble, and he had to do it alone. "My body responds to you, Dallas, but there's nothing inside my soul. Eventually, you'd hate me. Eventually, you'd want someone else."

"I'd never hate you, Jake. And I'd never leave. I think you know that I love you. I'll say it, this once, just so that you'll know the truth. But I don't ask anything from you that you don't want to give."

"You aren't considering the consequences."

"There won't be any consequences." She played with his fingertips, drawing his hand to her stomach, reveling in the immediate rush of heat that came with his touch.

"There are always consequences, Dallas." He pulled away from her grasp and spread his fingers across her stomach. "What if there is a child?"

She felt the air rush from her lungs. She'd never once thought about that. She was a grown woman, considered to be a worldly woman, but having a child was so far from the life she'd envisioned for herself that she'd never once considered the possibility.

"A child?" She couldn't keep the wonder from her voice.

"Dallas, in spite of your strength there are times when you're such an innocent. You must know that what we've done could make a baby."

Dallas laid her hand on top of his, sliding it lower as her body began to move beneath his touch.

"It would be a boy," she said confidently, "a son for the Honorable House of Silver."

Jake's fingers played through the soft hair that rippled beneath his touch, exploring her intimately.

"Jake," she gasped.

"Tell me about our son," he demanded in a voice that he didn't even recognize as his own. He moved his finger lower and lower, until it found its way inside her most secret place and felt it being opened freely to him.

"He'd have his father's name," she said between pants. "He'd be proud to be Jacob Silver's son."

Jake rolled over her and took her body again. After all, he thought, the damage was already done.

Jake was silent the next morning as they were driving back to town. He had been since he waked before dawn and pulled away from Dallas, removing her cheek from his chest and her leg from across his thighs. He didn't know what to do. For the first time in his life, he'd run into an immovable wall, a prison from which he couldn't escape, a woman who loved him, even when he told her that he would hurt her.

But she was right about one thing. In spite of everything he'd done, the battle lines were drawn. The gunfighters brought in by both sides were growing impatient, and confrontation was imminent. He'd never intended to get involved with another war or another woman. Until someone shot Wu.

Now he was involved. He'd have to find a way to keep Dallas away from the fight, and nothing he'd said up to now had made any impression on her. She was a woman of words and action, but out here, words were useless. It was the survival of the fittest, the strongest became the victors. The law of the West was still the gun. But he couldn't do it alone. He needed Elliott.

"You know," Dallas said, "I found some of Jamie's notes. He said that there were two men who stood to gain by winning the range war. That would be you and Elliott."

That caught Jake by surprise. "Me and Elliott?"

"If you defeat the farmers, their land remains free. You can buy it cheap and expand your empire. If Elliott wins, the farmers have the same choice."

"You expect them to buy our ranches?"

"No, but it doesn't matter. They won't have to buy land. They already have access to the creek. All they have to do is what they came here for, plant their crops."

Dallas didn't have to tell Jake that this was the growing season, for the signs were all around them. Jake didn't tell her that he didn't believe anything would grow except range grass, for nobody would believe him.

The morning was golden. As far as Dallas could see, the grass was growing green against the mountain ranges that surrounded the plains like meringue-frosted hard candies. There was a humming when the wind ruffled the grass, as if the earth were breathing. Birds flew overhead. Insects flew below, and the sunshine was warm against her face.

She couldn't stop happiness from welling up inside her like a fountain.

"You don't understand about cattle, Dallas," Jake explained. "They must have grass to live. If fences are erected, the cattle won't survive."

"There must be a way, Jake. This problem can't be new. There has to be an answer."

"None that you want to hear, Dallas." He'd spent the early hours of the morning working out what he would say to her.

"You know that I'll have to join with the ranchers; it's a matter of honor. In a way I brought them here, just as Elliott brought the farmers. I'll have to defend their right to the land. But it won't be easy. And when it's over, I'll be moving on. Alone. I want to see the Pacific ocean, maybe get on one of those sailing ships and see the rest of the world."

Dallas sat very still. "You're choosing to be alone, then."

"I've always been alone, Dallas. Ever since I was a kid. My father didn't want me. He never even married my mother. She was his housekeeper, not his wife. Even later, after she was carrying me, he could have married her, but he refused."

"But you were his son, Jake. How could he do that?"

"I was his second son, his illegitimate second son. He already had an heir; I was simply an inconvenience. If I'd been a slave child I'd have been given the family name. But I was white. When I got old enough to ask questions, he sent me away to school."

Dallas could see so much more clearly now. Jake had desperately wanted to be loved by the man who was his father. Instead, he'd been abandoned.

"Oh, Jake, I'm so sorry."

"The Confederacy called me a hero. I wasn't.

Elliott and I were both misfits. I was a nobody, a bully, and he was a gentleman who was also a coward. Together we became a killing team. Not because I gave a damn about defending the Confederacy. I didn't. I just wanted to prove to my father that I was a better man than my brother. I was, but you know what?" Jake gave a bitter laugh. "My father didn't care. In the end it was all for nothing."

Dallas wanted to say something, but the words wouldn't have penetrated the walls of ice that Jake was carefully reconstructing.

"I went back home afterward. The plantation was burned to the ground. My father couldn't pay the taxes, and he was going to lose it. I offered to help, but he refused. He and my brother just walked away, let them take our land, and never looked back."

"What about your mother?"

"He left her, too. She was sick, living in a burned-out shed. Mercifully, she died quickly. I buried her in the family plot and left. In Missouri I ran into Elliott again. He was as lost as me. We headed west, together."

"What happened between you and Elliott, Jake?"

He laughed bitterly. "Elliott was the only friend I ever had. I thought we knew each other. I thought he was something he wasn't."

"He let you down?"

"Yes. Or maybe I let him down." He told her about Sarah, the woman they had both loved.

"It seemed she loved us both. She didn't want to choose. Elliott and I swore an oath to treat her like a sister. But we both fell in love with her. She chose Elliott and I left."

Dallas sensed there was more, much more to the story. She couldn't hold back one question. "How could she have let you go?"

"She didn't think I needed her. Elliott did need her. He had something to offer—an honorable name. She deserved that at least. I thought he'd take care of her."

"And he didn't?"

"No. He wasn't ready to accept the responsibility. When she died, she took the last bit of decency left in me. I wanted to kill him for what happened, but I'd promised her that I wouldn't. So you see, it's fitting that I'm on one side of this and Elliott is on the other."

Jake didn't have to tell her about his pain. But until now she hadn't understood. She thought that it wasn't Elliott he held responsible for Sarah's death, it was himself. If he'd admitted that he cared, she might still be alive. He couldn't save his mother, or his land, but he could have saved Sarah. What that knowledge must have done to a man like Jake.

Elliott wasn't Jake's enemy. Elliott was Jake's guilt.

Dallas swallowed the lump in her throat. "I knew there was someone else, someone who'd hurt you, someone who haunted you. Now I understand. You couldn't make room in your heart for me, for that would displace Sarah."

"Yes," he forced himself to say. "You were always a replacement for Sarah."

They'd reached the newspaper office without Dallas even being aware. She climbed stiffly down from the wagon, her heart thudding coldly against the walls of her chest.

"And you'd rather drive me away than take a chance on being hurt again. Say it, Jake. Tell me the truth."

"Yes. History does repeat itself. If I could keep you safe, it somehow made up for Sarah."

"And what about the possibility that I might be carrying your child?"

"You needn't worry. I'll take care of you. I'm deeding my land to you, Dallas, when I go. No matter the outcome, you'll be a wealthy woman. If you don't want to stay here, sell it to Lawson Pickens."

Dallas heard his words. She wanted to scream out that he was a fool, that he would be doing the same thing to his child that his father had done to him. But she kept silent.

"I don't need your money, Jake. I have more than I'll ever need. And I have a newspaper to publish, and a range war to report on. Goodbye, Jake."

She went inside and closed the door behind her. She heard the horse pull away, make a circle, and head back the way they'd come. He was gone. Jake was leaving her, just as he'd left Sarah.

Only Dallas wasn't Sarah, and she had no intention of giving up. Something wasn't quite right about Jake's story. Despite everything that he'd gone to such pains to tell her, Jake Silver was her future, and if he didn't destroy it, she intended to share it with him.

Inside the office, Willie was whistling a tune, waiting for Dallas to give some indication of what she intended to do. She would have, except she didn't know. Instead, she began to pace back and forth, around and around the chair near the stove.

An hour later she was still pacing, but she'd altered her direction, moving across the room toward the bookcase, running her fingers back and forth across the spines of Jamie's books in growing agitation. Until she finally dislodged one volume that came crashing to the floor at her feet.

With an oath she reached down and picked it up, closing it with a slam. Then, realizing what she'd done, she clasped it to her chest and rested her chin on its edge. The anger began to recede. She'd been charging about like one of those calves to which Jake had compared her.

Maverick.

She took the book and started to reshelve it, glancing absently at its title, *The Plays of Aristophanes*. The scholars called his plays about the Peloponnesian War comedies, but Dallas had always called them tragedies. The Greeks, with all their great wisdom, weren't any smarter than the residents of Green Willow Creek.

The men from Athens and Sparta fought for control of the Peloponnesian peninsula for over twenty-five years, losing their brave young men and draining their treasury dry. Until, according to the playwright, a woman from Athens, called Lysistrata, found a way to end the war.

At least the ranchers and the farmers in Green Willow Creek wouldn't take twenty-five years to kill each other. They'd accomplish the same thing much sooner.

Unless—

Dallas sat and flipped to the last play in the series. She hadn't been particularly fond of early Greek writings, but plays were easier to read than the *Iliad* and the *Odyssey*, and if her brothers read Greek literature, Dallas also read it. Now, if she remembered the Aristophanes tale of Lysistrata, it just might provide a solution to the problem in Wyoming.

An hour later, to Willie's amazement, Dallas began to laugh. It started with a snicker and burst out into a full, deep laugh.

"Are you all right? Shall I call Dr. Horn?" Willie asked anxiously. "He could give you a sleeping powder."

"No, Willie. Absolutely not. I need to be in complete control of my faculties. I have decisions to make."

"Is it about Jake?"

"In a way." She came to her feet and began to pace anew. "In a very big way."

"Shall I go and fetch him?"

"Jake? No! Go get Miss Miranda. If she's not up yet, wake her. Tell her that—never mind. Just tell her to hurry."

"Yes, ma'am."

"Then, when you're done, get a fast horse and take this message to Miss Shadow." She scribbled her note, folded and sealed it. "Be certain that she's the one to get it—not Jake. I think she'll come back with you."

"But what about Jake? He'll have my hide."

"Willie, if we pull this off, I'll make you the assistant editor of the *Gazette* and pay you a salary big enough so that you can buy yourself a new one."

"Yes, ma'am."

As Willie went for Miranda, Dallas started composing the next issue of the *Green Willow Gazette*. It might not be the truth yet, but it would be, when she and Miranda were done.

Jamie was right. Two men stood to gain. But they also stood to lose. Dr. Horn had also been right. The present could learn from the past. The citizens of ancient Athens didn't have a thing on the citizens of Green Willow Creek.

And anything men could do, women would do just as well. Dallas smiled and touched her stomach. It was time for the men to learn another way to fight. And it didn't take a Greek play to show them the way. A few provocative clothes and a one-page small-town newspaper would work just as well.

Chapter 20

Miranda arrived at the newspaper office in minutes. "Is it Wu?"

"No, he's fine. The shot grazed his head and knocked him out, but thank heavens, it didn't do any real damage. At least not as much as Jake and the ranchers are about to do."

Miranda frowned and took her friend's hand. "I talked to Elliott, Dallas, but I don't think it's going to do much good. He's ready to face Jake and the ranchers' gunfighters. They've set up a showdown at the schoolhouse tomorrow night."

"You mean they're going to war?"

"Not yet. This meeting is to be a last chance to settle the problem."

"Oh, Miranda, we're going to have to work faster than I thought."

"To do what?"

Dallas pursed her lips, considering how best to word her question. The wrong answer meant that her plan would fail. "Tell me the truth, Miranda. It's important. Are you convinced that Elliott loves you?"

"Yes, but that doesn't seem to hold any weight in the fight."

"And I'm convinced that Jake . . . cares about me.

He won't admit it, but he does. Effie spoke to you because she is worried about Lawson, and Wu went to get a pig for Shadow."

"Dallas, I think it was you that got the lick on the head. What does all this mean?"

"It means that the women of Greece figured out the answer over two thousand years ago. And they did it without firing a single shot." She smiled. "They may even have enjoyed the campaign."

"I don't understand. How did the women of Greece know about a Wyoming range war?"

"It doesn't matter. I know. What I want you to do is go out to the settlement house. Find Lena. After those cowboys caused Adolph's leg to be broken, I think she'll agree to join us."

"And do what, Dallas?"

"Tell Lena to get the women to bring firearms and their most provocative clothing and come into town tomorrow afternoon. They mustn't tell the men. If this works, we'll keep those hotheads from killing each other and have a little fun at the same time."

Miranda shook her head. She still wasn't certain that Dallas hadn't been the one who was injured. "Are you sure you know what you're doing?"

"I'm sure."

"All right, I'll try. Where do you want them?"

"The men are coming to the school? Bring the women to the saloon. And send for Effie Pickens. Tell her to get the local wives. We're going to have a little meeting of our own. Just the women."

"And what will you be doing?" Miranda asked.

"I'm going after the ranchers' wives."

"You're inviting the ranchers' wives, the immigrants' wives, and the merchants' wives all to the same meeting?"

"That I am. If the men can't settle this thing, the women will."

Dallas pulled on Willie's spare trousers once more and found some of Jamie's clothes for Miranda. Moments later they slipped around the buildings and headed for the livery stable to rent horses.

"Are you sure we'll be safe, Dallas? Hadn't you ought to take Willie with you?"

"No, I'll risk another meeting with the Devil of the Plains if it means keeping Jake from interfering with our plans. Are you worried?"

"I've faced devils all my life. At least now I have someone to face them for," Miranda answered confidently.

Before anyone else knew what they were doing, Dallas and Miranda were on their way. Miranda turned toward the settlement house and Dallas kept going.

Dallas's task would be easier, for the ranchers would be away from their houses in the middle of the morning. She was banking on Miranda's relationship with Elliott getting her to the farmers' wives.

At the first house, the Trendle ranch, she was met with suspicion by Amy Trendle, until Dallas outlined her plan. The rawboned woman listened and grinned, then agreed to take part.

There was hostility from the second woman, until she learned that Amy Trendle would be there. This woman heard Dallas out and admitted to having already lost one husband to a disagreement over a land dispute. She didn't want to lose another. She'd come.

To Dallas's surprise, one woman after another agreed, until she'd covered all the ranches she could reach in one day. The last woman, the Widow Potter, was sitting on her porch, rocking and spitting tobacco juice in the yard.

"Sounds like you got a good plan, chile. But you need a little help. I'll just ride out in the morning and gather up the rest of 'em. We'll be there, younguns and all."

"Thank you, Mrs. Potter. I'll be very grateful for your help."

"T'ain't nothing I like better than a good fight, unless it's putting a man in his place." She laughed and slapped her thigh. "One thing. You tell that— Miranda, she'd better lay in a supply of blankets, a little liquid refreshments, and plenty of cake."

"Cake? Why do we need cake?"

"To keep our spirits up, o'course. A little cake and spirits do wonders for a body when it's worried."

Having Widow Potter's support was going to make the meeting smoother. She hoped that Miranda had done as well with the wives and sweethearts to whom she'd spoken.

Shadow was the only one Dallas worried about. She hoped the Indian woman understood what Dallas was asking her to do. It would mean making a hard choice and sticking to her decision. But it might mean an end to the danger.

It could also mean that the pig could be accepted as a gift and not turned into someone's meal.

The next morning, Dallas alternated between apprehension and euphoria. She warded off Willie's curiosity about the type she was setting. Finally she had to make up an excuse to send him away. She composed a handwritten note to be delivered to Jake before the meeting, asking him to stop by the office.

Willie accepted his task, but it was clear that he was puzzled about why Dallas didn't tell Jake whatever was so important in person. She'd stayed over-night at the Double J, so they'd obviously spent some time together. And she knew that Jake would be in town later. Having Willie ride out alone was something he didn't consider smart.

"Don't come back by yourself, Willie. Stay and ride in with Jake and Wu."

Once she was rid of Willie, she went about setting the type for her flyer.

> ATTENTION: MEN OF
> GREEN WILLOW CREEK!
> *Effective immediately* . . .

She wanted the flyer ready for the women's meeting. Hurrying now, she located the proper let-ters, spelling out one word at a time. Finally, she read it over. It wasn't the best article ever written, but it would serve the purpose.

"Oh, Jamie, if you could only see what I've done with the *Gazette*. You'd love it. If you're up there watching, just hold on. I'm still going to get the man who shot you. But I figure you can wait a bit, and I don't think these men down here now can."

By late afternoon, Miranda's saloon was full. Drifters and regular customers meandered up, caught sight of the sign tacked up beside the doors, and backed away. When Dallas reached the entrance and read Miranda's message, she smiled.

> *Angry disease inside. Men affected worst. Stay Away!*
> *Signed*
> *Miranda Carmichael, Proprietor*

Like Dallas's flyer, Miranda's wording was a bit awkward, but it served the purpose. Dallas swallowed her smile, pushed open the door and went inside. She'd expected a handful of women, but to her surprise, the room was filled with concerned women. Ranchers' wives sat on one side. The farmers' wives sat on the other, and in the middle were Effie Lawson and the women whose husbands ran the businesses in town.

Dallas took a deep breath and hoped that she wasn't making a big mistake.

"Good afternoon, ladies," she began, speaking slowly so that Lena could translate for the women who didn't feel comfortable with English. "I've called you here to enlist your support."

"What makes you think we're interested in anything you have to say?" one of the ranchers' wives said. "My man is gonna have my hide when he finds out I'm gone. I still don't know why I was supposed to bring a gun."

"His hide is what I hope to save," Dallas said. "What I want to do is convince you that we should be the ones declaring war."

"Hot damn!" Widow Potter said, slapping the tabletop with such force that she upset her spitting cup.

A baby cried, and a murmur started among the farmers' wives.

"Wait," Miranda called out. "Let's hear what she has to say. Then we'll all have the refreshments I've prepared."

"Refreshments?" Effie Pickens glanced at the cloth-covered bar skeptically.

"Fruit punch and little cakes," Miranda said.

Widow Potter nodded her approval. "Let her talk, 'less you all want to end up a widow like me."

As they quieted, Dallas continued. "All right. This is what I hope we'll do. Are any of you familiar with the Greek comedies of Aristophanes?"

This time the skeptical looks ranged across the faces of all the women.

"No, of course not. That's all right. I didn't expect you to. But the Greek men of Athens and Sparta went to war. At the end of thirty years, most of their young men were dead and their treasury was bare."

"The treasury?" Effie spoke up. "You mean like the bank?"

"That's exactly what I mean," Dallas said. "And that's what is going to happen here. The men are going to withdraw their money to hire gunfighters. They're going to kill each other, and we women will be left with no way to look after our families."

"What'd them Greek women do?" Widow Potter asked.

"The same thing we've done. They begged and pleaded with their husbands and lovers to stop the fighting. But they wouldn't. Finally, the women took matters into their own hands. This is what they did."

Dallas outlined her plan.

Mrs. Trendle, the rancher's wife, protested. "I can't do that. It ain't that I wouldn't want to, but it's branding time and I have to cook for the men."

Miranda posed the real issue. "If they start fighting, there may not be any men to feed."

But it was Shadow who ultimately brought the women together.

"I am new to your town," she said as she walked from her place in the corner of the room to stand beside Dallas. "But I am not new to this place. My people were here long before you came, and they fought to keep you out, to hold on to this land for themselves, just as your men now fight. And my people all died. Now I am the only one left. I will join with Miss Banning, for I believe she has the only answer that the men will understand."

"And I'll do it," Miranda said, joining the other two women. "But if it's going to work, we all have to stand firm. No matter what."

After a long, low discussion among the farmers' wives, Lena stood and joined Miranda, Shadow and Dallas. "Ja! I join you," she said simply.

"Hot damn! It's settled," Widow Potter said. "Now, let's get to that punch and cake while you give us our jobs."

"Just a minute." Dallas stopped the widow's progress. "There may be some of you who choose not to join us, and we can't force you. But we would ask you to keep our plan secret. It will do the men no good to know until we're ready to tell them. Those of you who don't want to stay are excused without ill feelings."

"Speak for yourself, Dallas," the widow snapped, "I'll be plenty ill at any woman who can't stand up to her man for his own good."

"No, we must not force anyone," Shadow said softly. "We would be as bad as those we hope to subdue."

Two women left, but the rest voted to stay.

Dallas looked around, studying her troops in satisfaction.

The war had begun.

Rejo heard about the showdown being called in town. The ranchers and the farmers were having a little meeting to settle the problem face to face. But it was too late for talk. Shooting Wu had been the thing that sealed the fate of any peace talks. Rejo began to whistle.

But the Devil hadn't played any part in Wu's injury. The yellow-eyed little man had fallen off his seat and knocked himself out in the back of the wagon. The only one to see the Devil had been the pig, and he, apparently, hadn't been impressed.

Now, tired of walking the obstinate creature back and forth to water, Rejo decided that the men were so involved in the feud that they wouldn't be out looking for the Devil. Rejo moved his little herd out of the mountains and back to the canyon. He replaced the fence and covered it with brush so that unless someone knew where to go, he'd ride right by. Rejo decided he'd just hole up here until things heated up in town; then he'd make his move. Maybe he'd help things along.

Soon the boss would have what he wanted, and Rejo would claim his reward.

Elliott paced the porch of the settlement house. The two gunfighters were cleaning their weapons. The farmers were trying to carry on their normal activities, stringing wire around their tracts of land, and praying for rain.

With the use of his mechanical plow, they'd managed to get the fields plowed and the seed planted. But the damp ground had dried hard, and the first spurt of growth had slowed. It was becoming obvious to Elliott and the more experienced farmers that they were never going to grow cabbages as big as dishpans. The only crop that was showing promise was Elliott's field of oats. But even that would need irrigation if it didn't rain.

Elliott sighed. Now, more than ever, it was important that he succeed. For now, there was Miranda. The beautiful, golden woman who'd come to fill his thoughts and make him believe in his failed dreams of having his own place.

He and Miranda both had a new chance at a real life. And this time he wouldn't mess it up.

Unless Jake refused to see reason.

Unless Jake wanted to do what he hadn't done five years ago.

Unless Jake had made up his mind that it was time for Elliott to die.

Willie delivered Dallas's message to Jake and passed on her wish that Willie ride back into town with Jake and Wu when they came to the meeting.

"She knows about the meeting?"

"All the women know. They're really worried."

"So am I," Jake admitted. He had been ever since someone took a shot at Wu. Wu could have been killed, and it would have been his fault for not stepping forward sooner.

Just like Sarah's death.

Jake hadn't told Dallas all his plans because he didn't want anyone to know yet. But he'd already decided to share the water supply without dispute. He would accept limited fences if an agreement could be made that would allow the cattle access to the farmers' fallow land. If they compromised, he thought he could get the other ranchers to at least give it a try.

Providing Elliott could convince his farmers. Elliott himself was the biggest obstacle of all. He led the farmers. He was the sheriff. But most important of all, Green Willow Creek crossed the northernmost tip of Elliott's land, and if he chose, he could divert it away from its flow to the town.

Nobody knew that better than Lawson Pickens, who stood to lose his own access to water. If Elliott wanted to, he could keep Green Willow Creek from ever reaching the town. Without water there would be no town. Without a town there would be no need for a banker.

Lawson Pickens had been invited to the meeting.

Now, Dallas's note warned that the women would be in town as well. They'd be at Miranda's, awaiting the outcome of the showdown.

"Damn! I should have known she'd do some fool thing."

"Miss Dallas?" Wu asked. "What did she do now?"

"She's called a meeting of the women for tonight. They'll be at Miranda's. Did you know about this, Willie?"

"No, but I knew she was up to something. She and Miss Miranda rode out yesterday. They were gone all day. Then this morning she was setting the type to print something."

"What?"

"She wouldn't let me see. But I think it might be a new issue of the *Gazette*."

"Tell me more about the whistle you heard, Wu. Did you recognize the song?"

"Just whistle, like call turkey to eat."

Something in the back of Jake's mind had been bothering him ever since Wu mentioned the whistle. Whistling was not unusual, but the ranchers didn't do it for fear of spooking the horses. Except for—and then it hit him: except for Doak. But Doak was dead. And calling turkeys didn't make any sense.

Jake was more worried that the women were in town than he was about the contents of her newspaper. They ought to be safe from attack, but Green Willow Creek had turned into a bubbling cauldron, and he wasn't sure who was stirring the pot.

"Where is Shadow, Wu?"

"Wu not know, Mister Jake. Wu plenty worry. She say she go to think about future."

Jake wasn't sure he liked the sound of that. He was torn between riding into town early to call on

Dallas and searching for Shadow. The pained look on Wu's face made the decision for him.

"Let's saddle up, Wu. We'll look for Shadow on the way into town."

The sky was still light when they rode into town. There had been no sign of Shadow. The street was empty, the businesses shuttered and closed. The women had hidden their wagons and carts well. Jake's men, and the ranchers waiting at the edge of town, fell into lines of three across and walked their horses down the street toward the schoolhouse. Already waiting, silent and distrustful, were the farmers. Their two gunfighters were leaning lazily against one of the wagons, waiting and watching.

A dog barked and let out a surprised yelp as it encountered the tip of somebody's boot.

Jake dismounted, tied his horse to the wheel of one of the wagons, and motioned for the others to follow. One by one the ranchers climbed down from their horses. Mules swished their tails and shuffled their feet, and the wagons creaked in the resulting movements.

Elliott stepped forward. "Jake?"

"Yes. Are we all here?"

"I judge so."

Wu and Willie stood by the horses, listening. The tension was as electric as the air before a storm. The men had drawn closer, forming a semicircle around the two leaders. Two of the farmers' gunfighters carried special rifles with fancy stocks and shiny new barrels. Others carried pistols.

"Wu," Willy whispered, "Jake ain't carrying no gun."

"Neither is Mr. Parnell."

A third man walked to the center of the circle. "Good evening, gentlemen. I'm glad you all came."

"Pickens," somebody murmured, "what are you doing here?"

"I stand to lose or gain as much as any of you if this misunderstanding isn't cleared up," the banker answered.

"Nein! You already got money, now you get land back."

"Ja!"

"You're misinformed. I only collect your loan payments."

"He holds the mortgages on our land, too," one of the ranchers said. "And if this cattle stealing keeps up, he'll be getting the rest of 'em."

"Yeah, I say we run all the thieving foreigners out right now, Pickens included. Get the territory back the way it ought to be."

One gunfighter stepped forward, lifting his rifle menacingly in one hand and holding a pistol in the other. "I wouldn't try it, boys."

It only took the suggestion of a hand move and one of the outsiders defending the ranchers fired.

The first man swore and dropped the gun.

Another rifle was cocked. The man started to fall back.

"Now, wait a minute," Mr. Pickens said nervously. "We're here to find a way to settle this, not turn the meeting into a free-for-all."

A second shot was fired and found its target, the arm of Wade Trendle. Wade hadn't even worn a gun.

Jake quickly stepped forward and jerked a pistol away from one of his men, firing into the air. "Put your guns away!" Jake ordered. "I have a plan."

"We don't need to hear your plan, Jake," a rancher called out. "If you'd helped us run those Germans out in the beginning, none of this would have happened."

The men fell farther away from the circle, leaving Jake, Elliott, and Lawson Pickens standing alone.

Elliott looked at Jake's gun. "Damn it, Jake," Elliott said, "we agreed not to use guns. We don't need to kill each other."

"We won't."

The school was so silent that Jake could hear Elliott breathing.

"The past is gone, Jake. This is about the future and what we want it to be. We don't have to repeat past mistakes."

They weren't talking about a range war. Jake knew it. They were talking about Sarah. Elliott was right. He wasn't saying anything that Jake hadn't already thought about. He couldn't forgive, but maybe it was time to put the past behind them.

"Where is the monster, Elliott?"

"I don't know anything about the monster, Jake. Send your gunfighters home and we'll do the same."

"No!" a rancher shouted. "We're standing firm until all you foreigners are gone."

"Wait," Jake said in a voice that dared contradiction.

"Not any more, Jake," the same man insisted. "We're through waiting."

Willie looked desperately around. The ranchers and the farmers weren't even going to give Jake a chance to talk. So far two men had been shot, but the fight wasn't going to stop there. Willie whirled around and ran back to the saloon, bursting through the door.

"Miss Banning! You've got to come quick. They're going to kill each other down there. You've got to stop them."

Then Willie blinked in amazement and broke out in a red face. The women were all dressed, or rather half-dressed. They looked like the girls who entertained the customers of Miranda's saloon.

"Gol darn," he said, letting out a deep breath in surprise. "I guess you ladies ain't dressed for going anywhere."

"On the contrary, Willie, we're dressed for battle."

"Whoopee!" Widow Potter said, dragging herself to her full height. "I say, let's go, ladies. Charge!"

Willie watched openmouthed as the women, holding guns, sticks, rifles, and torches, marched out the door and down the street. In loud voices they began to sing a hymn, drawing the townspeople to the sidewalk to watch.

"What in hell?" Elliott saw them first.

Jake turned to see who was causing the new commotion.

"That can't be Effie!" Lawson Pickens said in a daze.

If it hadn't been such a stunning sight, Jake Silver would have laughed. The women, all the wives and sweethearts, were wearing only petticoats or pantalets. Widow Potter was wearing something that vaguely resembled an army tent, except it had no sleeves and its hem fell just below her knees. And Effie Pickens was wearing a glittery boa around her neck.

"Effie Pickens, what do you think you're doing? Cover yourself, woman!"

Lawson Pickens took off his coat and started toward his wife, looking everywhere but at her half-bare bosom.

"Get back, Lawson! Don't you take a step closer if you ever expect to share my bed again!"

There was a collective gasp.

"Lena? Is that you?"

One by one the men started forward, momentarily forgetting the impending confrontation as their wives and sweethearts formed a half-circle around them. Their movement came to an abrupt halt as they watched each woman assume a provocative stance and draw her weapon.

"Stop right there!" Lucy Trendle said.

"Ja!" one of the German women said. "Men must listen. Women speak!"

"Miranda?"

"I'm with the women, Elliott. We're united in a common purpose." A chorus of yesses rang out until Dallas held out her flyer and began to read.

"Like the women of ancient Greece, we, the women of Green Willow Creek, in the territory of Wyoming, hereby declare a state of self-denial to be in effect immediately. No man will be welcome in our beds so long as the dispute between the ranchers and the farmers is unresolved."

"Now, wait just a minute," a loud voice called out. "Agnes, you get yourself home right now!"

"No!"

"And Louise, what do you think you're doing dressed like some dance-hall girl?" This voice came from one of the merchants.

"Effective immediately, Wiley Lewis, that's just what I am, a dance-hall girl."

"I forbid you!" said one of the farmers and started toward the girl he planned to marry.

A shot rang out as Widow Potter took an answering step forward. "Now hold on here, boys. I think you'd better let Dallas finish reading our demands. Go on, child."

Dallas hadn't looked at Jake until her reading was interrupted. Now she found him, caught sight of his narrowed lips and what, for one brief second, looked like silent admiration. Then he turned the full force of his fury on her, glowering with all the rage he'd apparently been holding back.

"Yes . . ." she said, swallowed hard, and began to read again. "Furthermore, let it be understood that until a settlement is reached, we are now in control of the saloon and the bank. No monies, endearments, or liquid refreshments will be made available to any man involved in the disagreement."

"Now, wait just a minute," Lawson Pickens sputtered. "You women can't just take over the town!"

"We already have," Irene, the dressmaker, answered, then lowered her voice seductively and looked straight at Pete. "Unless you all are ready to send those gunfighters packing and listen to reason."

Jake suspected the women were enjoying their surprise attack. He couldn't decide whether or not he was glad. He was the one expected to assume leadership, not Dallas. "Dallas, you know this isn't going to work."

"What, Jake, stopping the war, or keeping you out of our beds?"

"Either one."

Dallas watched as resignation set in on Jake's face. The bluster of the other men quickly melted in the face of the women's opposition. Most of them were clearly stunned to see the women's bodies in such a public state of undress. Some, Dallas guessed, were seeing their wives in seductive attire for the first time in their lives. They'd all been made up to look their best. Women who had no provocative clothing had been provided with whatever Miranda could scavenge, and now all the wives and sweethearts were practicing the kind of feminine wiles they'd been cautioned against for all their lives.

Dallas glanced back at her flyer and read the final line. "Signed this last day of June, 1874, by——"

and each of the women stated her name. The last woman to come forward was Shadow.

"No," Wu whispered. "Shadow not belong here."

"Looks like you're gonna have to hold on to that pig for a while, Wu," Willie said with a grin. "Looks like the honorable bride has postponed the wedding."

Chapter 21

Satisfied that they'd made their point, the women turned and marched away from the schoolhouse. Though Dallas was more than satisfied with the train of events, she didn't miss the longing glances that young Harriet Brown directed at one of the ranch hands.

Possible problem here, Dallas decided. It wouldn't do for the youngest of their group to let romance interfere with the greater good. Still, so long as she, Miranda, and Widow Potter were diligent in their observances, they could likely shame any of the fainthearted among them, at least for a time.

The final challenge to the men—negotiate a peace treaty or sleep alone—had met with derisive comments and blustering threats. With the men finally saying that the women could stay in town until they "learned which side their bread was buttered on."

Widow Potter instantly responded by making the churning motion used to turn cream into butter and chanting, "Come butter come, come butter come, come butter come."

Effie Pickens and the merchants' wives peeled off toward the bank, keeping the beat of their march with the chant of their churning. The farmers' wives, making up the other regiment, headed for their duty station, the saloon.

The newspaper office had been designated as the command post, where Dallas formulated the plans for the siege. Beds were set up for the children in the upstairs quarters of the saloon. One troop would care for all the children. One troop would man the bank and another the saloon, twenty-four hours a day. The commanders of the individual troops were to be Effie, Irene, Lena, Widow Potter, and Amy Trendle. The rest of the women were divided up among the units.

"How long do you think it will take?" Miranda asked Dallas.

"Not long, I hope. I don't know how steadfast some of our soldiers are. I saw a couple of soulful looks as we marched away."

"Yes, and I saw another couple of obvious responses from the other side. I think they got the message."

Dallas murmured her agreement. She smiled. "I think they got exactly the message we were sending."

Shadow sat on the floor of Dallas's office and began to plait her braid. "Now," she said softly, "we wait."

But Dallas didn't know what she was waiting for. Jake had made his feelings clear. He'd never cared for her. She'd always been a substitute for Sarah, the woman he'd lost. He couldn't punish Elliott for Sarah's death because he'd promised Sarah. Now he had another chance to even the score.

To Jake, Elliott was the target now. Jake's solitary actions were all tied up with the people he'd been disappointed by, all the people he'd loved. Jake had loved his mother, and she died. His father had never acknowledged him. And Sarah had chosen someone else. There was no reason for Jake to risk exposing his feelings. Instead, he closed them out. Now that someone had pierced that wall of ice, he was afraid. He wanted her to think that he'd leave rather than face being hurt again. And she didn't believe that for one minute.

It was time, she decided, that Jake learned a lesson. He'd expected too much of the people he'd cared about in the past. But Dallas wasn't some lily-livered soul who couldn't make up her mind. She didn't play games. She never expected to find a man she could love, but she had, and tonight, when she'd seen that fleeting look in his eyes, she'd sworn by all the fires in hell that he'd understand that he belonged to her.

Dallas Banning had come to Green Willow Creek with the reputation of being a woman who always got her man. She just changed her sights a little. She'd claim Jake and she'd find Jamie's killer. It had come down to a showdown, all right. For an oath was the measure of her honor as well.

While Dallas was setting her sights, Jake Silver was trying to focus on his feelings. He feared neither man nor beast. But he had the most to forfeit if the master of the Devil of the Plains wasn't found. For Jake had thought he'd lost the capacity to love. Now Dallas had restored it.

Jake and Elliott watched the women walk away.

"Come butter come. Come butter come. Come butter come," they chanted.

Elliott groaned. "Damn it, Jake, how'd you let her do something like this?"

"As I interpret the note Dallas sent me, Miranda was just as much involved."

"Well, they're right about one thing," Wade Trendle said as Dr. Horn worked on his shoulder, "I'm

for sending these gunfighters away. If we can't get in
the bank, we can't pay them anyway. Now it looks
like I'll have to take on another hand to help me
out."

"Ja!" Adolph agreed. "I have no time to make
war. Must replant my crops, else I have no need to
put up wire to guard land that does not grow. Tell
fighters to go."

"But, men, men . . ." Lawson Pickens wrung his
hands. "We must look at the situation logically."

Jake decided Lawson was more upset than the
men who'd called for the showdown.

"What's really bothering you, Lawson?" Elliott
snapped.

Lawson Pickens looked distinctly uncomfortable.
"We have to talk about this. I mean . . . we don't
know who controls the Devil of the Plains. The kill-
ers are still loose."

"And the cattle are still being rustled," one
rancher agreed.

"Ja! And beef cows still churn our plowed
ground."

"And tear down our fences!" a farmer charged.

"And we still need water," Adolph said. "It costs
much to dig well and well goes dry."

"Listen," Pete finally said, "the truth is, we've
been outfoxed by our women. They've turned our
attention away from settling a land dispute."

"Yes," Elliott agreed with the beginning of a smile
curling his lips as his gaze met Jake's, and the two
men saw a possible way out. "They've issued a challenge. What it's come to now is, are we going to allow the women to run the show, or are we in
charge?"

"We are!" Trendle stamped his foot.

Hans, the blacksmith, spoke up. "Hans have no

woman now, but I think women need to go back to settlement house."

"I hate to say it, Jake," Elliott went on innocently, "but I believe all this is your fault. It's your woman who's organizing this."

"She's not my woman, Elliott," Jake snapped, seeing the direction Elliott was heading and playing along by refusing to take control of the new battle lines that were being laid out.

"Ah, but I've seen you look at her, and I don't think I believe your claim of indifference, my old friend."

"I'm not your old—" but Jake broke off, stunned by the realization that everything had changed. Though the men were on opposite sides, the women had forced them to join their efforts. He couldn't blame Elliott for all the trouble anymore, no more than he could blame Elliott for what had happened to Sarah. Slowly but surely he'd been forced to see the truth. He'd always known in the back of his mind that Sarah would have tempted him into her bed if he'd allowed it. Elliott wasn't so strong then. But Elliott had changed. It was time that Jake stopped blaming Elliott for something that he couldn't have changed.

Yes, Elliott was his old friend. They'd been through too much together to let past hurt make new pain. And they needed each other now.

The two men simply stared at each other, each reliving the incident that had ripped them apart. Each forced to deal with the reality of how things were now.

Jake finally nodded. "Maybe you're right, Elliott," he said, jumping the real issue of the war and focusing on the women's ultimatum. "But what do you intend to do? From where I stand, Miranda is just as guilty as Dallas."

"Yeah," Elliott said, "and it looks like the rest of the women aren't holding guns to each other's heads. We have a mutiny here, men. It's a matter of our livelihood or our ladies. Anybody got any ideas?"

After a grumbling discussion that reached no conclusion, the meeting broke up. The problem with the open range issue was still unresolved, but for now, the ranchers and the farmers were united against the women.

"At least the gunfighters are going, Wu," Jake said as they watched the men return home.

"Yes, but women gone, too."

"What are you so long-faced about? According to you, you've lost your manhood and couldn't take care of a woman anyhow."

"Wu is very proud man, Mr. Jake, and very . . . righteous man. His manhood is very disturbed."

Jake's manhood was disturbed as well. It had only taken one look at Dallas's body beneath the thin lawn garment she called her chemise. She'd known exactly what she was doing when she took deep breaths before reading each sentence. She'd known too that the sun was setting directly behind them, that they'd all appeared as silhouettes before its golden rays.

"What do you say we go have a drink and talk about it?" Elliott suggested.

Jake gave a dry laugh. "Where?"

"Well, we could—" Elliott began. "No, we couldn't. The women have taken over the saloon."

"How about the general store?"

"No, that's right across from the saloon," Lawson said. "Too easy to be spied upon."

They ended up in Dr. Horn's office, Jake and Elliott taking the two patient chairs, Hans and Pete on the examining table, and Mr. Lewis and Mr.

Trendle on the floor. After standing around for two drinks, Lawson Pickens gave it up and went home, swearing that he'd find some new games to play with Effie if she weren't there waiting for him. And these wouldn't be so pleasant.

She wasn't at home.

At the end of the second bottle, Dr. Horn sent Pete for more.

At the end of a fifteen-minute discussion with one of those foreign women at the door to the saloon, Pete gave up trying to buy a bottle and settled for trying to catch a glimpse of Irene's ruffled drawers.

"Dallas, they're down in Dr. Horn's office," Irene confided later in the saloon. "I think they're getting drunk, from the sounds of their conversation."

"Who?" Miranda asked, trying to conceal her longing to know about Elliott.

"Jake, Peter, Elliott, Hans, Mr. Lewis, Mr. Trendle, Dr. Horn, and Wu. Lawson Pickens was there, but he left."

"Are they still threatening to fight?" Dallas asked.

Irene grinned. "No. They're trying to figure out how to outsmart us. They think they'll catch us alone and sweet-talk us into jumping ship."

"Sweet-talk?" The women couldn't miss the yearning in Harriet's voice. "How do they talk sweet?"

"They promise you things you want in exchange for a kiss, then kiss you so silly that you don't even want them anymore," Miranda answered, only a bit breathlessly.

"And is that easy?" Harriet asked.

God knew, Dallas thought, it had been easy enough with her. Jake hadn't even had to sweet-talk her. All he did was look and she melted. He'd made no promises and she'd asked for none. Which was just as well, since she hadn't figured out any other way to stop him from leaving. Prolonging the stand-off between the men and the women served two purposes; it stopped the war, for now, and it kept Jake from leaving.

She touched her stomach and allowed herself to remember Jake's warning that she might be with child. She hoped he was right. If not, as soon as the conflict was ended, she intended to find a private way to make his fears a reality. Still, she felt guilty about what she was thinking. She was ready to do the very thing she'd told the other women not to do. Her plan of self-denial had gone right out the window the moment she saw Jake.

"Sometimes," she said quietly, "sometimes, Harriet, being sweet-talked is easy. Now, ladies, for the second part of our plan. Tomorrow we print our invitations and let Willie deliver them."

Irene went to the window and looked out. "Are you sure about inviting the men to a party, Dallas? I mean it's one thing to keep them away when they're away. But keeping them away when you're dancing with them, that might be hard."

Miranda groaned, then giggled. "That's the idea, Irene. That's exactly the idea. We want it to stay hard until they give in."

Jake didn't come by Dallas's office as the note had asked. Instead, he met Elliott by Green Willow Creek, at the point where it crossed over Elliott's land into Jake's.

While he waited, Jake studied the open prairie in the moonlight, letting the muted sounds of the night surround them. He loved Wyoming. He hadn't expected to, hadn't cared whether he did or not, never expected to stay. But now that his ranch was in jeopardy, he was ready to acknowledge how he felt.

Elliott rode up, drew his horse to a stop, and waited.

"Looks like somebody is trying to force a show-down," Jake finally said.

"Looks like it. Any ideas, Jake?"

"Maybe," Jake answered.

"So, are we in this together, or are you working alone?"

"I always work alone, Elliott. And I think our troublemaker is counting on that. Maybe we ought not to disappoint him just yet."

"I see." Elliott's voice was tired. "I'd hoped you'd agree to a truce between us, at least until this is settled."

"I might," Jake said.

"The way I see it," Elliott explained, "we can let this war go on and eventually a lot of people will get killed. But for every farmer who goes, two more will come. I've heard that in some areas, the new-comers are bringing in sheep."

"I heard that too. Sheep and cattle can't graze the same range, Elliott. You know that."

"That's why I say this may be our best chance of controlling the future of the territory peacefully."

Jake considered Elliott's request. The man was right. There was nowhere to go. He'd left South Carolina, left Kansas, and now he was contemplating leaving Wyoming. Six months ago, he might have gone. Before he'd met Dallas.

But joining forces with Elliott was something he wasn't ready to do—not yet. Still, enough people had died or been hurt.

"All right, Elliott. I think that there is one person behind all the trouble. I don't think it's one of your people, and I don't think it's a rancher."

"Then who?"

"That's the problem. As much as I hate to admit

it, I think it's Lawson Pickens. He stands to gain the most. He collects the payments for the land for a fee. Then when the farmers can't pay, he buys their land for a pittance. He's becoming the largest land-owner in the area."

"But what good is that? I'm beginning to believe that their land is practically worthless for farming, and Pickens is no rancher. He's not a farmer, either."

Jake slapped the reins against his knee. "That's the problem. That's why I can't figure it out. If I could find out who controls the Devil, it might help. But so far, there's been no trace of him. For now, I think we ought to let the world think we're bitter enemies. You try and keep the peace and I'll keep looking."

"Personally, I don't like what the women are doing," Elliott said, "but this standoff might keep things quiet for a few days."

"Maybe, if it lasts. At least the women and children are in town, where they're safe."

"So where do we go from here?" Elliott asked.

"Let's just play the hand as it's dealt, until somebody makes a mistake. You watch your people and I'll have Pete watch mine."

"Agreed. And you'll keep me informed?"

"I will."

Both were dissatisfied with the results of their meeting, but both agreed that until they came up with a better idea, this was the best they could do. Neither admitted that their own standoff had been ignored. Neither was sure whether their decision to remain public enemies was for the benefit of the participants or because they weren't ready to end the bitterness between them.

The next day Elliott took over the schoolhouse as his office. The farmers gathered around the building, proclaiming the north end of town as the unofficial headquarters for the farmers. Dr. Horn's office on the south end of the street became the meeting place for the townspeople and the ranchers, with Miranda's saloon and Dallas's newspaper office in the center. During the next day the farmers and the ranchers rode in and out of town, exchanging sharp slurs and verbal jabs. The union of the ranchers and the farmers in opposition to the wives was weaker, but still holding.

Effie Pickens stood in the doorway, holding Wade Trendle at bay with a shotgun.

"You can't be serious, woman. You don't really mean I can't withdraw any money," Wade roared, red-faced and disbelieving. "Here I am wounded and in need."

"In need, maybe; when have you not been, Wade Trendle? But the women have agreed that no man can withdraw money from this bank until a treaty between the ranchers and the farmers is signed."

"Excuse me, please." Amy Trendle slid past Effie, pocketing a wad of bills. "Hello, Wade. Nice day, isn't it?"

"Amy Trendle, is that our money?"

"Absolutely not, Wade, it's my money. You don't have any money; I've withdrawn it all."

If Wade's face was red a moment ago, it was fiery now. He sputtered, slammed his hands in his pocket and whirled around. "This has gone too far, woman. When you get home, you're going to be sorry."

"If I get home," Amy said airily and kept going.

Moments later she hurried back to the bank and handed the money to Effie.

"I think that worked just the way we wanted it to," Effie said, clapping her hands. "We refused service to Hans Dornier this morning and Wiley Lewis this afternoon. I guess by now they know we mean business."

Amy giggled. "You should have seen Pete trying to talk Miranda into selling him a bottle last night. Even Dr. Horn came by, said he needed some whiskey, strictly for medicinal purposes."

"Did you give it to him?" Effie asked.

"Absolutely not. Miranda told him that anybody sick had to check into the children's ward to be treated."

When Dallas heard the report, she agreed with Effie. Their plan was working. At least it was on the surface. She couldn't be sure that it had forced the warring factions to change their positions, but at least it gave them something else to be mad about.

The party invitations for the men of Green Willow Creek were delivered the next day to the farmers at the schoolhouse and the ranchers and the merchants at Dr. Horn's office.

> *You are cordially invited to a party at Miranda's Saturday evening from eight o'clock until twelve midnight. Refreshments will be served.*
> *The Wives and Sweethearts of Green Willow Creek*

*   *   *

Jake was still puzzled about Wu's assault and his claim that he'd heard whistling. "Calling the turkey to eat," was the way he explained it. *Turkey?* It made no sense.

When Pete brought the invitation to the party, Jake let go a reluctant smile. She was pulling it off, keeping the women united in their purpose. Jake didn't know about the other men, but he missed being with Dallas, and they weren't married. He suspected the other men were missing their wives as well. Maybe a little party was a good idea. At least

if everybody was in one place he wouldn't have to
worry about someone being burned out or shot.

The weather cooperated by continuing its bright
sunshine in the daytime and temperatures that
stayed above freezing at night. The men wandered
into town, the ranchers heading for Dr. Horn's office and the farmers for the school. They didn't
hurry to the saloon, but ambled about as if they
were unsure of their destination.

Dr. Horn, always the calming influence in the
community, cautioned the ranchers about attending
the party. "They're just trying to tease us."

"Don't take much to do that," one rancher observed.

"I'm coming in for the refreshments," another observed.

"Anybody seen Jake?" the doctor asked.

"Nope," they all agreed.

"Haven't seen him much since that Chinaman of
his got shot," Wade Trendle said. "I think he's out
looking for the monster."

Dr. Horn nodded. "Has he seen any signs of the
creature?"

"Not so far as anybody knows," somebody answered.

"There's an awful lot of territory out there. Even
the posse couldn't find it. It's like the creature knew
where we would look. Where's Jake searching?"

The answer to that question came from Pete,
who'd just come in. "Along the base of the mountains, I think. He goes out alone most of the time.
Personally, I don't think there is a monster."

"You're wrong," Wade contradicted. "I have it on
good authority that there was an old miner who
saw a herd of them monsters in the Green Mountains."

"A herd?" Pete questioned.

"You ought to remember him, Doc," Wade said, "didn't he break a leg or something back last fall?"

Dr. Horn nodded. "Yes, I believe he did. I set his leg and he insisted on going right back to his mine. Had to get a wagon and carry him."

Wade's eyes widened. "Did you see the herd?"

"I saw a crazy old man who'd been by himself too long," the doctor answered.

"What happened to him?" someone asked. "Did he ever find gold?"

"Nobody knows. He disappeared and nobody ever found his mine."

Dr. Horn listened to the men discuss all the reasons why they shouldn't attend the party, but in the end, they did just what the women expected. They came.

Chapter 22

Dallas studied herself in Miranda's mirror. She and the other women had, again, decked themselves in their most provocative clothing. The more alluring they were, the shorter the war.

Effie added a red petticoat to match the red boa around her neck. Always considered to be a meek little partridge controlled by her husband, the banker's wife had become a surprisingly creative accomplice.

"Do you think it's safe to leave the bank unguarded, Effie?" Miranda asked.

"Oh, yes. I didn't even lock the door."

"But Mrs. Pickens," young Harriet asked, "what if the men take over the building?"

Effie laughed and took a suggestive pose. "Let 'em. They won't find any money. I hid it."

"You hid the money? But wasn't it heavy?"

"Nope; Lawson got scared about this range war and sent it over to Laramie until everything is settled. All the money in Lawson's bank is paper, and right now, he couldn't find it if he looked."

This time it was Amy Trendle who showed her surprise. "Effie Pickens, aren't you afraid that Mr. Lawson will be upset?"

"It's time that Lawson learned that he isn't the only one who knows how to play games."

The women shook their heads and joined in the laughter. For most of the day they'd worked together preparing the food and, with Irene's help, planning their costumes. The children had been fed and put to bed early, and Lena was applying lard to her fingers so that they'd soften enough for her to play the piano.

The Widow Potter suddenly spoke up. "Dallas, as part of our entertainment I think you should read some of that Greek play we're going by."

"Oh, I doubt anybody would want to listen," Dallas protested.

"The men won't," Amy agreed. "All the more reason to read it. And every woman here should make certain that her man gets his stomach full and thinks that he's forgiven."

"Yes," Irene agreed, "then we make them listen to Dallas read."

All the women concurred.

"Well, if you're sure. I'll have to go back to the newspaper office and get the book. Make certain things here are ready," she instructed Miranda. "When the men come, we proceed just as we planned."

Dallas pulled on her long opera cloak and slipped out the door of the saloon. She hurried down the sidewalk and crossed the street to the newspaper office. She unlocked the door and slipped inside.

She knew immediately that she wasn't alone.

Jake was standing by the stove, the thin curl of smoke snaking upward from the cigar clenched between his teeth.

"Not going to your own party?" he asked.

"Jake! How'd you get in?"

"I have my ways."

"What are you doing here?"

"Your note asked me to come."

"But that was two days ago."

"I got held up by a group of women running around in their underwear."

She was wary of him, her eyes sending the kind of signals that a trapped animal sent, not the forward, provocative ones the men were receiving from their wives and sweethearts. He took a step toward her, closing the distance between them, then stopped. "I've missed you, maverick."

She drew in a deep breath. *Good!* Her plan was working. "You shouldn't be here, Jake. You're supposed to come to the party at Miranda's."

"I know. Why?"

Dallas pulled her cape closer. "What do you mean, why?"

"Why a party? Don't you know that it's dangerous inviting the ranchers and the farmers to the same place? Anything could set them off."

"I don't think so. Enemies ought to be able to meet on neutral ground. Besides, all we're trying to do is bring an end to the hostilities."

"I don't think this is the way to do it, Dallas. Why couldn't you talk it over with me, let us work out a plan?"

Jake took the cigar from his mouth and spit a loose piece of tobacco into the air. Dallas's dark hair was loose across her shoulders, as it had been the night she wore Miranda's Russian dressing gown. But tonight she'd caught it up with a green ribbon that matched the green flecks in her eyes. Her lips, pink and full, were trembling as she tried to keep her emotions from showing.

"You made it clear that you wanted no part of me, Jake. You work alone. So why are you really here?"

"You know that isn't true," he admitted. "I just didn't want you to be hurt."

"I know. I knew that at the time. What kind of plan did you have in mind, Jake?"

"I'm not sure. I just can't get a handle on who the man is behind the killings. I was certain it was Lawson Pickens, but I can't see what he gains. So he does buy up all the farmer's land; he can't farm it, and I don't think there are enough ranchers hurrying out here for him to sell it off. There's no water supply for half of it, no timber, no wildlife."

"Jake, could it be someone else? What about an outsider who's just using the monster to cover his rustling?"

"The only man who stands ready to make money is the man who is selling the land to the farmers, the land agent. But according to Pickens, he's back in Chicago. I can't see him going to the trouble to steal cattle. And I'm not sure there are enough cattle involved to take the risks he's taking. Are you certain you didn't recognize the men at the camp when you found the monster?"

Dallas saw no reason to conceal the truth any longer. She'd long ago decided that Jake wasn't behind the trouble. If he'd made any effort to make her a part of his investigation, she would have told him before. "It was Doak."

"Doak?" Jake was surprised. His mind went to Wu's story of the man whistling. Doak was the only one who routinely whistled. But even if Doak had been involved with the monster, he wasn't now. And he couldn't have been the one to take a shot at Wu. By then, Doak was already dead.

"Dallas, Wu said the only thing he heard the night he was shot was a man whistling. He thought it was a signal to someone who answered with the call of a coyote."

"Does that mean anything to you?" she asked.

"No. But knowing it was Doak in the camp might, if I can figure out who gave the signal. Wu said he was whistling for the turkey to eat. That makes no sense."

Dallas couldn't make any sense of that either.

Jake flipped the cigar inside the stove and said. "The only person I ever heard whistle was Doak, and he's dead. You saw his body yourself."

Dallas shivered visibly. "And unless we believe in ghosts, we have to keep looking."

"About this party, Dallas," Jake began, "why aren't you down there, getting ready?"

"I came back to get a book."

Jake lifted one eyebrow. "I'm afraid to ask what kind of book. Is it some erotic poetry, designed to drive the men even crazier?"

Her voice caught in a throat so tight that she could barely breathe. "Something like that," she managed to say.

He reached out and unfastened the catch of her cape, pulling it open. He knew, even as he peeled the cape away to reveal the white petticoat beneath, that he was making a mistake. He'd already told her he wasn't interested. He'd found a way to send her away from him.

There was only one problem.

He couldn't seem to let her go.

"Is this what the rest of the men can expect at the party?" he asked in a low voice.

"Yes."

"I don't want other men looking at you, Dallas."

"I don't want other men looking at me, Jake."

"Then call off this campaign."

"I will, as soon as you make a truce with the farmers."

"Dallas, it may surprise you to know that I don't

give a hoot about the farmers planting crops here. They can take over Wyoming tomorrow. But nobody fires a gun at someone I care about. And somebody damned near killed Wu."

"So you're still determined to hurt someone in return?"

Jake touched his fingertip to Dallas's throat, running it down the hollow beneath her chin and rimming the top of her camisole. He could see her nipples, now hard little cherries pressed against the thin fabric. Her breath was coming in quick, shallow pants.

"I'll hurt anyone who hurts anything of mine."

"But I'm not yours, am I?"

"You're a witch," he said in little more than a growl, drawing her into his embrace. "A witch who is driving me crazy. Is that what you want to hear?"

"Oh yes," she whispered, pressing herself against him, feeling the evidence of his desire throbbing between them. "I want that. I want you to touch me, Jake. I want you to take me to bed and give me a child."

"Now?"

Oh yes, now and tomorrow and every day. But she couldn't let that happen. She had to remember the plan. "Oh no!" she said gaily, jerking herself from his grip and dancing away. "Remember our vow of self-denial? It applies to me and you, most especially you."

"Don't do this, Dallas!" Jake roared. "I don't want you involved in your women's war. Why must you always be rebellious?"

"Why, Jake? I'm a rebellious woman. You ought to know that by now. But why are you worried? You're leaving anyway. You want to see the ocean. Don't concern yourself about me. I'll do fine."

Dallas grabbed the book of Greek plays, refastened her cape, and left the newspaper office.

"Don't miss the party, Jake. We have special entertainment. Lena is playing the piano and Effie Pickens is going to sing."

"And you," he said as he watched her walk away, "what are you going to do?"

"I don't think I'll tell you, Jake Silver. You'll have to come and see."

The light of a rising moon spattered the town, casting a familiar silver glow across the rutted street. She remembered the first time she'd walked down that street. Had it really been so few weeks ago? Jake had thrown her across his shoulder like some primitive caveman, carrying her out of danger.

He'd continued to rescue her, care for her, and fight his attraction to her. But it was too strong. He'd been no more able to stay away from her than she'd been able to stay away from him. It was as if they were destined to be together.

Jake would come to the party; she was sure of that. Then later, when the women had woven their spell, the men would agree to settle the trouble and peace would prevail.

But from the first, the men were quarrelsome and argumentative. Lena's piano playing seemed jarring in the silence. Effie's song met stares of disbelief as the men grumbled among themselves about the women's provocative dress. Instead of enticing the men into a state of submission, the women were being ogled and stared at.

"I saw you looking at my woman," Wade Trendle said, grabbing the shoulder of one of the immigrants. "Do that again and I'll kill you!"

"Stop that, Wade Trendle!" Amy snapped.

"Ja!" Lena agreed. "Men who want their women home must make agreement, not fight."

"I wouldn't agree with anything one of those for-eigners said," a rancher called out. "And I want some whiskey to drink, not this sweet water you call punch!"

"Let's not get all wrought up, boys," Elliott said quietly. "This is a party, remember? I think the women want to make us see what we're missing."

"That's the trouble," Wiley Lewis called out from the back of the room, "they're showing us too much."

"Don't you fellows like what you see?" Widow Potter asked. "Look what you're missing. 'Pears to me you ought to be talking about making peace, not more fighting."

"Effie Pickens, you get down from that piano and put some clothes on, or I'm sending all your furni-ture back East!"

"You'd better not, Lawson! Besides, if you do, I'll just buy some more. I have plenty of money."

"You wouldn't dare spend the bank's money!" her husband challenged.

"Try me," Effie said.

"Stop drooling at Effie, you old fool!" Lawson Pickens said to Dr. Horn.

"I'm just admiring your wife, Lawson," the doc-tor answered. "I didn't know she was so—lovely."

Dallas looked at Miranda. This wasn't working out the way she'd envisioned. It was time for some kind of intervention. "Just a minute, men," she said, "I have a story to tell you. A story that might ex-plain the terms of our surrender."

"Oh? And what are they?" This time the veiled threat came from one of the ranchers who rarely spoke out.

"Not speak harsh to Miss Dallas," Wu said softly. "We listen."

"I'm rather enjoying looking," Pete confessed, casting a rueful grin toward Irene.

"I want to read from a play, written by a Greek playwright in the year four eleven B.C. He'd watched the great minds of Greece try to find an end to the Peloponnesian War for over twenty-five years. He found a simple solution that didn't cost anybody's life."

"This is where you get idea?" Hans Dornier asked incredulously. "A play written over two thousand years ago?"

"Nein!" Adolph Schmahl shouted. "We not listen to play. We want wives home, now!"

Dallas looked helplessly at the women. She wasn't about to let the women lose their purpose and give in. There had to be an answer. She looked up to see Jake's familiar face. He was standing by the door, with one foot propped lazily against the frame.

"Jake?" she said, then realized that she couldn't expect him to come to her aid now. This was her showdown, and she had to find a way to follow through. After all, she was the maverick. "You came."

"I wouldn't miss this for the world. I want to see how the women plan to run the town."

That statement brought an immediate roar of disapproval from the party-goers.

But it was Dr. Horn who stopped the hostilities from becoming more heated when he stepped forward. "Miss Lena, I wonder if you know a tune called 'Turkey in the Straw?' I have a hankering to dance to it."

" 'Turkey in Straw'? Nein." She shook her head, glancing at her husband out of the corner of her eye.

"It goes like this." And Dr. Horn began to whistle the tune.

Dallas found Jake. He took a quick look at Wu,

who nodded, then turned back to Dallas. Wu's signal. This was what Wu had heard, someone whistling "Turkey in the Straw."

Dr. Horn was whistling "Turkey in the Straw."

Jake couldn't make any sense out of what he was thinking. Why would the man who'd been the town peacemaker be responsible for stirring up trouble that led to murder? He couldn't be. Everybody knew that Dr. Horn couldn't hit the broad side of a barn. He always used his buggy because he was such a poor rider. No, it was simply a coincidence. Like Doak, he'd heard the song somewhere and it had stuck in his memory.

Lena got the gist of the song and began to play it. Dr. Horn stepped up, took Dallas's hand in his and began whirling her around the hall. She was too stunned to resist. One by one, the men claimed their women for a dance. By the time the music came to a close, the tension had eased. Dr. Horn was winded, and Jake had disappeared.

During the next hour, one of the men pilfered a bottle of whisky from behind the bar and added it to the punch. Afterward, the dancers became more lively, more argumentative, and more outspoken.

Dallas was determined to force the issue of a truce. Accompanied by Widow Potter, she circulated, cajoling the women into sticking to the plan. She watched the women flirting with the men, then pushing them away. It was working, except for young Harriet Wood, who disappeared with her cowboy, returning later with lips that were red and swollen.

About that time Hans Dornier jostled Wade Trendle, causing him to stumble against Effie Pickens. In Wade's attempt not to fall, he caught Effie's red petticoat and pulled it down. Whereupon Lawson Pickens took a swing at Hans, while Effie hit Lawson over the head with a beer mug. The free-for-all that followed brought an end to any possibility of peace between the warring factions. Now, in addition to the ranchers and the farmers being at odds, the husbands and wives were engaged in physical combat.

Elliott fired his gun in the air, bringing instant calm to the fracas. Then the stunned party-goers heard a scream followed by a second gunshot, and they watched Dallas crumple to the floor.

There was a roar from the balcony as Jake swung over the railing and dropped to the floor where Dallas had collapsed. Nobody except Shadow noticed the very big man standing in the doorway who was buttoning his coat as he backed out into the darkness. Nobody but Shadow, who felt a heaviness settle over her heart.

Before Dr. Horn could examine Dallas's injury, the men had separated into groups and were facing each other with pure hatred in their eyes. Any hope of a peaceful settlement died as the blood seeped into a teardrop-shaped crimson splotch on the white of Dallas's chemise.

"See to her, Horn!" Jake snapped. "Shadow, help him."

He stood as the Indian woman came and knelt beside her friend. Jake tried to still the wild thunder of his heart. He'd never known such rage as he'd felt when he saw Dallas fall. The shot hadn't been fired by Dr. Horn. He'd been in Jake's line of vision. The only other gun in evidence at that moment was the one that belonged to Elliott.

But Elliott couldn't have shot Dallas. In spite of all that had happened in the past, Jake knew that Elliott would never deliberately hurt anyone. But the men in the saloon didn't know that, and the tension was so thick that nobody was moving.

One look at Elliott's shocked face confirmed Jake's belief that Elliott hadn't shot Dallas. But someone expected Jake to think so. *Remember, Elliott, we'll play the hand as it's dealt.*

Jake took a step toward his old friend. "I saw another woman die when I didn't act, Elliott. Now, because of your immigrants, Dallas has been hurt. Right and wrong don't matter now. I'll give you and your farmers five days to pack up and get out. You have until noon on Friday. If they're still here, you're a dead man."

The farmers moved in behind Elliott, silently, but with little room for doubt that they would come to his aid if needed.

Elliott shook his head. "No, Jake. We didn't have anything to do with the trouble, and in your heart, you know it. I'm the sheriff here, and I won't have you issue an ultimatum. We've already seen what that does. We aren't leaving."

"Not now, Jake," Miranda said quietly. "Let's get Dallas upstairs to my bedroom. Now, Jake!"

Jake leaned down and lifted Dallas in his arms and mounted the stairs. At the top, he turned back. "The party is over, folks. Go home, all of you, and stay there."

To Elliott he said, "Remember, Friday, noon."

Chapter 23

It was too much to hope that Dallas's wound was as insignificant as Wu's had been. Yet, surprisingly enough, it was. The bullet had entered and exited her shoulder, leaving a clean wound that Shadow was able to stop bleeding in a matter of minutes. She and Dr. Horn washed the wound carefully and cauterized it, then filled it with powdered herbs, bound it, and put Dallas to bed.

Now, Dr. Horn was studying Jake's grim expression. "She'll be fine, Jake."

"This time," Shadow added softly.

Jake jerked his chin up and looked at Shadow. "There won't be another," he pledged, adding sternly, "Once those farmers are gone, the territory will be at peace again."

"You think they'll really leave, Jake?" Dr. Horn asked as he gathered up his instruments.

"They'll leave. I'll see to it."

"Mr. Jake, you think that what bad men want?"

"What do you mean, Wu?"

"Old Chinese proverb say to make mother panda angry, you attack her cub."

"You think all this was to force me into action?" Jake wasn't surprised at Wu's observation. It was the same one he and Elliott had made.

Wu nodded; his expression, always hard to read, was even more stoic.

Dallas, swimming in a haze of pain, heard Jake's words and tried to protest. She whimpered and fought the effects of the sleeping potion that she'd been given. But her fighting was in vain, for in the end she slept.

Through the night, Jake sat beside her, never moving. He'd long ago decided that Shadow's knowledge was as great as that of the doctor, but there was something reassuring about Horn's presence. He had no family, at least none that anybody knew of. He'd come at the same time as the railroad, and like Miranda had stayed on. Through the years the doctor had earned his reputation as a caring man.

Jake swore softly. He, too, had earned a reputation, that of turning his back on anything that didn't pertain to him or his ranch. Always before he'd protected his own, until Dallas came to Green Willow Creek. This time he'd failed. He hadn't been able to keep her from being shot. He hadn't even been able to find the Devil of the Plains. The next morning, finally convinced that Dallas would be all right, Jake stopped by the bank to have a look at Lawson's land map.

The posse had borrowed it and marked off the valley to be searched a quadrant at a time. Between him and the ranchers they'd found several places where the creature had been kept, but it was always gone.

Time was running out. Jake decided earlier in the day that it was time to call in a few debts, starting with a telegram to the Pinkerton Agency back East. They ought to be able to find out about the land agent. To conceal his suspicions, he'd included the names of several others, including Elliott Parnell,

Lawson Pickens, Dr. Horn, and even Miranda. Spence sent the telegram and swore he'd keep the request under his hat.

Continuing the ruse that he and Elliott were ready to meet in a showdown, both men made certain that everyone still believed that the farmers had five days to pack up their belongings and leave. Lawson Pickens had agreed to work with them on selling their land. It might take some time, but nobody would be cheated; Jake would see to that. In the meantime, the ranchers had been instructed to stay close to their homes and leave any further action to Jake. There'd been too many deaths.

When Dallas opened her eyes the next morning, she felt as if she'd been roped and branded. She was in Miranda's bed, wearing Miranda's nightclothes, and looking out through the gauzy bed hangings at a concerned Shadow.

"Where's Jake?" Dallas asked.

"He was here for most of the night."

"Help me up, Shadow," Dallas said, forcing herself to try to sit as she fought the swimming headache that racked her brain.

"No, you stay quiet!"

"No. I won't stay quiet. I didn't believe it until I heard Jake threaten the farmers. He's finally decided to take a side, and I don't want that."

Shadow gave her support and helped her to sit up. "Don't you? Haven't you tried to force him to become involved?"

"Yes, but I didn't mean that he should run the farmers out. I wanted him to act as a peacemaker."

Shadow just looked at Dallas. "Jake Silver is many things, but there is nothing peaceful about him. He is a man with a tortured soul, a soul he protects carefully. You forced him to open up. Now he is at risk."

"No, he isn't, Shadow. Don't be melodramatic. All he needs to do is work out some kind of agreement with Elliott."

"So long as one man leads and one man follows, two men can agree. But when two men try to lead, one must fail. Which man do you want to fail, Dallas?"

There was a dull ache in Dallas's shoulder, but no real pain. She was weak, but no more so than she'd been after an illness. Still, standing and walking to the window were more taxing than she'd expected. As she reached the glass pane, she caught at the frame and rested her forehead on the wooden crosspiece.

Breathing deeply for a few seconds, she lifted her head and looked down into the empty street. Only one horse was tied at the rail, Jake's horse, Blackjack.

"Where is he, Shadow?"

"At Dr. Horn's office. Maybe the school. He walks the street, back and forth."

"Where is everybody else?" Dallas asked.

"The ranchers stay home. The farmers don't come into town. The merchants remain inside. The gunfighters have all left. The women have gone home. Now, everyone waits."

Dallas felt a lurch in her heart. "Waits? For what?"

"The—I think you call it—showdown."

Dallas groaned. She hadn't been wrong in her remembering. Her grand scheme to force the men to settle their battle like the women in ancient Greece had been a fiasco. In the end, someone had made the final push, forcing Jake into the fracas, bringing the war to a final confrontation.

"So much for your great plans, Dallas," she said to herself. "You couldn't even settle a difference of opinion with one man. You couldn't even make him believe that you love him, that you want all this to end so that you can convince him that mavericks can be branded, if they allow themselves to be."

"I do not understand this talk about mavericks," Shadow said. "Now, come back to bed. The bullet did no great damage, but you are weak."

"Not yet," Dallas insisted, holding on gamely. "How long was I out?"

"Only one night and this morning."

"So there are four days left before the war begins in earnest?"

"Four days before the Germans have to be gone, yes."

Dallas leaned against Shadow and started to turn. Then she saw him, Jake, walking down the center of the street as if he were the only man left in the world.

For Dallas he was.

Wearing the same canvas duster with the split in the back, he was a lean, desperate figure. He hadn't shaved, and his two-day growth of beard seemed to set off the thin black cigar that he clasped in the corner of his mouth. She hadn't noticed it before, but now it came to her that he was wearing his spurs once again, the silver spurs with the turquoise stones in the design.

Around his waist was a gunbelt. She could see his hand resting lightly on the gun as he walked, keeping back the coat in order to give himself quick access if needed.

Dallas shivered, not from the cold, but from fear.

"Please, Dallas, come back to bed."

"Yes," she whispered, but did not move, waiting for Jake to turn and look up at her window as he had that first night when their gazes had connected with such force.

But he never did. And Dallas Banning had never felt so alone in her life.

All day Monday, Dallas was forced to remain in bed. She took the time to review the case in her mind, determined to separate fact from rumor. Dallas Banning was an ex-operative for the finest detective agency in the world. She'd solved other crimes; she could solve this one.

Just follow the greed and the power, Allan Pinkerton always said. So, who stood to gain money and power from a range war? Someone who wanted the land? They'd explored that possibility endlessly without finding a reasonable answer. The land wouldn't grow anything except range grass, at least it hadn't so far.

Ranchers? That didn't make sense, for they couldn't afford to buy it, even if the farmers let it go. But if the farmers were gone, the range would remain open. Open range land was good for the cattle. Still, the ranchers had lost as much as the farmers.

Or had they?

Some cattle and a couple of ranch hands had died. There was no making light of death, but somehow the ranchers' losses didn't compare with the farmers'.

Wu had been shot and now someone had tried to kill Dallas. Or had they? She couldn't avoid the thought that if someone had really wanted to kill her, he wouldn't have missed. They hadn't missed when they'd shot Jamie. She'd been a clear target, as had Wu.

No, someone had been deliberately goading Jake, forcing him to take a stand. She followed that thought through. If someone wanted Jake to enter the war, it was because they wanted the Germans to be run out.

Now she was back where she started.

Why would anybody want their land?

There had been no gold strikes in the mountains.

Dallas forced herself to get up and move around, pacing the room as she thought.

Then there was the Devil of the Plains. She'd seen him; at least she'd seen his shape and shadow in a cloud of dust. Why couldn't Jake find him? Had he really looked? Had he known all along about the creature and faked his searches?

No. Jake was many things. But he wasn't a liar. And he wasn't a killer, either.

And then there was the whistler. Who was he? Not Dr. Horn; he only wanted a tune for a lively dance.

Dallas was missing something. In the back of her mind she knew there was something she'd heard that she ought to recall, some important conversation. But it wouldn't come to her. In desperation she sent Willie to the newspaper office for Jamie's papers and his notes. She read them again. Two men, he'd said, but Jake held the key.

Everything came back to Jake Silver.

Jake refused to set foot inside the saloon. Not only did he feel Miranda's censure, Dallas was upstairs, and if he went inside, he'd keep going straight up the steps.

Jake Silver was a man at war with himself. Every step he'd taken since he watched Lee surrender to Grant had served to send him farther from his past and any hope of a future. He'd tried to keep the territory wild and unsettled. But once the railroad came, reality invaded his solitude.

And nothing would ever be the same again.

He stayed in town, leaving Pete in charge at the ranch, while he waited for the answer from the Pinkerton people. Whoever wanted to get to him had a clear target. There were no loyal hands around, nobody to take a stand or interfere. He couldn't do anything about the families of the Germans who'd been burned out or killed, but he could do his best to see that there were no other threats. By focusing attention on himself, he believed that he was keeping everyone else safe.

If only he'd stepped forward in time to save Dallas from pain.

"She's fine," Dr. Horn kept telling Jake.

"She needs you," Shadow pleaded.

Her request fell on deaf ears. Dallas might have survived one bullet. The next one would find its target, if Jake didn't provide a better one.

Though Elliott had pleaded with them not to do so, some of the immigrants had ridden into town and surrendered their deeds to Lawson Pickens. With Lawson in charge of the bank again, Jake arranged to have funds withdrawn from his account to advance the farmers enough money to get back east or to move farther west. A promise was made to send other funds gained from reselling the land to wherever the farmer directed. If his account was emptied before this was settled, Jake didn't know what he'd do.

The Germans had three more days, until Friday noon.

On Tuesday afternoon, Dallas dressed and slipped out of the saloon. Hugging the doorways of the businesses, she dashed down the wooden sidewalk and across the street to the newspaper office. As soon as she stepped inside the door, she felt a great weight lift from her. This was her place, a place she'd made for herself that was uniquely hers. This was where she'd spent so many hours with Jake.

She'd never known what love was like, until now.

Never known that it was so good, nor that it could hurt so badly.

Until he'd kissed her and she'd felt the danger in his soul. The emptiness. The need. The ice had begun to melt. And she suspected that he'd been as astonished with the fire they'd created between themselves as she.

Dallas didn't believe for one minute that he'd walk away and leave her, leave his land and the great herd of cattle he'd bred. He was only making one last attempt to keep her safe. She didn't believe he'd force the Germans out either, unless it was the only way he could save their lives.

She stood inside the door, leaning against it, breathing slowly as she allowed her body to find its own way back to the demands of rapid movement.

"Willie?"

"Dallas? What the hell are you doing here?"

It wasn't Willie who answered, but Jake. He was sitting in her chair, by the stove, smoking in the twilight.

"Oh, Jake, I'm so sorry." She allowed a sob to break through the lump in her throat. She was just so glad to hear his voice again.

"Don't cry, darling," he said, coming swiftly to his feet and catching her as she took a step forward.

"I'm not crying, you jaybird, I'm happy."

"Yes, I remember how you get hysterical with laughter when I hold you."

She felt his arms go around her, pulling her tightly against him as his mouth captured her lips. An answering rumble of sound swept through the silence as he groaned and explored her willing mouth, feeling her open herself up to him, just as she always did.

Dallas kept her eyes open, feeling the pain of contradiction in his stance, registering the tension that fought with desire as he pulled back.

"What are you doing here, maverick?"

"I had to think. I couldn't do it any longer in Miranda's bedroom."

His chin touched her cheek. She could feel the tickle of his mustache against her forehead, the warmth of his breath feathering her hair.

"What did you need to think about, Dallas?"

"This. Us. What we're going to do to make things right."

"You can't do anything," he said. "You aren't supposed to do anything. I forbid you to do anything."

"Of course you do," she whispered happily. "You always do, Jake Silver."

"And you never pay any attention to me. I'm glad you didn't break your leg. You'd probably be hobbling down the street on the other one."

"But I failed so miserably. And I thought my idea about the women banding together could fix everything."

"It almost did," Jake said, nuzzling the side of Dallas's face. "You brought all the women together as equals, and that's something that's never been done before."

She let out a deep sigh. "But it didn't work."

Jake was so damned glad to be holding Dallas that all his plans not to do so went straight out the window. "Only because someone didn't want it to work."

"So we're back to where we started, aren't we, Jake?"

He leaned back and gave her a resigned grin.

"Not quite," he answered. "But I think I like where we are a whole lot better."

So did Dallas, even if, several hours later, it did mean telling both Willie and Miranda to go away!

"Why did you tell me you were going away?" Dallas asked later, as they lay in the darkness of her sleeping loft.

"I didn't want you to be hurt," he answered simply.

There had been a relaxed quality about his body in the aftermath of their lovemaking, until now. Now the tension was returning.

He gently disentangled himself from her and stood.

"Where are you going?"

"I have to get back outside," he answered, pulling on his clothes.

"Why? Do you expect something to happen?" A flash of fear swept over Dallas. He did expect something to happen. Of course—he was offering himself as a target. He'd become the lightning rod, deliberately reaching for the storm in the sky.

"Of course," he admitted, pausing at the head of the stairs. "That's what it has come down to, hasn't it? I can't find the person behind the trouble, so I'm waiting for him to find me."

Long after Jake left, Dallas lay in the darkness, thinking. There had to be an answer. Follow the power, the money, Allan Pinkerton had taught her. Look for the false word, the casual conversation that isn't quite right, her newspaperman father had always said.

And it was there, somewhere in her subconscious. She knew it. She felt it. In her mind she went back over the incidents. The pulling down of the sod houses, the killing of the cattle, the attack on the wagon that resulted in Adolph's leg injury.

Leg injury. What was said about another leg injury? Jake had said he was glad she hadn't broken her leg because she'd have hopped home on her good one. Adolph's leg had been broken, but it was practically healed. But there'd been another broken leg.

The miner. Everybody knew about the miner who'd broken his leg and forced Dr. Horn to take him back to his claim in the mountains in a wagon. Nobody had ever seen the man again. Dallas didn't know what that had to do with anything, but it stuck in her mind. And a good detective paid attention to hunches. A good newspaper editor paid attention as well.

She wondered where the doctor took the miner.

That was when she decided to call on Mr. Pickens. Maybe they'd been going about this all wrong. Somebody wanted to keep people away, all right, but maybe their reason was something nobody had thought about yet.

But Dallas would have to work quickly and quietly. There were only two days left before the showdown between Elliott and his farmers and Jake and his ranchers.

The map of the valley was tacked on the wall of the banker's office. There were sections marked off with names written in the center. Some of the names had been marked through.

"Now let me make sure I understand this, Mr. Pickens. This line along here is the railroad."

"Yes. And the government originally offered the railroad companies great amounts of land on either side of the site free. These sections of land often became favors bestowed on investors."

"And that's how the land agent acquired the land

around Green Willow Creek? It was part of the land given to the railroad as a bribe to build it?"

Lawson nodded his head, glancing occasionally at the door that opened into the banking area behind them. He didn't often have a woman asking these kinds of questions. It must be a characteristic of a newspaperman's mind. Her brother had been just as probing when he'd asked to see the map. Then two days later, James Banning had been found shot and mauled by that Devil.

"Yes, ma'am. That was common practice. It was considered an incentive to get the railroads to build through areas that were expensive and possibly financially unprofitable."

"If that's the case, did the railroad holding company also own the land on which Green Willow Creek is built? Who owns my newspaper office, me or the railroad?"

Lawson cleared his throat uneasily, "Well, you do, of course. Your brother bought the land. You have a title, a deed."

"I do? I'd like to see it, Mr. Pickens. Where is it filed?"

"It's filed over in the territory office in Laramie. I'm afraid I don't know where your copy of the deed is. Wherever your brother kept his papers, I suppose."

The banker was clearly uncomfortable, but unless the entire settlement of Green Willow Creek was built on fraudulent land sales, she couldn't see what that had to do with the farmers or the Devil of the Plains. Maybe she was going down the wrong path, even if it was one that ought to be explored. She walked closer to the map.

"All right. The farmers' block of land begins here at the edge of town and curves like a crescent around to the base of the Green Mountains near Bitter Butte."

"That's correct."

"So, starting with this little section tagged 'Parnell' near the butte, the farmers' land curves back and lies along the body of land that makes up the town. It's a bit like two people shaking hands; the farmers' hand is on the bottom with one thumb sticking up into the mountains."

"I don't think the ranchers look at it quite that way. Why are you so interested in this map, Miss Banning?"

"I don't know yet, Mr. Pickens, but the land seems to have triggered the trouble here, and I want to see how the incidents of death and mutilation plot on the map."

The more she looked, the more she changed her mind. The entire map was more like waves along the shore, the farmers' wave washing away from town, curving up and heading back. Then there was the next section, being towered over by the farmers, then the rest of the smaller waves washing toward these mountains here on the right. "Who owns this large middle section of land here, the one the farmers' land borders? It almost makes a barrier between them and the other ranchers."

"That's Jake's ranch. He bought that center section from one of the ranchers that sold out last fall. But I can't see what that has to do with anything."

Jake didn't own all the land along the mountain, but he owned a large section of it, and most of the land bordered by the farmers as well. Still, as she began to plot in the incidents of destruction and murder she could see a pattern emerging. In every case, except that of her brother, the houses and cattle that had been attacked bordered the areas nearest to Bitter Butte.

Bitter Butte, where she'd discovered the monster. If Dallas could find the monster again, she could use it to lead her to the criminal behind all this.

But she didn't have much time left, and with Jake stalking the streets, she'd have to work quickly and quietly. Going alone probably wasn't a smart idea. If something happened to her, she wanted someone to know what she was beginning to understand.

Chapter 24

This time Dallas couldn't take a chance on hiring a horse. After the last fiasco, she wouldn't depend on the livery stable operator's discretion. Instead, dressed in Willie's clothing, she waited until midday, when it was easy to claim a horse tied to the rail outside Lucy Jarrett's boarding house.

Taking the route behind the buildings, she made her way out of town. Even then she had to go out of her way to avoid ranchers who were drifting into Green Willow Creek. Then, because of the delay, she was forced to ride furiously to reach Jake's ranch.

Shadow and Wu were skeptical about her plan, but when she threatened to go alone if they didn't join her, Wu finally agreed.

"We not gunfighters, Miss Dallas," Wu argued. "Mr. Jake will remove the last of Wu's pigtail if he finds out."

"If we don't find the answer to the monster, Wu, Mr. Jake is going to be killed, and probably others as well. Please hurry. I have a gun and I'm a very good shot. You'll be safe, I promise."

As they rode toward Bitter Butte in the late afternoon light, Dallas wished she were as confident as she'd sounded. Too many people had already been killed to keep the monster and what he guarded a secret, and she didn't believe that it had anything to do with rustling cattle. That was simply a convenient cover.

The butte began to grow larger. They finally reached it and began to make their way around it as clouds began to slide across the sky, obliterating the dying sun.

"About here was where I made my camp," she explained, "and then I started to the mountains in search of wood. Let's get off the horses and walk, like I did."

Shadow slid from her horse and glanced uneasily at the bleak face of the rock before them. "Dallas, are you sure you don't want to make camp here tonight and let Wu go for Jake?"

"No, we don't have time. The monster has killed your family. If you're uncomfortable and would rather return to the ranch, I won't hold you."

"I am afraid," she admitted. "This is where my people came to seek answers from Mother Earth. But in the end they became afraid, believing that she'd turned her back on them, refusing their pleas for the return of their land and the buffalo."

Dallas turned to face her friend. "Is this where you were when your uncle and your brother were killed?"

"I was up there, on the mountain. They waited here for me to return. I heard the monster when it came, but I couldn't see it."

"Jake was right about the criminals being lazy," Dallas said, "and if I'm right they'll be in the canyon. They'll think it's safe to come back."

"How you find, Miss Dallas?" Wu asked.

"I followed my nose to the fire and then slipped along the edge of the rocks. There's a tiny stream. You can hear the water falling."

Dallas fastened her horse's reins to a bush in the base of the funnel-shaped outcropping of rock and started toward the jumble of granite boulders that were strewn like crumbs along the fierce protrusions of snow-tipped mountains. In the sunlight they might look green. But at close range, in the growing darkness, their color was gunmetal gray.

Wu and Shadow stared at each other in dismay, then tied their horses alongside Dallas's mount and started after the woman who was hurrying through the grass. By the time they caught up, she was standing statue-still, turning her head from side to side like some weather vane in a waning breeze.

"What is it?" Shadow asked.

"Shush!" Dallas replied. "Listen."

"Cattle," Shadow said.

"Yes, and something more." Dallas sniffed. "Do you smell it?"

Wu took a deep breath, then again. "Yes. Wood smoke and something musky, like ancient bird's nest."

Dallas turned and began to move toward the rocks, quickly but quietly. As she came to a pile of wind-driven brush she stopped, studying the barrier thoughtfully. "This wasn't here before," she whispered. "Can we move it?"

"Not without making noise," Shadow said. "Wait." She hurried to the other side of the brush, walked up and down for a moment, they started up the side of the mountain, motioning for Wu and Dallas to follow.

"Where you go, woman?" Wu asked in a low voice.

"There is a way to go up, here, the way my mother showed me long ago. I remember climbing this way when she came to talk to the spirit gods. Hurry, before all the light is gone."

Suddenly a stone dislodged and rolled down, setting off a smaller chain of rocks.

"Who goes there?" A voice called out from the canyon below.

The three climbers froze, bent in crouched position.

There was a long silence, then the evening seemed to come back to life and they heard the same voice swear, "Damned coyotes, creeping around up there."

"They're down there," Dallas finally whispered. "And I'll bet the monster is, too. We've got to find out who the mastermind is. He's the one we're after. Him and the creature."

"But how?" Wu asked. "If we keep moving, they're going to hear us, and then Wu will enter the Celestial kingdom of heaven before he is ready to go."

"Just a little farther," Shadow said, "then we'll wait until the moon is full overhead. We'll be above the valley and we can see who is there."

"But what about the clouds? And what if he leaves?" Dallas asked, her fear very real. They were too close to fail. If it became necessary, she'd just let herself be captured. Then they'd know the man's identity and Wu and Shadow could go back and tell Jake.

"The clouds come and go again. The spirit of the wind moves through the night sky. The man won't leave," Shadow assured her. "If he'd been planning to leave quickly, he wouldn't have re-covered the entrance to the canyon. Come!"

Slowly, Shadow picked her way along, followed by Wu and Dallas. They made their way steadily upward and across the side of the mountain until the flicker of the campfire below came into view. There was only one man, drinking from a cup and talking to himself.

"Just hold on to your spit, you sorry animal. He'll be here soon, and we'll find out where we stand."

"It's him," Shadow said softly. "He's the one who shot you."

Dallas gasped. "You saw him? Why didn't you say anything?"

"I'd never seen the man before, and I didn't see him actually fire the shot. But when I looked up, he was hiding something beneath his coat, and afterward he was gone. I was never certain, but it was him."

"I kill him," Wu said and made a move toward the fire.

Dallas caught his arm. "Not yet, Wu. I want to know who the other man is. We have to wait until he comes."

But the second man didn't make it easy for them. The moon rose, playing tag with the clouds. The three watchers waited, cramped and cold, but unable to move for fear of giving themselves away.

It was very late when they finally heard the sound of the brush being moved and the buggy being driven into the canyon. The moon made slivers of light through the clouds, but the newcomer remained inside the buggy. With a big, dark hat covering his head and a heavy jacket that concealed his size, he could have been anybody, including Elliott or Jake. The buggy was identical to the one at the livery stable, so identification was impossible from where the viewers were watching.

"I thought I told you to shoot the sheriff," the newcomer said.

"You did, but I don't cotton to killing a lawman. Too risky. They'd bring in the marshal."

"You fool. You're going to ruin everything. What does one more murder matter at this point?"

"I guess it don't matter when it isn't you doing the killing." The big man's laugh bespoke his disbelief. "You have me do your dirty work, then use a dumb animal to cover up the killing. It took me a while, but I finally figured it out."

"What do you mean?"

"I followed you the last time you left here. You went up in the mountains, and you weren't talking to the spirits. You don't want all those farmers' land. You just want one farmer's land."

"You don't know what you're talking about."

"I think I do. You see, I found the skeleton. It was that miner, wasn't it? He struck it rich, didn't he? What was it, gold or silver?"

"You're crazy, Rejo. You've been out here too long."

"I don't think so. That's what you wanted all the time, not the cattle, or the land. You've got a mine, and somebody else already owns the site. Well, as of now, I'm cutting myself in. Tell me, boss, what did that prospector find?"

The answer was long in coming. "Silver," he finally answered, and climbed down from the buggy.

Dallas listened, more mystified than ever. Dr. Horn's miner with the broken leg. He'd insisted on returning to his stake. But nobody had ever seen him again. Everybody had assumed the old man just moved on. If there had been a strike someone would have known.

Someone would have staked a claim.

But wait, not if the land belonged to the railroad. The whole problem was beginning to come clear. The miner found something, but he couldn't claim it because the land in question already belonged to someone else. So long as nobody knew the truth, his discovery could remain secret.

But the railroad had sold the land to a speculator. And the speculator had paid Elliott to bring the immigrants by giving him the section of land in question. In order to conceal his real purpose, the master criminal had come up with a way to scare everybody away.

The Devil of the Plains.

And Jamie had figured it out. That's why he'd been killed. Now Jake's life was being threatened, and the immigrants were being eliminated. Dallas wanted to scream out in rage. She wanted to race down the mountain and confront the mastermind.

"I think I'll buy some land of my own with my share," Rejo was saying. "When do we start mining it?"

The reply was inaudible.

"Why wait? All hell is about to break out. Who'd ever know?"

"I said we wait."

"I don't think so," Rejo said. "I've done your dirty work all this time. Now I want my reward."

"Sounds like they're about to come to a parting of the ways," Shadow observed. "Let's hope the leader doesn't decide to shoot that big man and take off in the dark."

"No, he not do that yet," Wu observed. "Not finished."

The moon suddenly broke through in full force. It cast a beam of light on the corral, showering a big piebald horse with illumination. As if he knew, the horse flicked his white ears uneasily.

"Jamie's missing horse," Dallas whispered. "It has to be. That's why it never came back." For a moment, she couldn't breathe. She'd found her answer, but who was the killer?

The circle of light widened to reveal the man called Rejo wiping his bushy head with a large handkerchief. The second man, now standing in the shadow of the overhang, lifted a tin dipper from a bucket and took a deep swallow of the water that was falling from between the cracks in the rocks.

The drinker replaced the dipper, removed his hat, and wiped his forehead with his lower arm.

"You're right, Rejo, you deserve a reward." The speaker took several steps toward the fire and looked up at the mountain, almost as if he could see Dallas, Shadow, and Wu. He gave a satisfied smile. "I'll soon have it all, and before I'm finished I'll own the entire valley as well. Not bad for a man who was cashiered out of the Union army for drunkenness, is it?"

Dallas gasped. "Dr. Horn." She couldn't believe what she was seeing. The man who'd concocted the entire scheme *was* Dr. Horn. One of the most respected men in Green Willow Creek was killing its citizens and stealing their land. Jamie must have learned the truth.

"I think the time has come to get rid of the animal," the doctor said, "before he's discovered."

"No," Dallas whispered. "We can't let him kill the creature. I'm going down there."

"Wait," Wu snapped in a low, firm voice. "You not go alone. We all go." He stood and started down the mountain, setting off a landslide of rock that peppered the clearing below.

Dallas drew her gun and fell in behind the two. "At least I can stop *one* of them. Let's split up."

"Who's there?" Dr. Horn called out, turning to the buggy.

"That ain't coyotes," Rejo said, turning his gun toward the mountain, pointing it directly at Wu.

Dallas, standing beside a large rock, pulled back

the hammer of Jamie's gun. It would only be justice
if Jamie's killer was killed with Jamie's gun.

"I see you!" Rejo shouted. "Come down or I'll
shoot."

"No," Shadow called out, leaping past Wu to the
ground. "You see the spirits who live here. They
have come to bring the mountain down on you and
punish you for your evil ways."

Rejo hesitated. That gave Dallas all the time she
needed. She gave the rock a shove. It groaned, then
gave way. This time the entire section of ground on
which it was resting followed, raining down a mass
of debris toward the people below.

"What the—?"

"Hello, good Dr. Horn," Wu said, giving a small
bow before he danced away and allowed the rock
bearing down on him to find Dr. Horn instead.

The doctor groaned and staggered backward, col-
lapsing in a crumpled heap beside the tiny waterfall,
his gun falling to the ground beside him. Wu picked
it up and moved away.

In the meantime, Dallas scrambled around the
loose earth and started down the mountain, firing
her gun in warning. The cattle, already agitated by
the rock slide, began to run back and forth. The
creature, surrounded by cows, was hidden by the
shadow of a rock that extended out over the crude
corral.

"Shadow, be careful!" Dallas yelled, trying to
keep Rejo's attention while she hid behind one outcropping, then another, on the way down. Rejo got
off one shot that pinged off the wall beside her.

Just as she reached the bottom, the monster
cleared the shadows and let out a low guttural cry
of annoyance. It moved toward Dallas, obscuring
Rejo's view so that his second shot went wild. At
that point, Wu fired Dr. Horn's gun, catching the

357

murderer in the side. Rejo turned a look of astonishment on Wu, then slumped to the ground.

Inside the cattle pen, Dallas looked up at the creature and let out an incredulous laugh. The Devil of the Plains *was* as tall as a building. He did have long legs and probably did look as if he were flying when he moved rapidly. The monster that had terrorized Green Willow Creek was a huge brown camel.

The creature came leisurely toward Dallas, stopped and chewed, clearly curious. He snorted and shuffled his feet.

"Dallas, be careful," Shadow called out. "He might hurt you."

"I don't think he's a killer, Wu. Help me. I need to catch him."

"What about the doctor?" Shadow asked. "He's still alive. Shall I tie him up?"

"Yes," Dallas answered and continued studying the camel. She had the feeling that as long as she didn't lose eye contact, he'd stand still.

"Wu, we have to get him down so that I can mount."

Wu climbed the fence and warily entered the pen. "Down?" he said.

"Down?" Shadow echoed.

"Down!" Dallas snapped in aggravation, and watched in amazement as the animal bent his gangly legs and sank to the ground.

Dallas and Wu looked at each other in disbelief. "He's been trained for riding," she said as she watched Wu lift a rope from the fence and attach it to the camel's harness. The camel started to fidget.

"We've got him now," Dallas said triumphantly.

"But what we do with him? Wu not feel good about travel in dark."

Dallas thought about his concerns. He might be

right. They didn't want to take any chances of getting lost or losing the animal now that they had him. By waiting a few hours, they'd stand a better chance.

"You're right, Wu. We'll wait. I'll tie the camel to the fence. Shadow, check on the man Wu shot. Wu, make certain that the doctor is tied up good and tight."

"The big man is dead, Dallas."

"And the doctor sleeps like a babe."

"Fine, we'll wait."

They did. By the time the sun began sending streaks of light over the mountains in the east, the doctor had come to, found himself securely bound, and began an unsuccessful attempt to buy his way free.

"Sorry, Dr. Horn, but I made a promise to my brother that I'd find his killer. You may not have fired the shot, but you're responsible."

"Your brother was a fool, sticking his nose into something that was none of his business."

"My brother was an honest, decent man, and you'll pay for his death."

"Perhaps, Miss Banning," the doctor said in a threatening tone, "but if you don't let me go, you'll pay an even greater price."

"I can't see how. Your henchman is dead and you're tied up. What can you do now?"

"Let's just say that I've arranged a little incident in town to make certain that Jake Silver and Elliott Parnell don't survive the showdown."

Dallas felt her heart twist. What had he done? How could he arrange Jake's and Elliott's death?"

"How?"

"Oh, I don't think I'll tell you. But if you let me go, I still have time to stop them."

Shadow came up to stand beside the doctor. "It is

said that the viper throws the mouse into a trance before he swallows him."

"Yes, but if the doctor can stop the bloodshed by getting to town, let's see that he does. Let's get him into the buggy and tie him to the seat."

While Wu and Shadow complied, Dallas untied the camel and gave the "down" command. After several attempts to throw off the lead, he finally complied and sank to the ground.

"Stay!" Dallas snapped and handed Wu the rope while she climbed on the animal, settling her body in the curve of his neck. She'd never ridden a camel, but as a girl, she'd dismayed her father by riding bareback along with her brothers. They had to get him back to town, and she wasn't certain that they could control him only with the rope. Besides, she'd read that camels could travel faster than horses, and time was running out.

"Let's hope I can stay on long enough to get him back to town."

"How you get animal up?"

But Dallas didn't have to try. Apparently the words "down" and "up" were the proper commands, for the great gangly beast lurched to his feet, causing Dallas to slide precariously from side to side before she got a good hold with her legs.

"Quick, Wu. Give me the rope."

The creature waited until Wu had complied before reaching out to nip him.

Wu's resounding oath needed no translation.

It took Dallas several miles to learn how to roll with the camel's gait. The ride wasn't smooth, but they managed.

Rejo's body was draped across Dallas's horse. Dr. Horn offered again to make all three of his captors rich, then sat in stony silence. The buggy made good progress, but Dallas and the camel soon left Wu and Shadow behind.

The sun was almost overhead now. It was almost noon of the fifth day, the morning of the ultimatum issued to the farmers.

The confrontation between Jake and Elliott.

But that wasn't necessary now. The whole range war had been an effort by Dr. Horn to scare off the farmers and keep the mine secret until he could claim the land. He was a greedy man who wanted wealth and respect so badly that he was willing to kill for it.

Dallas shuddered.

Jamie had been to see Mr. Pickens and studied the land map, then had gone in search of something. He must have discovered the same secret that Dallas had found, and he'd had to die for it.

Now Dr. Horn would pay for his greed.

Jake wouldn't have to keep her safe any longer, if she could get there soon enough to stop the showdown.

A sudden sense of dread swept over her. Suppose she didn't make it in time? Suppose something terrible happened to Jake? Nudging the camel and slapping his side, she urged him into a full gallop. Overhead the gray hawk swooped down out of a pale sky and flew toward town.

"Where is she, Elliott?"

Jake was standing in the street, across from Elliott, his legs spread, his hand resting on his gun. His eyes were as cold as the snow on the mountain peaks beyond the town.

"I told you, Jake. I don't know. I was eating at Lucy's. When I came out, my horse was gone. I've been looking for it ever since. I don't even know that she took it, and neither do you."

Logically, Jake knew that Elliott wouldn't hurt Dallas, but all rational thinking had disappeared when he found out that she was gone. And the only thing he had to go on was Elliott's missing horse.

"Elliott, I said we'd play the cards we were dealt, but if I find out that you know where Dallas is and didn't tell me, I'll kill you on the spot."

"Boss," Pete came riding up the street, yelling. "Boss! Wait! Shadow and Wu are gone, too. Nobody at the ranch has seen them since yesterday."

Jake let out a sigh of relief, followed by a new fear. She'd gone off on her own again, and she'd taken Wu and Shadow with her. "Did anybody see them leave?"

"No. But I sent the men out to look for them."

"We'll go, too, Jake," Elliott said. "I would never hurt Dallas for any reason. I think you know me better than that."

But the women in Green Willow Creek didn't know who had shot Dallas. They'd gone home after the shooting, but they hadn't stayed. Individually, without being called, they'd returned to the saloon. They knew about the deadline and about Dallas's disappearance. Dallas had become their champion, and they intended to carry out her orders. After a hasty meeting, they decided that their original plan had been to stop the men from fighting, and that hadn't changed. They separated into two columns and silently marched along the street through the center of town, forming a human barrier that forced the men to remain on the wooden sidewalks, leaving Elliott and Jake facing each other in the middle of the street.

"Now then, you two hotheads," Widow Potter called out. "I don't know what your problem is, but it's time it was settled. We have to find Dallas, and we need you to do it. If you want to kill yourselves, do it quick! But any of the rest of you men who fires risks hitting his own woman."

"Go home, Amy!"

"Irene!"

"Effie, I thought we had all this settled."

"Not on your life, you heathens," Widow Potter snapped. "We're going to stop this fight right now! Then we're going after Dallas, together!"

Jake had waited in town for a reply to the telegram. But it still hadn't come. The Devil of the Plains and his leader were still a mystery. All he could do now was hope that the confrontation would force the guilty party to commit himself. Otherwise, the showdown was doomed to fail. The last thing he intended was for anybody to get hurt.

Then he saw them, on the roof of the general store, two rifle barrels shining in the sun. He glanced around, checking the ranchers. He didn't miss anybody, though he couldn't be sure.

"Elliott," he said, under his breath, "do any of your farmers own fancy rifles?"

"Not that I know of. Why?"

"I believe our mastermind is on top of the store behind you. And he's brought a friend."

"You were right. Somebody plans to be sure we don't settle this war."

"Let's see if we can force their hand. When I challenge you, one on one. I'll count real loud. We'll draw and fire. Just make sure it isn't me you hit."

"Let's do it!"

Jake spread his legs and snarled, "We're here to settle this fight, Elliott, and I guess I'm going to have to kill you to do it!"

"I don't think so, Jake. I'm the sheriff, remember. I don't believe you'll fire on an officer of the law."

"I'll do whatever I have to, to protect my land.

On the count of three, Elliott. Either you draw or I do. One. Two."

Jake never got to the third number. The riflemen weren't taking any chances. One shot caught Elliott in the arm, sending him sprawling in the street. Another churned up the dirt where Jake had been standing a second earlier.

Screams broke out from the women. The men swore and dived for cover as Jake returned fire with one hand while grabbing Elliott by the shirt collar with the other and dragging him toward shelter behind the horse's water trough.

"Are you hurt bad?" Jake asked.

"It burns like hell, but I'll live. Who are they?" Elliott asked in a tight voice. "Did you get a look?"

"Those two gunfighters you sent for. Somebody kept them on after you fired them."

"Who?"

"I don't know."

On the opposite side of the street, the farmers were busy getting the women to safety. Behind Jake and Elliott, the ranchers were pinned down by gunfire.

"Just like it was at the Battle of Shiloh, isn't it?" Jake said dryly, "except it's you that's hurt. Here, tie this bandana around your arm."

"What are we going to do, Captain?" For Jake, with that one question, the last doubt went away. It was Jake and Elliott again, a team, as they once were. A woman had come between them. Now another woman had brought them back together.

"Cover me!" Jake dashed down to the next water trough as Elliott laid down a barrage of bullets in the direction of their attackers.

Under cover of Jake's fire, Elliott followed.

There was one more thing Jake had to do. While

reloading, in a voice so low that only Elliott could hear, Jake began to speak.

"I can't let you bleed to death without squaring things between us, Elliott. Sarah's death wasn't your fault. You went for help. That's all anyone could have done."

There was a flash of emotion in Elliott's eyes. "I'm not going to bleed to death, Jake." He winced and tightened the bandana to stop the flow of blood. His shirt was soaked and his arm was growing numb. There was a weakness surging through him. He focused on the pain, using it to hold on. Jake needed him. He'd be damned if he'd allow himself to pass out now.

Behind them some ranchers had joined in the fight, keeping the riflemen pinned down. Jake twisted back into firing position, studying the situation. He had to get to the steps leading to the second-floor porch. From there he could pull himself up to the roof.

"Somebody throw me another gun," Jake yelled to the ranchers behind him.

Elliott gave up any attempt to fire, leaning his head back against the water trough as he watched Jake. "You wouldn't allow yourself to care. You turned us both away. You were the fool, Jake. Sarah loved me, yes, like a brother. You were the man she wanted to marry."

There had been a time when this statement would have punched Jake in the gut. But now, Elliott was hurt and Jake couldn't worry about Sarah. He couldn't change the past. He couldn't save his mother, nor could he save Sarah. But this time he wouldn't walk away.

"Cover me, boys," Jake yelled and in a hail of bullets, made a wild dash toward the store.

ᐦ *Sandra Chastain* ᐦ

There were screams from the women and a shout from the end of the street.

Elliott, summoning up a desperate show of strength, forced himself to stand, firing the last of his bullets toward the rooftop as he staggered forward.

As Dallas rode into town, she saw Elliott collapse in the street. Jake was nowhere in sight.

"Jake!"

Every eye turned toward the spectacle of Dallas Banning galloping down the street between the enemy lines, her feet drumming against the sides of the camel. The distraction was enough that Jake was able to reach the roof, felling one of the gunmen with a single well-aimed shot. The other one took one look at the flint-gray of Jake's eyes and turned to run, tripped over the body of his fallen companion, and toppled over the bannister to the ground below, where he was clobbered with a shovel by the Widow Potter.

Miranda ran to Elliott's side, cradling his head in her lap while Effie Pickens examined his arm.

The monster, carrying Dallas, charged down the street, slobbering and slinging his head, flinging great globs of spittle toward the dodging women.

"The Devil of the Plains!" someone called out and hid behind a post.

"It's Judgment Day!" Mr. Bowker said solemnly.

Panic ensued as Dallas reached Elliott, reined the beast to a stop and announced in a loud voice, "Elliott, you're hurt! Down, Devil!"

To everyone's amazement, the beast folded its legs and sank to the dusty street. Dallas lifted her leg over his neck and scrambled to the ground. "Where's Jake?"

"A camel," Jake said, making his way down the steps to the street.

366

"An ordinary camel," Elliott repeated in amazement. "The Devil of the Plains is an ordinary camel."

"Would you look at that," one of the ranchers said in amazement.

"I never see such an animal," one of the immigrants said in amazement.

Dallas handed the camel's rope to a startled rancher and flung herself into Jake's arms. "You're still alive?"

"I'm fine, but Elliott managed to get himself shot."

"Someone get Doc Horn," a voice called out.

"No!" Dallas shouted. "It was Dr. Horn who did all this. I was so afraid. He said you and Elliott would die."

"We almost did," Elliott said grimly. "He must've hired the gunfighters that shot me. Where'd you find the monster?"

"Just where Doctor Horn's flunky, Rejo, hid it," Dallas answered, "in a blind canyon near Bitter Butte. Oh, Jake, darling, it wasn't the immigrants behind the trouble. It was Dr. Horn. He was crazy. He killed Jamie and he might have killed both of you."

Jake tightened his grip around Dallas. "He tried. I should have guessed when I heard him whistling 'Turkey in the Straw,' but I didn't."

The onlookers weren't convinced. "Not Doc Horn," one said. "Where'd he get the Devil?" another asked.

Dallas nodded. "I'm sorry, friends. I don't know how he captured the camel; maybe the miner used it. But it was Dr. Horn. I heard him. He admitted his guilt. Shadow and Wu are bringing him now, in his own buggy. It's finally over, Jake."

She said it with such calm pride. As if capturing

the killer and the Devil of the Plains were an every-day occurrence.

But it took Spence's arrival, bringing the answer to Jake's telegram, to finally convince the people.

"It says," Jake relayed, "that Dr. Horn was court-martialed from the Union army for selling medicine to the Confederates. He served time in prison and disappeared. Over a year ago he returned to St. Louis with silver ore that he claimed to have taken in payment from the Indians."

"Silver?" A murmur of excitement ran through the crowd.

Lawson Pickens spoke up. "It makes sense, folks. Dr. Horn must have learned about the discovery of silver in the Green Mountains from the prospector who broke his leg. He probably tried to claim the land legally at the federal land office in Laramie, but by that time it belonged to the land speculator who gave it to Elliott."

Jake took up the story. "Then Horn tried to conceal the mine by trying to run all the settlers off, using this camel to heighten the mystery and fear. When that was too slow, he arranged to have Elliott appointed sheriff, hoping he'd be killed. Then he'd claim the land. I expect the fellow that Widow Potter captured will be happy to testify."

"You mean there's silver on my land?" Elliott asked in amazement.

"We're going to be rich," Miranda said and planted a kiss on Elliott's forehead. "And when Shadow gets here she'll fix your wound and we'll get married and . . ."

"It's over, maverick," Jake said softly. "Because of you, we found the truth."

"It's over? Oh, Jake!" She'd come so close to losing him. The strain of the night and her unorthodox ride into town swept over her. She began to sway. "I don't feel—"

"Catch her, Jake," Elliott snapped weakly. "She's about to collapse."

Jake dropped the gun he was still holding in the street, catching Dallas just as she fell. This time when he lifted Dallas in his arms, he smiled.

"Were you really going to faint?" he asked skeptically.

"I don't think I'll answer that, Jake. Maybe I just like being held. But if you don't get us out of here quick, I'm going to kiss you, right here in front of all these people."

Moments later they were on his horse, riding toward the ranch, the camel loping casually behind as if he'd been invited to come along.

"I'm sorry I took so long to admit my feelings, Dallas. It's hard for me to talk about them."

"You don't have to say anything, Jake."

Dallas bit her lower lip. She didn't have to be told why Jake had become a man of ice. He'd found the only way he could to survive. He'd simply closed off his ability to love. If he didn't care, he couldn't be hurt. If he didn't take a risk, he couldn't lose. Well she wasn't going to let him find a way to close her out. There was a tiny crack in his icy plate of armor and she intended to chip away until she could come inside.

"I love you, Jake Silver. And I'm not going anywhere unless you go with me. If you want to see the Pacific Ocean, I'm ready. If you want to live on the Double J, I'll be happy. But what you aren't going to do is walk out that door without me."

"But, I'm . . . I'm afraid I'll lose you, just as I lost Sarah."

"Well, you'll lose me for sure if you don't tell me

you love me, Jake. Tell me you want me by your side. Say the words, Jake."

"But suppose something happens to you?"

"What do you want, a guarantee? I think the only guarantee is that we're human and that we make mistakes. If loving you is a mistake, it won't be the first one I've made. I'm a maverick, remember, like you. I'll never follow the herd. But two mavericks together? That's the best either of us can expect."

"I love you, Dallas Banning."

She could see his pain melt away, the cold steel of his eyes turn into a soft gray. The last of his icy shell was gone.

Suddenly the sun brightened. The sky was an endless expanse of blue. Overhead the hawk swept across the late afternoon sky, growing smaller and smaller as it flew toward the Green Mountains. A quick, warm breeze sprang up, ruffling Jake's hair. A good day for new beginnings, Dallas thought. "You told me once that you'd come into town for a woman and you asked me if I was available. You told me to set my price, Jake Silver."

"That I did, maverick."

"I have. I want to get married, to you, and live here in Green Willow Creek. I want to belong to you forever."

"Too late," he said in a low voice. "You already belong to me. Just as I belonged to you, from that first moment."

"Is that a problem for you, Jake?"

"Probably," he said with a dry smile. "But I think I prefer my lady to be a maverick. There are some wild things that ought never to be tamed."

"My thoughts exactly," she said and surrendered herself to Jake's kiss.

Epilogue

Willie came into the newspaper office shaking his head. "Miss Banning, you're not going to believe this, but there's a pig tied to your front door."

"A pig?"

"A fat, pink pig, with a white bow tied around its neck."

"Oh, Jake," she whispered, "you sweet, foolish man."

"Jake did this? Why?"

"It's my bride's gift, Willie. Wu explained it to me. Now I have to find a rabbit's foot to send to him. Can you help me?"

"Sure, I'll bet Miranda has one hanging on the wall. Lots of gamblers think they're good-luck charms. I'll go and ask."

Dallas heard the door slam behind Willie and gave a deep sigh of contentment. She had printed the most important edition of the *Gazette* she'd ever edited and it lay stacked on the counter to be distributed throughout the day.

LOCAL DOCTOR
BEHIND RANGE WAR.
To protect the location of a silver strike, local doctor Lorenzo Horn is accused of murdering the

*prospector who discovered the strike and setting off
a war between local ranchers and farmers by per-
petuating the myth of a mountain monster as the
villain.*

*For months, the Devil of the Plains, a lone camel
abandoned by the Union Army after an unsuccessful attempt to use the animals for transportation
during the Civil War, has been forced to take part in
the killing of innocent people, cattle rustling, and
the destruction of homes.*

*Dr. Horn has been sent to Laramie, accused of
multiple murders, including that of James Augustus
Banning, owner of the* Willow Creek Gazette.

"Well, Jamie, I did it, I found the man who killed
you. And, you know what, little brother, I'm staying
out here in this wild land you picked. We're setting
up a school and bringing in a real teacher. The farmers and the ranchers have worked out a solution.
Elliott's immigrants will grow oats and Jake's ranchers will buy them.

"And somehow, the settling of the range war
brought Elliott and Jake back together. We have
peace in Green Willow Creek, at least until the word
gets out about the discovery of silver.

"I'm getting married, Jamie. And Jake doesn't
know it yet, but I have a few plans of my own. After our baby comes, I may run for public office. So,
you see, everything is going to work out. And it's all
because of you. Thank you, James Augustus Banning."

Two hours later, Dallas and Jake, along with
Elliot and Miranda, assumed the status of family to
Shadow of the Eagle and Sun Wu of the House of
Qing.

Jake, dressed in his black coat and brocade vest,
was wearing polished boots and had a fresh shave
and haircut. He was still a dangerous-looking man,

with steel in his eyes, until he looked at Dallas, and the granite color turned to silver.

Dallas, wearing a bright yellow dress, had pinned her hair back with a cascade of spring wildflowers. Her face was filled with joy, and her mouth curved into a wicked smile. She lowered her eyes and gave the suggestion of a curtsy, whispering, "I thank you, my lord, for your kind and generous gift of a pig. I have gift for honorable bridegroom in return."

"You do? I'm afraid to ask what."

"Give me your hand, Jake." She took it, curving it under her arm and sliding it beneath the arm full of wildflowers she was carrying.

Moments later Jake let out a moan as his hand touched the curve of her breast.

"Do you want me to unwrap my gift now?" he asked innocently as he watched Wu and Shadow kneel before each other.

"Yes, very much."

And then he found it, the furry appendage resting in the valley between her breasts.

Jake held back a grin. "Is it alive?"

"Not now."

"A rabbit's foot?"

"For luck, Jake, an acceptance gift from this worthless woman you have chosen."

Wu and Shadow entered the hallway, bowing to heaven and earth, then to the friends who represented their family. They knelt before a table on which two red candles were burning and repeated their vows in low voices. Afterward they drank cups of green tea and stood to face their friends.

Wu beamed. "Shadow has now turned her back on her people. She has joined her life with that of Wu. We are now part of the House of Silver and we invite you to celebrate in this most happy occasion."

Jake held out his hand to Wu. "I am honored that my friend chooses to join his family with mine."

Special foods followed—green tea, dumplings, fish, and rice. Following the long feast, Wu led the guests to the creek, where each was provided with a paper boat.

Wu explained. "In China, honorable wife would now cry pitifully and show how unhappy she is to leave her family."

"But I'm not unhappy," Shadow insisted, "and I refuse to have the kind of marriage where I'm not allowed to go beyond the gate for three years."

"Due to your influence, no doubt," Jake said and planted a kiss on Dallas's forehead.

"On this occasion," Wu went on, "each member of family choose paper boat. On boat put past troubles and heartaches. Then let current carry them away. Make for happy life."

Jake looked past Dallas to where Elliott and Miranda were standing. He lifted his paper boat as if in salute and placed it in the water. Elliott did the same.

Dallas watched as both men followed the path of their boats, cheering as they miraculously avoided rocks and twigs that made little barriers in the water, eventually disappearing from sight.

Later, back at the house, the sweet scent of the budding pink roses on the picket fences was in the air as the wedding party gathered in the courtyard to watch the fireworks that had been Elliott's contribution to the festivities. Brilliant sunbursts of color began to explode overhead, leaving trails of light across the darkening horizon.

Beyond the courtyard, in the corral, the camel chewed his cud and spit occasionally at the two pigs now occupying a recently built pen in the corner.

Dallas began to fidget. "By the way, you never told me who sent you the wire."

"A very nice Pinkerton agent. By the way, he insists that I tell Miss Dallas Banning that they all miss her. Would you care to explain that?"

"Not at the moment," she whispered in Jake's ear. "Can't we get away from here?"

"No more siege of self-denial?" Jake asked with a straight face.

"Not necessary. Just like the women in ancient Greece, we won. Besides," she added with an impish grin, "Miranda made me a present of the Russian dressing gown. I have a great need to feel fur against my bare skin."

Jake looked out over the wedding guests at Wu and Shadow, at Elliott and Miranda, and felt an odd warm sensation inside his chest. *Thank you, Sarah. Because of you, we've come to this place where love can grow wild and free.*

"I love you, maverick." As Dallas slipped her hand in Jake's, he smiled. The emptiness inside him had been filled.

If you liked Rebel in Silk,
look for Sandra Chastain's next
Bantam Once Upon a Time Romance

SCANDAL IN SILVER
coming at the end of 1994

About the Author

SANDRA CHASTAIN is the bestselling, award-winning
author of 32 romances. She lives in Smyrna, Georgia.